MARIA J. HART

Born Anew in Blood

The author of this work is a staunch supporter of human rights and freedom for all oppressed peoples. If you have at any point in time found yourself on the side of the aisle that supports, enables, or turns a blind eye to humanitarian crises, up to and including genocide and ethnic cleansing, and have been comfortable staying on that side of the aisle, place this book back on the shelf. This book is not for you, and neither is this author — and she doesn't want you as a reader. If, however, you have raised your voice - in whatever capacity you may have - to oppose oppression, then please do stay and enjoy.

If you've driven your car to the lookout.
But managed not to follow your fears down.
If you've watched your pages turn.
And felt the heat of your bridges burn.
If you can go anywhere you want, but just not home.
You are not on your own.

Contents

Pronunciation Guide

Arkenvale: ARK-en-veil
Auberon Danodraic: OH-ber-on DAN-oh-drake
Azaeroria: az-uh-ROAR-ee-uh
Bastet: BAS-tet
Bleddyn: BLEV-in
Cuhloch: KOO-lock
Dhabiha: va-BEE-ha
Diego Vidales: dee-AY-go vee-DAL-ays
Eilidh Shaw: AY-lee SHAW
Himesh: hih-MAISH
Imane: ee-MON-ee
Jang Hyun-Joo: JAHNG HYUN-joo
Kianga Nabil: kee-AHN-gah na-BEEL
Mallory Smith: MAL-or-ree SMITH
Martín Peña: mar-TEEN PEN-yuh
Nabeyha: na-BAY-ha
New Camlann: New CAM-lin
Ousmane: oos-MAH-nee
Saif Rahim: sigh-EEF ra-HEEM
Tenazeryth: ten-AZ-uh-rith
Valentina Peña: val-en-TEEN-uh PEN-yuh

Content Warnings

Anxiety, BDSM, Bigotry (in a fantasy context), Blood (no, really), Body Image Issues, Daddy Issues, Death, Depression, Drugging (nonconsensual), Explicit Language, Knives/Cuts, Mommy Issues, Morning People, PTSD, Sexual Encounters (all consensual and *very* explicit; 18+ only!), Social Commentary, Suicidal Ideations (discussed; call 988 in the US, or visit 988lifeline.org for help), Transphobic Parent, Vehicle Accident (mentioned), Zucchini Brownies

BORN ANEW IN BLOOD

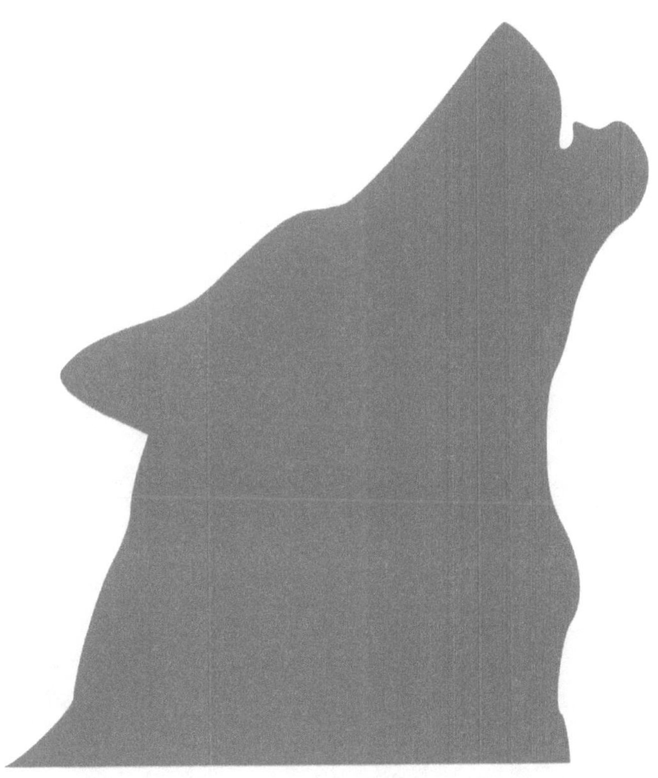

~ Waxing Gibbous ~

Fateful Meeting

The woman running behind me is definitely checking out my ass. I can see her staring at me in the giant mirror that takes up the entire wall of the gym. Most gyms just have a mirror on the wall by the free weight benches, but the owners of this gym have decided in their infinite wisdom that there should also be one in front of the cardio machines, presumably so you can watch yourself become increasingly red and disheveled by the minute.

I've been on the elliptical for almost twenty minutes, and it definitely shows. My hair is slowly but surely revolting from the constraints of the scrunchie that tries desperately to keep my ponytail in check. My cheeks are bright red, and there is a healthy layer of sweat on my forehead, as well as in my sports bra.

But the woman on the treadmill does not seem to care. I sneak a peek at her and nearly fall off the elliptical when I see her gazing directly back at me. She flashes a radiant smile, and my legs turn to rubber.

I didn't know it was physically possible, but my cheeks flare even more crimson than before.

I had hoped these new leggings would do my curves some favors. I spent way too much money on them, but I was feeling particularly sad last week, I had been walking around a mall, and they had pockets. How could I resist the instant dopamine? Although, I definitely hadn't been expecting *this* kind of reaction.

What the hell is this woman who looks like she puts on lingerie and walks down a runway for a living doing flashing that blinding smile at *me?* She's a tanned white woman with a tall, athletic build, and is running in a black sports bra and skin-tight pink spandex shorts. Sweat glistens off her toned abs, and I try desperately not to stare.

Her dark eyes definitely seemed to twinkle when she smiled at me. Her jet-black hair is somehow immaculate, and it isn't even in a ponytail. The laws of physics do not appear to apply to her.

I practically jump off the elliptical when my timer beeps at me. Pointedly looking away from Treadmill Model, I scurry to the weight training area. There are a few other people here, but not too many. Wednesday nights are usually - mercifully - not terribly crowded by this time. I had tried coming before work one morning, long ago. Never. Again.

I put on a metal playlist to blast through my earphones, then do my arms circuit before heading back to the treadmills. When I realize Treadmill Model is *still* running, I debate skipping this portion of my workout entirely and just heading home.

Goddamn. She was running when I got here more than forty minutes ago. She must be a marathoner. Or seriously disturbed. But maybe that's redundant.

Despite my anxiety, I take a deep breath and steady my gait. My therapist has been telling me that I need to gain confidence, and get out of my comfort zone. I should be able to be on a treadmill within the same vicinity as a hot woman without convincing myself that she's judging everything about me. *This is for you, Susan.*

I jog on and off for thirty minutes on the treadmill, then do my post-workout stretches while I mentally prepare to head home for a wild night filled with a post-workout shake and a trashy monster movie before bed. As I'm stretching, Treadmill Model finally begins to slow down and gets off the machine.

As soon as she's off, she makes a beeline for me. Before I have time to decide whether I should try to dissolve into the floor, or perhaps just flat-out run for the locker room, she's standing in front of me, motioning for me to take my headphones out.

I comply immediately.

"Hey," she says simply. Her sultry voice jumpstarts my heart rate. That killer smile is back. She's a couple of inches taller than me; she must be about exactly six feet.

I must look like a deer caught in headlights. If only I would soon be granted the sweet relief of a vehicle putting me out of my misery.

Instead, I have to think of how to respond, but all ability to produce words has vacated my brain. *What language do I even speak?* My mouth opens a few times, but nothing comes out. A few more seconds go by, and I realize I've stopped breathing, so I take a gulp and squeak "Hey!"

She chuckles musically. "I just wanted to apologize for staring at you since you got here. I've just never seen someone so gorgeous in here before." She tilts her head and raises one sculpted eyebrow.

"Oh," I breathe out shakily. *May I direct your attention to any one of these giant fucking mirrors?* "Um . . . oh."

My hand flies to where a pendant usually hangs between my breasts, but it's in my gym locker, and I awkwardly clasp my hands together in front of me. I cast my eyes down to the ground. Maybe one day I will be able to utter more than mono-syllabic words again, but I fear today is not that day.

She sticks her foot out, directly into my line of vision, and motions up with the tips of her white sneakers. When my eyes meet hers, she raises her eyebrows, her expression teasing.

"I'm Mallory," she says, putting both hands out like she's showing a frightened stray kitten that she means no harm. "Mallory Smith.

What about you?"

"Eilidh, uh, Shaw?" I ask quietly, as if I need confirmation from her. *I did it!* Four whole syllables.

She leans back, palms turning skyward like she's greeting an old friend. "Scottish, huh?" I blink confusedly, and she elaborates.

"Oh, I spent last summer in Edinburgh. Met a few Eilidhs there. It's such a beautiful place. Beautiful people." She looks me up and down once, quickly. "Also the uh . . ." She trails off, pointing to my hair.

"That bright auburn can*not* come from a bottle, I just know it." As she says this last bit, she steps forward and brushes her fingertips over the end of my long ponytail. She pulls it forward and lets it go gently, her hand hovering inches over my breast. Her touch is like an electric shock that releases me from the spell I was under. I shake my head in an attempt to clear it.

"Yeah, actually, I am Scottish! I mean, well, I was born here in Rochester, but I . . . well, my mom's side of the family is all Scottish. But I've actually never been there, but it's something I've always wanted to do."

You're rambling, Shaw. My cheeks redden again.

"That's so cool," she says, and it sounds sincere. Her intensity makes me blink.

"Yeah, I . . . I guess it is," I say lamely.

She forges ahead after an awkward beat. "So hey, I'm kind of new to the city, and I've been searching for the best coffee shop. Any suggestions? Maybe you could show me one tomorrow." She tilts her head to the side again and *bites her lip.*

Dear sweet lord.

"Well, there's a cool little bookshop a few blocks away from here with a café that has a killer iced macchiato." I attempt a smile, but it comes out more pained than anything.

She grins. "A bookshop date? That sounds awesome!"

~ Full Moon ~

A Date with Destiny

The next morning, we meet outside my favorite indie bookshop and stroll inside. I wave a greeting to the owner, a fifty-something Black woman named Tia, with whom I've spent endless hours chatting about books over countless cups of coffee.

She sees Mallory at my side, and her eyes widen. She smiles at me knowingly, and I can tell exactly what she's thinking. *Damn!*

Okay, so I'm not the only one who can see how hot this woman is.

I had convinced myself overnight that I had been hallucinating, and was still convinced of this as she walked up to me wearing a white crop top with puff sleeves that sets off her tan skin, and the shortest jean shorts I've ever seen.

Mallory eyes the shelves laden with books like she's a kid in a candy store. After a moment, she spots what she had been searching for, takes my hand, and guides me straight to the fantasy section.

The shelves are arranged by creature, and her face lights up as she reads a title on a shelf near the top.

I smile at her. "Werewolves, huh?" My voice is just a bit more steady than it had been last night at the gym.

She nods. "I've loved them for as long as I can remember." I nod slowly in approval and point to the shelf just under the werewolves.

"Personally, my weakness has always been vampires." I shrug and smile meekly. "I know it's cliché, but I can't help it."

Mallory gives a flirty chuckle and squeezes my hand. My heart skips a beat.

"Too bad for me, just basic human teeth in here." She flashes a grin at me like she wants me to confirm that she does indeed only have perfectly straight, blazing white teeth.

I giggle.

"But don't worry baby," she says, and my stomach explodes with butterflies. "There's always dental implants." She smirks and tucks a hair behind my ear.

I had tried to do a cute half-updo this morning with my braid secured in a knot at the back of my head that took me at least twenty minutes to figure out, cursing into the bathroom mirror of my tiny apartment. But my hair - as usual - has other plans, and is slowly falling out.

Her fingers trail over my chin. "So, about that coffee."

I nod, suppressing a shiver.

I lead her toward the café in the back corner of the bookstore. Tia's partner, a Japanese American guy named Kenji, is working behind the counter. He turns to me as he hears us approach, and the corners of his eyes crinkle as he smiles.

"Hey there Eilidh! Your macchiato is waiting for you!" He slides an iced cup of pure heaven across the counter at me as we approach.

"You're a lifesaver. Thanks!" I grab the glass and take a sip. *Perfect.*

Kenji turns to Mallory. "Sorry, didn't know what you would want. What'll you have? I'll whip it up quick."

"Just a black coffee, hot." I shift awkwardly as Mallory waits for her coffee, unsure if I should move to the chairs, or wait for her.

Mercifully, Kenji is a seasoned pro. Seconds later, he sits a hot mug on the counter, and Mallory picks it up. "What do I owe ya?" She asks Kenji.

"No, I can pay," I say, unzipping the purse. "My drink is way more than yours —"

She cuts me off. "My treat. I insist." Mallory's dark eyes bore into mine.

"Okay," I blink rapidly as she turns away, and give myself a small shake. *Get your shit together, Shaw.*

She pays him in cash, leaves a five dollar bill in the tip jar - *brownie points* - and we walk to a pair of upholstered armchairs and sit.

She takes a sip of her coffee, and her bright red lipstick doesn't even leave a mark on the white mug. "So, you must come here pretty often. Favorite haunt?"

I take another sip and let out a satisfied sound. I flush after realizing it might sound a little too suggestive. I clear my throat. "Oh yeah, I'm here pretty much every weekend. It's an addiction."

She lets out an amused sound. "Books are like, your thing, huh?"

"Well, I guess you could say that," I say sheepishly. "I'm actually a librarian. At an elementary school."

Her eyes widen and she grins. "A librarian? That's hot."

My cheeks burn. Have they *not* been red since last night? I sip my macchiato, hoping the cup covers at least some of my blushing face.

"What about you?" I finally manage. Her smile falters, only for a moment, but then returns like the sun emerging from behind a cloud.

"I'm actually self-employed," she says vaguely, before taking a sip of her coffee.

How are her teeth so white when she drinks black coffee?

"Oh," I say. I'm surprised to hear she isn't a runway model. Or a princess. "That sounds interesting. Must be nice to set your own hours."

She nods, but her eyes are unfocused. "It's . . . definitely an adventure." I don't pry any further.

The rest of our conversation is more of the same. Where we spent our early adulthoods (I got my Master's here on the East Coast, and she skipped college to travel Europe), our ages (I choke a bit on my macchiato when she says twenty-five; she doesn't bat a perfect eyelash when I say thirty), and so on.

When our cups are drained, we return them to the counter, and I thank Kenji, who gives me a thumbs up when Mallory turns away. I give him a small smile and a wave, and then I'm back out in the bright morning light.

It's not quite lunchtime, but the streets are still pretty crowded with people going in and out of the local shops. A farmer's market nearby is bustling, and the sound of an electric guitar lilts through the air on a warm breeze.

"Hey," Mallory says, and I turn to her. "Can I give you a kiss goodbye?" She asks, her voice low and slightly husky.

I blush again, but there's no hiding it this time. I stammer something nonsensical but manage a small nod, which is all the permission she needs.

Before I can blink, her mouth is on mine. She tastes of black coffee, and her red lips are warm and soft.

Finally, we pull apart, and I sway for a moment. My vision has gone blurry; I have to blink several times to bring the world back into focus. Her eyelids are heavy, and she reaches for my hand, rubbing her thumb back and forth across my palm. I shiver.

"You know," she says. "I was actually hoping to get out for a hike today, and I think I'll just go there next if you want to tag along. We could . . . spend some more time together." She stares into my eyes, her intent crystal clear.

This is absurd. And fast. Normally, I don't mind fast. In fact, I had made every romantic encounter I've had for the last decade as fast as I could.

But there's something about Mallory that is unlike anyone I've been with before. I can't identify what, but something deep inside me flutters when I look at her. It draws me to her.

I do not want this to be like every other encounter.

Still, it's definitely not the smartest thing to go into the woods with someone I just met. I'd much rather just go back to her place. But it's broad daylight. There will probably be plenty of people there, and I've got my pepper spray tucked in my small crossbody purse.

Her deep brown eyes bore into my soul as I hesitate. For a moment, her irises look dark enough to be completely black.

"Um, I'm not really sure —"

She pulls me into another quick kiss.

Fuck it, I think, as I blink rapidly once again, pushing back the haze that seems to be fogging my mind.

"Okay, yeah," I breathe.

What could happen?

<div align="center">~~~~~~~~~~</div>

I had walked to the bookstore, but she had driven, so we make our way to the parking lot to find her car. As she unlocks her doors with the fob, she glances at me. Her expression changes abruptly to one of concern.

"Hey, you okay?"

I attempt a smile. "Yup."

She's not convinced. "You seem a little pale."

I wring my hands and look away, embarrassed. "I'm just, I kind of have a . . . a thing about being in cars. I was in a bad accident as a kid, and I just have to hype myself up to be in them."

She says nothing for a moment, then puts her arm around my shoulder and squeezes me tightly. "Don't worry baby. I can go slow."

She opens the door for me and I sit down jerkily. When she sits in the driver seat, she quickly rolls all the windows down. "Get some fresh air. We'll be there soon."

As her sedan makes its way up the winding road to the hills, she engages me in more small talk as I try not to panic. *You're being ridiculous*, I chide myself. Why the hell did I agree to do this? *Idiot.*

She drives with one hand; the other one grips mine tightly over the center console. Her hands are soft. I hope mine aren't as sweaty as I think they are.

Finally, she pulls into a parking area, and I clamber out of the vehicle as soon as she comes to a stop. I turn to gaze around the parking area as I take deep breaths to calm myself. There are, as I predicted, a good number of people here. The late June air is hot, but a small breeze offers some relief.

"You good to go?" Mallory asks, and I nod, a little less shaky than I had been. We walk to the trail head, hand in hand.

After about twenty minutes of walking, we branch off from the main path and down a small side trail, where we come upon a tree in a small clearing that forms a sort of natural bench. It's bent almost perfectly horizontal near the base, then curves back on itself before shooting upward.

I wonder if it was guided to grow this way, rather than being allowed to follow its natural progression, and the thought brings with it a twinge of sadness.

I sit on the tree trunk and stretch my calves out, pulling my toes toward me as I reach for them. I'm glad I wore sneakers for our coffee date. I had debated an outfit that involved pumps, but decided that my beat-up sneakers, jean shorts, and a flowy tank top were perfect for a casual coffee.

I had grabbed a light flannel as I walked out the door, which I now have wrapped around my waist, using it to wipe the sweat from my brow when Mallory isn't looking.

She plunks down next to me. "Well, now that we're alone . . ." She trails off, a devilish gleam in her eye, and a smirk on her lips. I glance around and realize she's right.

We're definitely not *far* from the main trail, but it is a nice little secluded spot. I can faintly hear voices coming from the people walking up and down the hill. They're all far enough away for a few minutes of privacy.

I bite my lip and tug on my crescent moon pendant.

She pulls me onto her lap and kisses me slowly. I kiss her back breathlessly, straddling her hips as she puts her hand up into my hair, sending tiny bolts of lightning into my scalp and down my spine.

She parts my lips with her tongue. She's gentle, and tender, and her movements are slow and deliberate. She runs her fingers down the sides of my neck, rubs her thumb over my collarbones, and puts her hands on my breasts.

I moan my pleasure into her mouth.

Her hands move away from my breast for a moment, and I whimper my disappointment, making her grin. She moves one hand up under my tank top, then down the top of my bralette to cup my bare skin. I exhale slowly against her lips.

She begins rubbing my nipples while she wraps her other hand around the back of my neck and pulls my mouth down onto hers again.

After a moment, she lies down and pulls me on top of her. Luckily, this tree trunk is wide enough to accommodate the new position.

My breasts dangle above her face for a moment while she takes in the view, then puts one in her mouth. She tugs on my hips to bear down on her, and I follow her direction.

She begins to move her hips back and forth, rubbing hard against me, sending jolts of pleasure up from my clit into my stomach. A moan escapes my lips when her devilish gaze pierces me.

"Shhhh," she chides. I clamp my mouth shut.

I close my eyes and tilt my head back and forth, feeling drunk. When I open them again, another pair is staring straight back at me from the edge of the brush.

I yelp and scramble off Mallory, hastily pulling my clothes back into place.

She blinks rapidly and follows my gaze to the brush. I had blinked for just a moment while I was moving, and now the eyes are gone.

"What's wrong?" She asks, sitting up.

"I . . ." My voice shakes pathetically. I'm incredibly embarrassed at the thought of getting caught in public. It's not something I've really done before, except for a few drunken hours in college in the back seats of cars with engines that were way too loud and men that were way too toxic.

What the hell are you doing? I scream at myself internally.

I clear my throat to steady myself. "There were eyes staring at me from the brush."

She turns, sees nothing, then glances back at me with one eyebrow raised. "I don't see anything. You sure it wasn't a trick of the light on the leaves?"

I furrow my brow and frown at her, annoyance prickling. *I know what I saw.* At least . . . I think I do? My confidence wavers. Maybe it *was* just my imagination. My vision *had* been a bit hazy from pleasure, after all.

The eyes were huge, and yellow, and more than six feet off the ground; they definitely weren't human, whatever they were. But maybe it was just a yellowing leaf fluttering in the light breeze?

Shadows are still bouncing all over the place as the leaves dance in the wind. It's entirely possible that I imagined them.

"I . . . I guess it could have been the light," I say, feeling utterly foolish. Mallory tilts her head sympathetically, her gaze thick with pity.

My annoyance flares up again. I walk past her, toward where I had seen the eyes, unsure if I would rather see them or *not* see them. I scan back and forth between the trees, but see nothing but leaves.

"Maybe it was a coyote or something?" She says behind me.

After a few moments, I let out a small sigh, and cast my gaze downward in defeat.

But then I yelp.

There's a giant paw print right near the edge of the brush, bigger than my head. My eyes widen. "That's definitely not a coyote," I whisper. My heart hammers against my chest.

Mallory materializes at my side, and I jump. I hadn't even heard her get up. Her eyes grow wide as she spots the print, and she whistles softly. "Well, I don't want to run into whatever it *is*."

Just then, we hear a deep, rumbling growl in the brush, directly ahead of us.

I snap my head up to the source of the growl, frozen, and see Mallory from the corner of my eye, pulling something from her pocket.

Does she have a fucking gun on her? I think wildly.

I swear I see that pair of eyes glaring hungrily back at me from the depths of the brush when Mallory suddenly whips a hand across my mouth and nose, clamping a damp cloth over them.

She wraps her other arm around my chest, squeezing so tightly I think she's going to crack my ribs.

Holy shit, she's strong, I think frantically.

I try to hold my breath, but my panic surges. I take a few struggling breaths and kick backward at her, but her stance is wide and firm. Even as I connect with her kneecap, her leg barely buckles, and her grip on my face stays firm.

The world begins to spin, and my vision blurs. Just before I slump to the ground and tumble into oblivion, I hear a booming voice scrape through my own head like hammers being dragged across a metal roof.

Primal, icy fear shoots through my veins.

Well done.

The world goes black.

Sacrifice

When I come to, my head is throbbing. *What the hell did she do to me?* I think groggily, blinking to reorient myself to the waking world.

I attempt to pull my arms across my chest, but I can only move them a fraction of an inch before searing pain erupts in my wrists. Fear shoots through me, and I struggle for a moment, desperate to escape my binds. They don't budge. My ankles are bound just as tightly.

I look around to figure out where I am, and realize that I'm tied to a giant stone slab. The harsh ropes cut viciously into my flesh, and they're connected to something below the slab that I can't see.

I'm about four feet off the ground in the middle of a giant clearing ringed by trees. *Giant* trees. Massive pines that are too big to be natural. Towering maples and oaks that have to be a thousand years old at least.

Where the hell am I? But I don't have time to wonder for long before I realize that the tops of the trees are bathed in golden light instead of there being a glaring sun boring down on me from overhead.

It's the golden hour. We got to the trail around eleven in the morning. *How long have I been out?* I fight through the fog in my brain to do the math. *About ten hours?* How is that even possible?

I'm sick to my stomach, whether due to whatever I was drugged with, my anxiety, or the fact that I haven't eaten in over twelve hours, I'm not sure. Probably all three.

Then, belatedly, I realize that I am wearing only my pendant and a thin, white slip that barely covers my ass. My skin is frozen where it touches the cold stone, and I am splayed open for all to see — not that anyone is here. I begin to struggle once more, desperate to cover myself somehow.

"Shit." I hear Mallory's voice from somewhere above my head. I try to twist to see her, but I don't make it very far.

She walks to my side. Her face has transformed into a cruel mask. "Guess I need to up the dosage," she says mildly.

She grabs something from below the slab, and as she straightens up, she's holding the cloth again, and she's got a glass bottle tipped against it, drenching it.

"Wait," I cry out. "Please. What's going on?"

"I've been keeping you out all day, but you're waking up sooner now, so obviously you're building up a tolerance, and now you're getting more." She says this with no emotion, like she's a robot.

"But why —?" But it's too late. She presses the cloth against my face, and it's like I'm drowning. The world fades away once again.

~~~~~~~~~

The next time my eyes open, a full moon hangs in the sky, almost directly overhead. It's far too big, and too close. If I reach up, I may be able to touch it.

I'm groggy, but I'm afraid to move or make a noise in case Mallory is watching, waiting to plunge me into the inky darkness once more.

Tears well up in my eyes and spill out, streaming down my temples to pool in my ears. I can't move to wipe them; I can't move to do anything. My lip trembles, but I suppress a sob. *I'm going to die.*
~~~~~~~~~

The minutes pass, and I have nothing else to do but watch the too-big moon lilt toward its zenith. Soon though, I hear movement above my head once again. I tremble.

"No sign of any trouble," I hear Mallory say. *Is she talking to me? I think indignantly. She doesn't consider this trouble?*

A beat passes, but then she speaks again as if responding to someone, though no one else had spoken.

"Yes, sir."

There is silence once more. I don't even hear her walk away. *Maybe she was on a phone call?* The thought twists my stomach. *Oh god, are more people coming? Am I going to be some kind of ritual sacrifice?*

My brain only has a moment to begin thinking up terrifying worst-case scenarios before a giant shadow blocks out the light of the moon. *What the hell?*

I blink, and let out an involuntary, piercing scream. The same eyes I had seen in the brush earlier, beaming yellow and as big as saucers, are staring down at me, unblinking.

It's a massive wolf. I've only seen wolves up close in captivity, and they were big, but this wolf is *monstrous*. Its fur is jet-black, and its hot breath blows on my face in heavy streams that move my hair, even dampened as it is with my sweat.

Silence. The command booms in my head like a thunder clap; it echoes and rattles around, scattering my thoughts. I stop screaming, but my mouth hangs open in fear; my entire body trembles like a leaf.

It will be over soon. I realize that the wolf is talking to me.

The wolf. Is talking.

In my head.

"Wha . . . what?" I whisper.

Soon you will be changed, and then you will be my mate. For eternity. It states this as if it's telling me its dinner plans. *Just a small salad, then I'll see how I feel.*

But then my brain hooks into one particular word it had said. "Changed?" I hiss.

The moon is nearly in position. Just another minute or so, then I will change you, and we will be mated for life. The wolf brings a massive paw up to my cheek. His paw pads are rough, and they scrape my cheek as he rubs it once before moving it away again. He has yet to blink during this exchange.

A squeak bubbles up from my throat. "No, I won't let you." *As if you can stop him, idiot.*

Fear not, beloved, the wolf booms. *It will only hurt for a few weeks.*

My blood runs cold with fury.

Like hell. I begin tugging madly at the ropes binding my arms and legs. The rope twists tighter, cutting into my flesh, but I don't stop. I scream with rage.

The wolf only glances up at the moon, then moves down the stone slab to stand beside my legs. I thought it was on its hind legs this whole time - as if *that* made more sense - but I realize that it's on all fours, and still, the tips of its ears are definitely more than six feet from the ground.

It is time. He bares his teeth, massive canines the length of my hand poised to bite into my thigh. My scream reaches a fever pitch, and I thrash wildly as his jaws widen.

His hot breath hits my thigh, and I prepare for searing pain when several things happen at once. Something small and sharp flies past my head and buries itself into the wolf's shoulder. It rears back and snarls in rage.

Then I hear shouting all around me, and Mallory screeches somewhere above my head where I can't see. There's a sound like a gas stove being ignited, and flames flare up around me in a ring, about three feet away.

The wolf jumps back farther, and I see thorny vines twist viciously around his neck and snout as if they're alive. He's yanked sharply to the ground, and out of my field of vision.

The clearing is in calamity. I see three shadows darting around, converging on the wolf. More arrows fly through the air. The sound of a tidal wave crashes nearby, and I begin to think that the heat of the flames is going to cook me alive.

Suddenly, a woman holding a dagger materializes out of thin air directly beside me. I don't know when I had stopped screaming, but I start again instantly.

"Shut up!" She bellows at me, and I do. "Hold still!"

She grabs my wrist and cuts through the rope, then moves quickly to my other three limbs, slicing those ropes as well.

"Sit up," she barks, and I do, shakily.

She yanks on a large piece of fabric which is tied around her waist, then throws it around my shoulders.

I realize distantly that it's a cloak, and that it's deliciously warm, as if it's just come out of a dryer. The heat warms me instantly, and some control comes back into my limbs.

She grabs my hand, yanks me off the slab, and I tumble off, nearly crushing her in the process. I'm barely standing on my unsteady feet before she pulls me toward the ring of fire.

"No!" I scream in terror. But even as I do, the flames part like the Red Sea, and she drags me through the opening. As soon as we're through, the flames slide away in various directions like living things, serpentine in their movements.

"Run into the trees!" The woman yells at me as she sprints next to me. She's at least half a foot shorter than me, but she keeps pace with my long stride. "Don't look back!"

I fully intend to listen to her, but then I hear a piercing, otherworldly scream somewhere behind me. It starts low and angry, then rises in pitch, becoming more frantic.

I screech to a halt, but the woman keeps running, apparently unaware that I have stopped. I whip my head toward the source of the scream. It's Mallory. At least, I think it is.

Walls of flames snake back and forth behind her, backlighting her into nothing but a shadow as each one passes. But when she's lit by only the blazing moon, it's clearly her, except . . . it's also *not* her. I can't quite comprehend what I'm seeing.

Her skin has turned blood red, and giant bat wings have sprouted from her back. Each section of her wings is tipped with a long, razor-sharp talon. She's struggling with another figure that dwarfs her — Mallory may be six feet tall, but the man she's fighting has nearly a foot on her.

His shoulders are impossibly wide, and his muscles ripple under a blue, skin-tight suit. Dark hair falls around his ears in shaggy waves that stick out wildly. A wall of flame flares up behind them and halts in place, casting the pair into shadow.

As I watch, the man seizes her by her two short horns, and he pulls her close. I think wildly that he's going to kiss her, but then he opens his mouth, and I see four long fangs glint in the light just before they sink into Mallory's neck. They stay there for only a moment before he rips back viciously, blood and flesh tearing away with his fangs.

I sink to my knees as bile rises in my throat; I clench the cloak around me like it's going to hold me together. Then, all at once, the woman is back, clutching at my shoulder, trying desperately to get me to move.

"What the hell are you *doing*?" She screeches. "You have to fucking *run!*" She heaves me up and I cling to her numbly. She's much stronger than she looks, but she can't move my legs for me.

I'm still staring at the gory scene in front of me. The fire has moved on, and I see everything in the harsh light of the blazing moon.

The man - the monster - who just ripped out Mallory's throat straightens to his full, mountainous height, and tosses the ravaged body down with a sickening *thump*. Her limbs lay at unnatural angles, but she can't feel the discomfort anymore.

The man turns to glare at me as blood runs down either side of his mouth in rivulets. Long fangs hang out of his lips, slicked in Mallory's blood. His irises are gleaming rubies, and his hungry glare makes me certain that I'm his next victim.

My legs suddenly move of their own accord. I release the woman and begin running, but I can't think, and I'm not moving toward the trees as she had instructed. I don't know where the hell I'm going, only that I need to get away from that monster.

The woman screams at me again, but then she's drowned out by a loud wailing, like a siren, that rends my mind in two. The volume and intensity cause me to slow as I clutch my ears in a vain attempt to block out the sound.

What the fuck?

I cringe in the direction of the noise and realize with a chill that freezes me where I stand that the wolf is racing toward me as he howls in rage. I had been so preoccupied with one monster, that I had temporarily forgotten about this one.

It is going to be my final, fatal mistake.

I see several other figures running toward us, but the wolf is too fast. It's on me in another second, and it slams me into the ground. All the air explodes from my lungs at once, and I'm in too much pain to suck any more back in.

Four blade-like claws drag from my left shoulder to my right ribs as the wolf tosses me like a rag doll, but though the pain is the worst that I have ever felt, I have no air left to scream. Hot blood gushes out from the cuts, soaking my torso in seconds, and I begin to feel light-headed.

An instant later, that pain is overshadowed by an explosion of agony erupting from my right thigh. The wolf's jaw is wrapped entirely around it, his fangs sinking deep into my flesh. My vision flashes white, and my ears begin to ring piercingly.

More sticky blood spurts out of me. I can't believe I have more to give. Somehow, my lungs find a reserve of air, and an echoing scream rips from my throat. It sounds, for one wild moment, like a howl.

Another sharp arrow hits the wolf's flank, and he releases my thigh before sprinting away in a flash.

Don't worry, beloved, I will find you again. The wolf's voice echoes through my head as consciousness begins to slip away from me. *If you survive.*

I distantly register two people falling to their knees on either side of me.

"*¿Qué carajo?* I thought you had him!" A man roars far above me.

"He broke through my vines!" Another man snarls in response. "He's gotten stronger!"

"Or you've gotten weaker!" The first man barks.

"Not now you two!" Yells a woman, but her voice is different than the one who had cut my bindings.

Their yelling continues, but the sound grows more and more distant as I slip away.

The last thing I see before my vision goes black is the full moon hanging directly above me, bathing me in her beams.

She's the most beautiful thing I've ever seen.

~ Third Quarter ~

Dreams

My frenzied dreams drip with blood. I dream of vampires ripping my throat out, and monstrous wolves the size of buses clawing me to pieces. I dream of Mallory, her ravishing smile twisting unnaturally, elongating until her mouth is as wide as her whole face, before black sludge erupts from her throat, coating me until I drown.

I dream of a young Black woman with the sun shining on her rich mahogany skin. Her eyes are closed, and she's turned half away from me, smiling up at the sky, soaking in the warmth. She's radiant, and though my hand is over hers, we may as well be a world apart.

I can't touch her like I really want to. I can't say three small words to her without tossing the world off its axis. She'll never want me the way I want her, but I will love the pieces of her that she gives me with everything I have.

Part of her is better than none, and I would never ask for more than she can give.

Her eyes open and she turns to me, smiling. Her eye sockets are pools of blood, and the side of her face is mangled; bits of bone stick out of gashes through which flesh and gore ooze. I scream and flail backward as she disappears into inky nothingness.

I dream of screeching car tires and blaring horns. Of metal crunching, melting in a blazing inferno, and two people screaming for me to run. To run, and never look back. And just like I had done in the clearing under the full moon, I do.

I don't ever stop running.

28

~ New Moon ~

Waking

I wake with a giant gasp as I sit fully upright, and fling a sweat-soaked sheet off of me. I press my face into my hands, and I realize my cheeks are wet with tears. A strangled sound erupts from my lips, and my shoulders shake as I'm wracked with sobs.

I don't know how long this goes on, but eventually, I run out of tears. As I wipe my eyes and try to return my breathing to normal, I assess my surroundings.

I'm in a firm, twin bed, pressed snugly in the corner of the room, covered with crisp white sheets. There's a large window on the opposite wall, through which I see that the sun is beginning to rise.

The room itself is sparsely furnished, and the walls are deep brown. Beyond the foot of the bed is a large cedar wardrobe. A small nightstand sits to my right, and there's a wooden stool near the foot of the bed that sits deep in grooves in a thick, white carpet that takes up the area between the bed and a door. A small writing desk sits against the wall in the corner opposite me.

I try to swing my legs over the side of the bed, but a sharp pain shoots through my right leg and throughout my chest. I suck air through my teeth, curl in on myself, and see that bandages wrap around my right thigh, and all around my chest and shoulders.

I dimly realize that I'm wearing only the bandages and plain white underwear that are *not*, in fact, mine. But they fit nicely, at least. I groan as the memories flood my head. My dreams had been bad enough, but reality is so much worse.

The knob turns in the door abruptly, and a tall, bespectacled man walks in. He flips on the light and stops short when he sees me sitting up, pulling the sheet hastily back over myself. He's wearing a white V-neck shirt that sets off his rich bronze complexion, dark jeans, and loafers.

He smiles warmly, and the corners of his eyes crinkle. "*Sabah al-khair*. Good morning. I hope you slept well." He steps into the room, and I see that his toned arms are laden with medical supplies: fresh bandages, tape, and a jar that is filled with some kind of poultice. He's also holding a mug full of steaming green tea.

His accent tells me that he's likely Middle Eastern, and he seems to be about my age. He's got a defined and close-cropped beard and mustache. His black hair is short on the sides, but there's a mop of thick curls on the top of his head. His warm brown eyes are soft, but the rest of him is as hard as chiseled stone; he has the body of a warrior.

He is, in short, incredibly handsome.

"How are you feeling?" He asks as he walks toward the desk.

My eyes follow him of their own volition. "Who are you?" I finally manage.

He chuckles. "Sorry, of course. My name is Saif Rahim. At your service."

He sets the supplies down on the desk and tosses me a two-fingered salute, then pushes his round glasses back up his nose by their thin black frames.

A small smile creeps onto my lips. "I'm Eilidh. Eilidh Shaw."

He returns my smile. "How are you feeling, Eilidh?" He asks, pulling the stool close to my side as he sits lithely upon it.

"Like shit," I say simply, gesturing at, well, all of me.

He barks a sudden, booming laugh that warms my bones. "I can imagine!" He says. "You took one hell of a beating, but you're a tough one. Your wounds are healing up nicely. I was just coming in to see if the bandaging needs changed."

I look down at myself, feeling like a mummy, and see a faint reddish-brown seeping through the gauze.

I wince. "I guess they probably do." Then, thinking about this handsome stranger seeing my bare chest, my eyes widen and I blush. He notices.

"If it makes you uncomfortable . . . " He begins gently.

But I cut him off, embarrassed. "No, I'm sorry, it's fine." I'm not sure why exposing my breasts feels so embarrassing. I've had a male gynecologist before, so this should be much easier. Of course that had been an old man and this man is . . . young. And incredibly attractive. I gulp.

He hesitates, but then nods. "If you want me to stop at any point, just tell me. Okay?" I nod, so he pulls the sheet down, and begins to unravel the bandages from around my thigh.

I wince more with fear than actual pain. *What is my leg going to look like under there?* But when the bandages are removed, it's surprisingly not as bad as I expected.

Deep purple bruising blooms in a kaleidoscopic pattern across my thigh, but that seems to be the worst of it. The puncture wounds are nearly healed, and they aren't actively bleeding. Saif gently rotates my leg as he inspects it closely, his thick brows drawn together in concentration. The bruises are tender, but his touch is skilled and gentle.

"The bites are definitely better than yesterday," he murmurs, almost to himself. "Maybe one more round of the poultice." Our eyes meet, and I look away quickly.

He stands and leans over me, reaching toward my left shoulder.

"Still okay?" He asks, and I nod stiffly.

He carefully begins undoing the bandages from around my torso. I close my eyes and his scent hits me; it's a mixture of floral sweetness and charcoal soap. When the bandages are completely off, I open my eyes, assuming it will be relatively okay, just like my thigh.

My assumption is wildly incorrect.

I inhale sharply as I see the mess that is my torso. Four long, angry, wounds rake from my left shoulder, across my sternum, and end just under my bottom right rib, almost in line with my navel.

The gashes have all been stitched, but blood oozes from the wounds regardless. I forget entirely about my breasts being exposed, and utter a strangled sob.

Saif's warm eyes are filled with sympathy. "I know," he says softly, his voice full of regret. "I'm so sorry. I stitched them as soon as I could, but I had to clean them all out first, and that took some time, and they were so *deep*." He takes my hand and squeezes it tightly. He must have noticed that I'm shaking.

I take my other hand and slowly, tenderly, run a few fingers over the bumpy stitches that are quite literally holding me together. I hiss, my teeth bared like a wounded animal.

"That wolf," I whisper. "He said he would find me again." Saif looks sick at the thought. "Why would he try to rip me in half if he wanted me alive? I don't understand." I shake my head numbly and think briefly that I may be going back into shock.

Saif clears his throat and pushes his glasses up his strong nose. "I'm not sure," he says dimly. "Maybe it was an accident. It all happened so fast. The bite was intentional, but he was dragging you around for a few seconds before that. I don't think he meant to claw you like *this*."

More tears sting my eyes, and I finally tear my gaze from the claw marks. "Please put the bandages on," I plead quietly.

He doesn't hesitate. He gently presses on my right shoulder to lay me down, opens the jar of poultice, and rubs it gently over my wounds. It's heavy and clay-like, and smells like honey and chamomile. A cooling sensation sinks into my chest and dulls the pain to a tolerable level.

When he's done, and my new bandages are secured, he tosses the old bandages in a garbage can in the corner and wipes his hands on a small towel.

He walks over to the desk, grabs the mug of tea, and brings it to me. "This is the tea that I have every morning," he says. "It will perk you up."

I take a grateful sip and savor the refreshing minty taste that hits my tongue. As I gulp it down, he stands next to the head of the bed, though I can't bring myself to look at him.

"Which do you prefer, roses or dahlias?" He asks.

I blink at him in confusion. "What?"

He winks. "Humor me."

I flush. "Dahlias," I squeak.

He nods, puts his hand in his pocket, and pulls out a seed. It sits in his outstretched hand for only a moment before it sprouts before my eyes, growing into a beautiful, though unnaturally green, dahlia.

"To match your eyes," he says, and tucks it behind my ear.

I'm frozen, my mug of tea hovering in the air a few inches from my lips. "How did you do that?" I whisper.

His eyes sparkle. "I'm a Mage."

A beat passes as I blink at him.

"Like, a magician?" I ask.

He smiles sideways and shakes his head. I frown.

"What happened to you was a terrible thing, Eilidh. But I want you to know that things here can be beautiful as well."

"And where is 'here?'" I ask quietly. *Please don't say New Jersey.*

He gestures to the room around us. "This is Arkenvale Castle, the seat of King Auberon Danodraic. This kingdom, this dimension, is called Tenazeryth."

Those are certainly . . . words. I can't do anything but stare.

He smiles sympathetically. "It will all make more sense soon. Let's take a short walk. We can go to the kitchen and get some breakfast, then it will be time for you to meet everyone else."

I'm utterly drained, but at the mention of food, my stomach growls loudly.

"Okay, sure." I glance down at my current outfit. "But I think I need some clothes first."

He chuckles and points to the wardrobe. "That's been filled for you. I'll be just outside. Let me know if you need help getting anything on," he says before he closes the door.

I get up gingerly and slowly make my way to the wardrobe. I pull it open, and my eyes widen as I see the contents. He wasn't kidding. It's packed to the brim with clothes of various styles; it's like a high school drama club's dream.

Long skirts, short shorts, tank tops, flowy blouses, hoodies, and even a leather jacket are stuffed inside. I grimace and stuff that toward the back.

I pull hangers out at random, becoming quickly overwhelmed, though it helps that each hanger contains an entire outfit. Whoever chose these clothes must have sensed that I have no idea how to dress myself if it's not for work. These outfits were chosen with an expert eye.

One piece catches my eye, and I pull the hanger out. It's a long, emerald green collared dress with a built-in belt, and buttons running almost the entire length of it. I decide this may be the closest thing to a hospital gown I can find in the wardrobe, so I wrap it around myself and button it up.

The process is slow; I'm terrified to so much as brush my ravaged chest with my hand, and so I pull each button through shakily.

Finally, when it's buttoned, I tie the belt loosely, then grab some simple brown sandals from the floor of the wardrobe and shove them onto my feet. A few scrunchies hang on a hook inside, and I pull my bedraggled hair into a low knot at the back of my neck. I grimace at the mirror that hangs on the inside of the wardrobe door, but I guess this is as good as it's going to get.

I totter over to the window to glance outside. I'm on the second floor of the castle, and the sun is rising to my left. Long grass ripples in the light breeze across rolling hills as far as the eye can see.

I walk to the door and open it. Saif is leaning up against a railing that runs around the entirety a balcony which is arranged in a square around a massive spiral staircase. I'm in one corner, next to a short hallway that leads diagonally away. There are three doors on each of the four walls, which, I assume, lead to more bedrooms like mine. All the walls are smooth, gray stone.

"Everything go okay?" He asks. I smile and nod faintly, taking in our surroundings. "Great," he says. He leads me straight ahead, then to the right, and we head down the spiral staircase.

It's a work of art. Each baluster is carved from iron to resemble vines, down to small thorns spaced periodically. The entire thing is covered in lush green vines - live ones - with fragrant purple flowers that cascade to the ground below.

"What is this?" I ask, running a finger gently over a delicate petal.

"Wisteria," he says, and touches one section of the plant lovingly. "It's my favorite."

My mind begins to race as we follow the winding stairs. Who else is here with me? Did the wolf succeed in changing me, or did he mean that he would find me later to finish the job? I'm fine other than the wounds on my chest and thigh. I don't have a sudden craving for raw meat. I don't have the urge to sit under a full moon and howl at it. Maybe these people - whoever they are - had saved me in time?

Hope flutters deep in my chest. *Maybe.*

As we get to the lower portion of the staircase, I can see two sets of large wooden doors, one each on the front and back walls. The area we walk into is fairly large, with several more doors spaced along the side walls.

When we get to the very bottom of the staircase, Saif points to the right. "That's the washroom. Everything is in stalls, so no need to knock when you need to shower or something." He smiles. "There's already a toothbrush in there for you. They're all bamboo; yours has a green handle. And the toothpaste is homemade; there's a jar on your sink for you. You'll see what I mean."

Homemade toothpaste? "Okay, thanks."

He leads me to the left and we go through the wooden door. As it swings open, I see a large room, in the middle of which sits a wooden dining table with long benches running parallel to it. All the wood is a deep cherry that has been polished so much I can quite literally see my reflection in parts of it.

The wall opposite us is mostly taken up by three rectangular stained-glass windows. They're minimalist designs - a sword on a blue background, a simple yellow chalice, and a red gemstone with swirls of black and gray - but the craftsmanship is impeccable. In between the windows hang two long tapestries featuring a bear and a dragon.

Saif gestures to the table. "Sit anywhere you like." I decide to perch on the end of the closest bench and face the stained-glass windows, through which the light is coming in brighter and brighter with each passing moment. Judging by the amount of light, I think we're facing East. *If the sun follows the same rules here as it does at home.*

"What would you like to eat?" He nods toward a door to my left. "I'll whip something up for you in the kitchen. What'll it be? Toast?

Eggs?"

My stomach flips at the thought. "Just toast please."

His forehead creases. "You need some protein to start rebuilding your strength," he says.

I bite the inside of my lip. "Have any peanut butter in there?" I ask hopefully.

He's satisfied with that. "Of course. Be back in a flash. You just sit and rest."

I do as I'm told.

Not more than five minutes go by, and then he's back, holding a tray piled high with what must be about half a loaf of toasted bread, a water pitcher, a chalice, and glass jars full of peanut butter and some kind of jam.

He sets the tray down in front of me and begins slathering peanut butter on a slice. I wave him off when he attempts to hand it to me. "Please, I can do it myself," I say sheepishly. "You've already done too much for me."

But he's stubborn.

"I already ate. This is all yours." He brandishes the toast toward me again, and this time I take it. I nearly cry when I take a bite. It's the best damn peanut butter toast I have ever had. I moan a bit, too hungry to try to hide my flush when I hear the sound I had made.

"This is so fucking good."

His booming laugh reverberates through the large dining hall. "I'm glad you like it. All homemade," he says.

"You're amazing!" I say, one hand in front of my mouth.

He shakes his head, but smiles crookedly. "It's nothing."

After he returns the jars to the kitchen, we sit in companionable silence while I eat another two pieces of toast, but then I'm ready to get some answers. "So . . . what's next?"

He rises and beckons me to follow him. "Now, you meet King

Auberon."

Assignment

We leave the dining hall and he turns left, toward the next room. When we walk in, my eyes widen in awe.

The curving walls of the huge, circular room are made entirely of thick glass, and the sun blazes into the room from our left; it will set on the right side of the tower. *I bet the sunsets in this room are gorgeous.*

Green leaves fill a significant portion of the room; giant monsteras, ferns, and even a small lemon tree soak in the sun through the glass tower. Hanging baskets abound, overflowing with spider plants, pothos, and a trailing plant with purple leaves that I recognize, but don't know the name of. I assume Saif is responsible for them all.

In the center of the room is a huge, circular table. At the far end of the table, directly opposite of me, sits a large, ornate wooden chair.

But I don't have time to admire the furniture any longer. A man who can only be King Auberon sits on the chair, and he's staring directly at me, analyzing me with one squinting, blazing golden eye; his other eye is covered with a black patch.

He's a handsome white man who appears to be in his sixties; his shoulder-length hair and his close-cropped beard are salt and pepper. A simple golden crown adorns his head. He's wearing a deep blue tunic over a beige long-sleeve shirt.

There are three other people and three empty chairs sitting around the table. To the King's right is an empty chair, but to that chair's right is a familiar woman.

"You!" I say. "You're the one who saved me." She's East Asian, and her features are sharp and beautiful, like a gleaming dagger. Her clothes are sharp, too. She's got on a cream cashmere sweater and black pleated slacks. A simple but elegant gold ring with a violet gem gleams on her right middle finger.

Her mouth twists in a grimace, and she narrows her eyes. "I'm the one who failed to save you from *yourself*," she says curtly. Her tone is icy, and I flinch like she hit me.

My cheeks burn.

The chair to her right is empty as well, but in the two chairs just to my right sit a man and woman; they're an attractive pair who might be in their mid-twenties or so. They're both Black, and have the same exact broad nose and twinkling brown eyes. Siblings, perhaps?

The man's hair is in long box braids with a fade, he's got the braids wrapped up in a bun on top of his head, and his facial hair is close-cropped. A silver piercing adorns his left eyebrow. He's wearing a black jean jacket with an orange hoodie underneath, and his tight, dark jeans have holes in the knees.

The woman has long locs that cascade around her shoulders and back, interwoven with gold beads and coils. She's wearing a red tunic with a leather corset around her thin waist. She's got numerous gold piercings on the one ear I can see, and her dark lipstick is immaculate.

Saif moves to sit in the chair to the King's left. I realize I haven't moved an inch, and am standing directly in the doorway. I should probably sit, but just as I take my first step, I hear the door open behind me. I turn, and nearly smack into the widest pair of shoulders I've ever seen.

I take a step back involuntarily and, intending to apologize, open my mouth and look up into the man's eyes. Mine widen in terror as

I recognize them. The last time I had seen them, they were glinting horrifically at me in the light of the full moon, the same color as the blood that was running from his mouth.

I scream, and the monster that ripped out Mallory's throat smiles at me wickedly, his fangs on full display.

I fall to the ground, still screaming, and begin to scurry backward the moment I hit the stone floor. My chest is on fire with the effort, but I have to get away from this monster. He almost caught me that night, and now he's found me.

He must work for the wolf. He's here to kill me, or kidnap me.

I back into something and look up wildly, finally clamping my mouth shut. I realize that I have backed directly into Saif, who crouches down behind me. He grips my right shoulder and motions for me to calm down with his other hand.

"Hey, hey. It's okay. Don't worry about him." He glares up at the man as he finishes his sentence.

I stare at him in bewilderment, then snap my gaze back to the man standing in the doorway, and as I catch my breath, my eyes wander up his towering form.

He's wearing black combat boots, black jeans with rips all throughout them, and a dark blue cowl neck hoodie with an asymmetrical hem. It's so tight I'm not sure how he got it over his massive shoulders, or how he's currently able to breathe. Solid muscles bulge beneath the fabric.

When my eyes reach his face, my heart starts hammering all over again. *You've gotta be kidding me.*

After my initial shock, I register that in the light of the day, without blood dripping down his face, this man is *devastatingly* handsome. He's definitely ruined some lives over the years.

His shaggy, chestnut brown hair falls around his ears, but wild pieces stick up and curl at the ends; his square jaw and high cheekbones look like they could cut glass. His lips are thick, and his bright red irises set off his deep tan skin.

He puts both hands on his slender waist. "Oh, great. This one's skittish, isn't she? This should be interesting." He cocks an eyebrow scathingly, his fangs still bared at me in a condescending grin. His voice is fairly deep, almost musical, and a faint Hispanic accent breaks through on certain syllables.

I take it back. He's ruined *many* lives over the years.

Heat rushes to my cheeks. As Saif helps me to my feet and directs me to the empty chair closest to me, the man saunters over and sits down at King Auberon's right hand. He slouches back comfortably, and I can practically see his long legs manspreading under the table.

I sit down heavily and squeeze the legs of my chair. I stare hard at the wooden table in front of me, begging every power in the universe to open a hole in the floor and let me sink into it for the rest of eternity.

I reach for the pendant that normally hangs between my breasts, then realize with a sharp twist of my heart that it isn't there. *Of course it isn't there.* It probably got ripped to shreds when I was attacked. I take a shuddering breath.

Everything is excruciatingly awkward for several beats.

The man to my right clears his throat. "Sorry guys," he says, his bass tone breaking the silence. "I left my tension-cutting knife in my other pants." The woman I presume to be his sister punches him in the arm.

Auberon scowls faintly for a moment, but then he clears his throat and all other sounds cease. "Eilidh." His strong, baritone voice reverberates around the room. "My apologies for the . . ." He glances at the man to his right. "Unorthodox introduction."

I blink, then realize he's waiting for a response, his one, gleaming golden eye boring into me. I stammer. "I'm not — I mean, it's okay . .

. I'm sorry for screaming," I finish lamely. I flick my gaze around the room, but no one else moves.

A beat.

Oh. "Your Majesty," I squeak.

Auberon nods. "We have much to go over, so if you have questions, please keep them until the end."

Am I about to be quizzed on something? I think frantically. He makes a circular motion, starting with the mountainous man to his right, and ending with Saif. "I am King Auberon Danodraic, and these people are my paladins. They call themselves the Order." He glances to his right once more.

The other man's smirk is gone now; he's all business. "My name is Diego Vidales," he says, standing. "I lead the Order." He says it as if he's expecting me to either compliment him, or argue with him about it.

I stay silent and stare at the wall behind him.

He puts his hand lightly on the shoulder of the woman next to him, who looks coolly down her nose at me. "This is Jang Hyun-Joo." His voice changes when he says her name. It deepens just a fraction, and turns protective.

Obvious what's going on there. I shift in my chair.

He points at the Jokester with one long finger. I wonder distantly if he plays piano, then shake myself. *Focus, Shaw.*

"That one is Martín Peña, and his sister, Valentina." Martín gives me a quick up-and-down glance and winks at me. Valentina gives a friendly smile and a small, furtive wave as she punches her brother again. I don't think she is even at the right angle to have seen him wink, but she saw it somehow.

He finishes with a glance at Saif, but doesn't say anything. It might be my imagination, but his lip seems to curl for just a fraction of a second at Saif before he sits down and leans back once more.

"Um . . . hi." I fill the silence.

"Eilidh," Auberon says. "Tell us what you remember of the day you were attacked." My palms immediately feel clammy. I bring a hand to my left shoulder, where the claw marks feel deepest, and wince.

"I —" My voice falters. I clear my throat, squeeze my eyes shut, and continue. My heart starts racing and I have to take a deep breath. "I went with Mallory that morning to get coffee after she had asked me out the night before —" Diego snorts, and I can't help but glare at him and bite the inside of my lip for a moment.

"After that we . . ." I pause. "We went for a hike in the woods. We had walked onto a smaller trail when I saw a pair of yellow eyes staring at me from the brush. Then Mallory came up behind me and put some kind of cloth over my face. I —"

I blink hard. "I passed out. And when I woke up I was tied to that rock, and the sun was setting. I tried to get up, but she came back and told me that she'd been keeping me out all day. Then she put the cloth over my face again, and I didn't wake up again until it was dark."

I plead silently for Auberon not to make me continue the story. *You can guess the rest*, I want to say. But he motions for me to go on. "When I woke up again, it was dark, and I heard Mallory saying something behind me. Saying there was no sign of trouble."

I clench my hands in my lap.

"She was talking to someone, but I didn't hear any replies. Then a giant wolf was standing over me, telling me . . ." I suppress a gag. "Telling me he was going to turn me into his mate." I finish in a whisper.

A suffocating silence blankets the room. Valentina stares at me with deep sorrow in her dark eyes. Martín looks mildly ill. Diego speaks first.

"At what point did you fuck her?" His voice is clipped and low. I whip my head up and wince at the pain it elicits in the claw marks on my torso.

"Excuse you?" I ask him indignantly. "I did no such thing! Why do you th—" Auberon holds up a hand, silencing me.

"Unfortunately, Eilidh, you don't have all the facts correct." I stare at him, my mouth parted slightly.

I'm sorry, were you *there?* I want to ask, but I hold my tongue. He sighs heavily.

"The woman you call Mallory, was in fact, not that." He suddenly sounds exhausted.

I blink. "Not . . . a Mallory?" I'm lost.

"Not a woman," he says simply. "She was a succubus whose real name was Azaeroria. She was a mercenary who we have been hunting for months now. She's been luring women to their untimely demise, selling them off to the wolf, though we are not yet sure what more she was getting out of the arrangement."

I shudder. *I don't want to know.* "But what does that have to do with . . . anything physical?" I ask, avoiding Diego's scathing gaze.

"While humans *can* technically cross the wards into Tenazeryth, it is usually impossible unless they are one of us; unless they have supernatural blood in their veins, or have, shall we say, become acquainted with someone who does."

I shrug my right shoulder helplessly. "We made out, but —"

Auberon cuts me off with a raised palm. "Your decisions about your body are yours to make," he says curtly. "And it's not entirely impossible that it was a malfunction of the wards. Regardless of how it happened, the wards that guard our dimension recognized you as one of our own, and Azaeroria was able to bring you here to the wolf to perform his ritual. That wolf is in fact, someone I have been at odds with for far too long. Some time ago, I killed his mate in battle, and he has been a thorn in my side ever since. His name is Bleddyn.

He's a werewolf."

I laugh out loud, and everyone around the table freezes. Auberon narrows his eye, and I clamp my hands over my mouth. I stare at him in horror.

"I am . . . so sorry," I say meekly. The King closes his eye for a moment, clearly annoyed. But maybe he decides to give me a break due to the insanity of what I am trying to process.

"He —" I glance around at the others seated around me. "He wasn't a *werewolf*. He was just a *big* wolf. He didn't change into a man, and I saw him in broad daylight! He was a wolf then, too. And why bring me all the way to a new dimension?"

My eyes rove around this table of strangers who have, for some reason, taken me in, silently pleading with them to put an end to this joke. They're wrong. About all of it.

Maybe I'm still unconscious. Maybe I just fainted in the woods, and Mallory is dragging me back to the trail for help as we speak. I bite the inside of my lip hard, and taste a warm gush of copper.

Auberon explains. "Bleddyn has a flair for the dramatic; that clearing is where I killed his mate. Though this was the first time he's used it for his ritual."

I place my head in my hands, too numb to cry. I press my palms into my eyelids as I try to feel three things, smell two, and taste one without moving. I tap my foot against the cold floor.

Wait.

"Then why am I not a wolf right now?" I ask. "If Bleddyn is one all the time, why am I not?"

Bingo, I think triumphantly. But then my heart sinks.

"Bleddyn is old. *Very* old. Werewolves have virtually infinite lifespans, just like vampires." He glances at Diego, who is scowling at the table, and my eyes widen.

Vampire? I gulp as the King continues.

"In fact, you're the only two Shifters who have that power, due to your strong healing factors. With time, werewolves can eventually control their shifting, and morph at will. But that takes years."

I'm going to throw up. *I'm going to live forever?* That sounds like my own personal form of hell.

"Why am I here?" My words are hollow. I start to feel the sensation that I am not in the room at all, that I'm not sitting at this godforsaken table being told that I've been changed into an out-of-control monster. That's happening to someone else.

Unfortunate for her, but at least it isn't me.

Auberon holds out his hand in answer; he's clutching a silver dagger. He releases the dagger, and it floats as if hanging by an invisible string.

Then, as if snatched into the air by a bird of prey, it flies up at an angle, spins at its zenith, and rockets toward me. I can't even blink before it lands with a loud *thunk*, not six inches from me, the blade piercing at least an inch deep into the wood.

I watch, terrified, as the dagger sways back and forth hypnotically. The hilt is black with a thin silver chain snaking around it. Two silver wolf heads face away from each other to act as the crossguard, and a third wolf's face stares at me from the round pommel with eyes made of the darkest sapphires I've ever seen.

"With training, you can become a member of this Order, and once an Order member, always an Order member. Diego is your commander from here on out."

Auberon rises, clearly done with this meeting. He heads toward a narrow spiral staircase behind his throne which leads up to the second floor of the tower.

"You can't go back to Earth; your life is here now. Rest for today. Tomorrow, your training begins. You're going to kill Bleddyn."

~~~~~~~~~
~~~~~~~~~

I follow Saif numbly out of the meeting room and up the staircase to my bedroom. Finally, we make it to my room, and he helps me lie down.

After stepping out for a moment, he comes back with a steaming mug in his hands. I accept it and drink without question, desperate for relief from my throbbing head and chest. The tea this time is lavender and chamomile.

He sets the dagger and a holster down on my nightstand. I hadn't even grabbed it out of the table as I left the tower, as my mind had been too preoccupied with not having a panic attack.

"Is it silver? Won't touching that hurt me?" My voice is a strangled whisper.

He grimaces at the dagger. "It won't burn you if you touch it or anything. It will hurt like hell if you cut yourself with it, but it won't be fatal unless it's in your heart. But yes, it will take more strength and endurance for you to wield it. A blade must be pure silver for it to kill a werewolf. Just think of it as building up a tolerance." He doesn't sound any happier about the arrangement than I feel.

An absurd laugh bubbles up from deep within me. "I've spent the last few years building up an immunity.'"

Saif blinks at me, uncomprehendingly.

"Never mind," I mutter.

He quietly watches me drain the mug, then takes it from me when I finish. He helps me lay back against the pillow and smiles warmly as he pulls the comforter up over me. "Sleep well, Eilidh."

I don't.

~ Waxing Crescent ~

;

The next day, I am awoken by Saif knocking on the door before the light of dawn has even peeked above the horizon. He walks in wearing a cream-colored, short-sleeved running top that hugs his pecs, black cuffed joggers, and black running shoes.

I groan and roll onto my back. "Who do I petition to move training to the afternoon?"

He chuckles lightly. "The King."

I run my hands roughly over my face and groan again.

I try not to stare as he brings me another mug of mint tea, which he hands to me to sip. It's quite refreshing. It's no espresso, but it's delicious nonetheless.

He also has a notebook in his hand, which he sets on the nightstand. I tilt my head at it. The cover is emerald green, with the outline of a daisy on it.

"It's a journal to press your flowers in," he says, gesturing at the dahlia, which is lying on the nightstand, slightly wilted.

I move to put a hand over my heart, then remember my wounds at the last second. "Thank you," I say.

"Of course." He smiles and reaches into his pocket. He pulls out a seed, and then I watch in awe as it sprouts and grows and branches off into several clusters of small, purple petals.

He hands it to me, and I cradle it gently in my hands. "They're beautiful. What are they?"

He chuckles. "Alfalfa."

"Wow." I didn't even know alfalfa could flower. I set the precious little plant down on the journal, and he clears his throat.

"I was hoping to check your bandages again before we head out for the day," he says. I acquiesce, every fiber of my being wanting to lay back down and sleep.

As he's re-wrapping my right thigh, he taps a finger on the outside of my right ankle. "This tattoo," he says tentatively. My lips tighten. "I just, I wanted to let you know that if you ever need to talk, especially now, feel free to talk to me." His smile is a bit sad, and his dark eyes are heavy with empathy.

"I appreciate it," I say quietly.

"Do you mind if I ask," he says softly. "Why the top part of the semicolon is a cat's head?"

I sigh, and he backtracks. "Oh shit, I'm sorry that's way too personal."

I shake my head. "No, you're fine. Sorry. I just." I sigh again. "When I was twenty, my best friend was killed in a car accident." His eyes widen.

"Black cats were her favorite animal; she grew up with them. Her parents let her keep whatever cats she found that would follow her home. A few months after she died, I . . . didn't think I'd be able to keep living without her."

I clear my throat. "But then, as I was standing on the edge of the bridge, just trying to get my fingers to let go, this fuzzy black cat comes out of nowhere, perches on the ledge right in front of me, and just *stares*."

I turn to Saif, and my eyes well up. "It was like she had sent it. She was saying, 'Don't you dare!'" I wag my finger at nothing in particular, a wistful smile playing at my lips, lost in memories. I can see the cat's bright green eyes as clear as day.

"That cat sat with me all night, and I fell asleep with it curled in my lap. When I woke up the next morning, it was gone. I walked home and decided to keep living. For her." When I look at him again, I think he's about to well up too. I quickly swipe a tear from my eye. He takes my hand and runs his thumb over my skin.

"What was her name?" He asks quietly.

"Kianga," I reply wistfully. Her name is sweet on my tongue.

A loud rap on the door makes us both jump. Saif pulls his hand out of mine as the door opens.

My stomach drops when Diego steps into the room. I bring the sheet up over myself quickly, but he doesn't even acknowledge me; he just glares at Saif.

"Have her outside in fifteen minutes so we can see what she can do." He turns on his heel and walks out, slamming the door behind him.

"What the fuck is his *deal*?" I hiss to myself, then remember I am not alone. I wince at Saif, but he just shakes his head back and forth and rolls his eyes.

"Don't mind him, he's just in one of his moods. Doesn't want to train someone new." He mumbles more things under his breath as he stands and throws my old bandaging into the trash.

"Don't worry," he says. "His bark is worse than his bite."

I blanch, and a slightly deranged laugh bubbles up from my throat. He tilts his head at me quizzically. I take the bottom knuckles of my pointer fingers and press them against my top lip, waggling my fingers back and forth.

"But . . . fangs." I stare at him a moment longer while he realizes what I mean. His booming laugh warms me, and I smile.

"Okay, maybe not *that* much worse."

Lobita

After another quick breakfast of delectable peanut butter, jam, and fresh bread, Saif leads me out of the large doors at the back of the castle into a large yard surrounded by high stone walls.

I realize immediately that it is way too breezy and cold for the capri leggings and loose tank top I have on, though Saif seems completely unaffected. My toes go numb almost instantaneously through the running shoes I had found in the wardrobe.

I consider for a moment taking my hair out of its bun just for some warmth against my shoulders, but if I do that, I may never get it to cooperate again. It will fight back just to spite me.

Despite the cold, the morning is gorgeous. The sun shines brightly in a cloudless sky, and I can hear waves crashing somewhere far below us; we must be on a cliffside.

The rest of the Order members are already here, and they're all wearing various types of athletic clothes as well. Hyun-Joo and Valentina are both wearing tight leggings and sports bras, their hair tied back. They're both flawless. I shift back and forth, tugging at the hem of my tank top.

Diego is wearing a baby blue hoodie with a quilted design that runs down each sleeve to the thumb holes, gray cuffed sweatpants, and bright red sneakers that match his eyes.

He and Hyun-Joo stand a bit off from Martín and Valentina, deep in conversation. He's bent nearly in half to get his head close to hers, but if it hurts to hunch over like that, he shows no sign of it. She's gesturing animatedly, and he's got a small smile on his face. His eyes flick to me, and I look away quickly.

Martín has a burnt orange short-sleeve compression shirt on, black athletic shorts over black leggings, and white and black high-top shoes. He jogs in place and does a few high knee touches, probably to warm himself against the breeze.

The yard itself is almost like an adult playground, or an outdoor gymnastics facility. Monkey bars that are at least twelve feet off the ground, horizontal bars, some with rings dangling from them, a pommel horse, wooden dummies and bales of straw, balance beams, a line of stumps, and further off, archery targets fill the square area.

Several long, wooden tables near the castle wall are laden with a plethora of weapons. There are swords of numerous styles, axes, flails, crossbows, some wooden clubs that have short blades protruding from either side, and on and on.

The sight makes me green. *I hope they don't expect me to know how to use any of that.*

I blink, and Valentina appears at my side. I start. "Hey there!" She smiles at me brightly.

Oh no. This one's a morning person.

"Hi," I say simply.

She hands me a large metal water bottle. I grab it, expecting it to be full, and nearly yank it out of her hand when it comes away, empty and light as a feather.

"Oh, fuck!" I yelp, and Valentina grimaces.

"Sorry! I haven't filled it yet!" She flourishes a hand, and water streams from her fingertips. It snakes through the air and glides into the open mouth of the lid.

I stare at her in wonder. "Woah. Um, thanks."

She gives a small smile and waves her hand. "No problem. You'll need to stay hydrated for this." An extra-strong breeze blows, and I cross my arms and huddle in on myself.

She frowns and smacks her palm against her forehead. "Oh, right." She turns to her brother, who is focused on stretching his glutes. "Martín!"

He rolls his head to the side. "*Qué deseas?*" He asks, annoyed.

She rolls her eyes. "*Qué deseas*," she mocks. She gestures both hands to me as if showing off the prize on a game show. "We've got a walking ice pop over here! Do your job *tonto.*"

He straightens up and saunters over to us, hands in the pockets of his shorts. He grins at me mischievously.

"Don't worry *roja*, I'll get you hot." My eyes widen as he puts his fingers to my temples.

He closes his eyes in concentration, and warmth blooms from his fingertips, spreading over me like I've stepped face-first into a warm shower. I blink slowly and gasp as he pulls away, flashing white teeth at me.

"That barrier will only last a few hours, but you won't freeze in the meantime," he says.

"How . . ." My gaze shifts from him to Valentina. She grins.

"My brother and I are diametrically opposed." She shoves her shoulder into him playfully. He, being about six feet of solid muscle, doesn't budge much.

Valentina herself is a few inches shorter than me, but her outfit shows me that she, too, is solid muscle. I get the sense that she won all their fights as kids. "I got the water powers, and he's a hot mess. Ignore everything he says to you forever, by the way. He's an idiot."

He clutches one hand to his heart and throws the other over his forehead, palm splayed up toward the sky. "You wound me, sister."

She rolls her eyes and turns back to me. "See?" She shakes herself suddenly. "Oh! Do you like your clothes?"

I put a hand to my head; I'm getting whiplash from this conversation. "Um, yes?"

Martín laughs. "Valentina was over the *entire* moon when Auberon told her to find clothes for you."

"Oh!" I turn to her. "Thank you so much! Everything so far fits perfectly. I love them."

"There's also lavender soap for you in the bathroom. You looked like a lavender person," she says, smiling.

I chuckle. "I saw, and I *am*, in fact, a lavender person."

She laughs. "I knew it! Oh, and if you need a menstrual cup, I can go pick one up for you."

I glance sidelong at Saif and Martín, but neither of them seems phased at this topic of discussion. *That's refreshing.*

I turn back to Valentina. "Actually, I had a hysterectomy a few years ago. No worries in that department."

She nods and opens her mouth to reply when a shadow falls over me, and I turn to see Diego looming. His expression is pinched, like he's annoyed, and has better places to be.

One corner of my mouth tightens involuntarily. It isn't my fault that he's been charged with training me. *I didn't ask to be here.*

He jerks his head toward the equipment spaced throughout the field. "Not to interrupt your girl talk, but we've got work to do. Let's see what you've got, *Lobita*." He turns and marches away without looking back. I cross my arms and stalk after him silently.

I study his back as we walk. *This guy's shoulder-to-waist ratio doesn't look human,* I think, then chide myself. *No shit. Because he* isn't *human.*

I'm lost in my observations when I abruptly realize he has stopped, and I halt, nearly bumping into him. He turns, and I scramble back a few steps. He cocks an eyebrow at me but says nothing.

"Up," he says simply.

Yours, I think automatically. But then I see the equipment we're standing next to, and snort at him.

"You expect me to hang from monkey bars right now?" I ask derisively. I pull the left strap of my tank top closer to my neck, revealing more of my shoulder.

Diego's eyes slide to the bandages. "Yes."

I bite the inside of my lips and resist the urge to roll my eyes at him. I blink a few times instead.

"Well, I can't," I bite out.

He puts his hands on his waist. "How do you know?"

I throw my hands up, making sure to leave my left elbow steady to not aggravate the very shoulder injury he is unconcerned about.

"Maybe because moving my upper arm at *all* is impossible? Maybe because I almost got ripped in half the other day?"

"Actually, it was more like two weeks ago," I hear Hyun-Joo say nearby. I turn to her, and see that she's on a balance beam doing an effortless cartwheel.

I goggle at her for a moment. *I was out for two weeks?* They hadn't mentioned that yesterday. But I don't have time to process that right now. I shake the thought from my mind for the time being.

Diego is still glaring at me as if he expects me to perform this impossible task. "You have to start sometime. Might as well be now."

I look around for a moment and see that Saif is watching our exchange, tight-lipped. I catch his eye.

"I'm not ready for this," I say to him. It sounds like a whine, even to my own ears.

He glances at Diego, who glares back at him, then sighs and casts his gaze to the ground. "Some activity might be good for it," he relents.

"There you have it," Diego says, as if the matter is settled. "Up."

"Wow," I scoff. "*Et tu*, Saif?"

He doesn't meet my eyes again; he just pushes his glasses up the bridge of his nose.

I approach the ladder reluctantly and gingerly lift myself onto it. Climbing it is excruciating, but a few agonizing moments later, I reach the top. I lean heavily into the bars, gritting my teeth at the pain.

"Now cross." Diego says from below me.

I look down at him, wishing with all my might that I had something to throw at him. Just something harmless. Like a lightning bolt. If I stretched my foot just a few inches back, I could probably kick him in his stupid square jaw.

"Fuck *that*."

The pain must be blurring my vision, because I swear I see a small smile flick across his lips. But then he barks at me again.

"The correct response is 'Yes, sir.' You'll never know your limits if you don't push against them. If you're wounded in a battle, the enemy isn't going to give you time to heal. Shit hurts sometimes, darling. Toughen up."

Despite Martín's magical barrier keeping me warm, my blood runs cold with rage. *How dare he.* Like this total stranger knows how much I have or haven't hurt in my life. He has no idea what I've been through. How much toughening up I've had to do.

I turn to face the first horizontal bar and, adrenaline pumping, reach out to it. My biceps scream in protest at first; it's apparently been weeks since I've so much as lifted my arms, let alone worked out, but then they settle into the activity.

The claw marks over my torso, however, are a different story. My entire center is on fire, and I break into a sweat within moments. I growl loudly through clenched teeth.

I make it four bars across before I can't take it anymore. My left shoulder seizes as I reach for the next bar, and my right fingertips slip off. For a few frightening seconds, there's nothing around me but whooshing air, and then I hit the ground in a heap at Diego's feet. All the breath leaves my lungs, and I wheeze.

Saif runs over to help me reach a sitting position as I fight to gulp enough air to make my lungs inflate again. I glance up and shoot daggers at Diego with my gaze. The wild urge to claw at his face slashes through my mind.

He looks down his nose at me for a moment, his hands on his waist. But then he crouches down to get closer to me.

"Diego —" Saif begins to say, his tone dangerous, but Diego just holds up a palm, cutting him off. Then he reaches that hand out and *pats me on the head*.

I flinch back away from him, baring my teeth, and he actually smiles at me. The smile drips with condescension.

"Entertaining start, *Lobita*," he mocks in a sing-song tone. "Now do it again."

I move to stand, and he holds his palm out at me this time. "What do you say?"

Is this guy fucking serious right now?

"Yes," I bite out. Saif's grip tightens on my good shoulder.

Diego's smile widens. He looks like a snake who has just spotted a mouse. "Yes, what?"

I glare at him for several heartbeats, then exhale slowly through my nose. "Yes. Sir," I say quietly.

Diego stands to his full height and gazes down at me, smirking. "Good girl."

Solarium

After training is over that day, Saif leads me up the spiral staircase inside, but instead of rounding the corner to head to my room, he opens one of the doors directly in front of us on the second floor, and motions for me to enter ahead of him.

I step across the threshold and gasp. It's like I've entered a jungle. It's a huge solarium that spans the width of Arkenvale Castle, and it's packed to the brim with plants and flowers.

The late afternoon sun shines in through the glass of the ceiling and walls, and despite this room being north-facing, it's blindingly bright in here. There are several large open windows on the ceiling, allowing air to circulate, but it's still much warmer in here than in the rest of the castle.

I can feel my hair frizz increasingly by the second, puffing up like an angry cat. I run my hands over it in vain as I spot a ladder that leads to one of the open windows on the roof, covered in vines of thorny roses.

"This is gorgeous," I say, looking around the room all over again, trying to see what I missed the first time. He walks a few steps in and holds one hand out wide, the other tucked in the pocket of his joggers. The hem of his shirt lifts just an inch, revealing the "V" outline of his lower abs, and I'm suddenly exceedingly grateful that the heat of the room has already turned my cheeks pink. I look away hastily.

"This is the source of almost all our food." He pauses. "And tea, of course," he says, gesturing to a bed of herbs. His eyes light up with his next sentences, and I find myself smiling at his joy.

"Most evenings, I'm in here working, tending to everything. I make all the soaps and things like that, too. It took me a couple of years to get the recipes just right, but now everything we use in the castle, from cleaning products to shampoo, is made right here."

I glance around the room. There's purple wisteria, its vines climbing up trellises, and smaller vines flowing down from hanging baskets, laden with fruits and vegetables in varying stages of growth and ripeness. I see a raised garden bed against one wall that's full of an array of different grains, and another full of lavender. Drying herbs and flowers hang throughout the room, strung off thick twine that crisscrosses the air above us.

Signs stick up in the dirt with the names of the plants written in a neat, rounded handwriting. I read signs that say, "zucchini, pumpkins, strawberries," and even one sign in a tall planter that reads, "peanuts" before I'm overwhelmed and can't read any more.

I walk to the far wall, which is almost entirely glass, other than beams of wood that are spaced out to enforce the structure. I stare out over the training yard, and beyond.

"Is that the ocean?" I point at the deep blue water that I had heard crashing in waves when we were outside.

Saif appears at my side. "Oh, that little thing? That's Nabeyha Lake."

I gawk at him before turning back to the vast expanse of water. The waves are huge. *How is that a lake?*

But then I chide myself silently. *You're in an alternate dimension with a whole group of Mages, and you've caught a case of lycanthropy. So maybe the waves on a lake here can be a little fucking big.*

Saif lets me wander around for a bit, and even picks a ripe strawberry for me. I take a bite, and it's heavenly. The berry is deliciously crisp on the outside, but when I bite into it, sweet juice bursts over my lips as I make a satisfied noise deep in my throat.

I wipe my hand unceremoniously across my chin and then on my pants. Saif has a small, sideways smile on his face. I blush, and he chuckles.

"I'll take that as a compliment." He turns and gestures at the various plants. "Please, feel free to come get anything you'd like whenever you want. Just be careful of that area." He points to a small area on the Eastern wall that is separated from the rest of the solarium with a tall bamboo divider.

I blink at him quizzically. "Why?"

"That's where I grow the more, eh, unfriendly plants." I don't ask any further questions.

When we leave the solarium hours later, just after sunset, he stops at the door just to the left of the exit.

"This is my room," he says, and a shiver runs down my spine. "If you need me for anything, don't hesitate to knock on my door." He smiles warmly.

I nod gratefully as he steps inside, then make my way to the balcony opposite the solarium to my door, thinking of his sideways smile.

Ignition

Years of darkness.
Lifeless and cold.
Paying my penance.
But then, a spark.
Me, a flicker.
Her, an inferno.
That blazes like the dawn.

Celebration

A few days later, Saif enters my room and hands me another mug of mint tea, which I sip absently.

"What day is it?" I ask quietly.

He frowns at the barren walls of my bedroom. "I'll have to get you a calendar," he mutters to himself. "The thirteenth," he says then, putting fresh bandaging on the nightstand. "Why?"

I exhale quickly through my nose. "I thought so." I could sense it.

He sits down on the stool. "Is something wrong?"

I sniff. "Today's my birthday," I say quietly.

He looks relieved. "Oh, well, happy birthday!"

I want to smile at him, but I can't. "Thanks," I whisper.

A beat passes.

He puts a hand on my knee tentatively. "If you have a thing about getting older, I can assure you that you're still b—"

"It's not that," I say. "I *like* getting older. It means I'm still here." My mouth twists. "But it's also the anniversary of Kianga's death. She died on this day, eleven years ago."

He inhales sharply and squeezes my knee. "I'm sorry," he says softly.

"Thank you," I murmur.

We sit in silence for a few long moments. He doesn't try to fill it with awkward conversation; he just sits with me, letting me know that he's here.

Finally, I take a shuddering breath. "Thank you," I say again.

He smiles. "Of course. Now, let's try to make this a good day, shall we? After training, I'll whip up some zucchini brownies for you to celebrate."

I chuckle. "Why not just regular brownies?"

His smile drops and he frowns at me gravely. "Eilidh, you don't understand. I have *so many* zucchinis in the solarium right now. I've been putting them in everything I can think of. I'm about to start tossing them into the lake for the fish. Or at Diego's head."

I laugh then, and he smiles triumphantly.

"Okay, okay, zucchini brownies it is," I say.

~~~~~~~~~~

That evening, I sit in the dining hall with the Peñas as Saif brings me a pan of brownies from the kitchen with a single candle in it. They all sing to me, and it's all I can do to keep from crying. I barely know these people, but here they are, the first ones to celebrate my birthday with me in over a decade. My first *reason* to celebrate my birthday in over a decade.

I look between the three of them, overwhelmed. "Thank you," I rasp.

Valentina puts her arm around me after the song is done. "Make a wish."

I stare at the candle for a long moment. *Please, Universe, let me keep these ones.*

I blow out the candle just as the dining hall door opens, and the King enters, talking with Diego and Hyun-Joo.

He looks at the four of us curiously. "What's all this for?"

Martín speaks first. "*Señorita* Shaw's birthday is today. The big . . ." He trails off and squints at me. "Two-one?" He asks teasingly.
~~~~~~~~~~

I smile and roll my eyes at him. "Well, you're only an entire decade off."

He shakes his head obstinately. "No, that's simply not possible."

I shake my head too, and my gaze lands on the King, but he isn't paying attention to me. His close-knit brow and unfocused eyes tell me he is thinking intensely about something.

Saif clears his throat. "There's enough for everyone."

I cut the pan of brownies into squares, and everyone takes one. We eat them quickly, making idle conversation.

"When is your birthday?" I ask Saif. "I'm not much of a baker, but I can buy a *really* cool candle for you."

He chuckles. "February 29th," he says.

"Oof. That's rough."

He shrugs. "I always just celebrate a day early."

"How very glass-half-full of you." I smile at him, and he returns it.

Once we've finished, Saif takes the pan into the kitchen, and Auberon motions to Diego. "Join me in the East Tower for a moment, Diego. I have an assignment for you that I would like to discuss."

Diego follows him without another word.

Hyun-Joo lingers for just a second, then turns to me. "Happy birthday," she says, then follows Diego and Auberon.

My eyes widen. "Thank you," I say as she closes the dining hall door behind her.

I turn to Valentina, and she raises an eyebrow at me. "What's that face for?" She asks as she takes the last bite of her brownie.

"Hyun-Joo acknowledged me," I say. "And she didn't even sound mad at me for existing."

Martín chuckles and saves Valentina from having to respond. "Hyun-Joo is one of the kindest souls you'll ever meet," he says, and Valentina nods silently as she chews. "She's just been a bit stressed since you got he—"

Valentina kicks him under the table, and he yelps.

An awkward beat crawls by.

"Wait, what did I do?" I look between them, my gut twisting.

Valentina looks at her brother for a moment like she's going to drop the lake on his head. "You didn't do anything." She says to me, still glaring at him. He has the grace to look ashamed. "It's just an adjustment having a new recruit - there hasn't been one since we got here six years ago - and your training just . . . takes up a lot of time."

Realization hits me, and I shake my head in horror. *Of course.*

"Oh, god. She knows I have *no* interest in him, right?" My eyes flick between them, and they look at one another with expressions that only two people who grew up attached at the hip could fully discern.

"Of course," Valentina says, a little too brightly, then stands. She narrows her eyes at her brother and puckers her lips to point at kitchen door, which Saif is just exiting. "Come on, *cabrón*, wash the plates with me." She begins stacking the plates in her hand.

I offer to help clean things up, hoping to talk more, maybe even get her to talk to Hyun-Joo for me, but she waves me off.

"I can wash them in a flash." She twists a small rivulet of water through her fingers. "It's no problem."

I nod, biting my lip. "Okay. Thank you."

Martín slaps me on the back, smiling a bit too wide. "Happy birthday, *roja*." He follows his sister into the kitchen.

"Thanks," I murmur as the door closes behind him.

Saif and I head upstairs and he walks me to my room. Our shoulders brush as we walk, and by the time we're halfway across the balcony, thoughts of Hyun-Joo are the farthest things from my mind.

"Thank you for everything today," I say to Saif as we stand on the balcony outside my door. I pick at the fabric of my pants. "You didn't have to do that."

He adjusts his glasses, even though they are already perched in the exact spot he likes. "You're welcome," he says, smiling sideways at me. "And yes, I did."

He takes my hand, brings it to his lips, and gives the back of it a quick peck. My pulse quickens instantly. "Good night." He holds my hand another moment longer, running his thumb back and forth across my skin before he drops it and turns to walk around the balcony to his room.

I watch him until he reaches the balcony opposite me, then slip into my room and lean back against the door. I have to take a few deep breaths to slow my racing heart before I can move.

I get changed into a baggy long-sleeved shirt and some soft shorts, then turn the light off and bury myself in my blankets. I fall asleep still feeling his lips on my hand.

~ Waxing Gibbous ~

Blades

I've gotten more bruises and scrapes this week than I ever have in my life. I've also cried tears of frustration nearly every night as Saif tends to my wounds, trying not to let the tears drip into whatever tea he has given me. *Am I a tea person now?*

No, that's heresy.

He comforts me every time, explaining that it's perfectly understandable for me to be bad at these things this early, and that Diego doesn't believe in easing people into things.

"He's a very sink-or-swim kind of man. He just doesn't understand that some people sink for a bit longer than others before they learn to swim. You should have seen the way he picked up fighting and swordplay; it was practically instantaneous. But he's never realized that not everyone is like him."

Something I *do* pick up quickly is that Saif is the most skilled swordsman of the Order. I've watched him swing his scimitar every chance I can get, admiring the way he moves, graceful, but disciplined, like he and his blade are partners dancing. Watching him wield his blade is probably what it was like to watch Van Gogh paint sunflowers.

"Does it have a name?" I ask him one day, as we walk back inside after training is done.

"*Dhabiha*," he replies, lovingly patting his scabbard. "It means 'sacrifice' or 'offering.'"

I tilt my head at him. "Was it an offering to you?"

He exhales quickly through his nose. "No, I had it commissioned long ago from a smith in the city. This blade is *my* offering to the world. It's how I can serve my King, protect the innocent, and do good for my people."

He's like a knight in shining armor. "How did you learn sword fighting? Or did you know it when you came here?"

He licks his lips, and I swallow hard. "Auberon."

When I just look at him questioningly, he continues. "When I first got here, there was no Order, but Auberon had been looking to build one. It was more than a year before anyone else was chosen, and in the meantime, he trained me himself. He was . . . terrifying."

My eyes widen in alarm, but he explains quickly. "With a sword, I mean. He was incredible. I've never seen anything like him, before or since. He was like something out of a legend, like Achilles, or Zorro. It was like he and his sword had known each other for a millennium. Like they were one being, or could actually *talk* to one another."

He shakes himself slightly. "I never beat him, not once, but now, no one can beat me." He says this without a trace of hubris; it's just a fact. And after my careful - research - on his skills, I believe it.

"Wow," I say, my eyes still wide. "Remind me to never get on his bad side."

Saif laughs heartily. "I don't think you have anything to worry about. He's pretty even-tempered, all things considered."

"Phew. That's a relief," I say, smiling at him. He returns it, and we head inside to get some lunch.

It's possible that my habit of watching him may have resulted in me falling off the equipment a few extra times by the end of the week. Once, while Hyun-Joo is trying to show me how to do a walking handstand, I must have been staring too long, because she pretends to knock into me, and kicks me onto my ass. Funnily enough, she never bumps into me again after that.

I bite my tongue, just managing not to ask her who she would rather I stare at.

Usually, Saif spars against Diego, since the two men are the closest in size and physical strength. Diego still has half a foot on Saif, but Saif's the only one who can beat the towering vampire with a weapon. Diego, I observe over the days, still has the advantage in hand-to-hand combat.

Watching them clash is terrifying, but exhilarating. They don't fight like they're sparring, they fight like they may actually kill each other. It's only at the last second when either of them shows restraint, either with Saif's blade hovering an inch away from Diego's jugular, or Diego's claws poised to shred Saif to ribbons as Diego pins him roughly to the ground.

Saif's experience with blades has come with just as much experience tending to cuts, puncture wounds, infections, and so on, making him the designated healer of the Order.

"There *is* a hospital in the city, but they can't do more for you than I can do here," he says one night. "Don't worry, my dear, I can take care of you." His eyes twinkle as he pushes my hair back behind my ear, and I have to hide my blush with my mug.

One morning, Saif is busy tossing knives up in the air for Valentina so she can use her water to propel them at frightening speeds into a target, so Diego tries to show me how to wield my dagger, which I have been terrified to so much as unsheathe.

The lesson does not go well.

"Why are you holding it like a letter opener?" He runs an exasperated hand over his face.

"Because it basically *is* a letter opener," I spit. "The thing is eight inches long. Am I supposed to wield it with two hands?" I demonstrate how this would look, jabbing with two hands at the space in front of me, and he pinches the bridge of his nose.

"*No puedo más,*" he mumbles under his breath. I don't know what that means, but he sounds done with me already.

He sighs. "It's nine inches long. Here, hold it like *this.*" He grabs the hilt from me and flips it around so that the blade points back at his elbow.

"One inch doesn't make any difference," I say, and he raises an eyebrow at me before I realize what I said. I clear my throat. "How do I stab with that?" I ask, gesturing to the backward blade.

He blinks at me, his gaze full of condescension. "Have you ever experienced carpal tunnel?"

"Do I have a copay for this visit, Doctor?"

He doesn't indulge me. "The average person's wrist isn't strong enough to go stabbing into werewolves like they're slicing a fucking cake. You'll want to slash. Use your whole arm." He demonstrates, then holds the dagger out to me.

I take it and mumble to myself. "The average person doesn't get *bitten* by a damn werewolf either."

But he just frowns at me, so I flip the blade toward my elbow and mirror his actions slowly.

The blade feels heavy in my hand, and I swear it zaps the energy from me like I'm a battery, but I don't complain. I almost think for a moment that he'll say I'm doing well.

He doesn't.

"Now slash me."

I raise my eyebrow at his command.

He puts a fist on one hip and motions once with his other hand. *Bring it.*

"Yes, *sir.*" I inject the second word with as much sarcasm as I can manage as I get into position, and then move to slash at him as instructed.

When my arm has barely moved, he twirls in a flash and sweeps my legs out from under me.

I cry out in pain as I hit the ground and my dagger clatters away from me. "What the *fuck*?"

"You were way too slow, and left yourself wide open. Speed means survival. Now get up, and let's go again."

I spend much of the rest of that morning crashing to the ground, hissing curses into the blades of grass before I rise.

Poison

Later that day, Saif takes me back to the solarium, which has become my favorite room in Arkenvale.

"I'm glad you enjoy it in here," he says to me once I've wandered around for several minutes, smelling the blossoms.

"I always wanted to have a giant greenhouse and grow all my own food in it. But, considering I live in an apartment, and I can't even keep a succulent alive, that dream has yet to become a reality." I run my fingers lightly over the spines of a huge aloe plant.

He smiles. "Maybe I should teach you some gardening tricks."

I smile back at him. "I'd like that." I examine some bell peppers in various stages of ripeness: green, yellow, orange, and red. "Who takes care of the plants if you have to go somewhere?"

He picks a dead head off a petunia plant. "Well, I'm not usually gone more than a few days. But when I am, Martín is the one who picks the things that are ready, and Valentina waters things for me. We catch a lot of gray water throughout the castle, and she can just direct it up here. But of course, when we don't have any, she just . . ." He wiggles his fingers, and I chuckle.

"And, this is probably a stupid question." I pause, considering my words. "But if you can grow things from seeds in an instant, why do you even need all this?" I gesture widely. "Can't you just grow whatever you want right when you need it?"

He nods. "I *can* do that, but honestly, whenever I use my powers to grow food, it tastes . . . off somehow. My powers work fine on flowers and herbs, but for a fruit or vegetable to grow to its full potential, it needs to be given the time and space to do so. They're a lot like people that way."

He frowns at me sympathetically. "That's something Diego has never really understood."

My mouth twists and I rub a bruise I received just a few hours ago that is already starting to turn as purple as Saif's petunias.

"Yeah, I can tell." I walk toward the partitioned-off area, trying to see around the bamboo and perhaps catch a glimpse of what lies behind it.

"Don't go in there," Saif reminds me cautiously.

"I won't. I was just wondering what 'less friendly' plants you have. Poppies? Deadly Nightshade? Belladonna?"

He chuckles, walking toward me with his hands in the pockets of his dark jeans. "Deadly Nightshade *is* Belladonna. But yes, actually, I do have that. Though you're way too excited about that prospect." His dark eyes glitter with amusement.

I grin sheepishly. "I just think it's a cool name."

"I've got a lot of plants in there that have cool names. Aconitum, Catha Edulis, Ricinus Communis. And they have even *cooler* effects. Which is why I don't want you going anywhere near it."

He puts an arm around my waist and turns me to one of the large garden beds in the opposite corner.

"Would you like to pick some corn for dinner?"

He doesn't remove his arm from around my waist as we walk. Butterflies explode in my stomach, and the unfriendly plants and their cool names disappear instantly to the back of my mind.

~~~~~~~~~
~~~~~~~~~

One evening, after I had dropped from a balance beam more times than I could count, Saif rubs some kind of soothing balm onto my scraped knees as I sip a cinnamon tea. I watch him as his hands move with steady, practiced motions.

"Were you a nurse?" I ask him quietly. "Before, I mean."

He glances at me, but his hands keep moving, rubbing the balm into my skin. "Well," he begins, "I was *going* to be one. I had actually moved to North Carolina when I was eighteen so I could go to school there." He removes his hands from my knee and wipes them on a small towel.

"What made you want to be a nurse?" I ask.

He drops my gaze, frowning, and his eyes tighten at the corners. "When I was a kid in Iraq, there were . . . a lot of people who could have used a nurse, but never got one."

His voice wavers, and my heart aches for him. "I wanted to be able to help people like that. But I only made it through one year of school before I was attacked by a couple of thugs who didn't like that I was in *their* country."

His mouth twists at that word like it's poison.

I suppose, in a way, it is.

"It wasn't a great time to be a Brown man in America," he says bitterly.

I can't even begin to imagine.

"One of them had a knife. I didn't know I had any magic inside me at the time, and we happened to be standing next to a building that was covered in ivy. He lunged at me, and my powers took over. I blacked out, and a minute later, I was standing over their bodies, and they had been strangled by the vines." His shoulders sag.

I realize I've stopped breathing, and inhale shakily.

"One of them was the dean's son, and I had nowhere to go. I stumbled into the woods nearby, and the next thing I knew, I was in

Tenazeryth. One of Auberon's scouts found me, and he took me in. Offered me a spot at his table, as long as I was willing to fight for him. That was fourteen years ago."

"You were just a kid," I say quietly. An adult, technically, but really, still just a kid.

"So were they," he says sadly. He stands abruptly and turns to walk away.

I reach for him before I even realize I'm doing it. He stops and turns back to me, his eyes on our clasped hands. My pulse quickens.

"I'm so sorry," I say. It isn't enough. There is so much unsaid in those three words, so much pain that I can't make better, as much as I wish I could.

There are no ample words to heal the wounds dealt to a kind young man whose only transgression was being born in a different place. There is nothing I can say to him to give him justice, or to give him back the life he should have had.

"Thank you," he whispers hoarsely.

He clenches my hand tightly, and I don't mind that it hurts.

Rubicon

For so long I stood.
On the banks of the Rubicon.
But her flames are close.
Do I take the plunge?
Or let myself burn?
Oh, how wonderful it would be.
To burn.

Mongrels

It's been nearly one month since I was bitten, and the full moon is approaching in just a few days, but I've only seen the King that one time in the dining hall on my birthday since he had thrown the dagger at me. *Levitated it at me? Telekinetically whipped it at me?*

I shake my head to stop my thoughts from running away from me. "Are you sure?" I ask dubiously.

Diego, standing next to me in the dining hall, cocks an eyebrow at me. "Am I sure that the king I take orders from every day told me to bring you to him?" He asks scathingly. "Yeah, *Lobita*, I'm pretty fucking positive."

I take a quick, deep breath and exhale through my nose. I reach for my pendant that I still forget is no longer there, and his eyes lower to where my hand is reaching between my breasts. I cross my arms, and he flicks his gaze upward once more.

"Fine," I bite out.

He stares, unmoving.

I grumble. "Yes, sir."

I cast a glance at Saif and the Peñas to nod goodbye, and follow him out of the dining hall. He turns left and heads toward the wooden door diagonal from us, and I follow sullenly. He knocks when we reach it.

"Enter," Auberon's voice comes from inside.

I walk into the West Tower and am nearly blinded by the setting sunlight blazing into the room, casting reflections off nearly every polished surface. The walls of this tower, too, are made entirely of glass. It's at least ten degrees warmer in here than the dining hall had been, and sweat beads up on my brow almost immediately.

I walk into the room, squinting at Auberon, who is seated at a massive table piled high with books and papers. I blink, and then I realize that we're in a library.

Towering bookshelves stand all throughout the room, and a balcony not unlike the one that leads to the bedrooms is wrapped around the walls, about halfway up the tower. Several rolling ladders stand against the shelves, giving access to even the loftiest tomes.

Some shelves tilt at impossible angles; only Auberon's magic keeps them and their contents from toppling to the stone floor. Scrolls and books flutter through the air like butterflies from his desk to various shelves, and back.

Just like the East Tower, the West one is flush with plants. Vines trail up and down the bookcases, and a small orange tree sits along the glass wall. Saif's signature seems to be in every room of this castle.

I exhale slowly in wonder, trying to take in every inch of the room as Diego looks at me from the corner of his eye. But his patronizing gaze be damned; I will not let him ruin this for me. I have just entered my own personal heaven.

It's so beautiful I could cry. For a moment, I think I might, but then Auberon clears his throat, and I turn to see him motioning for me to take a seat across the table from him.

I do so, and Diego sits as well, and leans back comfortably in his chair.

Great, he's part of this conversation too, I think as the King sips red wine out of a simple golden chalice. He sets it down and turns to me.

"I hear your training is going remarkably well," Auberon says finally.

I blink rapidly at him. *What?*

It's been going terribly. I'm clumsy and awkward. Just yesterday, I nearly shot a window out of the castle with an arrow. Martín had found this an extremely impressive and amusing feat, given that the archery targets are in the *opposite* direction of the castle.

Diego had quickly snatched the bow from me and taken it back to the table laden with weapons.

Saif had smiled reassuringly. "Maybe your strength just lies in blades."

And of course, my wounds are still severely restricting my motion, which gives Diego ample opportunity to bark at me that nothing I do is good enough.

Diego says nothing. Clearly, he doesn't agree with Auberon's assessment, but doesn't want to contradict his king. Saif must have spoken with Auberon about my training and healing progress. I grab the end of my braid, which is resting over my shoulder, and twist it around my fingers nervously.

"Um . . ." I mumble something that sounds vaguely affirmative. Auberon's one eye just gazes at me unblinking. "I'm . . . learning so much," I say finally. He nods, leans back, and steeples his fingers in front of him.

"You've now had a few weeks to come to terms with your new life," he says, and I blink again.

I have done no such thing. I'm still not absolutely positive this is not some kind of coma-induced fever dream.

But he doesn't rephrase. "As such, I believe it is time you learn more about this dimension that is now your home."

My breath catches. 'Home' is such a loaded word, and certainly not one that applies to Arkenvale, but I nod.

"Okay," I whisper.

Diego glances sidelong at me, but then his gaze is back on Auberon, who is turning a book around for me to read the cover.

A Comprehensive Guide to Mongrels.

I raise an eyebrow in confusion. "Mongrels?"

Auberon looks at me for another beat. "You know now, obviously, that there are forces from this world that are not native to yours."

Like van-sized wolves and winged sex demons? I think, but say nothing. I nod.

"But they are not the only ones you share this world with," he says.

My eyes widen. It makes perfect sense, but I've been so preoccupied recently that it hadn't occurred to me that there are more than werewolves and succubuses out there.

I sense Diego's massive presence next to me. *And vampires*, I think, swallowing hard.

Auberon flips the book open to a Table of Contents. It's a list of creatures that are, presumably, discussed in this book. I scan the list, my brain trying to wrap around the words. There are many, but some jump out to me more than others. *Centaurs? Fae? Unicorns?*

"These are fairy tales," I choke out.

Diego scoffs beside me. "So is the Big Bad Wolf." For once, though, his eyes are not unkind. They almost appear — sympathetic? But then he blinks, and they are cold once more.

"All the stories are true, dear girl," Auberon says softly.

My mouth works as I try to find something to say. I let out a long breath as I look around the bookshelves to identify a book of each color of the rainbow. I make it to green before Auberon interrupts.

"I want you to take this book with you. Use it to familiarize yourself with the Mongrels of this world. The best defense against any enemy is knowledge of them." He says the word 'Mongrel' like a slur, and I wince. "You must learn their weaknesses, and exploit them."

"What exactly does 'Mongrel' entail?" I ask, not sure if I really want the answer.

The king's one golden eye lights up like he's about to discuss his favorite topic.

"Look at Diego," he tells me. I bite the inside of my lip as I comply. I turn to the man at my side, and he looks back at me, his mouth tight at the corners, but his expression otherwise blank. "What do you see?" Auberon asks.

A pompous asshole. I manage - miraculously - to say these words only in my head. I shrug. "A man who —"

But Auberon cuts me off before I have to figure out what to say next. "Exactly!" His voice is louder than I expected, and I jump, tearing my eyes away from Diego's crimson stare.

"He is a man," Auberon says. His eye blazes with passion as he turns to Diego. "What do you see in her?"

Diego and I lock eyes again. His Adam's apple bobs before he answers, like he has to physically swallow whatever insult he wants to unleash.

"A woman," he says finally.

"Precisely!" Auberon smacks an open palm against the table in emphasis, and Diego and I both flinch at the noise. "When I look at you two, I see your humanity first and foremost. You Shifters are simply humans who have been bestowed with precious gifts. In your cases, strength and durability."

I had not been feeling particularly durable as of late, but I keep quiet.

"But in the case of Mages, the gift is magic."

I think of Hyun-Joo materializing out of thin air, and the invisible barriers that she can produce. Of Martín and Valentina wielding powerful elements with nothing more than a wave of their hands. Of Saif, holding a seed and growing it into a beautiful dahlia that matches my eyes to cheer me up.

And Diego, well, I have not actually seen him do anything particularly superhuman since the night he ripped my would-be date's throat to ribbons. He's fast, and powerful, and has fangs and claws, but he hasn't transformed into a bat, and as far as I know, he doesn't sleep in a coffin. Not to mention, he's out in the sun every day, his skin glistening with sweat.

I blink away the image.

"The abilities you two have, the magic that flows through the rest of us, those things don't negate our basic humanity. We laugh, we cry, we hate, we love," Auberon pontificates.

Diego is as still as a statue beside me.

"We crave community, and continually progress as a species."

I'm not so sure humanity is progressing, necessarily, but I don't say so. I get the sense that he's not in the mood for my cynicism.

"Mongrels." He slurs the word again. "Have none of these things. They aren't capable of it. It's not their fault, of course." He shakes his head sadly. "They're little more than wild animals. But that's why it is our duty to maintain order within this dimension and, of course, the next, when they manage to break through the wards."

The thought of a unicorn pulling a carriage through a public park flashes through my mind, and I chide myself silently. *Focus, Shaw.*

I look down at the list again. Many *do* seem to be some kind of non-human animal, such as griffins and phoenixes. But not *all* of them. "Kelpies?" I ask. "Fae?" There are subsections for both Seelie and Unseelie, and I've read enough fantasy novels to know that neither is one I want to meet.

Auberon waves a hand at me dismissively. "Merely animals who happen to appear humanoid due to our habit of anthropomorphizing things." I furrow my brow, but it does make some sense, I suppose. Only . . .

"In a few days, I'm going to transform into a wolf." I pause, steeling myself. "Bleddyn never took his human form. What if I —" I choke back the rest of the sentence, too scared to utter it.

Auberon's gaze softens, if only a fraction. He reaches over and takes my hand, which I realize I have clenched on the table in front of me. His grip is rough and strong.

"Just because the werewolf that turned you has lost his humanity, doesn't mean you will too." His voice is fierce with conviction.

I squeeze my eyes shut and lower my head. I refuse to cry. I take a breath to steady myself. The king releases me, so I close the book and run my hand over the worn cover.

Books I know. Books I can do. I pull it toward me and hug it to my chest like it's a life preserver that's been thrown to me. At least this part of my training will be familiar.

Auberon leans back and gestures around him at the vast collection of tomes. "There are, of course, other forces that threaten the safety and stability of Tenazeryth, and not all the answers are in these books," he says ruefully. "There's a nasty pod of sirens to the East that have been disrupting trade routes for some time now. There is a guerrilla leader named Bastet who has been sacking every armory that she and her rag-tag circus of Mongrels can find." His face twists with a disdainful frown.

Diego tenses his jaw beside me.

I raise an eyebrow. "Bastet? Like, the Egyptian cat goddess? You're dealing with a cat goddess?"

He waves a hand dismissively once again. "Merely a moniker taken on by a meddlesome fool. But those are nuisances for another time. For now, your focus is on Bleddyn." He stands.

"You're dismissed," Auberon says, not unkindly.

Diego and I rise as well, then we walk out of the library tower and he heads up the spiral staircase. I follow him without thinking, staring down at the floor as I walk, lost in the echoes of Auberon's words, still clutching the book to my chest.

Then, when we reach the upper balcony, I collide abruptly with something rock-solid. *Are there suits of armor up here or something? I think to myself, annoyed, cursing at my own clumsiness.

"Ow! Fucking hell." I wince and realize that I had not, in fact, run into a suit of metal, but rather into Diego, who is stopped at a door adjacent to the wall of the solarium, directly across from Saif's room. He stares at me as I rub my tender nose.

"I don't think I've ever met someone who hurts themselves as much as you do," he says sincerely.

I dig my nails into the book. "It's not my fault you're so fucking dense," I snap up at him. He just stares back at me, and I gesture at the door for something else to talk about. Anything to stop talking about how inept he thinks I am.

"What's in here, are we going in here next?" I gesture at the door, and I can't read his expression when he replies; he doesn't meet my gaze, but stares inches above my head.

"This is my bedroom and, no, I think I will be going in alone," he says evenly. "I assume you can find your way to your room by yourself." He points to his left as if I actually need directions to my door.

Heat creeps up my neck. "Oh," I squeak, and clear my throat. "Yes. Obviously. Sure." I mumble some more affirmative sounds, and he doesn't say another word. He simply opens the door and walks through it, and I catch a quick glimpse inside.

The setting sun entering the West-facing window casts a cozy glow across the room. A row of worn-out books is lined up on a shelf above a desk, on which an open notebook lays.

Then I see Hyun-Joo sitting on the corner of the bed. Her eyes are narrow and her gaze would probably set me on fire if she had Martín's powers. My eyes widen at her, and then the door slams in my face.

The massive chandelier that hangs above the center of the spiral staircase hasn't turned on yet, and with the light from Diego's window no longer streaming onto the balcony, I am left alone in the dark.

~ First Full Moon ~

Bloodthirsty

On the morning of the full moon, I wake up with a raging headache. I've had only a few migraines in my life, and they were nothing compared to this. I lie in bed for about thirty minutes longer than usual until I hear a knock at the door. I mumble something incoherent, and someone walks in.

"I figured you'd have a hard time making it to the dining hall this morning, so I brought you some breakfast," I hear Saif say. I groan at the mention of food as my stomach ties itself into knots. I burrow myself deeper into the blankets.

I realize distantly that there are more blankets on me this morning than there were when I fell asleep; he must have brought me some extras in the night. The thought of his caring gesture distracts me from the ache in my head, just for a moment.

"I know, I know," he says in response to my groan. "But at some point today you *need* to eat something. Promise me you'll try." I stick a hand out from my cocoon and give him a thumbs up. He chuckles. "Okay, I'll leave you alone."

He leaves, closing the door gently behind him. I lie like this for several hours, drifting in and out of a fitful sleep.

Then, sometime in the late afternoon, it's like a switch flips in my brain. My head stops throbbing, and at the same moment, my stomach screams at me to put something into it.

I sit up and walk quickly over to the desk where Saif had put the tray of food. It's miso soup; bits of tofu and green onions float in a savory broth. It is normally one of my favorite comfort foods, which I must have mentioned to him in passing one day. It's an incredibly sweet gesture.

The sight of it turns my stomach.

I pull the first hanger I touch out of the wardrobe and throw the clothes on. It ends up being a collared blue and green plaid dress with three-quarter-length sleeves. I throw my hair into a wild bun on top of my head, then hurry down the stairs to the kitchen.

I don't bother stopping to sit in the dining hall, where almost everyone else is eating. All their eyes follow me, but I ignore them as I walk to the kitchen door and fling it open.

My first thought is how *modern* everything is. It looks like I've walked into a five-star restaurant's kitchen rather than one in an otherwise Medieval-style castle.

A massive, stainless-steel island occupies the center of the room. Shelves full of pots and pans, plates, bowls, and various small kitchen appliances line the walls. Along the far wall are three large refrigerators.

As I walk toward them, my second thought is, *How the hell have I not been in this kitchen in the month I've been here?* But of course, I have had a man waiting on my every need. It's a jarring and foreign thought, but my mind doesn't have time to dwell on it. I'm laser-focused.

As I swing open the doors of the first refrigerator, I hear the kitchen door open, and two sets of footsteps enter. His scent hits me, and my pulse quickens.

"Saif, do you know if there's any venison in here?" I ask, still rooting through the contents of the refrigerator. *Nothing.* I close it and move to the next one.

There's a pause behind me. "How did you know it was me?" Saif asks tentatively.

"I smelled you, obviously. You always smell like charcoal and flowers. It's intoxicating," I say absently. It strikes me faintly that this is not something one would typically say to someone else, but frankly, right now, I don't give a damn.

Another pause from behind me. "What are you looking for?" Hyun-Joo asks caustically. *What the hell does she want?* I think, more ferociously than I should.

"Venison!" I say again, my temper flaring. *Dammit!* I kick the door to the second refrigerator angrily and move to the third and final one.

There better be something in here.

I rip at the door and see several paper-wrapped packages on the bottom shelf. The smell hits me first, and my mouth begins watering instantly. *Bingo.*

I grab one, pause a moment in consideration, then grab a second. I kick the door shut and walk over to the electric stove.

I toss the steaks onto the counter, then begin tossing pans around, searching for one that's large enough for both steaks. The smell of the bloody meat grows stronger, and my search turns frantic. I still haven't deigned to look at Saif and Hyun-Joo.

Suddenly, I hear another voice behind me. I hadn't heard anyone else enter, what with the clattering around the stove searching in vain for a pan.

"Look at me." His tone leaves no room for negotiation. It never does.

I whip around angrily to face Diego, who is halfway between me and the door, taking slow steps in my direction. He's wearing some kind of ridiculous suit, royal blue and skin-tight. It's got built-in shoes and gloves and covers everything but his head. He's got a red metal contraption attached to each forearm from which a pair of long blades protrude back toward his shoulders.

I recognize them dimly from the other day when we were training, and he had been sparring with Saif. He had sliced through walls of vines and shot miniature arrows from the underside of the contraptions with the press of a button at the base of his palm. He's got pouches strapped around his waist and to one thigh like he's a secret agent in a superhero movie.

I snort at him derisively. "I love Halloween too, but you're a little early, don't you think?" I turn back to the stove, but my stomach growls loudly. It does *not* want to wait for the steaks to cook.

Fuck it.

I rip open one of the paper packages and tear into the steak. Blood drips down my chin and onto the floor, turning the stone red.

It's absolutely delicious.

Suddenly, Diego grabs my chin, heedless of the blood. He twists my face so that we're eye to eye. His are brighter than they had been the other night before he had slammed the door in my face.

The hairs on the back of my neck rise in fury at the memory, and a growl escapes from deep in my throat.

"Fuck," he says.

I lunge at him.

He crashes into the steel island and topples over it, pulling me with him. He holds me up as high above his face as he can reach, which, with his arms, is a decent distance. I'm on top of him, scratching wildly at his face with my claws, but I can't quite reach far enough to connect.

Claws? I think distantly. *I barely have nails. I don't have claws.* But there they are. They have sprouted out of my nail beds, and are growing longer with every swipe I take. My vision turns blood red.

Diego manages to throw me off of him; I land sharply on the cold stone floor and howl in pain. And I mean — I *howl* in pain. The sound reverberates against all the stainless steel in the room, and Saif and Hyun-Joo cover their ears in pain.

Diego doesn't have the luxury, but I see him grit his teeth, his fangs sliding out as he does so. It gives me a sick sense of satisfaction.

Then he's on top of me, and as he tries to pin me to the floor with a knee in my back, his cedar and aloe scent chokes me with its intensity. I struggle underneath him, but he grabs the knot of hair on top of my head and twists his fist into it to hold me still.

I snarl. I hear him yelling something at the other people in the room, but I can't understand what he's saying. I can smell fear on him, and it fills me with sadistic glee.

I roll over, throwing him off my back and into a shelf full of large pots and pans that crash down around him in a cacophony of clattering metal. Before he can move again, I run for the kitchen door. I crash through the wood and into the next room.

There are two more humans in this room, and they're both gawking at me. I growl, and all of us move at once. In a blink, I'm swimming upstream against a rushing wave that forces me against a wall. I see a door near me and wade toward it.

The geyser of water stops, and vines wrap around my four ankles. I break them easily and run for the door.

I hit an invisible barrier just before I reach the door, and snarl in anger. I try to move around the barrier, but it's surrounding me like a bubble. My mind becomes frenzied.

Outside. Need. Outside.

I howl again and scratch at the barrier. It wavers but doesn't give. I stop a moment, growling, and tense my muscles before ramming into the barrier with my large, furry head.

It breaks, and then I'm out the door as another wave chases me in vain. Now I'm in yet *another* room, but this one is devoid of humans, and I immediately see a door. I know, instinctually, that it leads outside. As I crash through it, bright light stops me for a moment, but then I see her in the sky, faint, but there.

The moon.

I howl in delight. *I'm here!* I call to her, and she gazes at me in acknowledgment, her love shining down on me in the form of her beaming light.

Hello, Daughter. I can't hear her with my ears, nor in my head like I know I've heard another creature speak before, though I can't remember who right now. The moon speaks to me in my heart; her voice rings throughout my soul. They aren't words, exactly, but I still know what she's saying, just as clearly as if she were sitting across the table from me sipping on a hot tea.

I'm only able to taste freedom for one more second; in the next instant, a large metal net falls onto me from out of nowhere. It doesn't feel heavy, but nonetheless, I struggle against it, as if it's zapping me of energy.

I roll frantically, tangling myself further. In the door that I had just crashed through, a man stands with his hand outstretched as if he had just cast the net over me. His eyes are different colors: one blazing gold, and one glowing red.

Or maybe that's just due to my blood-soaked vision.

I roll again, and then there's a large human on my back, the same one I had fought in the kitchen, but he feels smaller than he had just a minute ago, like he has gotten shorter. He's on the outside of the net, trying to hold me still. He's yelling something, but it's an uninterpretable garble.

I buck wildly and roll, trying to throw him, or crush him, whichever will work first.

His claws dig into me, and no matter how hard I thrash, he doesn't loosen his grip. He clutches my snout shut as he pulls my head to one side, and four sharp fangs sink deep into the base of my neck.

Nothing happens for a long moment as I thrash in vain, but then my body is flooded with a wave of the purest ecstasy, and I lose control of my muscles. I melt into a puddle as the world goes dark.

Hopeless

"You okay, *hermano?*" Martín sits down backward on the bench beside me and leans against the table.

I sigh and shake my head at the plate of *makhlama* in front of me. Hyun-Joo had made it for me, knowing it's one of my favorite comfort foods, but I haven't taken a bite of it yet.

He props his head on his fist and gives me a small, sympathetic smile. "She's okay. He won't let anything happen to her, and she'll probably just sleep for the rest of the night anyway."

I grimace as the memory flashes through my mind of Diego carrying Eilidh's limp form over the hill to the greenhouse. "I just feel so fucking useless," I grumble.

He punches me lightly on the arm. "We were *all* pretty useless tonight." He lights a spark in his hand and tosses a ball of flame back and forth several times as he talks. "None of us were able to stop her."

I turn around and lean back against the table as well, then cross my arms. "One of us did," I say sullenly.

He considers his next words, opens his mouth, but then shuts it again, apparently having thought better of it. I just raise my eyebrows at him, and he sighs. "Well, they're on a different level than the rest of us. Physically, anyway. It only makes sense that he was the only one who could help her."

I wince. *I should have let him stay silent.*

He taps his foot against mine. "So, what are you going to do about it?"

"About what?"

"About being hopelessly in love with a woman who could rip your head off."

I open my mouth to protest, but then Valentina enters the dining hall and jumps into the conversation like she has been in here the whole time. "Any woman could rip your head off, boys. Remember that."

I look between them quickly. "I'm not —" But they both tilt their heads and raise an eyebrow at me, in such perfect sync with each other that it's almost unnerving.

"We can tell you like her," Valentina says simply.

Martín snorts. "*Everyone* can tell you like her."

I push my glasses on top of my head and run my hands roughly over my face. "*Akh.*"

"It is *not* hopeless," Valentina says. "And neither are you. Just tell her how you feel."

Martín nods in agreement. "Hyun-Joo said she watches you while she's training more than she watches her own two feet."

My eyes widen, and he grins. "So," he says slowly.

Valentina puts a hand on her hip and stares at me as well.

I look between them and smirk. "I can always count on you two to bully me into making a move, can't I?"

Martín has the good grace to look sheepish for a moment. "Hey, I didn't know that woman was going to ask you for a threesome with me."

He crosses his arms and heaves a dramatic sigh. "But I'm still rather hurt that you turned her down," he teases, pouting.

I laugh easily at the memory from several years ago as Valentina makes an exaggerated gagging sound.

When she's done, her fierce gaze turns to me. "Anyway, you need to talk to Eilidh. She seems sweet. I think she could be good for you, and you deserve to be happy. *Really* happy."

I hold up a placating hand. "Okay, okay. I'll go talk to her first thing in the morning."

"Good man," Martín claps me on the back and gestures at Val. "We're going to go to the city tonight. Want to come?"

I smile and shake my head at them. "No, I'm going to turn in early. But thanks."

I turn around and finally take a bite of the *makhlama* as they exit the dining hall. It warms me, as do the scenarios that play out in my head about how tomorrow morning is going to go.

When I get to the greenhouse, Diego will probably be leering at Eilidh from outside the cell, and then he'll stalk away as soon as he sees me.

But then, I'll look into her emerald eyes, and tell her how I feel. *Well, maybe not* exactly *how I feel.* I don't want to scare her off. *Maybe I should just show her instead.*

Suddenly, I picture myself leaning in to kiss her, and I wonder what she might taste like. And, if she really does reciprocate my feelings like Martín implied she does, what will happen after that?

What would it feel like to run my fingers through the fiery waves of her hair? To run my hands over her curves, and the freckles that are peppered across her shoulders? What would it be like to have her underneath me?

Tension builds rapidly in my core, and I shake myself, desperately trying to banish the image of my fingers digging into those thighs of hers that I would do just about anything to be able to see more of. I take the last bite of food, then quickly take the plate to the kitchen sink and splash cold water on my face before I wash it.

I'm too old for this shit. I'm not twenty anymore; thoughts like these shouldn't be making sweat bead up on the back of my neck like they are. But then again, that's what Eilidh has been doing to me every time I've looked at her this past month — setting me on fire.

Once the plate is put away and I've made myself a black tea with a splash of honey and a dash of cinnamon, I head to my room for the night.

I sit at my desk and write while I sip the tea. Writing always helps. It's always been the most effective way to process my emotions.

After I've written several paragraphs about the events of the day, and what the Peñas had said, I set the pen down and look back over the page.

It does the trick. By the time I strip down and crawl into bed, I'm feeling much less hopeless than I had even an hour ago.

Tomorrow - hopefully, if she wants me - a new chapter will begin.

~ Waning Gibbous ~

The Morning After

When I open my eyes again, I'm lying in a bed, but not *my* bed. I look around to figure out where I am. It's a jail cell that has been dropped into a once-loved greenhouse that's now full of dead plants. There are bars surrounding me on all four sides, with thick glass walls on the other side of them. Early morning sunlight streams down around me.

I groan against the light and roll over onto my side. Diego is hunched over in a chair at my bedside, elbows propped against his knees, staring at me. I start, and he stands slowly, wincing.

"You kicked my ass last night, *Lobita*." He smirks, his eyes twinkling. "*Qué maravilla.*"

My head is still thick with fog; I don't have a response to whatever that means. It doesn't sound like an insult, though. Something flutters in my stomach.

He puts the back of his hand to my forehead, then to my cheek. It lingers there for a moment, and I close my eyes.

"Good. Your fever broke," he says quietly.

"Fever?" I ask dimly.

"First change is hell on the body, and the body fights back. A lot of people don't make it."

I press a hand to my forehead in relief. "My headache is gone, too. It was pounding like hell all day yesterday."

He frowns at the ground for a moment, as if trying to remember something, or making a mental note to remember something later.

"Were you out here with me all night?" I squint at him. "Don't you need sleep?"

He shrugs. "It's fine. I'm a night person."

That didn't really answer my question, but he apparently isn't planning to.

"Your healing factor kicked in." His hand brushes my left shoulder, and it doesn't hurt for what feels like the first time in years, even though it's only been a couple of weeks. I gasp and sit up quickly, which doesn't hurt either. I undo several of the buttons on the front of my dress, exposing my left collarbone.

There are only scars across my chest; the stitches have dissolved overnight. The scars are bumpy, and somehow more white than the rest of my skin. I'll have the marks forever, but relief washes over me anyway.

I run my right hand from my left shoulder to my sternum as hot tears of relief well up in my eyes. I hadn't realized until now how accustomed I had become to the pain. Now that it's gone, it's like a weight has been lifted from me, and I feel light as a feather.

I look up at Diego and realize he's standing unnaturally still, staring down at my chest. I realize with a jolt that my breasts are barely covered. I hasten to button back up, but he reaches toward me, and I freeze.

His hand moves, not to my breasts, where I thought he had been staring, but just above my right collarbone. He runs a finger over a few tiny bumps, and I shudder.

His face is utterly blank, but his *eyes*. A myriad of emotions flicks through them too fast for me to identify. They're tight at the corners, and the morning light glistens off his pupils. He appears to be in an enormous amount of pain. I can't look away from him, so I bring my hand up to feel what he's feeling, and our fingers brush for a moment.

He moves his hand back abruptly as if burned.

There are four puncture wounds in my trapezius muscle, two each on the front and back at the base of my throat. The memory of the previous evening hits me like a ton of bricks. I flinch away from him, and that snaps him out of his trance.

"You *bit* me!" I exclaim, my hand clutching my neck. "You *asshole!*"

In a blink, his expression switches from pained to indignant.

"You were rampaging all over the place!" He snaps back at me, throwing his hands into the air. "I didn't have any other way to stop you, and not even that silver net was going to hold you long. You shifted early! The fucking *sun* was still out. I've never seen that before." His thick brows knit together in thought.

"So what now, am I going to become some kind of . . . lycan-pire? A super-hybrid Shifter?"

He frowns at me and crosses his arms. "Don't be ridiculous. Our blood can't mix; it's like oil and water. My venom oozed back out of your wounds in a few minutes, but by then you were already out."

I flush for a moment at the thought of his venom oozing in either direction through my body. "Oh," I say lamely.

I think back for a moment over my red-tinged memories. "How did you know?" I ask quietly.

I don't need to explain what I mean. He sighs. "Your demeanor was the first clue. I was finishing getting suited up when Martín started banging on my door. He said you had just strode into the kitchen like a vengeful harpy hunting an ex-lover."

One side of his mouth quirks up at that. The imagery washes over me for a moment. I sound . . . like a badass. I hadn't realized Martín was so poetic.

Diego continues. "By the time I got to the kitchen, you were about to tear into those raw steaks, and as soon as I looked into your eyes,

I knew. They weren't like they normally are. They were cold and cruel. Bloodthirsty." He pauses. "Literally," he adds as an afterthought, raising his eyebrows briefly.

I think of his hand gripping my chin, turning my face to his, inches away, and quickly look away from him.

"What are they normally like?" I ask softly, twisting my hands together.

He puts his hands on his waist and turns to the side. "Not like that." His voice is clipped.

There's a beat of silence, and he says, his voice a bit lighter, "Then you were on top of me trying to claw my face off, and your eyes were glowing bright green. That was a pretty big clue."

I laugh out loud. I didn't know he knew how to be funny.

"Yeah well, I want to claw your face off all the time." I grin sideways at him.

He smirks back at me. "But you've never actually *done* it until yesterday."

I look down, and my smile fades as I consider my next words. "It — it didn't hurt." My voice is low. "I mean, I had a *raging* headache all day, but when I shifted, it felt amazing. Every horror novel depicts a werewolf's transformation to be excruciating, but I didn't feel that way at all. I felt . . . invincible." I finish in a whisper and clench my fists to stop my hands from shaking. I pull my legs up on either side of my stomach and hug them tight to my chest, which, I marvel again, is no longer throbbing.

His mouth tightens. "It's easy to feel invincible when you're high on power," he says. "The hard part is when you come back down. *If* you can come back down. Not everyone can." He sits down on the foot of the bed, and we just gaze at each other for a moment as I consider his words.

"What was it like for you?" I ask quietly. I don't need to elaborate.

His thick lips press into a hard line. "Hell," he grunts. "It was hell." He doesn't expound on this.

It's like trying to bleed a stone, I think in annoyance at his taciturn answer. *A giant, chiseled, fucking stone.*

"Is that it?" I bite. He surprisingly doesn't appear annoyed at my venomous tone. He just looks tired.

"Every member of the Order has a sad story that led us here. A lifetime of trauma, and nowhere else to go. The perfect soldiers." He scowls to himself, and then continues. "I'm nothing special. Some of the others had it much harder."

I think of Saif's tale and frown.

"But," I say quietly, and bite my lip before continuing. "Everyone else woke up one day with *magic*. I mean, I'm sure it was hard for them to adjust, but you and I are . . . monsters." I grimace, considering how to voice the rest of my thoughts.

He stares at me silently.

"The Universe didn't randomly grant us any wonderful powers. We were ravaged, and born anew in blood."

He doesn't break my gaze, but his eyes unfocus as he thinks. Finally, he sighs and throws himself back on the bed, lying with his hands clasped on his abdomen. I rock lightly with the motion of the mattress.

"You're right," he murmurs.

I make an incredulous sound and push his shoulder with my foot. He doesn't budge. "Can I get that in writing? Get the signature notarized?" I smile.

He tilts his head toward me, a small smile on his lips. This is an entirely different man than the one who finds a new way for me to nearly kill myself in the training yard every day.

This version is so easy to talk to.

He opens his mouth to respond, but then there's a sharp rapping on the glass. We both start and turn to see Saif opening the door at the opposite end of the greenhouse, his expression thunderous.

Lahabi

Saif enters the greenhouse, glaring hard at Diego, who sits up abruptly, and gets off the bed. The springs creak in relief, and there's a pang deep in my chest. My eyes follow him of their own volition.

He strides to the bars of the cell surrounding us, reaches into a pocket on the pack strapped to his thigh, and pulls out a key.

As he reaches through the bars and unlocks the cell door, Saif approaches the other side of it. His eyes glint dangerously up at Diego, whose back is to me.

The men look at each other for a few tense moments, and I have no idea what silent words are exchanged between them. Saif breaks the silence first.

"You said you would stay outside of the cell," he bites out through his teeth. I've never heard him use this tone before. He's *pissed*.

He lowers his voice. "You know the price if you don't." His words would normally be imperceptible, but I'm pretty sure my hearing is still heightened from the transformation.

Of course. He's worried about his colleague's safety, especially after seeing me lose it last night.

For the first time, I'm embarrassed at the thought of what I had done. I could have seriously hurt someone. I should have felt the change coming sooner than I did. Should have known as soon as I didn't want the soup Saif had prepared for me. I grip my knees to my chest harder.

Diego raises himself to his full height and his shoulders rise in a quick chuckle. "No need to worry about that." His voice drips with sarcasm once again, the gentleness from a moment ago completely gone. "I only entered a few minutes ago to see if her fever had broken, and we were just chatting."

I furrow my brow. *You were sitting in that chair like you hadn't moved all night when I woke up.* But I don't want to make the situation more tense than it already is. I say nothing.

Saif flicks his gaze to me, then back to Diego. He opens his mouth like he has more to say, but before he can, Diego grips his shoulder quickly and moves past him. "I appreciate your concern though."

As Diego leaves the greenhouse, Saif steps through the open cell door and makes his way to me. The corners of his mouth tighten at the sight of the chair by my bedside, but he says nothing about it.

I clear my throat, and he blinks at me, snapped from whatever direction his thoughts had started to go in.

"Good news, nurse," I say with a forced smile, trying to derail him from possibly picturing me gnawing on Diego's mangled corpse, or whatever else he's worried I would do. "I'm healed!" I pull my dress collar open again to reveal the scars on my left shoulder.

His eyes light up, and he runs his fingers over the scars. My pulse quickens at his touch.

"That's wonderful!" He sits on the edge of the bed next to me, his hand still on my shoulder. "Is the pain gone?" He starts running his thumb back and forth across my collarbone.

Suddenly, my skin is on fire. I'm not so sure Diego was correct when he said my fever had broken.

"Yeah," I say shakily. I must still be tired from the transformation. "I hadn't realized how used to it I had gotten."

His thumb stops moving, but now it's directly over the pulse in the hollow of my neck. Surely, he can feel it quickening. He takes a few beats to reply, then clears his throat and shifts closer to me.

"It's astounding how much pain people can adapt to when that's all they know." He finally tears his gaze from my shoulder, and his eyelids are heavy as he looks at me. I'm distantly aware that his face is now only inches from mine.

"Yeah," I say again, lamely. My brain does not seem to be able to form any other thoughts at the moment.

"I was so worried about you last night," he says finally, his voice thick. "I'm sorry I couldn't help you, *Lahabi.*"

I gulp. "What, um, does that mean?" I murmur.

He brushes my hair behind my ear and runs his fingers through the auburn strands. "My flame."

My heart slams against my rib cage so hard that I'm convinced it's going to break out of my chest entirely. I reach out to grab his other hand and squeeze it reassuringly; it's rough and warm, and mine fits perfectly in it. "I'm totally fine," I croak.

He doesn't break our gaze, just moves his hand from my hair to my cheek. I inhale shakily. The rising sun lights up his eyes; streaks of caramel and copper glint at me.

I lick my lips, which suddenly feel dry as a bone, and his gaze moves to them. "I'm better than I've ever been," I whisper.

"Good," he breathes. Then he leans the last few inches into me and kisses me tenderly. His warm, soft lips taste like mint tea. His mustache prickles me, but in a delightful way that shoots fireworks through my head.

After a few moments, he pushes into me and slowly guides me onto the mattress. When he's propped over me, he looks down at my lips again and brings his mouth down gently onto mine.

I drink him in as he lowers himself onto me slowly, as if not confident that my torso is actually healed, that he won't break me. I gasp against his mouth and try to pull him in closer by the front of his shirt, but he doesn't budge.

His kisses deepen, and he softly nudges my lips open with his tongue. I run my hands against his back, the muscles strong and solid as he moves against me slowly. He props himself up onto his elbow, and though I'm briefly in agony over the loss of his mouth on mine, it's immediately on the left side of my neck, and I whimper into his ear. He clutches his hand into my waist and licks from the base of my throat up to my ear, then kisses from my ear down to my left shoulder.

He kisses each of the four scars on my shoulder individually. His left hand moves up under the back of my head, and his right moves to the back of my left knee. He gives the smallest tug on my hair, and gradually brings my left leg up around his hip as he continues kissing my neck.

My body is screaming at him to go harder in his movements instead of being so delicate. *I'm not made of fine china*, I want to tell him. But I'm afraid if I say anything, the spell will be broken.

Instead, I move my hips up against him. I try to move him faster, but he sticks to his steady pace. He breathes out heavily and brings his mouth back onto mine. I kiss him hard, and he pulls back a bit. I halt for a moment, afraid to open my eyes, and then kiss him softly. He kisses me back fully once again.

He's so tender and deliberate in his movements, like he plans each one out before he makes it. He props himself up on his forearm again, then kisses my jaw, down the left side of my throat, and onto my chest between the open buttons of my plaid dress. His lowest kiss is directly on my sternum, where he lingers for a moment.

As he kisses his way back up my neck, he trails a finger up the inside of my thigh. I moan with anticipation, but he doesn't increase his speed.

Finally - *finally* - his hand reaches the top of my thigh, and he slips his fingers past my underwear. He rubs two fingers around my clit and kisses me deeply. I kiss him back, put both my hands into his hair, careful not to be too rough for him, and arch my body into his.

I'm dripping wet by now, and my pussy is throbbing with desire. At this rate, I almost wish he would skip right to fucking me, and not bother with his fingers, but he continues rubbing my clit as he kisses back down my neck, down to my sternum, then, this time, back up to the right side of my neck.

As he moves to plant another kiss, he tugs on the collar of my dress, which has been stretched to reveal the opposite shoulder until now. He freezes.

I grind against him another time before my brain catches on that he has stopped. I flutter my eyes open in confusion, breathing heavily. I run my fingers over my skin to see if there's something on me, then realize he's staring at the puncture wounds at the base of my throat.

They're less pronounced than they were even a bit ago when Diego had run his fingers over them, but they're definitely still there.

"Oh," I say breathlessly. "Don't worry, they don't hurt." I move to kiss him again, but he leans back farther, and looks at me in disgust. I sober up immediately. I've never seen that look on his face.

"That is not the problem," he says curtly. He rises quickly off the bed, and I quickly tug the dress back down around myself. I stare at him, bewildered, but he won't meet my gaze.

"Then what *is* the problem?" I ask, trying to slow my racing heart. "Because I'm lost."

But he ignores me; instead, he glares at the chair by the bedside.

"Saif, what —" I start to say, but then he kicks at the chair, and it clatters to the floor.

I jump, too shocked to say anything further. He stalks out of the cell, leaving the door open. In seconds, he's across the greenhouse; he rips that door open, and then he walks off into the distance without another glance back at me.

I stare after him until he disappears from sight over a hill. For a moment as I watch him, before I blink it away, my vision is once again coated in a blood-red film.

Transitions

I lie in the greenhouse in a daze after he storms off and watch the sun slowly march above me toward its zenith. My mind swirls, and I don't try to stop my thoughts as they come. My therapist would be proud. *I'm feeling my feelings, Susan*, I think ruefully.

No matter how I look at it, I can't understand Saif's reaction, and that makes me confused. *No*, I chide myself. *That makes you* angry.

But then guilt hits me for feeling angry, because what if he has a perfectly valid reason to be mad, and I just don't know what it is? I just wish he would have told me what that reason is, so I could fix the problem.

And what about Diego? Who the hell was that transformed version of him who joked with me and watched over me to make sure my fever had broken? What the hell is going *on* with those two? I wonder, sadly, if they had been close before I got here, and I had done something to drive a wedge between them, though I can't imagine what.

Finally, I decide to drag myself out of bed and figure out where in the hell I even am. My shoes are nowhere to be found - *Was I wearing shoes when I transformed?* - so I step out onto the grass, which is still just faintly wet with the last of the morning dew.

It's been so long since I've had the chance to be alone, other than when I'm falling into an exhausted sleep at night, and it's nice, in spite of the circumstances.

Alone isn't painful.

Alone is easily controlled.

Alone is familiar.

Suddenly weary despite having been in bed all morning, I sink to my knees, and the soft earth cradles me when I land. I run my hands back and forth over the blades of grass and pick delicately at the intermingled clovers. I close my eyes and take in the sounds of the birds singing their morning songs, and the waves crashing nearby.

I fold myself over and press my forehead into the earth as if Gaia herself will telepathically convey all the answers I need to the questions swirling in my mind. We had been so connected once, Mother Earth and I, but that had been a lifetime ago. I can't recall when last I sat and meditated during a thunderstorm, made cider for Mabon, or visited the cemetery for Yule.

The cemetery.

I breathe through gritted teeth and dig my nails into my palms. For five years I had lain between two austere stones, asking them in turn for advice that they'd never give me again. Then, in one horrible instant, there was another grave a few rows away that required my attention as well.

Kianga.

I sat by her grave for five years before I couldn't do it anymore — had simply laid my heart on the stone and walked away. I hadn't been back since. That was six years ago.

My body I could give to others, if only for a night. A nonbinary person with snake bite piercings that I had met at the bar. A woman who would sometimes substitute for the chemistry classroom across from the library at school. A guy who had reached for the same book as me in Tia's store, and had insisted I keep it, but only if I let him buy me a coffee.

Many other hazy memories drift through my head of stolen kisses and temporary highs. They'd been fun, but they'd never had my heart. That is still with her.

At least, that's what I had thought, until now.

Now, I've started having that feeling again. Someone had crept under my skin, cared for me, and shown me compassion. Had shared trauma with me, had seen me at my lowest, and made me feel like it didn't lower his view of me. That I was allowed to be vulnerable with him.

And look how that turned out.

I reach again for the pendant, and this time, when my hand passes through the air where once the last remnants of my heart had been, I scream with blind rage.

I scream, my forehead still pressed into the grass, as I clasp my hands behind my head, and tremble like a leaf. Hot tears fall heavy and fast onto the blades of grass that I've buried my face in. I scream again, and it sounds like an agonized howl.

When I finally lift my head again, the sun is higher still in the sky — it's nearly lunchtime. My eyes are dry, and my throat is raw. I'm spent, as though I've just shattered into pieces that I hadn't realized I had been trying desperately to hold together for the last six years.

But still, the earth cradles me. She, at least, hasn't left me. "Thank you," I murmur to the clovers. A soft breeze blows my hair off my face, kissing my cheeks.

A soft, tentative voice behind me yanks me from my reverie. "Eilidh."

I turn to see Valentina standing a few yards behind me, clutching her hands together in front of her. I've never seen her look abashed before, but she is now.

"I'm sorry," she says, her voice quiet and soothing. "I was outside walking when I heard you screaming, and I ran over the hill to make sure you were okay. I . . . I didn't want to interrupt," she finishes sheepishly.

I sniffle, expecting to feel embarrassed, but I don't. *She was here for you the whole time. You just had to look.*

"Thank you," I croak.

She squints in sympathy, then walks to me and sinks to the ground beside me. "I'm here if you want to talk," she says, throwing an arm around me tightly.

I'm grateful, but exhausted.

"I think . . . I think I just want breakfast," I say dully. She looks hurt, and I, in turn, feel like an asshole. I look away guiltily and dig the nails of my free hand into my palm.

"Okay," she says quietly, and pulls me to my feet.

She leads me back over the hill, her hand still holding mine, and as we crest it, I see the Eastern side of the castle. I realize, for the first time, that it's small, as far as castles go. I've seen bigger buildings at the end of rich cul-de-sacs.

"It's really more of a keep," I say aloud.

"What?"

"Saif called this place Arkenvale Castle when I first woke up, but it's really just a keep."

One corner of her mouth lifts. "I'll take your word for it. But either way, 'Arkenvale Keep' doesn't have the same ring to it."

I exhale quickly through my nose. "Yeah, that's true." Maybe Auberon just isn't one for bells and whistles.

We walk in silence for a minute, and then Valentina clears her throat. "Do you want me to make you something?"

I just nod, too exhausted to insist that I can do it myself. "Yes please." As we approach the front door on the South side of the castle, I see that it's been repaired.

She notices my confusion. "Oh, Auberon fixed the doors right away. No worries."

She waves her hand through the air like an orchestra conductor, and I assume it's supposed to mean his telekinesis can fuse shattered wood back together too, and isn't just used to hurl daggers at women. I don't know how that works, but no one asked me for input when the magical abilities were being designed.

After we eat some *arepas* that Valentina whips together in no time, I decide to grab a mug of hot tea from the kitchen, and then she walks with me to my room. Sensing she wants to talk more, I invite her inside.

"Take your pick of the ample seating," I say, gesturing with a smile at the stool. She smiles back and sits on the floor, her legs crossed.

I plop onto the floor across from her and lean against the bed, cradling my mug. As I take a sip, she clears her throat. She looks like she's hyping herself up to say whatever is coming next.

"So." She looks at me, and I don't interrupt. "I know I said earlier that you can talk to me if you need, and I meant that. But we've only known each other for a few weeks at this point, and I've come to realize that you're not the kind of person to trauma dump on strangers."

I look down into my mug. *I did with Saif.*

"So, instead of just saying that you can talk to me, I was hoping that we could, you know, actually do some talking. Get to know each other. And then, I hope you feel comfortable eventually opening up. It really can do wonders for one's mental health. And that's before you add 'lycanthrope' to the equation."

She finishes her monologue with a small smile. I return it weakly. "You first," she prompts. "Ask me anything you'd like to know."

I sip my tea as I think of something simple. "Where are you from?"

She responds immediately. "Miami. My parents immigrated there from Colombia soon after they got married, and then a few years later they were cursed with Martín." She clutches her chest in mock sympathy. "Luckily for them, I came along not even a year later."

A wistful smile lights up her face. "When we were growing up, Martín and I practically lived on the beach. I'd spend all day swimming, and he would build bonfires every night for people to crowd around." The smile tilts. "I miss it so much."

I nod sympathetically.

"My turn." She taps a finger to her chin thoughtfully. "So what did you do? Before you, ah, before coming here?" She recovers quickly.

My smile fades, remembering that I can't go back to my old life anymore. I don't have a family to miss, but I'll miss my library.

"Oh, uh, I was an elementary school librarian."

Her face lights up. "No. Way!"

My eyes widen in surprise at her enthusiasm.

"That's so awesome! I always wanted to work with kids. Their constant energy, their hilarious stories. I thought about becoming a teacher for a while, but then. Well." She twists a ribbon of water through her fingers quickly with a melancholy smile.

"Why can't you go back?" I ask quietly. "It's not like you'll snap and bite someone's head off," I say ruefully.

She considers this for a moment. When she seems unable, or perhaps unwilling, to provide an answer, I continue. "Your power could probably do so much good for the world. You could prevent floods. Bring water to dry wells." My mind reels with the things that just one woman could do. "Holy shit, Valentina, you're basically a superhero."

But her eyes are glinting in a way I haven't seen before, except during our sparring sessions: dangerously.

"Once an Order member, always an Order member," she says quietly. "Besides, the world pushed my brother and me out; we didn't ask to leave. But no matter where we went, once it got out what we were, suddenly there were a million reasons that we didn't belong.

If the world wanted our help, it shouldn't have made us outcasts." She hugs her arms to herself. "Our parents were the first ones who pushed us away."

I frown at her sadly. *I know that feeling all too well.*

"When I was twelve, my father and I got into a *huge* fight. He started to get physical, but then Martín . . . stepped in for me." Her voice breaks. "We ran away for a week or so, but child services returned us. They didn't care what we had to say. Things were tense for the rest of our time there, but nothing else quite so bad happened until I turned eighteen, and insisted that he call me by my proper name."

My brow furrows in confusion, and she breathes in deeply, steadying herself for her next words. "My father said that 'Valentina' is not a name that any *son* of his would ever be called."

My eyes widen as realization dawns on me. *Oh.*

"It was . . . bad. Again. Worse, actually, but Martín stepped in for me, just like he always did."

She sniffs. "And then his magic activated, and the house caught fire. Then *mine* activated, and I just barely managed to put the fire out before it spread to the neighbor's house. We left as soon as Martín had patched himself up. We still don't know if Dad made it out or not." Her voice is perfectly calm.

I look at her in stunned silence. At first, I regret that there's nothing I can say to help, but her eyes are dry. She doesn't need my help, anyway. I reach my foot out and press it against her knee. She looks at me guardedly, waiting for my response.

"I'm sorry you had to go through that, Valentina," I say firmly. Her grateful smile warms my heart.

We chat until dinnertime, and after that, we finally part ways. I lay on my pillow that night, deep in contemplation. I'm grateful that Valentina has shared her story with me. I think of Martín, practically glued to his sister's side whenever they are in the same room, watching her like a nervous mother hen.

No wonder. I suppose when you grow up protecting someone you love, being the one that steps in to take the blows aimed their way, that habit doesn't stop when you become adults.

Having someone love you so unconditionally, someone to protect you from the entire world. Someone who the universe doesn't rip away from you, leaving you with nothing. I fall asleep wondering what that would be like to have.

Fallen

She is a bonfire that lights up the world.
But to fall would end in ruin.
Naught but an echo of the past.
For now, I'll pretend.
Pretend that I haven't already fallen.

Arrogant

everal days later, Saif has still not turned up. When I get to the training grounds that morning and ask Martín if he knows where he has gone, he doesn't quite meet my eye.

"He said he was going on a mission for Auberon. I'm not sure when he'll be back, but he said your torso's all healed, and that you'd be fine without him."

I wince, and he places a hand on my shoulder, finally looking at me. "Just give him time, kid."

I cross my arms sullenly. "You know I'm older than you," I say with a smile that doesn't meet my eyes.

He punches me lightly on the arm. "Only in years."

I've just begun stretching when a shadow blocks out the sunlight at my back. I sigh, already sensing who it is. He hasn't talked to me outside the training yard since the morning he left the greenhouse, and not once when he *did* acknowledge me did he smile at me like he had then.

I'm starting to think I had imagined the whole thing.

I turn to see Diego wearing light gray cuffed sweatpants and a dark red muscle shirt with arm holes so wide it basically doesn't have sides. Instead, his chiseled abs poke out of it. I very pointedly do not look at them.

I've seen many jerks wearing similar shirts in many gyms over the years. Seeing a jerk wearing it in an alternate dimension is a first, though.

It's too early for him, and I'm already in a foul mood. I raise a questioning eyebrow.

"When you're done stretching, get in the circle." He jerks a thumb at the chalk circle on the ground a few yards away, where we typically do hand-to-hand sparring and wrestling.

I lean around him to see who I'll be sparring against, hoping it will be Hyun-Joo. The last time she and I had gone hand-to-hand, she nearly made me break my hand when she blocked a punch with one of her barriers, and I'm still itching to get her back.

Maybe I'll actually win a match against her for once.

But everyone else is occupied with their own routines. My other eyebrow shoots up as I realize he means for me to spar with *him*.

I gape at him. "Not uh. No way." I make a slashing motion with my hands.

His expression doesn't change. "Everyone else is busy, and Rahim, clearly, is still gone. It's been a week since I've sparred with someone other than Hyun-Joo, and I need a bigger opponent to stay sharp."

The idea of a vampire not being sharp enough makes me giggle madly, and he glares at me.

"Stretch. Then circle. That's an order, soldier." He stalks off.

I put my hands on my hips, just resisting the urge to stomp my foot. "I'm not a fucking soldier, I'm a librarian," I mumble to myself.

He whips around, and I instantly know by the look on his face that he heard me. "Sorry to remind you, *Lobita*," he says, walking backward, "but you quite literally *are* a soldier now."

I flush as he turns and continues walking away without missing a step.

I take at least five extra minutes to stretch, hoping he'll give up and ask Martín, but he just stands there, staring at me. Finally, I stop stalling and walk over to the chalk circle. If they have to get Auberon to levitate me away from this circle in pieces, I won't be surprised.

As soon as I'm in the circle, he grabs my hand and flings me around in a giant arch over his shoulder. I land with a loud *thud* in the grass and I cry out as the air rushes from my lungs.

"What the *fuck?*" I choke when I regain my breath.

He shrugs at me innocently. "I wanted to see if your reflexes are faster since you've transformed. Apparently not." I glare up at him from the ground. He turns away from me, and I seize my opportunity, fueled by rage.

I spin quickly on the ground and sweep his legs out from under him. He topples like a giant, landing face-first, barely catching himself before his nose smashes against the ground. I stand up, far enough away that I know I'll be out of his reach.

"That, *sir*, is a move I learned in soccer when I was twelve. How embarrassing for you," I taunt.

He looks up at me from the ground, and though I expect him to be pissed, he's smirking at me, and his eyes are — playful?

"Okay then," he says, and then he's a blur of motion. I had underestimated his reach, or maybe he just moved that fast. He grabs at the back of one of my knees and pulls it forward. At the same time, he shoves his shoulder into my stomach, and the ground rushes up to meet me again.

This time, though, I'm a bit faster to recover. I wrap my legs around his waist and twist him off of me. We roll.

For the next ninety seconds or so, we're a tangle of limbs. I get in a few good jabs, finally landing a solid kick to his shin that incapacitates him for enough time that I'm able to whip around, and climb onto his back to put him into a headlock. He slams me down into the ground, but though stars explode across my vision, I don't let go.

His wide shoulders are his disadvantage; he can only reach me enough to scratch at me a few times, but not far enough to actually grab me.

I notice for the first time, holding him as tightly as I can for those few seconds, that gray hairs are peppered throughout his chestnut waves. The scent of his cedar and aloe shampoo fills my nose.

Finally, he taps out, and I release him. He puts his hands on his knees and smiles up at me, panting hard. I look away from him and try to get my heart rate down.

We take a minute to recover. When we start our second round, he seems fully recharged, while I'm still panting, my movements slower and sloppy; he blocks my blows easily.

I realize quickly that I'm not winning this round with brawn. I try brains instead.

Or, at least, my mouth.

I go for the one thing I know is his weakness, praying it will distract him.

"Hyun-Joo never mentioned how quick your recovery time is," I say when he next comes in close. I try to twist away from him, but he gets both arms around me, and traps me in a bear hug, my back to his chest.

"What the fuck are you talking about?" He gasps into my ear. The sound sends a shiver down my spine.

He's trying to get his leg between mine to toss me off balance, but I use his momentary confusion to my advantage and launch myself as hard as I can off the ground, pushing us backward.

He lands hard on his back and his grip loosens. I scramble off him toward the other side of the ring to give myself time to breathe.

"Hey, I'm happy for her," I say, my hands on my knees. I want to hang my head and pant, but I'm not dumb enough to take my eyes off him. He gets up off the ground, a fraction slower than before, but that might just be because he's focusing on my words.

"You'd think she'd be less bitchy all the time, though," I say.

Harsh, my conscience pipes up, but I push it away. Now is not the time.

His eyes glint dangerously as he stands to his full height, trying to intimidate me. "Shut up and fight," he growls.

"Hey, Auberon told me that knowledge of the enemy is the best weapon. If I know their weakness, I should exploit it. And I know your weakness is her."

He comes at me again, and I can tell I've gotten to him. *Good, I think*, jumping quickly over his sweeping leg. *If he's upset, he'll get sloppy.*

I manage to side-step his next attack, and as I do, I jump and whip my elbow into the side of his head. I didn't even know I could do that. Maybe he was right to think that my reflexes had enhanced since the change. I had definitely not been this good in the ring before.

That move dazes him momentarily, so I kick into the back of one of his knees, and he buckles. My muscles are on fire, but I'm high on the adrenaline that is pumping through my veins.

I'm actually going to win this again.

I become arrogant, and that's my undoing.

Instead of just kicking him out of the ring and ending things, I taunt him again. "How many puncture wounds has she got on *her* shoulder? She's got magic, sure, but she can't heal like I can."

My brain is screaming at me to shut the fuck up, but my mouth ignores it entirely. "Your bite was euphoric for me. Does it hurt for her?" I sneer at him.

He hasn't yet moved from his kneeling position since he fell, but at that, he spins on his knees and launches himself at me. His claws are out, and I see his fangs flash at me before he slams into my chest. I barely have time to widen my eyes before he hits me so hard that we both fly several feet, and land well outside the chalk circle. Stars explode across my vision as my head makes contact with the earth.

He pushes into me with his full body weight, and I squirm under him, struggling in vain to push him off me. He yanks my shoulders and slams me back into the ground again, and I see more stars.

His claws cut through my hazy thoughts, deep into my arms, as he pins them to the ground beside me. "You have no idea what you're talking about," he growls, his speech slurring a bit around his fangs. His accent is stronger than normal; it rumbles in my ear and sends a chill down my spine. "Keep her name out of your mouth."

I open my stupid mouth immediately, though to say what, I'm not sure, when a sharp voice cuts off my thoughts.

"Diego!" Hyun-Joo snaps. My stomach drops.

He raises himself off me easily, and I lie there dazed for another few moments.

When I'm able to roll onto my side and prop myself up on my elbow, I see the two of them standing a few yards away. He's bent down over her protectively, and she's clutching his forearms, staring daggers at me.

I had been so focused on him that I had completely forgotten that other people were around us. It hits me that she had to have heard everything I said, and so had the Peñas, who are looking at each other with identical wide-eyed expressions. Shame washes over me as I look down at the ground.

No one else moves. Hyun-Joo is the one who finally breaks the awful silence.

"You're a mess. Go clean yourself up." Her voice drips with contempt, and I don't blame her. Right now, I hate myself too.

I don't look at anyone else as I stand up gingerly, wincing as my muscles protest. I clutch my arms around my chest as I walk back inside the castle.

Prodigal Daughter

I try to sit in my room after I've taken a hot shower, but the dark walls feel like they're closing in on me. I get up and pull on sweatpants and a crew neck sweater, then pull my damp hair back into a claw clip.

I briefly consider strapping my dagger onto my thigh in its holster, if only to feel its now-familiar weight, but I leave it laying on my nightstand. I open my door and peek onto the balcony to make sure no one else is nearby. I can't face anyone right now.

There's one place in Arkenvale that I know will welcome me. One place I'll be comfortable, and safe. At home.

I scurry down the spiral staircase and over to the door. I knock tentatively, hoping there's no answer.

There isn't.

I open it and enter quickly, then sink to the ground in the library. I sit against the door for a moment and just breathe in the scent of paper and ink. With Auberon gone, no papers or books flutter around; the tower is eerily silent.

Eventually, I rise and make my way around the shelves, pulling books at random to examine them before moving to the next shelf.

There are books here from what might as well be the last thousand years, though there seems to be no organization to them. I grimace at the chaos, but push away my instinct to grab a cart and start reorganizing.

Not your library, Shaw. My heart twists. I may never see *my* library again. *One more thing lost.*

I see some old scrolls near the top of a few of the shelves that are probably full of fascinating maps or charters, but no way am I going up there and risking wrecking them by accident.

I've fucked up enough lately.

Many of the books are historical accounts from all over the world. I flip through pages discussing various rulers, the lands they dedicated their lives to, and usually, the gruesome ways in which they met their ends.

One shelf contains an enormous collection of transcribed diaries starting around the seventh century. The same cramped handwriting describes numerous historical days throughout the years.

Some of the books themselves look too old to have been transcribed, but they must have just experienced rough treatment through the years; who knows what these books have gone through to end up in this collection.

That's one of the things I love about books. Each one *is* a story, but also, each one *has* a story that you can't find within its pages. Each old book has someone in its past who loved it. A string of lives it has touched. Show me a book, and I'll show you ripples left in the universe, and people forever changed.

I make it to the final bookcase in a long row, jammed haphazardly full of fairy tales. The most well-worn book is one about the life of King Arthur. I pluck it delicately off the shelf and thumb through it.

The thick pages are full of gorgeous illustrations of Arthur through-out various stages of his life, as well as Lancelot and Guinevere. They are eyeing one another secretly in every picture; clearly, the artist wanted to convey their hidden affair, and the tension between them.

A cloaked and bearded figure that can only be Merlin holds a gnarled staff in one picture, a rust-colored glow emitting from a large red gemstone on its top as the wizard casts a spell.

Another picture shows a hauntingly gorgeous white woman with jet-black hair that billows around her in thick waves.

Morgana.

Sinister black tendrils twist around her limbs. She's surrounded by swirling purple flames, and her eyes glow white. Her power practically radiates off the page; it's almost tangible.

Arthur's silhouette cowers at her feet. *Can't blame him.* I would do the same thing in the presence of the most powerful and terrifying sorceress in history.

I take the book to an armchair nestled in between two shelves and lose myself in it. Hours later, I blink and suddenly realize the sun outside is gone. Just as I think about how I have no clue where the light switch is in this tower, the door to the library opens, and a dark figure fills the doorway, backlit by the soft yellow light in the entrance hall.

I hear the click of a switch, and a massive chandelier overhead blazes to life. I blink as my eyes adjust, and realize that King Auberon is stepping inside. He sees me in the chair, and just as I wonder if I'm even allowed to be in here, he smiles at me.

"Eilidh. I wasn't expecting you." He closes the door behind him and makes his way over to me. I unfurl my legs from under me and scramble to my feet, assuming that's what I'm supposed to do when a king enters the room, but he motions for me to sit back down.

I do.

He leans lightly on the arm of the chair and points to the book in my lap. "A fan of old Pendragon, are you?"

I smile meekly. "I've always loved his story," I say quietly. "Ever since I was a little girl."

Auberon is contemplative for a moment. "What draws you to him?"

I think for a moment, gently running my hand over the cover of the well-loved book.

"I guess that he's just a random little orphan boy who proves himself worthy. He gains great power, but he isn't corrupted by it. He uses it to protect the innocent. To do good for his people."

My mouth twists as I think grimly of how Arthur's story usually ends. "I always hated that he lost the love of his life and his best friend at the same time. I like to imagine that those stories are wrong, and that they actually lived happily ever after."

If only they had heard of polyamory.

The King nods slowly, his golden eye unfocused. "That does sound like a better ending," he says solemnly.

"Your . . . Majesty?" I venture. He blinks and turns his warm gaze to me. "If I may, what's next for me? Really?"

He raises an eyebrow. "Once your training is complete, and we get intelligence on where Bleddyn is, you will be granted the chance to get your justice," he says in a tone that reminds me that we've already discussed this.

"Yes, but." I hesitate. I've barely spent an hour with this man since I've been here. He lets me stay here in his home and train with his paladins, but I'm still not sure *why*, or what it means I owe him.

"But after I get my 'justice,' what then?" I twist my hands. "What am I supposed to do?" My voice quivers. I don't ask him what I really mean. *What do I do if your paladins all hate me, and don't even want me in the Order?*

The king says nothing for a moment, then places a firm hand on my shoulder. "Find your place in your new world."

"So I just stay here at Arkenvale forever? Become a member of the Order? And then what?"

He rises, and I wince, afraid I've crossed some line, given that I have such a knack for doing that lately. But his eye is not unkind. "Then you will help me protect the innocent. And do good for your people."

I swallow hard as he clears his throat.

"Actually, Eilidh, I'm happy you're here. I was hoping that you and I could talk soon. I discovered something very recently that you should know."

I tug on a stray hair that had escaped from the claw clip. What could a king have to talk to *me* about?

He motions to a nearby table, and we both walk to it and sit.

"After you came to us, I had Diego dig into your past a bit. Merely a formality, you understand. I like to know what kind of people are under my roof."

I nod, slightly annoyed. I understand the need for a background check, but the fact that Diego was the one to do it prickles me. *That explains the couple of days he's been gone over the weeks.*

He continues. "You were raised by your grandparents." It's not a question.

I nod as grief grips me. No matter how many years it's been, it has never gotten any easier.

"Why is that?" He asks.

I bite the inside of my lip and take a deep breath. "My mother abandoned me when I was eight," I say finally. "She was never the nurturing type, and one day she just decided she was ready to move on with her life. She left me with her parents, and I haven't seen her since. I got cards for my birthday and some holidays, but that's it. The last I knew, she was living in Reno." My mouth twists at the memory of her cards throughout the years, cold and impersonal.

His gaze is laden with sadness. "Were they good to you?" He asks solemnly.

"My grandparents? They were the best thing to ever happen to me," I say earnestly.

He nods, seemingly relieved, but then his expression clouds once more. "And the accident?"

I shut my eyes and nod jerkily. I don't want to tell this story, but I suppose I have no choice.

"When I was fifteen," I say. "We were driving home from a soccer tournament. I had scored the winning goal, and the trophy was huge, but I squeezed in the back seat next to it."

I close my eyes, and the image is as clear as day in my mind. I can smell the leather and tobacco scent of the car perfectly.

"We were making plans to order pizza when we got home, and we were all laughing about something my grandfather had said. Then, we went through an intersection and got T-boned by a tractor-trailer. The guy had been driving for more than twenty-four hours and had fallen asleep at the wheel. He ran the red light and —" I breathe deeply as my pulse races.

"And the next thing I knew, our car was flipped over. I was lying on the ceiling, but they were still strapped to their seats. I could smell gas. Something was on fire. They screamed at me to run."

Shame washes over me, familiar as an old blanket. "I didn't even think about it. I just . . . ran away. I made it to a parking lot close by just as I heard the explosion."

The King is quiet for several long moments as my mind swirls with memories. My emancipation. Getting the check that was supposed to somehow make up for losing them. Sure, it had put me through school, had gotten me my Master's Degree. But I'd return it all in a heartbeat if I could have them back instead.

"I am terribly sorry for all the loss you have suffered," he says finally. I can only nod and stare at the lacquered table.

His voice turns acidic. "Your mother should never have left you."

"She did me a favor," I reply automatically, taken aback by his tone. "I'd be way more fucked up if she had tried to raise me. She had . . . problems."

He doesn't ask me to elaborate, and I don't volunteer any further information.

"You know," he says slowly, "when you first came to us, I assumed, like the others, that you had fallen victim to Azaeroria's spell."

My cheeks flush at the memory of my first meeting at the circular table, and Diego's harsh words ring through my mind. *At what point did you fuck her?*

Auberon continues. "But, when you insisted that you had not, I had the wards inspected for some kind of fault - anything that would have let you slip past the barrier. But there was nothing amiss."

I stare at him wordlessly, unsure what to say.

"Then, when Diego came back with this information a few days ago, I saw your mother's name, and it all made sense. How you had supernatural blood in you to make it here. Perhaps, even, why you had been a target in the first place; why Azaeroria was drawn to you."

My brows knit together.

He reaches into his pocket and pulls out a picture, then unfolds it and lays it on the table in front of us, facing me. It's a sepia-tone photograph of my mother, but from before I knew her.

She's young here, maybe eighteen, and her wide smile crinkles the corners of her eyes. Her wavy red hair, the hair she had passed on to me, is in a shaggy wolf cut. She looks . . . happy.

She had never looked at me like that. She had only ever looked at me like I was a burden, or a terrible reminder of some tragedy.

Did Diego find this somewhere? I've never seen this photo before. It's not one I recognize from my grandmother's albums. And anyway, those albums are probably still in the attic of the house owned by a woman I haven't spoken to in years.

I shake myself and push away the guilty thoughts that fog my mind. *Focus, Shaw.*

In the photo, my mother is sitting in the lap of a white man who is at least a decade older than her or more, but the way her body leans into him tells me that they are not just friends.

The man is familiar, though he's turned toward something out of frame, so I can only see the right side of his face. But there's something about his black hair, peppered with just a few grays, that I feel I should know, like there's some part of me that recognizes him instinctively.

I squint at the photo for another moment, trying to place him. And then realization strikes me like a thunderbolt, and I can't breathe. I can't even blink. My jaw hangs open.

King Auberon points to the picture. "Eilidh, if this is your mother, and you were born thirty-one years ago in July." His golden eye glistens.

"Then you are my daughter."

~~~~~~~~~

Hours later, long past midnight, I lie in my bed, utterly failing to get even a wink of sleep as Auberon's - my father's - words bounce around my mind.

He and my mother had met when she was in college, and he was a professor. I hadn't even known my mother had *gone* to college.

And of course, for that time, no one batted an eye at their relationship, though he seemed ashamed to admit it now.

He had been hiding his magical abilities, trying desperately to blend in with the rest of the world, thinking he could build a life on his own outside Tenazeryth.

But then, my mother told him she was pregnant, and he decided that he couldn't hide such a huge part of himself from her anymore.

She, of course, thought he was lying at first, but when he proved himself to her, she got scared and ran. He never saw her again.
~~~~~~~~~

Sounds like Mom, I had thought bitterly when he told me.

He never imagined he would find the child, and had even assumed after some time that she had terminated the pregnancy when she never turned back up looking for child support.

My eye had twitched at that as memories flashed through my mind of all the nights we ate nothing more than dry cereal or plain noodles for dinner, and the one-room apartment we had lived in that had more rat tenants than human ones. Her pride had obviously been more important than my well-being.

I chided myself silently at that. *It wouldn't have mattered anyway. You know exactly what any extra money would have been spent on.*

Not long after losing her, he had returned to Tenazeryth, and he never went back through the gateway again.

When I had asked if Diego knew, he shook his head and grabbed my hand, his grip rough and strong. "This is your secret to tell as you see fit," he had said.

But how do I even begin to tell anyone? My head reels as I stare at the ceiling of my room.

I have a father.

Bonding

By the end of the first week of August, I've gotten my ass kicked in the chalk circle several more times. Diego doesn't speak to me for two days after that first fiasco, but then, on the third day, he approaches me as I'm stretching, barks "Circle," and stalks away.

I follow without argument. We go three rounds; I don't say a word through any of them. Each one ends with me pinned or incapacitated in some fashion.

Hyun-Joo doesn't so much as glance in my direction while he and I spar. She's busy at the archery targets, working on her reaction time by using her barriers to stop arrows that Martín looses at random times. She stops almost every single one.

By the end of the third round, as Diego releases me after I tap out, he's glaring at me, disgusted.

That's fine. I just stare at the ground.

"Done?" I ask quietly. I swear I can hear his teeth grind, but he just stalks off.

I spend a lot of my time training solo. I work with my dagger, stabbing at a wooden dummy that is at the far end of the yard. Its sections move individually, and for a couple of hours, I'm pretty sure it lands more hits on me than I do on it.

The dagger still siphons energy from me, but just as Saif said would happen, I'm building up a tolerance. I'm able to wield it longer now than when I had started, though my hand still tingles after holding it all day.

Worse, though, is when I don't hold it all day, and my hand starts to feel its absence; this dagger is quickly becoming an extension of myself. I memorize the number of teeth in the wolves' mouths, and how the light glints off the sapphire eyes from every direction.

I work on my slashing technique and my agility. Hand-to-hand fights are fast, faster than I had ever imagined in my previous life. Diego also spars with Hyun-Joo while Saif is gone, but though he's got more than a foot on her, she is nearly an even match for him with her speed pitted against his hulking strength.

If Bleddyn's claws are that fast - and from everything I've been told, they'll be faster - then I need to gain a lot more speed. *And that's before I even factor in the teeth.*

Fear drives me to move my muscles faster and longer each day.

Valentina and Martín are the only ones who want anything to do with me, but most of our time together is spent with them trading insults and trying to loop me into their discussions. I chuckle at the appropriate times, and nod along when needed, but offer nothing more to the conversations.

I know how this goes. A line has been drawn in the sand between Diego, Hyun-Joo, and myself. Saif has effectively abandoned me - there's still no word on when he may return - and soon the Peñas would realize that they have no need to try to be around me, either.

Diego and Hyun-Joo are their family, and I'm just a stranger that landed on their doorstep. I've seen the way the four of them interact when I'm not in the immediate vicinity; their exchanges are easy and carefree.

I don't know how or why, but my showing up here had just made things harder and more tense for everyone. So, I do my best to remain invisible, and let them try to get back to normal.

It's one of the few things I'm good at.

Being alone in a room full of people has always been my superpower. Since losing Kianga, no one has put me first. She was the one who saved me seats at parties, made sure I was included in activities, hell, had even beat up some kid in third grade because he didn't pick me for the dodgeball team, making me last to be chosen.

She was my sun; she radiated warmth and love, and was always bright and full of energy. I was just her moon — I only shone because of her light. Without her, I have been shrouded in eternal darkness.

Kianga was my hero. She kept me tethered to other people, who had always flocked to her; she was a natural-born leader. Since losing her, I have simply been adrift, alone in a sea of humanity, jagged and cold.

The moon calls me her daughter now, but I've always belonged to her, I think bitterly.

Alone is fine. Alone is where I am most comfortable. At least, it had been. But now, despite my best efforts to not let it get to me, being alone hurts. It hurts like hell. But I do it for them.

Most afternoons, I find myself wandering around the solarium. I poke and prod idly at pots and dirt, and pick the produce that practically falls into my hand when I touch it.

I don't dare actually try to take care of any of the plants, lest they suffer from my curse of killing every green thing ever, but it's comforting, at least, to be in this place that Saif loves so much. Even if he isn't here with me.

I begin spending every evening in the library. It was awkward at first, but Auberon insisted I was welcome. He sits at the table, pouring over mountains of documents, and I sit opposite him, crack various books, and consume them hungrily.

I learn about my father, who has lived a full and rich life in his sixty-three years. I ask him about his parents, and he reveals that his mother, Egwene, had died in childbirth, and he was his father's only child.

He was raised here at Arkenvale, but then left when he was a teenager to seek a life on Earth after a fight with his father. He was convinced that he could make it on his own, in a new world, away from the pressure of the crown and the Danodraic name.

He shows me a book with paintings and names of his ancestors - *my* ancestors - for the last ten generations. The men, at least. No record of the prior years - nor the record of their wives - exists, apparently.

I roll my eyes. *Of course.*

I flip through the pages of past Danodraics: Adalbern, Gerben, Humbert, Bjorn, Barrett, Oberon, Armel, Torben, Orson, Espen. The family resemblance is incredibly strong; my father looks almost exactly like all of them. The most noticeable change from picture to picture is hair and clothing, and the same nose and strong jaw jump out at me from every page.

I rub a finger across my own round face and frown, wondering how such strong genetics did not shine through at all, and how I am nearly an exact replica of my mother — a painful fact of which I am reminded every time I see her face looking back at me from a mirror.

The Universe had granted me one small mercy, though; my mother's eyes are a brilliant blue. At least I don't have to see those staring back at me, too.

"Eilidh Joann Danodraic," I say slowly, my mouth twisting strangely around the foreign name. It just doesn't have the ring to it that "Eilidh Joann Shaw" does. And I certainly *look* more like a Shaw than a Danodraic.

My father beams. "It suits you."

I bite my tongue and nod, smiling politely.

I learn about Tenazeryth itself, this strange dimension that I've been thrown into. The weather here is held steady by magic; it never snows, has natural disasters, or so much as rains.

"The leaves never change here?" I ask him sadly.

He shakes his head excitedly. "Never. No need for it. Earth cycles and requires rest to grow new life every year. Tenazeryth is powered by magic; there's no need to rest and rejuvenate. Plants can grow constantly, and there's no danger of lives lost due to the whims of Mother Nature. It's a paradise."

I bite the inside of my lips. Stagnation doesn't sound like paradise to me, but I suppose there are worse things than no gorgeous fall leaves, and it *is* nice to never have to shovel snow again, or watch helplessly as natural disasters get worse every year.

I think sadly about the state of Earth. "No climate change here, I guess?"

His mouth twists angrily, and my heart skips a beat. *Shit, what did I do?*

"What humans have done to Earth is despicable," he growls at the table. Then he turns to me, and his eye softens. "No, dear girl, there certainly is no climate change here. Here, we know better. We work together with our land, and it rewards us."

I breathe a small sigh in relief. He isn't mad at me — he's mad at humanity. *That's understandable.*

I study a map of the continent. Arkenvale Castle - I ignore the voice in the back of my mind that pipes up that it's technically just a keep - is close to the center, and the capital city of New Camlann is ten miles away to the West, across one of Nabeyha Lake's inlets.

I ask my father why the castle isn't actually *in* the city, and he looks vaguely horrified at the suggestion.

"I value privacy, my dear. At my age, I just want peace and quiet with those closest to me."

I nod slowly. I can certainly appreciate that sentiment.

I tear through *A Comprehensive Guide to Mongrels* in one evening. It isn't a terribly long book, and there are a lot of illustrations. I also realize quickly that I don't particularly like the book itself, and so I skim more of it than I actually read. If it weren't for my father, I would DNF it for sure.

It has a nasty habit of confusing opinion for absolute fact, and it prickles me. Whenever I have a question about a statement it makes in defense of the subjugation of the 'Mongrel races,' the King is happy to answer it for me, eager to share his thoughts on what makes a creature "sentient."

Some days it seems like he had authored this book himself. It if hadn't been dated about two hundred years before now, I would be certain he had.

I question how Bleddyn had turned into such a monster when so many other other Shifters live peacefully in the cities alongside Mages.

"Bleddyn has lost his humanity," my father explains. "He's been in his wolf form for far too long. I doubt he even knows how to shift back at this point, and his mate was the same way. I never saw her human form. He has become a prime example of Mongrel behavior. Monsters, all of them."

I try to wrap my head around it, but I can't quite accept it as truth. It doesn't seem logical. "But if the centaurs have fought battles against Mages with bows and arrows, and organized their troops, then they know how to use tools and cooperate with one another. How much more of a leap is it to developed societies?" I ask one day after reading about a particularly bloody skirmish in a city on the East Coast known as Blumenthal.

Apparently, the Mages had angered a centaur herd that lived in the nearby Mordrenian Forest, and dozens had lost their lives.

His response is quick. "Do you think orangutans would be able to live in an apartment complex simply because they use sticks to dig bugs out of trees?"

"No, but orangutans can communicate with humans," I say stubbornly. "Several primates have been taught human languages, and they have their own societies. They're just *different* kinds of societies."

He strokes his salt and pepper beard, but he doesn't look annoyed, merely like he's trying to puzzle out how to answer.

"My dear girl, it's not just a matter of tools and rudimentary communication. Ravens can do that. Dogs can do that. The goal of humanity is achieving *civilization*, not just forming packs. Besides, the *ability* is merely one piece to achieving that goal. Morals are the other piece. Primates tend to bash the young of rivals against rocks. Animals will rip each other to pieces over a scrap of meat. They are simply not on our level. Mongrels are the same way. They have pack mentalities; they will never work as one peaceful, unified force."

I think briefly of the atrocities that have been committed by humans against one another in the name of their religions, skin colors, and social classes, but I bite my lip.

When my father isn't helping me learn about Tenazeryth and its magical occupants, he's telling me about my mother as she was when he knew her, or asking me about my life.

I recount some of the highlights of my once humdrum existence. Soccer trophies, softball scars, and a failed science experiment in high school that had resulted in my first ever failing grade - not to mention an afternoon standing outside the school, watching firefighters shoot water from thick hoses into the chemistry lab.

He laughs uproariously as I recount some of my worst dates, or of the antics that Kianga had dragged me into, such as sneaking into the city pool at midnight to fill it with shampoo because the lifeguard she was dating at the time had cheated on her.

To this day, I'm not sure how that was a punishment for *him* specifically, but she was not to be reasoned with at the time; she had wanted her revenge, and she got it.

She was *very* good at getting revenge. When she found out the girl who bullied me liked a certain football player, she literally stepped between them at a school dance and stole him out of her arms. They ended up dating for several months, and he actually turned out to be a huge fan of comic books, which we bonded over.

When my math teacher - perhaps justifiably, in hindsight - berated me in front of the class for not doing a long division problem correctly, she bought a fish from the store and put it in the drop ceiling just above his desk. It was a couple of weeks before the janitor found the fish. It was a couple of years before the stench came out of that room.

Kianga Nabil had been a hurricane of a human; an unstoppable force of nature, and terrifying - yet beautiful - to behold.

As the days pass, I begin to feel more at home in this library than I have anywhere else in the world since losing her. Though my grandparents had been wonderful, they had been ripped from me at such an early age that I hadn't had a chance to really *live* yet. They gave me advice every day, but I hadn't been able to sit with them and recount these tales.

I am finally feeling, for the first time in my adult life, kinship.

When I was a little girl I had dreamed that my father would find me one day. That he would pluck me from the rubble of my life and take me far away. And now he has, but I'm scared that he too will be ripped away from me, just like everyone else I have ever loved.

Fuck that.

I won't let anything - or anyone - take him from me now.

~ New Moon ~

Diego's Warning

One night, after I read through the diary of a man who lived through a rebellion against a king led by a hauntingly beautiful woman that resulted in dozens of deaths (the diary had failed to mention the name of the king or his would-be usurper, but she sounded like a hell of a leader, despite her ultimate failure), I say good night to my father and head out into the entrance hall.

As I turn to walk to the spiral staircase, my eyes land on Diego, who is just coming out of the dining hall. I expect him to ignore me, and decide to try to skirt by him without incident, but as I try to sneak past him, he speaks, and I jump.

"What are you doing?" His suspicious crimson gaze pins me in place.

"Me?" I ask dimly, shrinking back.

He closes his eyes and takes a deep breath like I annoy him so much he has to count to three before he replies.

You probably do.

"You," he says finally.

I cross my arms and huddle in on myself, suddenly cold despite the balmy summer evening.

Damn stone walls. "I was just reading. In the library."

He blinks. "Oh," he says simply. He scrunches his face like he's trying to recall something. "The King is usually in there at this time. He must be up —"

I cut him off. "Oh, he's in there if you need him," I say, and take a few steps sideways up the spiral staircase, assuming we're done. But Diego moves in two strides to my side and grabs my upper arm.

I freeze.

"You were in there alone with him?" He asks sharply. My eyes widen momentarily, then narrow at his hand on my arm.

"Unless there's a ghost in there too," I snap without thinking. Then, remembering his face as he had pinned me to the ground and growled at me about Hyun-Joo, I wipe my expression blank.

But he isn't angry with me now. In fact, he looks . . . concerned? I wait to see if he's going to elaborate on his question. He doesn't.

Then annoyance flares up, and I know it shows on my face. "I've been in there with him every evening this week. He doesn't mind. He's teaching me things." Diego's eyes widen in alarm.

He drags me up the spiral staircase without another word. I protest and sputter at him questioningly the whole way, but he doesn't break his stride. In seconds, he's pulling me into his bedroom and closing the door behind him, and the scent of aloe and cedar floods my nostrils.

"What is going on?" He asks finally when we're in his room. "Why are you alone with him? What is he teaching you?"

"I —"

But he cuts me off before I can answer him. "Are you okay?" He glances up and down my body as if searching for a knife sticking out of my flesh.

I look down at myself too, thinking for one wild second that there might actually *be* one. But no, I'm wearing a flowy, dark blue dress and white flats, but no sharp implements are protruding from my person.

I blink at him in utter confusion. He breathes in deeply though his nose.

"Are *you* okay?" I ask, bewildered. "He's the King, not a wild bear."

Diego flinches at that. "What is he teaching you?" He asks again, his voice clipped. He inhales again, raggedly.

I say the first thing that comes to mind. "Centaurs are basically orangutans."

Diego stares.

"I don't know!" I exclaim, throwing my hands up.

"*¡Cállate!*" He hisses, making a shushing gesture at me.

I literally bite my tongue so I don't tell him to fuck off.

"I've just been *reading*. When I have questions about things, he answers them. I can't do anything else right around here, but I can *read*," I say petulantly as I throw myself down in a huff to sit on the mattress.

Then I remember that we are in Diego's room, not mine. That I am sitting on his mattress. I bolt back up and nearly collide with him in my haste to step away from the bed.

He reaches his hands out to my arms to steady me, almost unconsciously, still lost in thought. The last time he had his hands on me like this, he was digging his claws into my arms. Those claws are retracted now, but it's like I can still feel them.

I flinch away from him, and he releases me.

He puts one hand on his waist and runs the other through his chestnut hair. I shove my hands into the pockets of my dress and stare pointedly at the wall. *Bless Valentina for only bringing me dresses with pockets.*

Diego is still staring at me as if trying to find a hole in my story, but finally, he seems satisfied. He nods.

"Okay then," he says stiffly. "But be careful. He's got a short temper and immense power. Just because he doesn't wield it openly doesn't mean it isn't there. You haven't seen what he's capable of." He grimaces at the floor.

Anger flares up in me. My father has been nothing but kind to me since I arrived here. Sure, he had flung the silver dagger at me during our first meeting, but he had been controlling it. It's fine.

"My fa—" I cut myself off. I still haven't figured out how I'm going to tell anyone, and when I do, Diego will certainly not be the first one. I scoff to cover myself. "My fucking god you're being paranoid," I say instead.

Then something else strange about his words occurs to me.

"Since when do you tell me to be careful?" This man has never once had regard for my safety. He's usually the one pushing me headlong into something that ends up with me flat on my ass.

He just stares at me for a moment like he doesn't understand the question. Whether he does or not, he doesn't answer it; he takes another deep breath in through his nose, shakes himself slightly, and blinks in realization as though he has just processed that he brought me into his bedroom, and that we're standing about a foot away from the bed itself.

The room suddenly feels exceedingly small, and my pulse races. I cast my gaze down to the floor to hide the heat creeping into my cheeks. *I shouldn't be in here.* Not that I had sauntered in — I had quite literally been dragged, but still. We stand like this for several long moments.

Finally, I can't take it anymore. "Look, I —" But I freeze when my eyes find his.

His irises are gone, and his pupils have taken over his gaze. He's looking hungrily at the base of my throat where he bit me during my transformation, inhaling deeply through his nose.

My heart begins hammering against my chest. *Is he smelling me?*

He seems to not be able to control his movements as he takes several steps toward me and backs me against a wall. My breath catches as he puts his hands on either side of my head. He leans in closer, inhaling. I squeeze my eyes shut and brace myself for the feeling of his fangs in my neck, but it doesn't come.

Instead, he clutches a hand to my cheek and his fourth and fifth nails push into my jawline. I open my eyes to his, mere inches away.

"You gave up." His voice rumbles against my ear, and I tremble.

I don't know what I had expected him to say, but it wasn't that.

"What?" I breathe.

He takes a shuddering breath. "During training. You aren't even trying. You're just letting me win every time. You gave up."

I scoff involuntarily. I am doing no such thing. "I'm not *letting* you do anything. I got lucky the first time, and then you kicked my ass," I hiss.

At that, his mouth twists angrily. "No, you didn't just get *lucky*. You used strategy and found my blind spot. You were confident in your abilities. But then you got cocky."

If I could back up any farther without having to dissolve through a wall, I would. I bare my teeth back at him instead.

"I'm not strong enough to beat you. If it makes you feel better to keep putting me in my place because of what I said about her —" My eyes flick to his bed beside us. "Then *fine*. I get it. But don't you *dare* tell me that I'm not trying."

With my final word, I shove against his chest, and he doesn't push back. He simply moves out of the way, blinking rapidly as if coming out of a trance. I stride from his room and slam the door behind me as I exit.

At the noise, Hyun-Joo emerges from her room, two doors down from Diego's, and perpendicular to mine across the hallway to the upper balcony of the library. She looks toward his door with concern, obviously thinking that Diego is the one having a meltdown on the balcony, but when her gaze meets mine instead, she reels back, her eyes narrowing dangerously.

I gape at her wordlessly for several agonizing moments while I try to figure out how to explain why I just emerged from her partner's room, flustered and breathing heavily. "Um, I —"

But then my father exits the library, headed toward his tower. He sees me panting on the balcony, gripping the railing, and raises his brows in alarm.

"Is everything well, dear girl?" He calls. My mouth works as I try to think of something to say when Diego bursts from his room. He nearly collides with me, but stops just short of doing so. Then he turns to Hyun-Joo and grimaces. Her gaze softens instantly when she looks at him, then she turns back to me, and her eyes blaze with rage like it's somehow *my* fault he looks like he's in agony.

He's the one you should be mad at, I want to scream indignantly at her, but I don't get the chance.

Diego clears his throat loudly, and his face morphs instantly into the square-jawed, chiseled mask it normally is. He's the perfect soldier once again. There's no sign of the shuddering mess he was just moments ago. His eyes are back to normal, but his irises are dark and dull.

"Your Majesty," he calls down to my father, with a bow at his upper back. "We were just discussing this week's training schedule." I look at him from the corner of my eye, but say nothing. Hyun-Joo just nods idly, going along with Diego's story without question.

Of course she does.

Auberon nods, satisfied. "Yes, keep up the excellent work, Eilidh. I am continually impressed by Diego's reports of your performance. I genuinely believe you'll be ready to fight Bleddyn when the time comes. Now, good night to you all."

He strides into the East Tower, presumably to head up the smaller staircase to his living quarters.

My ears begin ringing.

Diego's reports? I thought Saif had been the one to give my father the first report that I had been doing well. Had it been Diego the entire time? *That doesn't make any sense.*

Diego steps toward me and reaches a hand out, and Hyun-Joo opens her mouth, ready to berate me, I'm sure, but I can't be around them for another moment. I scurry away from him without looking back, stride past her, my head held high, and don't stop until I slam my bedroom door behind me.

They are silent for several long moments, but when they speak, I can hear them perfectly. My enhanced hearing is apparently a permanent change since I had transformed.

"You don't look so good," she says to him. Her loving tone twists my gut strangely.

He blows air quickly from his nostrils in agreement. "Yeah," he says absently, and it sounds like he's facing my door, but maybe that's my imagination.

Her voice is tight when she speaks again. "Do you need me to . . ." She trails off.

He breathes out heavily. "Yes," he says simply. I hear the two of them walk back toward his room and close the door.

I slump down to the ground against my own door, not bothering to turn the light on in the dark room. The furniture, at least, will not be able to see the tears sliding down my cheeks.

~ First Quarter ~

Honesty

Saif finally returns three weeks after my first transformation. I only find out when I'm summoned to the East Tower and see him seated at the circular table at my father's side. The sight of him nearly knocks me off my feet.

Our eyes meet briefly as I enter, but he turns from me abruptly, frowning.

I cross my arms and huddle into myself as I sit diagonally from him, my gaze downcast. The rest of the Order is already seated as well, other than Valentina, who had brought me here.

The King gets down to business immediately as she sits. "We've found Bleddyn's location."

I start, and my eyes dart around the room as if the monstrous wolf is hiding behind a nearby vase, waiting to pounce. I bring my right hand to my shoulder reflexively and run my fingers over the scars.

"Where?" I ask quietly.

"The Cuhloch Forest," Saif answers, adjusting his glasses. I peek at him from the corner of my eye, but he's speaking to the table between us.

He doesn't even want to look at you. A sharp pang echoes in my chest.

I nod, biting my lip as I think back on the maps I've studied of Tenazeryth. The Cuhloch Forest is far to the Southeast of the continent; it nearly borders the ocean on the maps.

"Okay," I say, thoughts forming. "So, how will we get to him? Do we walk there? How long . . ." I realize everyone - everyone except Saif, anyway - is looking at me with mixed degrees of incredulity.

Martín speaks first, raising his right hand as if under oath. "I'll keel over and die before I walk that far." Valentina kicks him under the table. Auberon ignores them.

"No, dear girl. When the time comes, you'll be going in a car."

"I don't understand," I reply. "There are cars here?"

"Correct," he says patiently as Diego rolls his eyes. "It's only about four hours by vehicle. That will save you a lot of precious time."

My head throbs and I put it in my hands, running my fingers through my hair for a moment as memories of the accident that took my grandparents from me flash through my head.

Several auburn strands come out as I do this, and I brush them to the floor. I realize I'm sweating. I alternate breathing and holding my breath in counts of four. I shake myself after a few silent moments.

"Okay, so we drive to the forest. Then what?" My leg bounces under the table.

Diego is the one who speaks, his eyes glittering brightly, shining like polished rubies in the light. "You'll be thrilled to hear that *then* we will walk." He gestures at Saif. "His source said that Bleddyn is holed up near the center of the forest. We'll make camp and rest when we need to. Then when we find him." He pauses and looks me up and down quickly. "You'll kill him." Does he sound dubious, or is that my imagination?

"When do we leave?" I'm already making a packing list in my head.

My father looks back at me levelly. "That will depend on your training, but I imagine no sooner than a few months."

"A few *months*?" I gape. "We can't wait that long! What if he moves his location?"

But my father puts a palm up, silencing me. "The source says that

Bleddyn will be in this location for the foreseeable future, and it's not unusual for him to go long stretches with little activity." He glances at Saif, who sits silently at his side, staring at the space above me, utterly unfocused. "We believe he may be biding his time, waiting to see if you will join him."

I shudder and bite down hard on the inside of my lip. This Auberon is a completely different person than the one I know from our evenings together in the library. He's not my father here in this room, surrounded by his paladins. He's the King.

I really, *really*, should not argue with a king.

"What if he kills more women?" I rasp, horrified.

"We don't have reason to believe that he has anyone to bring new victims to him, if he's even looking for any, but if he does, it makes no difference to me."

I gape at him wordlessly.

"The cost is unfortunate, but it is one I would be willing to pay to ensure that you are truly ready, not just to get your justice, and vanquish this foe who I've been at odds with for far too long, but to join the Order. I will not send you to fight him just to get yourself killed."

Saif makes a noise under his breath, and my father glances sidelong at him without a word. Saif glares down at the table, his eyes narrowed almost imperceptibly. His fist is clenched on the table so hard his knuckles are white.

I desperately wish that I could go to him and take his hand, but by the look of him, he's as furious at me as I am at myself.

If you were better at this shit, you could go after Bleddyn now, and no one else would be in danger.

"You're all dismissed."

Saif exits the room first, and he's halfway up the spiral staircase by the time I get to the entrance hall. I watch him forlornly until I hear his door close behind him.

I walk numbly to the dining hall for lunch. As I chew distractedly on a bowl of rice and beans that Martín had placed in front of me, Valentina sits beside me on the bench, squeezing my hand as she does so. It snaps me from my trance, and I look at her, eyes wide.

"So, are you going to talk about why you almost passed out when the King mentioned a car earlier?" Her voice is thick with worry.

I sigh. She's shared so much with me. It's only right that I finally repay her honesty with some of my own.

The words come slowly, and quietly. "I was in a bad accident when I was fifteen. I lost the two people I loved most in the world. We got T-boned by a tractor-trailer, and they were trapped. They told me to run, and I did. I just . . . left them there. Then the car went up in a gas-fueled inferno."

I think I see Diego out of the corner of my eye, staring hard at me from his seat farther down the other bench, but when I glance at him, he's focused on his mug of tea.

Valentina lays her head against my shoulder and puts an arm around my waist. "I'm so sorry," she says. I nod sadly. "But, you were just a kid. I'm glad you ran."

I wince. I had been told by many therapists over the years that survivor's guilt is normal, but that doesn't make it hurt less.

I put my head in my hands and take several deep breaths.

Valentina rubs my back. "Where are they buried?" She asks gently.

I say the name of the cemetery back in Rochester, and she nods slowly, looking contemplative.

Light a Fire

"How do I even begin to apologize?" I ask from my prone position on the floor.

Martín rolls his eyes at me over the magazine he's reading. "Maybe start off with something safe, like 'I'm.'"

"And then get wild with it and toss in a 'sorry' just to switch things up," Valentina remarks over the soft whirring of her sewing machine.

I groan into her plush, pink rug.

"She missed you," Martín says as he flips a page that has some American athlete on it. I don't recognize her, but apparently the petite Black gymnast is good at what she does — the picture shows her with at least a dozen medals around her neck.

"She's been sulking for weeks," Valentina says, concurring with her brother's assessment.

My stomach twists. "Great," I mutter. "That makes me feel so much better about it."

"I wasn't trying to make you feel better," she says simply, sewing a zipper into some thick emerald fabric. "I was trying to get you to move your ass and go get your woman."

I sigh and push myself up off the floor. "What if she hates me?" I ask quietly, rubbing the back of my neck. *I wouldn't blame her.* It would serve me right if she never wanted to speak to me again after I snapped on her for no reason and effectively abandoned her with a monster for three weeks.

I flex my hand, which is itching for *Dhabiha's* hilt, though she's stored safely in my room. After hearing what Diego did to Eilidh in the circle, he's lucky that I don't run him through, wait until he heals, and then do it again.

"She doesn't," Martín says, flipping the page once more. "So go, before I light a fire under your ass."

I exhale quickly through my nose. "Alright, alright, I'm going."

Saif's Warning

That evening, I take a walk outside in the training yard to watch the sunset instead of going to the library. I just can't face my father right now. I meander aimlessly around the grounds and find myself at the monkey bars. Suppressing a grimace at the memory of my first day of training, I climb them easily and perch on top of them to watch the sun go down over the wall.

Soft footsteps approach, and then someone starts climbing up the ladder beside me. Assuming it's Valentina, I reach down without looking to give her a hand up, but the hand that grabs mine is calloused from years of holding weapons.

I turn to Saif as he steps on the top rung of the ladder, then inhale sharply and withdraw my hand. I hope he hasn't come to tell me off for not insisting to the King that we leave now to go get Bleddyn. But when he speaks, he isn't angry at all.

My inner critic is much more cruel than this man could ever be.

"Mind if I join you?" He asks, and his tone says that he's expecting me to say, 'I do mind, as a matter of fact, and by the way, fuck you.'

"Of course not." I shift over a few more rungs and he climbs up to sit beside me. I chew the inside of my lip.

"*Shloonich*, Eilidh? How are you?"

I just shrug. "Okay," I mumble. He doesn't press me for a real answer.

We sit for several long moments, staring at the sunset.

Finally, I decide to be the one to break the silence. "Look, I'm sorry about what happened before." I'm still not sure what I had done exactly, but with all the ways I tend to fuck things up, I've come to accept that it must have been something. "I . . . I really missed you," I finish quietly.

He sighs, removing his glasses to rub his hand over his face and into his dark curls. "You didn't do anything wrong, Eilidh. *I* overreacted. I was jealous that *he* had been the one to help you and spend the night with you. I was already angry at him for lounging on the bed when he should have been outside of the cell, and then when I saw those bite marks I just —"

He grimaces, shaking his head. "I knew he had bitten you, obviously, but seeing the evidence just set me off. But that's no excuse for my behavior. I was a total asshole, and I'm sorry."

My jaw hangs open for a moment. Those weren't the words I had been expecting. Blame I can take, but apologies are foreign. "Oh," I say, unable to think of anything more substantial.

He reaches over and takes my hand again. "I missed you too, *Lahabi*."

His deep voice kick-starts my heart rate. I glance sidelong at him through my hair. The sunset sets fire to his bronze skin. *He looks like a god.*

I wish briefly that I could capture him in a photo, here in this moment. But no photo could ever do this man justice. No lifeless, two-dimensional snapshot could possibly capture his essence, the way he radiates warmth, or the way he moves with more grace than the most seasoned dancer.

His eyes meet mine, and he tucks my hair behind my ear, then cups my face and runs his thumb along my cheekbone. I close my eyes and lean into his touch, my pulse quickening.

When I open my eyes, his face is inches from mine. His eyes are narrowed and tight at the corners as if holding back is physically uncomfortable.

I can help with that, at least. I lean the rest of the way into him, and our lips meet. He puts one hand into my hair, and the other on my thigh. I grip the bars below me as if they're my only anchor to the world.

We're still kissing as the sun dips below the horizon.

~~~~~~~~~~

As dusk envelopes the world, we walk hand in hand back to the castle. We stop briefly in the kitchen, and he brews us each a cup of marjoram tea. When we get back to my room, we sit side-by-side on the bed, sipping on the steaming mugs.

After we've completed our drinks, and he's sat the mugs on the desk, he faces me with his legs crossed, and takes my hands. We haven't actually said any words since he had apologized earlier; we've just been in companionable silence — or our mouths otherwise occupied. Finally, he takes a steadying breath and speaks.

"I need you to promise me that you'll be cautious around Diego. Keep him at a distance as much as possible. *Al bab tejeek menh reeh sedh westereeh.*"

I blink. "What?" Of all the things I want to talk about with Saif, Diego is not one. "What does that mean?"

He tilts his head back and forth a few times. "Basically, close the door on people who are bad for you. Protect yourself."

He rubs his thumbs back and forth across my palms, and the repetitive motion makes me shiver.

"He's dangerous. And I know you two have more of a similar experience than us Mages, but please don't mistake similarity for safety."
~~~~~~~~~~

He takes a deep breath and his eyes glisten when he turns to me. "He's a murderer."

I furrow my brow. "I know that," I say quietly. "He ripped Azaeroria's throat out in front of me."

But Saif shakes his head. "No, that was a battle; that's not the same. I mean, he's gotten innocent people killed. As good as did it himself." The vehemence in his voice shocks me.

"What happened?" I'm not confident that I really want to know.

He takes another breath, steeling himself. "There was a woman who occupied your seat at the table several years ago. She had been attacked by a feral werecat, and she was taken in by the Order. Auberon said that she could train with us, and then find her attacker and get her justice."

I inhale sharply. This woman's story perfectly mirrors mine, but I have a feeling I don't want to know how it ends.

"She was magnificent." His eyes light up and a wistful smile touches his lips. "And . . . she thought *he* was too." His eyes go dark.

Oh. Realization dawns on me. His feud with Diego isn't just because of Diego's everyday callousness, and it is much older than I had thought.

"She trained with Diego, but he slacked off. He was too caught up with their personal relationship, and didn't spend as much time training her on the field as he did sharing her bed. He thought the two of them would waltz into the werecat's lair and slay it with no issues. He got cocky, and she paid the price. He came back from that mission alone." His voice has gone stony. I inhale shakily.

No wonder Saif hates Diego being around me at all. This man, this natural healer, who cares so deeply. I think of the small gestures he's made in my time here. The blankets during the last full moon. The flowers, and the brownies on my birthday. The endless care he's provided. How he's heard my deepest trauma and shared his own. It all - finally - makes so much sense.

I raise my hand to his cheek and wait for him to meet my gaze. "You've helped me heal so much," I say softly. "I wish I could do the same for you."

His warm brown gaze moves to my lips.

That, I can do.

Healing

I move to my knees and kneel against Saif as I press my mouth softly against his, then I push him gently back onto the bed, and he pulls me on top of him. I straddle his hips as I deepen our kisses.

I pull away for just a moment to take my top off, and he does the same, pulling his black V-neck off in one swift motion. He tosses the shirt on the floor and sets his glasses down on top of it.

I kiss him again, running a thumb over his beard as he unclasps my bra, then he tosses it to the floor beside his shirt and puts his hands on my soft waist. I want him to dig his nails into my back, to take his pain out on me, but that's not what he likes. His fingers trail up my back and tangle lightly in my hair.

He's too tall for me to put my breast in his mouth while I'm still grinding into his hips, so I settle for kissing his neck, breathing in his floral and charcoal scent as I run my hand through his curls. They've gotten a bit longer since he left, and I tug them gently, relishing the feel of them between my fingers. He runs his nails lightly down my bare back, and goosebumps form all along my skin.

When his hands reach my waistband, he tugs it down around my ass, and I stop kissing him long enough to pull my pants the rest of the way down and fling them away. I try to make eye contact as I take his pants off, but he's got his head thrown back on the mattress, sucking in his breath.

I take in the sight of him for a moment, positively dumbstruck that I get to see him like this. He's a work of art; he belongs in a museum, protected behind a thick pane of glass, so that nothing else can hurt him. He's too perfect to be walking around with the rest of us. He's too good for this world. For *either* world.

He's covered in various scars from his life as a warrior, but they don't diminish his perfection — they enhance it. A particularly ragged set of scars not terribly unlike my own claw marks runs from the top of his right pectoral muscle to his sternum, like he was clawed by a feral animal. I want to run my fingers over every one of them, and ask him how he earned each individual mark. I want to kiss them all, and memorize the pattern they create on him.

His muscles are taught against his skin, and the veins in his forearms stand out prominently. The deep "V" of his lower abdomen muscles points directly at his cock, which is throbbing, the tip already glistening with precum. He breathes out heavily, puts one hand behind his head, and looks back at me, tugging at his shaft with his other hand. Heat kicks on in my stomach like a gas stove being ignited.

I put my lips around his tip and move deliberately down his length until I meet his base. He stretches my lips wide, but, luckily, he's not so long that I'm gagging; he fits perfectly into my mouth.

I move up and down his length, moving my tongue side-to-side as I do. I increase my speed, hoping to get him moaning, but he's mostly silent other than his heavy breathing, and a few muttered curses.

After a few minutes, he reaches down and grips my shoulder. I look up at him, but keep my rhythm up and down his length as I do.

"Wait," he pants.

I remove him from my mouth and wipe my chin. "What's wrong?"

He motions for me to move upward, still breathing heavily. "If you keep that up, I'm going to come way too quickly. Get up here for a bit." I crawl up over him, and then he puts his hands behind my ass and pulls me up further until my knees are next to his ears.

His tongue moves in delicate circles around my clit, narrow and darting. I moan and grip the footboard, digging my nails into the wood.

"Shh," he breathes against my thigh, and I clamp my mouth shut. I suppose it would be pretty awkward if anyone else heard us. There is, after all, not much space between Hyun-Joo's wall and my own. I bite the inside of my lips instead, hovering over him as he eats me out until my legs are shaking.

"Are you close?" He asks softly a few minutes later.

"Yeah," I breathe, and wait for him to resume.

But instead, he says "Lean against the wall." I look down at him for a moment, then acquiesce. I swing one leg back over him and prop myself against the wall, my knees digging into the mattress. He gets on his knees behind me, and kisses between my shoulder blades, moving my hair out of the way as he plants each kiss.

I shiver.

Then he laces the fingers of one hand through mine against the wall, and he uses his other hand to rub his tip against my soaking entrance. I bite back my moan as he pushes inside me and grips into my hip. He thrusts against me in smooth, deliberate strokes, and I gasp with pleasure. I lean my forehead into the wall and take ragged breaths as he moves, stretching me wide.

Then I throw my head back, and he leans into the left side of my neck and kisses me delicately as he strokes in and out of me. I want him to bite me, but he's so gentle in every one of his movements. I move one hand to my clit and rub it in fast, steady circles.

He reaches around and circles one of my nipples with two fingers as he plants hot kisses on my skin, up and down my neck, across my shoulder, along my jaw. Before long, I begin quivering.

"Tell me when you come," he whispers.

I shiver in pleasure as his lips brush against the delicate and sensitive skin of my ear, and release a quiet, high-pitched moan. "I am."

He grunts, and his thrusting increases as I clench around him, then he gasps, "Oh, *fuck*," and pulls out. His warm cum hits my lower back and starts running down my ass.

I lean harder into the wall as he puts a hand between my legs and rubs my clit, providing delicious friction for me to ride out my pleasure. When I stop shuddering, he rests his head against my back, panting heavily against my skin.

We stay like this for a minute or two until our breathing returns to normal, then he gets off the bed, grabs one of the towels that hang from a peg on the door, and wipes me down, kissing my neck and shoulders as he does so.

He gathers his clothes from the floor and pulls them on, then hands me my top and I take it with a small smile. I pull my clothes back on quickly, and then we stand and look at each other for a moment, both still in a daze.

I break the silence first. "I'm, uh, gonna go get cleaned up," I say.

He nods. "Of course."

He takes a step toward me and kisses me tenderly on the forehead, and I can't help but smile. "I'm going to turn in for the night; it's way past my bedtime." He cracks a slightly teasing smile. "Not that I regret staying up a bit late for that. I'll see you in the morning, *Lahabi*."

I bid him a smirk in farewell.

~~~~~~~~~~

After a cool shower, I towel myself off in the bathroom and throw on the only robe that I had found in the wardrobe.
~~~~~~~~~~

It's a little, navy, satin number that looks suspiciously like it came from the lingerie section rather than the pajama section (Valentina is going to have to explain that), but it's a warm night, and there's not going to be anyone else up at this hour anyway.

I wrap my hair in the towel and pad back to my room, lost in thoughts of Saif as I circle the spiral staircase, running my fingers lightly over its thorny iron vines, careful not to disturb the trailing wisteria. I think of how deep his need to heal is, and how much trauma he's gone through.

I think of his bare skin on mine and the feeling of him inside me, but also of him simply holding my hand and sitting next to me, watching the sunset. I think of the man who has picked me fresh berries from the plants that he nurtures, and how he brings me tea every day just to comfort me.

I realize with a terrified jolt that I might be feeling more than just a crush on this man. It might be *much* more than that, which is outrageous. But I haven't felt that way about someone since — well, did it ever really stop? Just because she's gone, have my feelings changed? No, not really.

I frown, my eyes barely registering the stone of each step as I make the climb to the balcony. *You'll lose him eventually, you know.* Saif is a warrior, and I am immortal. One way or another, we will be separated. I bite the inside of my cheek, gazing hard at the ground.

When I bump into a wall in what I thought was the middle of the balcony leading to my room, I yelp in shock. Sure, I hadn't really been paying attention to where I was walking, but sheesh. I don't usually get *this* off course.

The wall in front of me turns around, and I inhale sharply when I realize that it's Diego. He's dressed entirely in black, standing just outside the middle solarium door, taking up the majority of the space with his massive shoulders.

He raises an eyebrow at me as he turns; his eyes practically glow in the dark, like the last embers of a fire that has finally burned through all its fuel, before it fades slowly, stubbornly, determined to shine for as long as it possibly can. Daring the darkness to try to claim it.

"We've got to stop meeting like this." His voice is a faint whisper. I'm probably the only other one in this castle who could hear him, even at this close distance. The only other Shifter.

I goggle at him.

His eyes move down to my robe for a split second, and then he snaps his gaze to a few inches above my head. I pull the robe around myself tightly.

"What the fuck are you doing, creeping around this late?" I hiss, hoping not to disturb Saif, whose door is just behind us.

He raises his other brow in genuine surprise. "I always make a few rounds at night. If you haven't noticed, we don't have any guards. Just trying to keep everyone from being slaughtered in their beds."

I hadn't considered that. "Well, there's no slaughtering occurring down this way," I say, gesturing at my door. I blush at the thought of what *had* just occurred in my bed, and I'm grateful for the dim light so that he can't see my cheeks redden.

He smirks. *Can vampires read minds?* I think wildly, but no, that's just his normal face.

"So it seems." He whispers slowly, elongating the "s" sound like he's a snake who is delighted to have finally caught sight of its next furry meal. He shoulders his way past me then, and stalks off down the staircase and into the darkness without another word.

I hurry to my room and shut the door behind me, firmly.

~ Second Full Moon ~

Sand

The morning of my second full moon as a werewolf is slightly less miserable than the first had been. I still feel nauseous, but my head only throbs every few seconds instead of constantly, and I'll take any improvement at this point. As I sit up in bed, I realize that Saif has once again piled extra blankets on top of me, and I smile.

I manage to wobble to my desk to watch the sun rise. There's a steaming mug of tea on my desk that I sip automatically, but instead of mint like Saif usually brings me, it tastes of hibiscus. After the initial confusion of a different taste than I had expected, I gulp down the tart, warm liquid in just a few swigs.

When I finish the tea, I toss on a black sleeveless turtleneck top with a gray plaid skirt that hugs my hips and hits just above my knees. It makes me feel put together, and at least a little in control of myself, if only for the next few hours. I leave my hair hanging loose around me in tousled waves.

Feeling a bit stronger - that tea must really have helped - I walk to the dining hall in search of something to eat. Everyone else is there already, and the hall stills as I walk in. I see Diego first, already in that skin-tight getup from last time. He's not wasting time on a wardrobe change this month.

He looks at me appraisingly as I enter the room, gives me a once-over and, apparently satisfied that I'm not going to attack anyone right this moment, returns to sipping his mug and speaking with Hyun-Joo. She doesn't deign to look at me as I approach the table and sit down next to Saif.

He puts a hand on my thigh, and my gaze is ripped from Diego. "How are you feeling?" He asks, worry lines etched on his brow.

I smile at him reassuringly. "I'm okay. That tea made me feel a lot better. Thanks for bringing it."

Confusion flicks across his face for a moment, but then Valentina ends her conversation with Martín and turns to us abruptly.

"Hey! What are you hungry for?" She asks.

Martín looks at me teasingly. "We don't want you starving today like last time. And before you ask, I know I'm handsome enough to eat, but I must graciously decline."

I snort and shake my head at him as Saif runs his thumb back and forth over my thigh. It strikes me how nice it is to have someone concerned for the little things, like if you're hungry, and if your headache feels better. It's been far too long since I've had that.

"Definitely not a steak, so that's a good sign, right?" I joke easily, here with these three people who have helped me for no reason other than because it is the right thing to do. Because they enjoy my presence, and want to make sure I am well. My heart warms in my chest. I have to look away from the three of them before I tear up with joy.

I look to the now-familiar stained glass windows that line the hall: the sword, the chalice, and the gemstone. Simple at first glance, but intricate and complex upon closer inspection. I've come to know each pane of glass like I've come to know these people, seeing their pieces individually, but also how those pieces make up the whole, larger picture. And those pictures are beautiful.

I take Saif's hand from my thigh, and lay it on the table, clasped in mine. Valentina's eyes briefly widen and dart to them, but she quickly looks back at me, grinning widely. Martín whistles softly and waggles his eyebrows at the pair of us. "About time."

I rub Saif's hand gently as the four of us talk about what's available and what sounds best for breakfast. Then we walk into the kitchen to prepare our food, Saif and I still hand in hand.

As we pass by the others, I see Diego from the corner of my eye, staring hard. I glance sidelong at him, and he's gripping his mug in two hands, his jaw tense, but his face otherwise blank.

Hyun-Joo whirls around in her seat to follow his gaze, and I can't help myself. I look right back at her. Her eyes land on my hand in Saif's, and her lips press into a thin line, then she turns her back to me again quickly.

I want to stalk to her and shake her by the front of her crisp onyx blouse. *You're mad when you see me with Diego. You're mad when you see me with Saif.* What *do you want from me?*

I rehearse the words over and over in my head as I close the kitchen door behind me, though I know I'll never have the courage to say them to her aloud.

When the four of us have finished prepping our food and return to the dining hall, the two of them are nowhere to be seen.

~~~~~~~~~

We spend the next few hours outside. The four of us walk down a narrow path that winds down the cliffside. It's nearly imperceptible to the average observer, but for once, my steps are steady. I know that I won't fall. I also know that if I stumble, my friends, and Saif, will be there to catch me.

The rocky area at the bottom is not a beach per se, as there are more stones and boulders than actual sand, but I enjoy it anyway.
~~~~~~~~~

The spray of Nabeyha Lake is deliciously refreshing, and the sunlight hits my skin with a delicious warmth. Saif takes my hand at one point and we walk in the shallows of the water together.

Valentina and Martín are sparring nearby. She whips spheres of lake water at him at steadily increasing velocities, and as he hits them in midair with walls of flame, they sizzle and evaporate.

Saif and I sit on a large boulder together, stealing occasional kisses. Eventually, after a particularly long kiss had apparently been deemed inappropriate for the public, Valentina douses the two of us with a wave of water, and I shriek in laughter. I slide off the boulder and chase her playfully, but then Martín steps in between the two of us, one hand on his hip, the other held out to me.

"Halt!" He commands with pompous bravado. I do so, grinning, just to see what he does next.

Then he kicks some of the only sand on the beach into the air, and flames whirl up abruptly in front of me in a blazing inferno, flaming out as quickly as they had come. I blink, and the sand he kicked up has turned into a curved glass barrier between us. I reach out and touch it in wonder.

"That is *amazing*," I breathe.

He takes an overly dramatic bow and flashes me a dazzling smile as he straightens. "Anything to protect my little sister."

"You should carry sand everywhere like Saif does with seeds!"

He cackles. "Maybe if sand wasn't so damn heavy."

Valentina walks over, giggling. She wicks the water off Saif and me just as quickly as she had doused us in it, but my hair is nonetheless a frizzy mess by the time we make our way back up the cliffside path.

We each go back to our rooms for a bit to relax and change into clean clothing for the rest of the day. I pick high-waisted jean shorts and a cropped tank top that make me feel sexy rather than self-conscious like they normally would.

If it's possible for a Mage to have two different kinds of powers, fashion is definitely Valentina's second.

I'm ready to kick this full moon's ass. *Carpe fucking noctem.*

178

What It Takes

n the late afternoon, Diego stalks into the dining hall where the four of us are finishing up a late lunch. He comes up to me and puts his hands on his waist.

"Time to go." His tone is flat, and he says nothing else. I glare at him, biting back the urge to argue.

I don't succeed.

"Actually, I want Saif with me tonight instead," I say. Diego's eyes narrow and Saif freezes beside me.

A beat passes, and Saif speaks first. "Eilidh, I . . . I can't. I'm sorry."

I turn to him, confused, and hurt. Isn't he the one who told me to be careful around Diego? To close the door? I open my mouth to argue, but Diego cuts in.

"He doesn't have what it takes."

Saif bristles, but doesn't look at Diego.

I have no such restraint.

I turn to the vampire, my head bent back to glare up at him. Looking up at him like this makes me feel like a petulant child, but my anger at his insult to Saif burns stronger than my shame.

"And what does that mean?" I narrow my eyes back at him, arms crossed.

He doesn't change his expression. "It means that I'm the only one you can bite without consequence if you lose control. His vines won't hold a werewolf, and the only other thing he's good for is weaponry. If you lose it, we need you *restrained*, not impaled on his scimitar."

Martín snorts behind us. "Too late for that, eh?" He doesn't bother lowering his voice.

My cheeks turn a darker crimson than Diego's eyes as I hear Valentina make contact with Martín, who yelps. "Ow!"

Diego's nostrils flare, but he doesn't react otherwise.

Embarrassed and defeated, I wave goodbye to Martín and Valentina, then, almost as an afterthought, lean down and kiss Saif goodbye. My mouth lingers on his, and I run my hand over his jaw, through his velvety beard. When we break apart, I look back at Diego, silently daring him to say something.

His face is blank, but his eyes are thunderous as he stares straight ahead at the wall. He turns and prowls back out the door. I follow behind him, arms crossed. He leads me to the greenhouse, which is as hot as an oven. I begin sweating almost immediately after entering.

"Why are we in here, anyway?" I ask, tying my hair in a knot on top of my head, desperate to get it off my neck and back.

He doesn't answer immediately, and I have the distinct feeling he has to unstick his locked jaw, given that he's been grinding his teeth since we left the castle.

I realize, abruptly, that I have actually been hearing his teeth clenching, and I can smell his cedar and aloe scent as strongly as if he had just emerged from the shower.

"Senses are sharpening," I mumble to myself under my breath.

He nods. "I figured that would start soon. It wasn't long after this time last month that you had blood dripping down your chin."

I wince at the memory, but my stomach growls instead of flipping.

"And we're in here because it provides cover, distance from everyone else, and because it lets in the most moonlight."

I look at him quizzically.

"What?" He asks scathingly. "Haven't come across the craving for moonlight in all those books yet?"

Maybe it had been so obvious that it hadn't been stated in the books. Or maybe I had simply forgotten? "I've been . . . preoccupied," I reply finally, thinking of my lengthy discussions with my father. It's possible I had read about it but been distracted by something he was saying.

He makes a disgusted noise. "Clearly."

A small growl rumbles in the back of my throat, and he looks at me, suddenly wary.

"What does *that* mean?" I ask, hackles rising.

"Never mind," he says quickly, holding out a placating palm. He reaches for something silver on a table nearby, and I balk when I see what it is.

"Is that a fucking *collar*?" I ask indignantly.

He grabs and unlatches it. It's several inches wide, and nearly as thick. It gleams brightly against the late afternoon light.

"It's just an extra layer of protection. For everyone." He says this like it's an extra layer of sunscreen. He steps toward me, and as he does, my vision flashes red.

"Not to kink shame, but that's not my thing," I say through bared teeth as my back hits the glass of the greenhouse wall. *What the fuck is with this man and backing me against walls?*

His mouth tightens at the corners, and then he moves in a flash. Before I have time to take a swipe at him, he kicks my feet out from under me, and I fall to the ground at his feet, where he quickly closes the collar around my neck and stands back up.

I breathe hard as I look up at him from my knees, my nails digging into my palms.

It's not a view I ever thought I would have of him.

"It's going to have to be your thing for tonight, *Lobita*," he says, and he clamps the other end of the chain around a bar of the cell. I struggle to unlock the collar, but my fingers feel too thick to maneuver correctly. I realize that they aren't fingers anymore; they've begun to morph into paws.

As my body starts to change, I notice that I definitely feel more in control than I had last month, though a primal anger still burns through me. I press my forehead to the ground and focus on feeling the transformation this time, just to see what it's like, and hoping it will distract me from the rage.

Shifting feels like slipping on an old, familiar sweatshirt. Like getting on a bicycle after a long time, but knowing exactly what to do. Like greeting an old friend who you know better than you know yourself.

My teeth elongate into points, and fur sprouts from my skin. A growl rumbles in my throat as claws slide out from my nail beds and curve to deadly, razor-sharp points. I grow an extra limb that juts off from my spine — a tail, I realize distantly. It comes with its own set of muscles, and the sensation is somehow strange and perfectly familiar at the same time.

When the transformation is complete, I lie growling on the ground. The rage that bubbles up inside me is just as intense as last time, but because I'm more aware, I can control it a little better.

Finally, after some time just getting used to this new form, I climb to my feet — all four of them. The sky above is on fire, a kaleidoscope of red and orange from the setting sun.

I realize as I stand that my eyes are several inches higher than they are as a human; I might even be eye-to-eye with Saif. But I'm still not eye-to-eye with Diego.

Diego. I recognize him this time. Last month, he had just been a human. Now I know exactly who he is.

I growl.

He leans against the glass wall and gazes warily at me, but says nothing.

I take a step to test my limbs and feel my powerful muscles rippling as I do so. The strength that courses through me gives me a delicious high. Suddenly, I see something else move out of the corner of my eye. I turn and step toward it, coming to the wall in just a few long strides.

I'm looking at a huge, auburn wolf. She has a white mark running from the top of her head, just between her ears, down to her nose. It's shaped vaguely like a dagger sticking out of a tawny stone. No, it seems a bit too big for that. It's a sword.

Her green eyes are glowing back at me. I realize, then, that it's my reflection. That the wolf is *me*.

"How are you feeling?" Diego asks, and I turn to look at him. It takes me a minute to process what he said; it sounds like he's talking to me from underwater, and from a distance at that.

I stare at him, unblinking. He repeats himself, louder this time, and slower. I flatten my ears and growl at him, teeth bared.

"Well, that's normal at least," he says, a strange expression on his face as he turns away from me. I try to move backward to get away from him, but then something pulls on my neck. I snarl in rage, looking for what is yanking on me, then realize there's a chain connecting me to the cell.

I pull backward more forcefully, trying in vain to break it. It holds fast.

I thrash and howl, but though the chain is light, it's too strong, and the collar is wicking my energy away faster the harder I move. I tire after a minute and sit back on my haunches, defeated.

Diego steps toward me, and I rumble at him wearily. He pauses a moment, then approaches again. Finally, when he's at my side, he reaches out and places a hand against my shoulder, and I look up at him silently.

He speaks loud and clear so I can hear him. "Do you understand me?" I consider ignoring him for a moment, but eventually nod.

He raises both eyebrows and whistles softly. "Usually it takes months for a new werewolf to have this much wherewithal. I don't understand why you're so different." His voice is devoid of the anger it held when I had argued with him in the dining hall. Now he sounds — impressed?

Would a Mage for a father have anything to do with it?

"Well," he says after a pause. "I hadn't planned on doing this yet, but maybe we could try something new."

I remember that Bleddyn had spoken in my head. I shout my thoughts at Diego, hoping it works for me too.

Is it you not being an asshole?

He has no reaction. I search my thoughts for something that would definitely get his attention. I think of Saif's head between my legs, and how he had fucked me slowly against the wall.

Diego still doesn't react. Apparently, that skill is more advanced, then. I huff in disappointment.

He pats my shoulder and unhooks the other end of the silver chain from the cell bar. He clamps the manacle around his own wrist, and then motions for me to follow. "Let's go for a stroll."

He leads me out into the twilight.

Moonlit Forest

We exit the greenhouse, and he leads me on my chain into the forest to the East of Arkenvale. After about fifteen minutes of walking, the only sounds being our footfalls and the crickets, we come upon a clearing that's bathed in cool moonlight; it's a training area, but not quite like the training yard at the castle.

Thick chains are hooked into giant boulders, and massive logs lie throughout the area. Large stumps are spaced at least twenty feet apart in a row for jumping between.

I glance at him silently, and he answers my unasked question. "The Mages have their magic. They don't have to focus on brute strength. You and I do."

I look around the clearing again. There is definitely nothing here that any of the other members of the Order could move on their own, perhaps even with their magic.

Except, perhaps, Hyun-Joo. *She could probably move the boulders with spite and her glare alone.*

Diego lets me process what I'm seeing, then reaches up and unlocks the silver chain from around my neck. As soon as it's loose, adrenaline pulses through my veins. I shake myself from snout to tail tip.

He grins. "Don't take off on me. I'm trusting you."

He walks off, and I watch him go for a moment, then follow behind him at a steady clip toward the boulder he's approaching.

When he reaches it, he points out the large handle that has been screwed into one side. "Bite that, and pull. Let's see what you've got."

Not being able to verbally argue with him saves us a considerable amount of time, I realize begrudgingly, as I take the large triangular handle into my mouth and clamp my teeth around it. I back up and pull at it, and it's as easy as opening a door.

He nods, a satisfied look on his face. "*No malo.*" I gather the general meaning of that. *Not bad.*

He points to another handle hanging nearby, but this one is connected to a rope that loops up and around a thick tree branch. At the other end of the makeshift pulley system is a massive log. I just stare for a moment.

He looks back at me evenly. "If you can move this boulder you can do that. Go." I bare my teeth at him but pad over to the handle, then take it in my teeth and pull. The log doesn't give. I let go and reassess.

I glance up at the moon to see if she has any advice. She does not, but I'm comforted nonetheless; her beams caress my glossy coat, and cool strength flows through me like water from a frozen stream. *Show him what you're made of, Daughter.*

Diego watches me as I inspect the section of the rope that loops around the tree branch, then walk over and nudge the log with my snout to see how heavy it feels. I can't make it budge.

"Stop stalling," he calls, but his tone is more excited than exasperated. It's almost like he *wants* to see me do this.

I walk back to the handle from the opposite direction this time, and then, with it clenched firmly in my mouth, I walk toward Diego instead of trying to back up.

For several moments, the log on the other end doesn't move, and I growl in frustration. I dig my claws into the dirt and my growl gets louder as I exert myself. Every muscle in my lupine body is tense and being pushed to its limit. The log is moving now, but only just.

Diego saunters closer to me, his hands on his hips, and clicks his tongue. "Well, I guess it's no surprise you're still so weak. It *is* only your second transformation. Maybe we'll try again next month, *Lobita*." He turns to walk away.

His words ignite a fire in my stomach, and I blink away a red haze from my vision.

Weak? I think furiously.

Fuck that.

I snarl around the handle of the rope and push with renewed vigor, staring straight at his back as I do so. A moment passes, then another. The log doesn't move. I rear up on my hind legs, then jump forward, aiming my paws at Diego's back.

The log flies into the air and crashes against the branch over which the rope had been looped. The branch breaks, and both it and the log fall to the ground in pieces. Diego turns just in time to see the wood splinter in a thunderous explosion behind me.

His face is not enveloped in shock like I had imagined it would be. Instead, he's got a self-satisfied smirk on his face.

"Good girl."

I shiver and shake my coat out.

He turns abruptly and walks toward two trees that mark an entrance to a path through the woods. I follow him automatically.

"This trail goes a few miles through the woods, then loops back around. Let's test your speed." With that, he takes off, and he's out of sight in a blink.

Is this a race?

I bare my teeth in a wolfy grin. *Oh, he has no idea what he's in for.* I've been running at the gym every day for the better part of a decade. Sure, I'm in a different body right now, but ninety percent of running is in your head.

I take off after him, and it's like I'm flying. My paws hardly touch the earth, but they're propelling me forward so quickly that the wind whistles in my ears as it flies by.

Diego is fast, but I am so much faster. No wonder he couldn't get between Bleddyn and me before I was bitten. His vampire blood lends him extra strength and endurance, but it can't fight evolution; he's still only got two legs.

And now, I have four.

As I overtake him, I howl triumphantly and leap over his head, landing just a few feet ahead of him. Then I'm tearing into the earth again, and I'm gone in a flash.

The wind is still whistling in my ears, but I'm almost certain, as I round a bend and leave him in the dust, that I hear him laughing.

~~~~~~~~~

Later, as we walk back toward the greenhouse, he says nothing. My muscles are totally drained, and by the time he leads me to the cell and locks the door behind me, I'm too tired to grumble - or, rather, growl - about it. I walk to an area near the bed and turn in circles, trying to get comfortable. Finally, I sink to the ground with a heavy *thwump*.

Diego sits hunched over in his chair gazing at me as he had been the morning after my first transformation. I wait for him to speak, but he doesn't say anything.

I stare back at him evenly for a long moment. I know better by now than to think he'll tell me I did well during my training, but it still needles me that he doesn't. I turn my back to him and huff air through my nose.

Eventually, as the first rays of dawn begin to lighten the sky, sleep finally overtakes my exhausted body. I hear him whisper something
~~~~~~~~~

behind me as I slip into the void. It sounds like, *"Dulces sueños."*

~~~~~~~~~~

I wake a few hours later on the bed with a thick, heavy blanket covering me. Diego is asleep on the ground next to me, curled up on his side, his arms folded under his head. I lie still and watch him. I hadn't even been sure he actually *does* sleep, and now that he is, I don't want to wake him.

His dark eyelashes rest on the tops of his cheekbones, and his mouth is open just slightly. The scowl that normally skews his features is completely gone, and he looks content for the first time since I've known him, like sleep is the only thing that can remove the weight of the world from his shoulders.

He shifts slightly, and a section of his shaggy hair falls over his face. I reach down to brush it behind his ear, and he turns his head in his sleep to lean into my touch.

My fingers linger on his cheekbone for several moments, but then he shifts once again as if to shake me off, a small frown on his face. I pull my hand back quickly as my stomach twists strangely.

I rise as quietly as I can and, after a moment of hesitation, lay the blanket gently over Diego's curled form before I exit the greenhouse and head back to Arkenvale.
~~~~~~~~~~

Dichotomous

Strong as iron.
Soft as silk.
More fiery than the sun.
More serene than the moon.
Swifter than the wind.
More immovable than a mountain.
How is she not pulled apart by these opposing forces?
This bewitching, dichotomous woman?

~ New Moon ~

Afraid of Falling

"You're out of your goddamn mind."

Diego rolls his eyes at me. "It's just one little jump. You'll be fine."

I scoff. "One little jump to snapping my neck in half."

Martín approaches, taking in the scene above him, his eyebrows raised. Diego and I are standing on top of the balance beam that has been set twelve feet off the ground. He stands steadily as I wobble back and forth.

"What's going on up there?" Martín calls up at us.

"She's afraid of heights," Diego says mildly.

"I am *not*," I snap, my arms splayed wide, my eyes on my feet. "I am afraid of *falling*."

"You won't fall if you stop expecting to."

"I don't think gravity gives a fuck if I'm confident or not," I growl at him.

I glance at Martín. "Diego is trying to get me to *jump* on this beam when I can barely stand upright on it."

Martín barks a laugh. "Come on, *mamacita*, you can do it," he encourages me.

My teeth chatter as I shoot a glare at him. "You've seen me try to do jumps on the short balance beam, right? How it always ends with me flat on my ass?"

Martín doesn't reply, he merely gives an abashed smile and walks off, apparently unwilling to watch my inevitable demise.

"We don't have all day, *Lobita*," Diego barks. "I've got plans tonight."

I squint at him, wobble, then look back at my feet. "Plans?"

I can't see it, but I know he rolls his eyes at me. I can hear it in his tone. "It's Hyun-Joo's birthday. We're going out."

I tilt dangerously to the right and have to bend myself in half and grip the beam with my hands for a second before I can right myself again. "Oh," I mutter lamely.

Don't ask. You don't want to know. Just keep your mouth shu—

"Where are you going?"

The voice of reason in my head officially clocks out for the day, probably to go cry itself to sleep.

Diego doesn't reply right away, as if it's a precious secret. "Baseball game," he says finally.

"Come again?" I teeter precariously as I peek at him.

He shrugs one heavy shoulder. "She likes baseball. I'm taking her to a game in Buffalo."

I knit my brow in consternation. *I like baseball, too.*

"Sorry, darling, I already got the tickets, and I doubt Rahim would let you out of his sight for a night."

My eyes widen and my cheeks burn instantly when I realize I had said that last sentence out loud. "No, I, I didn't mean . . . I wouldn't want to go with —"

He raises a thick brow at me, and I clamp my mouth shut.

An awkward beat crawls by.

"So, like I said, today would be splendid," he drawls.

I grit my teeth and stay crouched low.

"Okay." He steps toward me, and I hold out a hand as if it will ward him off, but it's no use. I think for one wild second that he's going to shove me off the beam, or kick my legs out from under me, but he takes my hands in his and holds me steady.

I'm too shocked to fight him.

He pulls me up so that I'm standing, inches from him, then releases my hands. The smell of his soap fills my nostrils.

I wobble immediately.

He places his hands on my hips, and my stomach lurches. I think briefly that I'm going to fall off this beam without him needing to shove me.

"Keep your center of gravity *here*," he says, patting my hips. "You're trying to balance with your arms. It's why you keep falling. Plant your feet, center yourself in your hips, and stand strong. It won't kill you to have some confidence." He releases me, but doesn't move back.

"Yes, sir," I whisper.

I breathe deep as I plant my feet one in front of the other and bring my awareness to my hips. I stop wobbling.

Diego's voice is low and rumbling. "Now, jump and turn. Keep your arms out when you land if you need to, but keep that awareness in your hips."

I am *very* aware of my hips at the moment, and of their general vicinity. I take a few quick breaths then hop into the air, turn 180 degrees, and land heavily. I crouch down, my arms held out, keeping my gravity low. I don't fall.

"Holy shit, I did it," I breathe.

He says nothing for a moment, then he presses his fingers into the underside of my arms and pulls me up slowly.

Neither of us moves for several seconds; the only motion between us is the wind whipping my ponytail back and forth across the base of his throat. I have the absurd feeling that we're on the prow of a boat. I had somehow moved closer to him in midair, and now as he breathes, I can feel his chest press against my back. He seems to be breathing quite heavily for just watching me try not to fall to my doom.

He leans down to my left ear. "Next time, don't crouch when you land," he murmurs. I'm pretty sure Valentina has doused me with cold lake water again, given my body's reaction to his words. An ache throbs in my chest as he removes his hands from my arms and takes a step back on the beam.

I force a blast of air through my nose. "Good job, Eilidh. Wow, you didn't fall to your death, Eilidh," I mutter to myself, looking back down at the beam.

He says nothing.

When we finish about fifteen minutes later, Diego hangs from his fingertips and drops the rest of the way to the ground. He lands softly on his feet like a cat, then turns and walks away without glancing back at me. I stare after him a moment, frowning, then climb down the ladder on the side of the beam.

Show off.

Saif meets me at the bottom of the ladder and looks me up and down. "Are you okay? You could have gotten really hurt."

I shrug. "Yeah, I'm fine. Did you see me? I did it!" I smile at him, eager for his congratulations. They don't come.

He continues fussing over me instead. "He shouldn't have made you do that. It's too dangerous. You aren't ready for that yet."

I frown. "I'm fine. I did it."

He frowns too, and sighs. "I just worry about you." He takes my hand and forces a smile. "Want to come spar with me? You can use your dagger, and I'll try to disarm you with vines." He pats the pocket where he keeps his wisteria seeds, and begins walking away.

I look after him for a moment, trying not to feel disappointed. But he's right. It had been risky for me to be up there. I wasn't ready for it.

"Sure," I say, following him. I grip the hilt of my dagger tightly as we walk. The familiar feeling of my energy being sucked into its hilt almost feels comforting.

~ Third Full Moon ~

Perseverance

O nce again, I wake with a headache, but, just as it had been last month, the pain is just a bit less than the previous full moon. I hope that by next month, it will be gone completely.

I disinter myself from the mountain of blankets and spot the tea mug on my desk. I sip on it as I get dressed for the day; it's another hibiscus brew. *Delicious.*

The day is quiet and comfortable. I spend most of it in the solarium with Saif as he tends to various plants. While he adds a nitrogen-rich fertilizer to a small fig tree, he tells me about how, when he was a teenager, he used to grow and then sell figs just like these to the soldiers occupying his town. Apparently, there had been quite the market for figs, as well as chewing gum and other small treats.

"What did you do with the money?" I ask. "Can't have been that much."

He shrugs. "It wasn't, not really. But it was enough, at the time. There were some kids in my neighborhood who needed shoes so they could walk comfortably to school, so I bought them some. The rest went to food."

My heart aches for him.

My stomach burns with anger.

That afternoon, Diego finds me as I'm exiting the solarium. He looks me up and down and minces no words. "Go get dressed and ready for tonight."

I look down at myself. I've got on a gray apron dress over a white cotton shirt. I had thrown my hair in a high bun on top of my head to keep it off my neck in the heat of the solarium. "What's wrong with my outfit?"

"Are you planning on shifting out on the prairie?" He asks sardonically.

I cross my arms. "Are you planning on taking me to a black-tie event? Because last I checked, my clothes disappear when I shift anyway."

He blinks, and if I didn't know better, I'd say some red creeps into his cheeks. He throws his hands up and turns away, heading back down the staircase. "Whatever, *Lobita*, just hurry up and let's get outside before you start scratching fleas off on the carpet."

I gape at his back for a moment, then stalk down the stairs after him. "I do not have *fleas!*" I say indignantly. I resist the urge to scratch my arm, which feels suddenly itchy at the thought.

He ignores me, and I follow him sullenly to the greenhouse. When we get inside, he gestures at the collar, which is once again lying on a table. "Do you feel like you'll need that this month?"

I frown at him and shake my head. "I was in perfect control last month. My headaches are better too, and I don't think it's just the special tea Saif makes me for full moons. I should be fine."

Diego stiffens. "Glad to hear it," he bites. Then he sneers. "If you want it on just for fun at any point, do let me know."

I flush, but he's - mercifully - already turned away from me. Soon, I fall to my knees, and the transformation ripples through my cells.

He leads me out into the night.

When we get to the training area in the forest, he points at a large rope ladder that's connected to a tree at a forty-five-degree angle. It looks rickety as fuck.

"Climb that."

I peer at the ladder apprehensively. The top of it isn't terribly high, perhaps fifteen feet, which will probably be fine as a wolf, but the problem is getting up to it.

I pad over to the bottom of the ladder, set a paw on one of the rungs, and then hold the paw up to him, hoping he understands. *I don't have any fucking thumbs to hold on with.*

He's unperturbed; he just stands with his hands on his slender waist, and raises his eyebrows. I let out a low growl, but I know it's no use trying to argue with him, particularly when he can't understand me.

I make it about three rungs off the ground before the entire ladder flips on me and I land on my back, letting out a yelp. Diego doesn't move.

After about ten tries, I'm halfway up the ladder, and he has moved on to his own workout. He's got some kind of rope and pulley system rigged up so that he can use logs almost exactly like you would a machine at the gym. It's actually pretty impressive, though I'd deny it if asked.

I make sure to keep my center of gravity low while I climb the ladder just as I had on the balance beam a couple of weeks ago. And while I thought the tail would throw me off, it actually helps as a counterweight.

I've stopped crashing to the ground in a furry heap after a few more attempts as well; when I get flipped off, I'm able to land on my feet. I see Diego watching me from the corner of my eye when he thinks I'm not looking.

On what seems like my fiftieth try, I finally reach the top of the ladder. I howl in triumph, scratch my claws into the trunk to mark my success, and jump down to the ground below.

I look up at the moon and yip happily. *I fucking did it!*

She beams at me in reply. *Of course you did.*

Diego walks over as I'm shaking my fur out, and I turn to him, waiting for him to tell me how well I have done. He looks up at my scratch marks and nods.

"Now do it upside down." He turns and walks away.

I glare after him, blinking away the red film that suddenly coats my vision.

I growl over and over as I try to get to the top of the rope ladder from the underside of it. I lose track of how many times I try before the sun comes up.

~ Waning Crescent ~

Boiling

After training and taking our showers, Saif and I head to the solarium to gather some produce for lunch.

We get a bit sidetracked.

"Oh fuck, just like that," I whimper. Saif breathes heavily into my neck in reply and keeps his fingers moving at just the right pace to set me ablaze.

He's got me pressed into the back left corner of the room, and the midday sun blazes into the room from above. I've got my right foot propped up on a metal shelf next to us, my dress hitched up around my hips, and he's got two fingers buried deep in my pussy.

He kisses down my neck and as far down my chest as the collar of my dress will allow before kneeling on the ground in front of me and licking my clit as his fingers find my G-spot.

I bite back my moans and coil my fingers into his dark curls.

He squeezes my ass with his free hand, then trails it up and down my thigh, shooting pleasure through me.

In what feels like no time, I come undone, and I bite into my lips as I quiver around his hand. "I'm coming," I pant.

He rips his jeans down, puts an arm under my other leg, and hoists me into the air to bring me down onto his throbbing erection. I kiss him deeply as he props me up against the wall, thrusting erratically, and then he comes as well, grunting heavily against my lips.

He removes himself from me, panting, and sets me down in a daze. I slide down the wall and sit there shivering, letting the last waves of pleasure crash over me. He sits down to my left and lets out a satisfied sigh.

"Well," he says after a few moments, "I suppose we should actually get the food for lunch, huh?"

I chuckle as he stands and reaches a hand out for me to grab. Once I'm on my feet, he pulls me into his arms and kisses me tenderly. When we finally break apart, I nuzzle my head under his chin.

"Or we could just stay in here for the rest of the day and bar the doors so no one can come looking for us." I trace a finger over his chest in tiny circles.

He chuckles, but a significant part of me had been serious. I cling to his shirt for a second longer as he pulls away, but then I release him, and after washing our hands in the solarium sink, we gather some vegetables to make lunch.

When we get to the kitchen, Valentina and Martín are there, playfully snapping at each other in Spanish. Martín is gesturing animatedly with an empty mug, and when he sees us enter the kitchen, he rushes to Saif.

"Finally, someone who knows what the hell he's doing. Please, *hermano*, tell this poor confused woman that you do not put the tea leaves into the kettle while it's boiling?"

Saif looks at Valentina in horror. "You did *what?*"

Valentina looks at me for backup. "Help me out here! It's more efficient, right?" Martín collapses dramatically to his knees, one hand thrown over his forehead.

I peek at Saif, and he, too, looks like he might collapse. I back away and put my hands up. "Sorry Val, I'm a coffee person. Leave me out of this!"

"This can't be happening!" Martín wails dramatically from the floor.

Valentina throws her hands in the air and stomps off. "Girl code violation! *Traición!*"

I collapse in laughter against the island in the center of the room.

~ Fourth Full Moon ~

Apology

"Well, now we know your bite is worse than your bark." Diego wraps a bandage around his forearm as we wait in the greenhouse, the light of dawn just starting to peek through the velvet blanket of night.

"I *said* I was sorry!" I say from the floor, where I'm sitting with my back against the outside of the cell bars. Even though I'm not *particularly* sorry.

Maybe just a fraction more than the moon had been. *Serves him right,* she had radiated. *Thinking he can best one of my children.*

And she wasn't entirely wrong; it had been his fault anyway. If he hadn't insisted on fist-fighting a damn werewolf, he wouldn't have gotten bitten. Or, if he had been wearing his crossbow-sword-vambrace contraptions, but he had taken those off prior to sparring.

"And *I* said that it's fine!" He says around clenched teeth as he bites into the bandage to tie it off. "It'll heal by tomorrow. You didn't get me that deep."

I cross my arms. "Wouldn't have happened at all if you hadn't been shouting orders at me the whole time, and had just let me focus."

He throws himself down on the ground beside me and leans back against the bars as well.

"In an actual fight, the opponent is most likely going to be talking. You have to learn to compartmentalize. Keep your mind and body separate."

I close my eyes. "I *know* how to dissociate, thank you very much."

It's a classic PTSD symptom, after all. Lucky me.

"What I *don't* know how to do is make you less annoying."

Diego breathes quickly out of his nose.

I gape at him. "Did — was that almost a laugh?"

He looks sideways at me, one thick eyebrow cocked, and then closes his eyes. "I didn't hear anything."

"Oh my *god*, it was!" I shove his shoulder. He doesn't budge.

"Holy shit. I wish there was a newspaper here I could alert." I spread my hands out in front of me as if centering a headline. "Giant Angry Vampire Nearly Cracks Smile."

He shakes his head softly against the bar behind him. *"Disparatada."*

I smirk up at him. I'll have to ask Valentina later what that means, but it didn't sound quite like he meant it as an insult.

We sit in silence for a few heartbeats, and maybe it's because I'm feeling guilty - a bit more guilty than I had a few minutes ago - about biting him, but I suddenly feel the need to say something to him that's been a long time coming.

I bring my knees up and wrap my arms around them. "I'm sorry," I say quietly.

He makes an exasperated sound. *"¡Ay por Dios!* If you apologize for this one more time, I swear I'm throwing you into the lake."

I have no doubt that he is one hundred percent serious about this. Diego Vidales is many things, but a man of idle threats is not one.

"I'm not apologizing for that," I say, nodding at his arm.

He raises that damn eyebrow at me again.

"I'm apologizing for what I said before. About Hyun-Joo. In the circle." I dig my thumb nails into the sides of my pointer fingers. "That was fucked up. I shouldn't have said any of it. I was just —"

What *had* I been, really?

"Angry. But that's no excuse."

His lips press into a thin line, and he's silent for a moment. "That was months ago."

I wince. "I know. I should have apologized sooner."

"That's not what I meant."

I peek up at him. "Oh." I pause. "Then what *did* you mean?"

He considers this for a moment as if he isn't totally sure himself. When he speaks, his voice is low and distant. "I just meant that I can't believe you still felt guilty about that."

"Well, I did. I *do*. And I'm sorry. I should have just let you beat my ass from the get-go instead of trying to taunt you into making a mistake. Or at the very least, not insulted the woman you love."

It's Diego's turn to wince.

"It was a major girl code violation. There's plenty about *you* I could have used before bringing her into it," I end with a small smile.

"Well, now you're just being hurtful." But I swear the corner of his mouth twitches upward just a fraction.

We sit in silence for another few moments. The light outside is starting to shine in earnest, but neither of us makes a move to leave. He looks lost in thought, and I'm lost in watching him.

"I didn't mean to snap on you like I did that day," he finally says, quietly. "She just —" He closes his eyes and sighs, putting his head back again. "She suffers so much because of me already, and your words on top of that just tipped me over the edge. But I'm sorry, too."

I don't think I'm breathing, but I can't focus on myself enough to check. His long dark eyelashes brush the tops of his cheekbones as he looks at the ground, and my senses are still sharpened, so his musky aloe and cedar scent fills my nostrils.

"I'm sure she can't suffer too much with you," I say quietly.

At that, he looks down at me from the corner of his eye, his head still leaning back against the bar. His gaze is dark. I'm suddenly acutely aware that my heart is pounding, and that he's seated only about six inches away from me.

"Being around me is nothing but bloodshed and pain. I hurt her over and over, and she takes all of that on without complaint. I'll never understand why." His voice is thick.

My shoulders rise and fall with my rapid breath. "Love makes people irrational," I say shakily.

His eyelids flutter, almost imperceptibly. "Yeah. It sure does."

I blink first and look at the ground, dizzy.

He stands. "Sun's up. Let's go get some sleep, *Lobita.*" He doesn't look back at me as he walks out of the greenhouse and back toward Arkenvale.

Curiosity

Just when I think I've got her figured out.
   Shocking.
   Confounding.
What a breathtaking curiosity.
This fiery Little Wolf.

~ Third Quarter ~

Concession

Martín crashes into the dining hall on the morning of October 28th, and closes the door behind him quickly. I turn around on the bench at the commotion, and he rushes over to me. "Do you have a plan?"

I swallow my bite of blueberry muffin and nod at him, holding up a placating hand. "Yes, I've got it covered. I'm taking her down to the lake to go swimming while Saif makes the dessert."

Martín bobs his head quickly. "Okay, great. Hyun-Joo is going to the city now for her present, and Diego's making the *ajiaco* and *empanadas*."

I glance at Saif. "Diego can cook?"

He rolls his eyes and nods. "Yes. Because of course he can."

Martín laughs. "Can he cook? *Chica*, that man's *pozole* is enough to curl your toes." He winks at me, and I clear my throat.

"Okay, cool. Is she still sleeping?" I look at the dining hall door.

Martín barks a deep laugh. "This late in the morning? No, she's in the training yard."

I roll my eyes at him. It's barely eight o'clock, and I'm not even fully awake yet. "Why is she training on her birthday?"

He throws his hands into the air. "Because she's *loca*. She said she doesn't want her muscles to atrophy in her old age."

Saif and I both groan. "I think I just felt my hair turn gray," he mumbles.

I reach across the table and pat his hand. "Don't worry, my little leap-year baby. Technically, you're only eight, right?"

His eyes widen. "Wow, you're right. You're *way* too old for me."

He smiles as I smack his hand.

~~~~~~~~~~

That evening, after a full day of swimming, I make Val take a long shower while the rest of us finish setting up.

"Am I being held prisoner?" She giggles as I shove her into the bathroom and shut the door behind her.

"Yes!" I say through the wood. "Stay put until someone comes to get you!"

When Martín brings her into the dining hall, we all yell, "Happy birthday!"

Dinner is a raucous affair, full of laughter and the clinking of six sets of silverware. I groan in delight as I bite into a bean *empanada*.

Damn. Diego really *can* cook.

Once dinner is cleared away, Saif walks out of the kitchen carrying a brown cake. Valentina's eyes are glassy as he sets it on the table in front of her. "Here you go, Val. *Torta Negra Colombiana.*"

I bump my shoulder against hers and point to the candles. "Not to brag, but *I* lit those. The two was easy, but that six put up a hell of a fight."

She laughs as she wipes a tear from her eyes. Once she blows them out and slices the cake, none of us say a word as we eat. It's the best damn dessert I've ever had.

After Valentina and Martín head upstairs, I move to follow Saif to the kitchen to help him wash up, but I don't know when I'll get the chance again - or the courage - to say what I need to say.
~~~~~~~~~~

"Hyun-Joo, can I talk to you?" I ask in a rush. Saif and Diego both stop in their tracks at opposite ends of the dining hall and look at me. Diego recovers first; he puts a hand gently on her shoulder and inclines his head as if to ask if she wants him to leave.

Or perhaps it's to ask if she wants him to throttle me. Though, she doesn't need him to do that for her; she's perfectly capable of doing it herself. She'd probably relish it, actually.

Focus, Shaw.

But she just puts her hand over his for a second and nods at him, and he exits the dining hall without another word.

I turn to Saif. "I'll be there in a second."

His gaze flicks between Hyun-Joo and me briefly, but he nods and heads into the kitchen.

I take a deep breath, gathering strength, and turn back to her.

"I'm sorry," I say. "For the stupid shit I said before when Diego and I were sparring." I don't elaborate. I know she knows exactly what I mean.

"I felt awful as soon as I said it. You didn't deserve any of that. I was trying to piss him off so I could win, but I shouldn't have done it like that."

She looks back at me evenly for several excruciating moments, and I tap my fingers against my thigh as I wait for her reply. She isn't obligated to forgive me, but I hope she at least says *something* to put an end to this awkward moment.

"Thank you," she says finally, looking me up and down quickly.

I nod at her. "I'm sorry it took me so long to apologize. I'm sorry for being such an asshole."

Her gaze begins to soften.

"And I just want you to know that there's *nothing* going on between Diego and I." I slice my hands through the air in front of me. "There never will be."

Her expression ices over in an instant. She turns on her heel without another word and exits the dining hall.

I stare after her in shocked silence for several long moments, shivering.

What the fuck? Was that not what she wanted to hear? I cannot figure this woman out no matter how hard I try. *So why bother continuing to try?*

Slowly, anger bubbles up in my core, and my shivering stops. I raise my chin at the closed door. "Fine," I whisper. "I give up."

I turn and stalk into the kitchen to help Saif do the dishes.

Eternity

That night, Saif and I sit on my bed, sipping on mugs of chamomile tea. My mind lingers dangerously on Hyun-Joo for a moment, so I turn my thoughts instead to birthday celebrations.

"Does it bother you?" I blurt suddenly into the silence.

He takes a swig of his tea and looks at me over the mug. "Going to need you to catch me up, dear."

I sigh into my mug. "That I'm going to live forever."

"Oh." He puts his mug into his lap. "No, not really. Does it bother you?"

I cringe. "Immensely."

He winces. "Oh," he says again. "Why?"

"*Why?*" I ask incredulously.

He takes my hand and rubs a thumb along my skin.

I take a deep breath. "I had my first existential crisis when I was four." I expect him to laugh; that's what everyone else I've ever told has done. Everyone except Kianga, at least. But he doesn't laugh; in fact, his gaze softens.

"I'm sorry to hear that," he says simply.

You don't deserve this man, I think for the millionth time.

"What was it about?" He asks.

I sigh. "Never mind; it's stupid."

He squeezes my hand. "Hey," he says, and I look up into his warm brown eyes. "Whatever it is, I'm sure it wasn't stupid."

My lips twist into a self-deprecating smile. "It was over the concept of eternity," I say quietly as I shift uncomfortably. "I told you it was stupid."

He still doesn't laugh, he just looks at me sincerely. "It's not stupid. That's a lot for a four-year-old. It's a lot for anyone."

I make a contemplative sound. "I had heard a kid at the park talking about heaven that day, so I asked my mom about it, and she said that when good people die, their spirits live on forever and ever and *ever*. And I freaked out."

"Why?" He asks gently.

I snort and raise a palm to the ceiling. "The thought of having no ending, no finality, kind of broke my little mind. It sounded *exhausting*. I couldn't figure out what the point of it was, or how eternity could ever be considered a blessing. Then I couldn't figure out why such a short time on Earth would determine our fate for the rest of time."

I nibble on a nail for a moment before I speak again. "I remember falling to the floor and crying into the carpet, and then my mom asking what the hell was wrong with me." I chuckle bitterly.

If she could only see me now that I'm a fucking werewolf. Though she'd probably react much the same as she had then: by walking away and making me pick myself up off the ground.

Saif pulls my hand to his lips and kisses it firmly, and I smile at him gratefully.

"So," he says softly, "living forever isn't exactly the power you wanted?"

I laugh humorlessly. "It's kind of the very last superpower I would have ever chosen, even *before* I tried to off myself." I drain my mug and lean into his shoulder. "Besides," I murmur. "It means I'll lose you someday."

He shifts and puts a finger under my chin to tilt my face up toward his. He kisses me deeply, and I lose myself in him.

It's always so easy to lose myself in him.

"Can I tell you something?" He asks as he pulls away.

"Yeah," I say breathlessly and smile as my eyes flutter open.

He pushes a strand of my hair behind my ear. "I'm pretty sure I'm falling in love with you," he says, looking deeply into my eyes.

I inhale sharply, and my heart instantly begins hammering against my chest. "I." I breathe shakily. "Um." I've never said the "L" word to someone. Not like this.

He puts a hand on my cheek and places his thumb gently against my lips. "You don't have to say anything back, *Lahabi*. I just wanted you to know."

I take a shuddering breath, and he kisses me again.

By the time he pushes me back onto the pillow, sets the mugs hastily on the bedside table, and begins kissing my neck, I've forgotten all about my worries of eternity.

After he takes my clothes off, he kisses down my chest as he runs his hands up and down my body. I wriggle and squirm under his touch as he settles himself between my legs, and moan softly as his wide tongue parts my lips.

He moves slowly, and I breathe heavily as I run my fingers through his dark curls. He wraps his arms around my legs and holds me tenderly, his fingers digging softly into my thick thighs.

I prop myself up on my elbows to get a better view of him, and he meets my gaze as he moves his tongue around my clit in steady circles. Then he turns his head side-to-side, licking me at angles I've never felt before. I throw my head back and breathe heavily at the ceiling. "Fucking hell," I whisper.

He pulls back from me, but only a few centimeters. "Lay back and relax," he murmurs against me. "I've got you."

I quiver under the vibrations of his deep voice against my clit, and more collapse than lay back down onto my pillow.

He runs his hands up over my stomach, and once he finds my hands, laces our fingers together. He holds my hands tenderly against the sheets, and rubs his thumbs across my palms in a circular motion, syncing the tempo with his tongue as electricity shoots up my center.

Delicious tension builds inside me, winding up tightly in my core. "I'm really close," I breathe.

"Good," he rumbles against me. He grabs my wrists and pushes them down against the mattress, and I tip over the edge.

"Fuck, I'm coming," I whimper, expecting him to increase his pace, or thrust himself into me. But he keeps going, and I release a high-pitched noise that I didn't even know I could make.

Blood pounds in my ears, and I blink dizzily when I finally come back to myself. "I'm done," I whisper. "You can —"

He kisses my clit harder, and I bite back a loud cry. "You need one more," he breathes.

I quiver against him. "You don't have to," I say quietly.

He releases one wrist, and a moment later, trails his fingers lightly up my thigh, closer to my opening. I exhale slowly. "I know. I *want* to," he says. He puts his first two fingers into me, and I have to bite my freed hand to keep from crying out loudly.

I utter a string of quiet curses and moans as he twists his wrists back and forth so that he fills me from various angles. I clench around his fingers, and he exhales shakily against me.

Soon, I'm gasping again. "Saif," I breathe heavily. "Oh fuck."

"Mmm," he rumbles. "Keep saying my name."

My stomach twists in delight, and I clench around his fingers once more. "Saif," I whimper. "Oh my *god*." I begin shaking uncontrollably.

He keeps moving for another few moments, then finally pulls his fingers from me, and pulls down his pants in a flash.

Between one shudder and the next, he thrusts his throbbing erection into me, hitting my G-spot sharply. He puts his mouth over mine, cutting off my pleasured cry. He moans against my mouth, and I twist my hands up into his hair as our tongues and bodies move together.

He utters a few curses in Arabic and then leans his forehead against mine. "Fuck, Eilidh, I . . . You're fucking amazing."

"Saif," I moan again, and my orgasm increases in intensity rather than dropping off. I begin gushing around him as he hits my G-spot over and over. He grunts heavily, then pulses inside me. I pull him into another kiss, and he moans quietly against my mouth as he comes inside me.

He kisses across my jaw and down my neck as his thrusts slow. He mutters something more in Arabic that sounds like *"Ana uhibbuki."*

"What?" I ask breathlessly as my heart pounds, and I try to shake the ringing out of my ears.

He pulls himself out of me slowly, and I moan once more. "Nothing, *Lahabi."* He smiles as he lays down beside me.

He plants a kiss into my hair and wraps an arm around me, pulling me close. I pant against his chest, catching my breath, and he brushes a strand of hair away from my face. When my heart is finally beating normally again, he murmurs into my hair.

"Can I tell you something else?" He asks.

I take a deep breath. "Yeah," I say quietly.

"You don't have to worry about losing me for a very long time, Eilidh. You'll have me for as long as you want me. I promise. I'll take as much of your eternity as I can."

I nuzzle into him sleepily. "Okay," I say quietly. *Tell him, you idiot.* I try to make my mouth cooperate and say what I actually want it to, but it refuses. No matter how hard I try, I can't say it out loud. The sentence echoes around my head as I drift off to sleep in the warmth of his arms.

I'm pretty sure I'm falling in love with you too.

~ Waning Crescent ~

Grounding

Saif glances up from his breakfast, and the corners of his mouth tighten. I know who has just entered the dining hall before Diego's shadow even falls over me. I exhale slowly and wait for him to bark whatever order he has for me.

But he speaks to Saif, ignoring me entirely. "No training today. Get dressed in something nice and meet me out front. Auberon wants us to show her around the city."

"Got it," I snap at my bowl of oatmeal. *I'm right fucking here.*

He leaves the dining hall without another word.

"What counts as 'nice' in the city?" I ask Saif.

He thinks for a moment. "Ren Faire."

My eyes sparkle.

After we're done eating, he helps me pick out an outfit. I marvel once again at how many different articles of clothing Valentina managed to stuff into the wardrobe as I look for something appropriate.

Finally, I pull on a cream off-the-shoulder top with puffy sleeves and tuck it into a sage green linen skirt.

Saif strokes his beard and looks me up and down. "Needs something else." He rummages through the wardrobe for a moment, then pulls out brown ankle boots and a wide, brown corset.

He helps me lace it, kissing me warmly as he does so. I smile against his lips as he knots it for me.

"I'll take this off you later," he teases, and I make a delighted noise.

"Can't wait." I find socks and step into the boots. After I strap my dagger to my right thigh and adjust my skirt over it, I reach into the wardrobe one last time and pull out a chestnut brown cloak. I throw it around my shoulders and look at myself in the mirror.

Despite having spent the last several months in a castle, I haven't had the chance to dress the part yet. In my previous life, trying on new clothes had only ever been a source of frustration, but right now, I feel . . . *hot*. Every piece Valentina found for me makes me feel confident in my body, and this outfit is no different.

I stand up straighter.

I head downstairs and brush my teeth while Saif gets changed, and then he meets me at the bottom of the spiral staircase. My pulse quickens at the sight of him.

He's got on an ivory, sleeveless, hooded vest that hits just above his knees. The sleeves of his dark gray tunic are rolled up, and my eyes linger on his forearms. His black linen pants are tucked into knee-high black boots. *Dhabiha* sits on his hip, her hilt gleaming.

He's stunning.

He smiles mischievously as he reaches the foot of the stairs. "I had to at least try to look half as good as you do."

I swallow hard. "That outfit looks good on you now, but it will look better on my floor later." It's the lamest line in the book, but still, his smile turns bashful, and he takes my hand before we walk out the front door. I smile to myself at how this man can put up such a confident facade, but the moment I match his energy, he crumbles.

The day is sunny but breezy, and we spot Diego lying in the grass a few yards away, his eyes closed, his arms thrown back behind his head. He rises without us announcing ourselves, and I look him up and down once before averting my gaze.

He's almost entirely in black; he's wearing a black, long-sleeved, tunic with a deep, open V-neck, black linen pants, and his combat boots. He isn't wearing his vambraces, but just like Saif, he's armed. I recognize the basic steel broadsword with a black hilt from the arsenal that stays in the training yard. He's also got a navy cloak thrown around his wide shoulders that flaps in the wind as he takes off, not bothering to make sure we're keeping up.

As we head West around the inlet toward New Camlann, I try to braid my hair to one side, but the wind makes it impossible, so I just pull the top half up to stop it from blowing in my face.

"How big is New Camlann anyway?" I ask Saif as we follow behind Diego's stalking form.

He thinks for a moment. "There's about a hundred thousand Mages there. It's the largest city in Tenazeryth."

I nod, mentally preparing myself for entering into an area with so many people after having been around only the Order and my father for months.

We crest a hill to the West of Arkenvale, and I spot a small building I've never seen before. Diego heads straight for it.

I tilt my head to the side. "What's that?"

Diego responds before Saif can. "Garage. I'd rather not walk ten miles to the city."

I stop in my tracks, and it takes the men a moment to realize. They both stop and turn to look at me. I swallow hard and half turn back toward the castle. Saif's brow knits together, his eyes full of concern. Diego closes his eyes and sighs, like a fight he knew was coming has finally started.

"On second thought, I'm not feeling very well today. I think I'll just go lay down." I say, my voice deliberately even.

Diego is in front of me in the blink of an eye, looking down at me with a disdainful expression. "You'll be fine."

I throw my hands up in the air, and my cloak billows around me.

"You don't even know what's wrong!"

He doesn't blink; he just tilts his head to the side slightly, as if he's silently waiting for me to catch up. Then I remember that not only did he almost certainly hear my story when I told Valentina in the dining hall, but he was the one who had given my father the information about the accident.

I glare at the ground and pull the cloak around myself tightly as if it can shield me from shame. "I can't," I finally whisper angrily.

"Yes, you can."

I turn my glare on him. "Look, you don't understand; you aren't afraid of anything. For us regular people —"

He snorts and glances up at the crescent moon, which is just visible in the clear, blue sky. She frowns at him in reply.

I growl. "For those of us who *experience* fear, it isn't always as easy as mind over matter."

"Birds." Diego puts his hands on his slender waist, still staring at me.

I shake my head at him. "Birds?" I shrug.

"Birds."

I glance at Saif, who lifts an exasperated palm to the sky. *No idea.*

I look back at our vampire companion, who I fear may be short-circuiting, and turn out the pockets of my skirt. "Sorry, I'm fresh out."

Diego closes his eyes, and I can practically see the numbers flitting through his mind as he counts while he gathers his patience.

"I'm afraid of birds," he says slowly after he's counted to at least five.

I rub my ear. "What?"

"I'm sure you've heard of them. Tiny dinosaurs. Scaly feet. Soulless eyes."

He's serious. A smile spreads across my face.

He closes his eyes and pinches the bridge of his nose.

"Birds?" I ask again, trying unsuccessfully to suppress the smile.

He glares at me. "It's a phobia. It doesn't need to be rational."

I cross my arms and frown at the ground. "You're right," I mumble. "Sorry."

His demeanor softens a fraction. "And I never said it's as easy as mind over matter. What it *is* is finding the right things that work for you, to do what you need to, despite the fear. What technique works best to ground yourself?"

I squint up at him quizzically. How in the world does this man know about grounding techniques? I can't exactly picture him reading a self-help book or attending a therapy session. *I don't think they even make chaise lounges in his size.*

But he's waiting for an answer, so I purse my lips for a moment as I think. "Finding all the colors of the rainbow, backwards if I really need to focus."

He nods and grabs my shoulder, pulling me along as he walks toward the garage. I glance at Saif, whose eyes are narrowed just slightly, but he says nothing. He prowls behind us silently.

"See anything violet?" Diego asks.

His hand, even through the cloak over my shoulder, burns against my skin. I swallow, look around, and see a batch of flowers. Close enough.

"Dead nettles."

He nods. "Indigo?"

I look out at Nabeyha Lake. "The water."

"Blue?"

I look up. "The sky."

"Green? Grass is cheating."

"And the sky *wasn't* cheating?" I raise an eyebrow.

He smirks. "You get one cheat. Green?"

I look down. "Skirt."

We approach the door, and he removes his hand from my shoulder to pull a key from his pocket. "Yellow?" He unlocks the door.

My eyes land on the weeds around the building. "Dandelions."

He flicks on the light, and the three of us enter the garage. With another flick of a switch, the garage door begins to rise. "Orange?" He unplugs the car from a large electrical box in the wall.

I tap the front bumper as I walk by. "Headlight."

"Red?" He unlocks the car, and Saif climbs into the back left seat silently. Diego looks at me from across the roof of the car as I prepare to get in the back right seat.

I glance around. The garage is surprisingly barren other than the car. Some metal shelves line the walls, but they're empty, and the car itself is a simple white sedan. I don't see anything red until I look back at Diego, who is staring at me intensely. Heat creeps up my neck.

"Your eyes," I say quietly.

He looks back at me evenly for a moment, but his Adam's apple bobs before he answers.

"There you go, *Lobita*. Feel grounded now?"

I very much do not; in fact, if I let go of this car handle, I'm probably going to float to the ceiling like I've just guzzled a magical carbonated drink. But I just grip it and nod.

"Good." He folds himself into the driver's seat without another word.

I get in the back seat next to Saif, who sits in the center with his long legs spread to either side of him. He takes my hand as I get situated.

"I've got you, *Lahabi*." He smiles reassuringly. "I believe in you." It strikes me that Saif doesn't even know what's wrong, but here he is, supporting me nonetheless. I make a mental note to fill him in later, squeeze his hand tightly, and lean into his strong shoulder.

Diego's crimson gaze lingers on me in the rearview mirror for several seconds, then he pulls out of the garage and drives down the dirt road in silence.

New Camlann

The wall surrounding New Camlann is a gray behemoth, at least five hundred feet tall. It comes into view as we crest one of the rolling hills, and I exhale in wonder.

A massive portcullis acts as the gate, and only a few other cars are going in or out. As Diego drives up to the security booth, the Mage standing there waves him through.

Saif answers my unasked question. "Most cars would get stopped, but since this is the King's personal vehicle . . ." He shrugs.

"Quite the perk," I say with a small, forced laugh. I'm ready to get out of this car.

Finally, Diego pulls into a square near the center of the city, and parks in a reserved spot. I jump out as soon as he puts the car in park, and Saif slides out behind me. He puts a hand on each of my shoulders and leans down to give me a quick kiss.

"You did wonderfully."

I smile back at him gratefully.

I notice Diego from the corner of my eye, standing with his hands on his waist, surveying the people around us as though on the lookout for threats. *That's probably exactly what he's doing,* I realize.

"Thank you," I say, and he glances sidelong at me.

"Don't mention it." He sounds like he means that literally. He strides away from us, and we follow.

New Camlann is absolutely breathtaking. The buildings are Romanesque and Gothic with a modern twist; glass and stone steeples reach toward the sky, intricate detailing bordering the edges. Every street is clean and bright.

Each building that I can see the top of has solar panels on its roof, and all of them are covered in greenery; there are rooftop gardens, walls covered in flowering vines, and trees covering any flat surface not already utilized. Many of the plants and trees bear fruit; I watch as a pair of children pick apples from a tree and take bites, laughing at one another.

The streets are narrow, but the sidewalks are wide, and Mages and Shifters greet one another amiably as they go about their business. Only a few vehicles drive past us, and almost all the ones that do are public transit buses. New Camlann must be quite the walkable city.

I turn in circles, taking everything in.

"This place is *amazing*," I breathe.

Saif smiles at me. "It's a paradise."

I gesture at the greenery covering the buildings. "Did you have anything to do with the eco-friendly architecture?"

He shakes his head as he admires a towering maple tree on the roof of a nearby three-story building. "The cities in Tenazeryth are all like this; they always have been. And all the power here is generated through renewable energy. Water, solar, that sort of thing. Wind, too, though that's still developing."

"No fossil fuels?" I ask in awe.

He smiles again. "None. We work *with* our land."

I blink at the echo of my father's words.

"Like I said, paradise. There are solar panels on the roof of Arkenvale, too, although I guess you wouldn't have seen those."

I certainly had not, but I'd like to. "That's spectacular," I say. He grins and takes my hand.

I squeeze his hand back and raise my voice to Diego, who is several steps ahead of us. "What does the King want me to see here?"

Diego turns, gesturing vaguely. "Everything. He said he wants you to see how perfect it is here." He rolls his eyes as he turns back around, but I'm not sure what he's rolling his eyes at; it *does* seem perfect.

I look around. "Everything looks so modern. Why doesn't Arkenvale look like this?" The castle looks like it has sat on that cliffside for the last thousand years, other than the lights, and the modern kitchen. Even the bathroom is filled with claw-foot tubs that had to have been there for at least a century. Shower pipes had been installed in all of them, but still.

"The King is old-fashioned," Diego says in reply, with just a note of hostility in his tone.

The reason for his mood clicks. *He's annoyed that he has to chaperone me all day.* I sigh through my nose.

We spend hours walking around the city, and the men take turns showing me their favorite places. Saif shows me a public park that is really more of a public garden. Food grows in abundance in neatly organized garden beds, and he tells me that everyone is welcome to whatever they need; it's all paid for and supplied by the King.

Diego leads us to a small building in a mostly residential area. Saif gets waylaid to help a couple with an arboreal emergency; the man had been pruning a large shrub with giant clippers as his partner gestured animatedly to direct him.

She describes to Saif what she had been trying to get the man to transform the shrub into, and he nods in understanding. He glances at me with a small smile and waves for me to follow Diego inside without him.

The small building turns out to be a library. I gasp in surprise as I look around the cozy space. A sharp-featured white person with a buzz cut and tattoos covering their bare arms looks up from the circulation desk and gives Diego a friendly wave as we enter. "Hey, Mr. Vidales!" They call jovially.

I blink in surprise.

Diego smiles at them, and I can't tear my eyes away from his face for several long seconds. "Hi, Kai. Just dropping this off." He pulls a worn paperback from a pocket on the inside of his cloak and slides it across the desk at the librarian.

I watch the exchange, slack-jawed, and peek at the book, which is a retelling of Robin Hood, judging by the cover. They slide another book back at Diego. It's a sci-fi novel; there's a spaceship on the cover, and a tractor beam illuminates the author's name. "You'll love this one," they say excitedly.

Diego gives another small smile and takes it. "Thanks," he says as he slides it into his pocket.

The librarian smiles at me as Diego turns to leave, and I smile and nod back at them in silent response. I'll have to come back soon and actually speak with them, once I have processed this first visit. I turn away and furrow my brow as I follow Diego back through the vestibule of the building.

"You look confused, *Lobita*," he says mildly. "I know you know how libraries work."

I roll my eyes. "Didn't know you were a reader is all. And the librarian seemed to actually be able to stand you," I mutter.

The corner of his mouth quirks slightly as he opens the door to the city street. "*Most* people can, but Kai only has to put up with me in small doses. They recommend books, and I read them. End of relationship."

I clear my throat. "Well, that explains it."

We rejoin Saif, who has just finished shaping the shrub outside the house next door into a Bengal Tiger that looks incredibly realistic, and continue our journey.

This city is utterly enchanting. Everyone we encounter throughout the day is friendly, and many even salute as we walk by.

I don't notice the pattern until the fourth person puts their hand to their forehead as we pass them, and Diego and Saif give curt nods in response.

"Are you guys like . . . celebrities?" I ask, looking at the person as they walk away from us. It seems absurd to think that these men are known to the masses, but I chide myself silently.

They're Auberon's paladins. Of course they're celebrities.

I had thought they were exceptional since I had known them, but this entire dimension must think the same thing.

Neither of them look particularly thrilled with the question I had asked. Or maybe, it's with the answer.

Diego speaks first. "Life as an Order member comes with an unfortunate amount of recognition."

Saif nods his agreement silently, his eyes downcast. My eyes widen. I don't think I've ever seen them agree with one another before.

I grimace as a strange feeling grips my stomach, and it takes me a minute to identify it. It's not something I've felt since losing Kianga. I realize that I'm feeling *possessive* over these two, though I have no good reason to, particularly with regard to Diego. But even Saif, as much as he might belong to me at Arkenvale, he belongs to Tenazeryth first. My heart twists.

You can only ever be second to his kingdom.

I clench my jaw and shove the thought away.

Sometime in the early afternoon, Diego leads us to a tavern for lunch. It's down a side alley and, despite the alley itself being wide and warm, the tavern somehow manages to look dark and seedy. Water from some indeterminable source collects in a puddle a few feet from the door, and pigeons splash happily in it.

Diego gives them a wide berth.

Vines crawl up the tavern's front, but unlike the other buildings, covered in plants that are obviously planned and controlled, these vines look wild, spreading in complete disorder across the tavern's facade.

The windows look dark and dirty, and the wooden door to the place looks to be about a hundred years old, spiderwebbed with cracks.

I look at the sign hanging above the door. "The Howling Jackal?" I raise an eyebrow at Saif, but he just shrugs and looks away. He must not have been here before. I turn back to the sign.

The silhouette of an animal sitting on a crescent moon is carved into it, but whoever made the sign was either not familiar with their canines, or was not a terribly good wood-carver. The animal looks more like the outline of a cat than a jackal. I trail my fingers over my sternum absently.

Diego answers. "I like their fries."

Skittish

The fries, admittedly, *are* good. Saif and I sit in a booth and split a basket while Diego sits at the bar, sipping a glass of white wine, and talks to the bartender. He's a thin South Asian man with silver hair who seems to be tolerating Diego's presence at best. He nods or shakes his head tersely at Diego's statements, his eyes darting back and forth between the vampire and Saif.

Poor guy must be feeling pretty intimidated around these two.

Saif's eyes also keep darting back and forth like he's expecting someone as he nurses a dark beer. Or maybe he's just expecting trouble.

I sip my tonic water and observe him for a moment. "Is there any crime in New Camlann?" I ask, and he jumps, just a fraction of an inch, before he looks at me.

"Sure there is," he says. "Theft, vandalism, rampant jaywalking."

I squint at him; he's only sarcastic when he's stressed or flustered. "Anything worse than that?"

He looks around again. "Not really," he says absently. "The punishment for breaking any serious laws is permanent banishment from Tenazeryth. I've never seen it happen as long as I've been working for the King, not in New Camlann anyway. We've had a few ne'er-do-wells over the years, but they're never brave enough to come to the capital."

Ask him about those stories sometime, I note to myself. "So, what's wrong?" I ask.

He looks at me again, widening his eyes. "Hmm?"

"You're as skittish as a mouse at a cat convention."

He quirks a smile. "What exactly is a cat convention?"

I try to frown, but a smile breaks through. "I don't know, it was the first thing I thought of. Just answer the question." I toss a fry at him, and he grabs it in midair before popping it in his mouth.

He finishes chewing and sighs. "Sorry, I'm just worn out. Ready to get back home."

I nod, understanding. "You're an introvert, aren't you?" I hadn't had the chance to see him around strangers before, and now that I have, I can tell that he's rather out of his element.

He smiles sideways. "Guilty as charged."

We both look at Diego, who is chatting up a blonde white woman who just came in. She laughs too loudly at something he said, twirling her hair around one finger as she looks up at him.

I drum my fingers on the table. "And that one's never met a stranger, has he?" I ask.

Saif's mouth is tight. "Not likely. He can instantly charm anyone he puts his mind to."

Charm? I look between Saif and Diego again, then give myself a shake. Saif is only half present in this conversation; he isn't thinking about what he's saying.

I reach across the table and squeeze his hand. He finally tears his gaze from Diego and smiles at me, but it doesn't reach his eyes. We reach for a fry at the same time, and that seems to distract him sufficiently. He takes one and pushes the basket toward me.

I take the last couple of fries and pop them in my mouth just as Diego approaches the table.

"Ready?" He asks, looking around the tavern just like Saif had been doing. I don't understand why these two men, who are a combined thirteen feet of deadly muscle - and have supernatural abilities on top of that - are so jumpy in a simple tavern.

I glance around the crowded room, but no imminent danger presents itself to my untrained eyes. "Yeah," I say, an eyebrow raised. Diego leads the way out, and Saif follows behind me. I nod in thanks to the bartender, but he ignores me. His intense gaze follows Saif, and as Diego opens the door, and sunlight beams into the tavern, the light plays tricks with my vision, because his eyes seem to flash entirely black.

Saif places a hand protectively on my shoulder and leads me outside. His hand doesn't leave my shoulder until we make it back to the main street.

Diego looks back and forth as if deciding where to go. "Want to go to the bookstore, *Lobita*?" He asks over his shoulder. "King's treat." He rattles a pouch on his belt, and the coins inside clink together.

I gasp in delight, looking around for the store.

Saif chuckles. "I don't think we have enough room in the car, Vidales."

I glare at him in mock indignation, but Diego doesn't miss a beat. "Don't worry, Rahim, she'll have room. I was planning on making you walk back anyway."

Saif's mouth twists in annoyance at that, but I laugh, forgetting momentarily how messy things can get between us some days. Here, away from Arkenvale, the three of us together with greasy tavern food in our bellies, it's almost . . . *nice*.

We walk down a couple of blocks and enter a tall building that is full of various business suites on the ground floor. Diego leads us down a few hallways, then pushes open a door, and the smell of paper and ink hits me like the scent of an old friend moving in for a hug.

I enter and look around, one hand over my heart. It's not unlike any other bookstore, but then again, every bookstore is unlike every other. There are sections for fiction, non-fiction, romance, and more. As I look through titles, I recognize some, but many I do not.

"It's a mix of books from both dimensions," Saif says as he meanders after me, trailing his fingers along the shelves.

"That's so cool," I say breathlessly, looking back at him. I see Diego then, who is busy talking with the bookseller, a short, plus-sized Black man with curly hair and a short, curly beard who is dressed vaguely like a pirate. He's got a rumpled tan button-up on over baggy brown pants, and a red knit hat rests lightly on his head.

The man is shaking his head at something Diego had asked, and then his gaze shifts to me. His eyes are friendly, but guarded. He looks like he's waiting for Diego to seize hold of the front of his baggy shirt and shake him.

Diego doesn't look particularly angry to me, but then again, Diego doesn't need to *try* to look intimidating. The poor bookseller probably doesn't get many six-foot-nine vampires stalking through his store.

Saif turns to follow my gaze, then looks away from the bookseller quickly. The man's eyes narrow almost imperceptibly when he sees Saif's face. I raise an eyebrow at Saif, preparing to ask him if he knows the bookseller, but then a giant wooden sign catches my eye, and my train of thought completely derails.

I walk to the sign and look around at the section.

Fantasy.

It takes up half of the store. I'm going to cry tears of joy.

About an hour later, I walk to the counter, Saif trailing behind me, weighed down by a large stack of books. I had offered to carry them myself, but, ever the martyr, he insisted that he would do it. I had simply shrugged and handed him three books. He didn't look concerned until I sat the ninth book on the pile.

I lost count after that.

I've never spent someone else's money as an adult, but I push away the guilt that prods at the back of my mind. My father owes me thirty-one years' worth of birthday and holiday gifts, after all.

Diego appears at our side by the register, a small stack of his own books in hand. He raises a thick eyebrow at me as Saif sets the teetering tower on the counter, trying to make sure it doesn't topple to the ground.

I meet his gaze evenly. "What?"

He smirks. "Nothing, *Lobita*, nothing."

The bookseller is wearing a name tag that reads "Ousmane." I smile at him, and he returns it.

"Your store is gorgeous," I say.

He beams with pride. "Thank you," he replies in a thick Cockney accent.

"Do you travel back to Earth to get the books there?" I'm fascinated by the prospect that there were always Mages wandering around my dimension, and I had just never known it.

He hesitates, his eyes flicking to Diego for a fraction of a second before he answers. "Oh, no, I have suppliers. I practically never leave the city."

I just nod politely, trying to dispel any anxiety this man has because of Diego's hulking form. "Well, they do a wonderful job; your selection is fantastic. I can't wait to come back again."

He smiles at me again, but he still looks anxious. His gaze turns to Saif, who is looking pointedly at a sign for the cookbook section. "I look forward to it," Ousmane says. "I hope to see you again very soon."

Diego pulls several gold and silver coins out of his belt pouch and pays for the books.

Ousmane finally tears his gaze from Saif as he processes the payment, and hands Diego a cloth tote bag with our purchases.

Diego takes it with a nod in thanks and a curious glance between the bookseller and Saif before he turns on his heel and walks toward the exit.

I lean in close to Saif as we exit behind Diego. "Do you know him? Ousmane?"

He waits a beat too long to answer. "No. Not other than from the couple of times I've been here."

I frown. "He seemed to know you."

He shrugs and looks at me sincerely. "Maybe I remind him of someone. Someone dashing." He winks, and I giggle despite myself.

"Well, if that's the case, I guess I have to agree with him." I shove him gently, and he takes that hand and plants a kiss on the back of it, looking deep into my eyes as we walk. Heat creeps up my neck.

As we wind our way back through the hallways to the main exit, I rush up and snatch one of my books from out of the bag. I crack it open as we walk, and I'm immediately engrossed with the novel.

Diego looks at the cover. "What in the world is that?" He asks, mildly alarmed.

I hold the book up as I read so he can get a better look at it. There are two men on the cover locked in a passionate kiss. One of them is translucent and floats a foot or so off the ground.

"Ghost romance," I say simply, then lower the book again and read as I walk. I see him shake his head out of the corner of my eye, but when I flick my gaze to him, he's smirking.

Saif puts an arm around my waist, and we walk like that all the way back to the car. By the time we reach it, I have several new ideas of what he and I can do that night when I finally get that outfit off of him and onto my floor.

Secrets

"What was all that yesterday?" Diego barks at me as soon as the solarium door shuts behind him.

I don't glance up from the herb bed where I'm harvesting some mint for Eilidh's tea. The first rays of dawn are just starting to break in the sky, and I need to wake her up soon, but I'm running later than usual, having tossed and turned last night in her bed long after she fell asleep.

"I didn't catch that blonde's name, if that's what you're looking for," I say mildly.

I can see his scowl from the corner of my eye. "Don't play coy with me, Rahim."

"Afraid I'll beat you at your own game?"

He crosses to me in a few strides and looms over me menacingly. I snip the stalk of mint and calmly lay it to the side before snipping a second.

"The bartender and the bookseller," he growls. "What do you know about them?"

I adjust my glasses, still not looking at him. "I know Himesh isn't your type. He's nothing like that guy from last summer, or the brunette woman before him. Ousmane might be good for you though."

Diego hisses through his teeth. "If you're keeping secrets that will put the King in danger —"

I cackle as I set the herb snips in their designated spot on the edge of the raised garden bed. "Please, Vidales. We both know you don't give a fuck about the King. And I'm nearsighted, not blind. The greatest danger to *her* is *you*." I finally turn to him so I can relish the effect of my words.

He stills and his face goes blank, even though he knows I can see right through that mask. "If either of them were going to put her in jeopardy, I would have sliced them both in half before you could even unsheathe your claws."

He just glares at me, inhaling deeply through his nose. His irises are dull.

I smirk. *He'll break easily.* And I know just how to do it.

"Is this interrogation over?" I ask, taking a step closer until we're only inches apart. I tilt my head up, dragging my gaze from the faint shadow of a beard on his jaw to his rapidly dilating pupils. He inhales again, but tenses his jaw; he's fighting it. I need to get him the hell out of here before I run out of excuses to avoid answering his questions.

Desperate times.

"Or is there something else you wanted to do while you're here?" I whisper, placing my palm against his solar plexus.

His Adam's apple bobs quickly and his eyelids flutter as he looks down at me, but then he turns on his heel, stalks back out of the solarium, and slams the door behind him.

As soon as the door closes, I lean heavily into the garden bed and grip the wood tightly as I pant to catch my breath. He'll be in a foul mood for the rest of the day.

Sorry, Hyun-Joo. Why she puts up with him is far beyond me. I know she thinks he's her soulmate, but surely she could find someone else to share her life with.

The things we do for love.

A million memories swirl through my mind as I wait for my heart rate to slow; some from only a few months ago, but others are more than a decade old. Soon, though, I straighten, run a hand through my hair, and grab the mint stalks.

By the time I open Eilidh's door to a wave of lavender and nudge her awake - despite her playful protests and requests for five more minutes - Diego's blazing eyes are tucked firmly away at the back of my mind.

~ First Quarter ~

Weakness

"What's wrong, no fight left in you?" Diego's taunt rumbles into my ear and down my spine. He's got a firm hold on my braid, immobilizing my head. His knee is in my back, and I'm positive I'm going to pass out.

I growl with the effort of trying to move any part of my upper body, but he's got his whole weight on me, pressing me into the grass of the sparring circle. My lungs burn, screaming at me for oxygen.

"Just tap out and I'll go easy on you, darling." His sing-song tone is laced with condescension.

Like hell.

Rage bubbles up in my stomach as I flail my legs, but try as I might, I can't connect with him with anything more than negligible force. I squirm a few more times, then go completely limp.

He waits a moment before climbing off me, then he rolls me over, and I feel him kneeling over me. "*Obstinada,* I told you to tap — " He doesn't get the chance to finish his sentence.

I wrap my legs around one of his massive thighs and yank as hard as I can while simultaneously wrapping my arms around his thick neck.

For a split second, he actually looks surprised. Then he rolls onto his back, trying to kick me off with his free leg, and drag me off his torso, his claws twisting tightly into the fabric of my tank top. But every time he tugs on my upper body, my arms wrap more tightly around his neck.

"Tap out, and I'll go easy, darling," I bite out from between clenched teeth. Instead of getting a growl in response like I had expected, he chuckles in my ear.

I shiver.

His claws dig into my waist, and I brace myself, expecting it to hurt, but it doesn't. In fact, it feels — good? Delicious even, but I don't have time to process this revelation.

Diego bucks against my hips, trying to flip me up over his head, but I cling to him with all four of my limbs for dear life.

Finally, he releases me and stops his frantic movements. I wait a moment before risking changing my position to look at his face, but he isn't feigning a blackout like I had; he's just staring at me intensely, a strange look on his face that I can't place. He's stopped moving other than his haggard breathing that bobs me up and down on top of him like I'm being tossed on waves.

His eyes glitter like rubies, the light of the sun revealing colors and depths to them that I had never noticed before. Streaks of vermilion, maroon, and rose explode in his irises like the echoes of a supernova. His wide pupils are black holes; if I look much longer, I'll be drawn down into their depths until I'm lost forever.

I look at his thick lips, which are parted slightly, his fangs just visible. My arms loosen from around his neck, and now I'm just lying on top of him, our faces separated by mere inches. I can smell his aloe and cedar scent mixed with his sweat. Right now, we're not sparring in a yard full of Order members. We're alone in our own universe.

He puts a hand on my hip, then runs it up my back as lightning shoots through me, frying whatever systems in my brain control rational thought. I can't look away from him as my pulse quickens.

When his hand reaches the bare skin at the nape of my neck, I inhale sharply. He trails one claw along my skin, and I stop breathing entirely.

Then he grabs the base of my braid and uses it to yank me off of him, slamming me to the ground. I yelp loudly.

In the next instant, he's on top of me, his knees squeezing my hips tightly; his right hand moves from the base of my braid to twist into the hair on my left temple. He yanks my head to my left and digs his claws into my right shoulder, rubbing his thumb along my neck. His claw leaves an intoxicating sting in its wake.

I arch up against him, trying in vain to throw him off me, then dig my right hand into the fabric of his shirt in an attempt to pull him off that way. He grabs my right hand, laces his fingers through mine, and pins it to the ground beside my head as I let out a high-pitched groan of . . . frustration.

He leans down until we're nearly nose to nose, and I pant in his face. "If you know their weakness, exploit it," he needles me, his eyes lidded heavily. His breath smells like a floral tea; I can't focus enough to place it. His skin is glistening, and I can feel his sweat through my thin top.

I lick my lips, which are suddenly uncomfortably dry, and his eyelids flutter. "And what's my weakness?" I whisper, breathless.

"*No es obvia?*" He flashes a fang at me, and I have to look away. He leans down into the right side of my neck, and one of his fangs slides against my delicate skin.

I shiver again and gasp quietly.

"I win," he whispers in my ear.

And then, all at once, the weight of him is gone. It had all happened in a matter of seconds, though it had felt like an eternity.

I lie on the ground catching my breath while he walks away to go do pull-ups on a horizontal bar.

As I stand, my muscles protesting, I sense a piercing gaze boring into me, and I turn to see Hyun-Joo glaring at me from atop a balance beam. Because of course she is.

I flush, but I hadn't done anything wrong; I don't know what her problem is. We were just sparring like we've done dozens of times. Anger flares up in my stomach.

I turn and stride toward Saif, who has had his back to me for some time, practicing weaving thin ivy vines through a maze of fire that Martín is controlling.

He turns to me and smiles tenderly as I approach. "Hello, my d—"

I grab the front of his compression shirt and pull him into a rough kiss, knocking his glasses askew. His vines whip in all directions, smashing through walls of flame as he wraps his arms around me, pulling me into him.

I faintly register Martín yelping and dousing the flames, but I'm too focused on Saif to care, willing him silently to dig his claws - *nails, his nails* - into me as hard as he can.

He doesn't.

When we break apart, Hyun-Joo is no longer staring. She's working on slicing hay bales in half with her force fields, whipping them like discs. Diego hasn't stopped doing his pull-ups.

Martín takes a few steps back and bows deeply. "Don't let me keep you."

He gives me a wink and walks off, and I chuckle at his back.

Saif takes a deep breath and blinks at me, slightly dazed. "Hi," he says weakly, smiling sideways.

I lick my lips, lean against him, and put my hands up into his hair. "Are you done for the day?" I ask, my voice low.

His Adam's apple bobs. "I can be."

I smirk up at him. "How about we go get our showers before everyone else is done?" I look him up and down quickly. "Or maybe we should just get one?"

His eyebrows raise in amusement. "I'm always on board for conserving water."

We do not, in fact, end up conserving any water.

251

Learning

"Eilidh," Saif moans my name as he throws his head back and grips the side of the tub tightly. Steam swirls around us throughout the small, enclosed space.

Despite the water from the shower splashing loudly around me against the bottom of the deep, wide tub, if there's anyone else in the bathroom outside my shower stall, they might be able to hear him.

The thought makes me move faster, and he curses rapidly in Arabic. I remove my right hand from his shaft and wrap both arms around his muscular thighs to hold him steady as my head bobs between his legs.

I take his cock as deep into my mouth as I can and moan loudly, hoping the vibrations will shoot through him.

They do.

"Oh fuck, stop, wait, *fuck*." He grabs a fistful of my wet hair and holds me tightly. The tip of his cock rests against my tongue as he pulls back as far as he can, and I grin wide and flick around it.

He pants desperately and releases my head as if he didn't realize he had even grabbed it. "You're going to make me come."

I dig my nails gently into his thighs and lick my lips in what I hope is a seductive manner. "What do you think I'm trying to do?" I ask as I rake my gaze from his fluttering eyes down over his glistening abs.

"Yeah, but I don't want to do it in your mouth," he explains.

I pout up at him. "Why?"

His eyes widen. "Do — do you want me to?"

I lean forward so that some of my wet hair falls across my face, then slowly lick from his base to his tip, fluttering my eyelashes at him as I do so. I'm pulling out all the stops, and it works.

"Holy fuck," he mutters dizzily.

"Is that enough of an answer for you?" I tease, then plant a few kisses on his wet thigh.

"Yeah," he breathes.

"Good." I take him back into my mouth and suck with renewed vigor. He stretches his long legs out and braces himself against the other side of the tub, still clutching desperately to this side with one hand.

He puts his other hand back into my hair, but doesn't grip it hard like he had a moment ago. *I bet I can make him.*

I moan loudly against him and move in steady, deep motions.

His thighs begin quivering, and there's the delicious tugging that I was looking for.

"Oh fuck, Eilidh, I —" He cuts off and grunts heavily as his cock begins pulsing in my mouth. I keep that steady pace as his cum hits the back of my throat, and continue until he's done.

Once he stops pulsing, I grab his shaft and slowly give him one long last lick before I swallow.

He slides down into the tub, and the water from the showerhead quickly soaks his curls as he moves to sit with his back against the far end of the tub.

I shift to straddle him and smile at him tenderly as I push some of them off his forehead. "We should probably actually take our showers now."

His brow furrows, and he wraps his arms around my waist to pull me tightly against him. "What about you?"

"I'm fine," I say automatically.

He looks at me dubiously. "If you *really* don't want to, then okay. But if there's something you want from me, I need you to tell me."

He cups my cheek, and I lean into his hand. "I can't read your mind, but I *want* to please you, Eilidh. I want to make *you* feel as good as you make *me* feel. I don't want you to feel bad for asking for something for yourself."

He pulls me in and kisses me firmly, and my heart flutters. He searches my eyes for permission, and once he finds it, puts a hand between my legs, and I moan as he pushes two fingers inside me. He licks water from my neck, and I shudder.

"Well," I say quietly, then whimper as his thumb begins circling my clit. "I really like it when you pull my hair."

He immediately tangles his other hand into my hair and tugs. "Like this?"

"Harder," I breathe.

His smile warms me more than the water cascading around us ever could. He pulls harder, and I cry out softly. "Too hard?" He asks.

"Just right," I purr.

He exhales shakily and curls his fingers deep inside me, finding just the right spot.

He kisses along my neck, and I moan in his ear. "Anything else?"

The only other thing he could do to make this better is something that I will absolutely *not* ask of him. I believe that he wants to make me feel good, but there is no manner in which I can ask him to be rough with me, to bite me and dig his nails into me, and not make his mind immediately go to someone else.

I've had plenty of rough sex over the years, and have enjoyed being bitten and marked long before coming here. But there's still no way I can ask Saif and not make it sound like *he's* not the one I really want.

It would hurt him, even though I wouldn't mean it to, and that is not something I'm willing to do.

"No, this is perfect," I whisper. "You're perfect."

And he is.

He kisses me deeply, and between his lips, his fingers, and his tugging on my hair, my pleasure soon crashes through me just like the water falling around us.

"Saif," I moan desperately in his ear.

He exhales heavily. "See? I can learn." He chuckles as I collapse onto his shoulder.

"Happy to teach," I say shakily.

When he removes his fingers from me, and I lower myself onto his lap, his erection presses against me. I widen my eyes at him, and he licks his lips.

"You're so beautiful, Eilidh." He pushes my wet hair out of my face. "And those sounds you make drive me fucking wild." We both chuckle, and I reach down to stroke him.

"I like the sounds you make, too," I say, and kiss his neck.

He moans softly as his cock grows in my hand. "Yeah, like that," I whisper.

He's a fast learner. As I shift and come down onto his erection, he moans in my ear, and then makes dozens of small noises as I ride him, slow and steady, gripping hard into the side of the tub.

It doesn't take long for us both to come again, and he moans against my mouth and tugs just right on my hair as he pulses inside me and I clench around his girth.

When Saif finally exits my shower stall to go to his own and actually get clean, I lie on the bottom of the deep tub for a moment, just thinking about him, and us, and how close we've grown despite the fact that we haven't even known each other for six months.

I think about how much I don't deserve him, and how much I may *never* deserve him. But really, who could? Who could *possibly* be good enough for him? I also think about how I know now that I'm *absolutely* falling in love with him, and though that scares the hell out of me, it also feels so *right*.

There's only one thing that doesn't feel right, one thing that chills me to my core, and causes the voice of the critic in my head to rise to a roaring crescendo.

Shut up. I turn the water of the shower to a scalding temperature, hoping to burn the voice out of my head, but it's no use. I can hear it screaming at me even as I stand under the showerhead, allowing the water to pool in my ears and wash away the guilty tears that sting my cheeks.

He isn't the only one you're falling for, is he?

~ Waxing Gibbous ~

Rooftop

I grab Saif's hand as I reach the top of the ladder, and he pulls me through the open window. I step up shakily onto the glass.

He flashes an encouraging smile. "You're okay, trust me. I've got you."

I smile back and stand a bit more firmly. "I can officially say I've gone through the glass ceiling now, so that's cool."

He snorts, and gestures toward the stone roof of Arkenvale behind us. "You continue to impress, my dear. Now how about we get you on solid ground."

He holds my hand as we walk to the large square area of stone. I squint at the tops of the East and West Towers; the setting sun glints brilliantly off the glass.

But the majority of the space on Arkenvale's roof is occupied by several large solar panels, and a giant metal cylinder that reminds me of a silo.

"What is that?" I ask, pointing to it.

"Water tank," he says, rubbing a thumb across the back of my hand.

I make a sound of understanding, and he grins at me mischievously. "Can I trust you to keep a secret?" He teases.

"Absolutely not," I deadpan.

His eyes crinkle at the corners as he kisses my forehead. "Okay then, tell the entire Order if you must." He pulls an acorn from his pocket and drops it at our feet. "This is my favorite spot in the world."

I glance down at the acorn and open my mouth to ask him what he means, but I don't get the chance. An oak tree springs forth from the acorn, and we're both caught up on a wide branch. I squeeze my eyes shut and cling to him as we're hoisted at least thirty feet into the air. A shriek escapes my throat, and I think it's fear at first. It isn't until he laughs that I realize that it's exhilaration.

I open my eyes as the tree gradually stops its ascent, and I exhale slowly in awe. He's got one arm wrapped protectively around me, and the other holding onto the trunk of the tree, but as I catch my breath, he releases me, and we sit down with our backs against the bark.

The view from here is breathtaking. We're facing West, looking out over the inlet of Nabeyha Lake, and I can just see the top of New Camlann's wall over one of the rolling hills. The water of the lake looks like molten lava.

"There's nothing better than a fiery sunset," I whisper. "They're always so unbelievably beautiful."

Saif gently tilts my chin toward him. "Yeah," he says quietly, looking into my eyes. "Beautiful."

He pulls me into his lap, and soon we're far too distracted with one another to even glance at the setting sun.

Vines

"You're blushing like a schoolgirl," I tease as we climb back down the ladder into the solarium.

"I am not," he says, turning so I can't see his burning cheeks. Unfortunately for him, moonlight is streaming into the solarium from above, and I can still see him perfectly. And though I can't hear the moon like I can when she's full, I know what she's trying to relay to me. *He certainly is.*

"Saif," I say gently. "We don't have to. It was just a suggestion, and I wanted to be honest with you, like you told me to do. But if domming isn't your thing, that's okay."

He turns back to me. "I didn't say it wasn't my thing," he says hastily. "I just didn't know that it's something you liked."

I bite my lip, hoping it looks seductive. "So, is that a yes?"

He shivers slightly and leans down to kiss me, cupping my cheek as he pulls back. "Absolutely."

Heat blooms in my stomach, and spreads down between my legs.

Saif kisses me again, and pushes me up against the back right wall of the solarium, a little harder than he normally would. It isn't quite as hard as I'd like, but it's a step. I'll give him time.

He slowly unbuttons the dark blue blouse that I had put on specifically so he could take it off. With each button he frees, he kisses my newly exposed skin, traveling farther and farther down to my navel. I arch into him, moaning quietly. I'm not wearing a bra underneath, and he squeezes my breasts as the blouse falls to the floor.

"Take my shirt off," he commands when he rises again.

I pluck his glasses off his face and set them on the closest shelf I can reach. I tug his black V-neck shirt over his head and run my hands down his chiseled chest.

He leans in to kiss my neck as he unzips my black jeans, and he pulls them to the ground, kissing down my body once more.

Every kiss he plants gets me increasingly excited. I'm practically panting by the time he tosses my jeans to the side. I reach for his belt, but he grabs my wrists to stop me. I look at him quizzically, and his eyes glint mischievously.

"I thought you wanted me in charge for tonight?" He smiles sideways.

My stomach flutters, and I lick my lips. "I do."

He runs a hand over my hair, twisting a few strands between his fingers. "And I get to do what I want with you?" His gaze darkens hungrily.

He's playing this role well. "Yes," I breathe.

He leans over and props an arm on the wall above me, and I shrink down under him, grinning idiotically as my heart hammers against my chest.

"Then there's no need to rush, *Lahabi*."

He waves his hands, and vines from several nearby plants shoot out toward me and snake around my ankles and wrists. I let out a small yelp, but he puts his mouth over mine to silence me.

The vines pull my limbs just enough so that I'm spread wide in an "X" formation. He pulls back and looks at me, and all the darkness is gone from his eyes.

"Is this okay?" He asks nervously.

I breathe a soft laugh. "It's *far* more than okay," I say huskily.

"And you remember the word you'll say if it's not?" He asks, still concerned.

I grin sideways at him. "Dahlia," I say firmly.

He hesitates another moment, but then nods. "Okay." He clears his throat and shakes himself like he's getting into character before stepping onto a stage. When he opens his eyes, he looks hungry again.

It shoots a carnal urge through me that I've never felt before. Desire pulses between my legs, and I tug against the vines as if I would be able to break free.

He quirks an eyebrow. "There'll be no getting out of that, my dear. Not until I say you can."

He puts a hand between my legs and circles my clit with his fingers. "You're already soaked for me. You can't wait to feel me inside you, can you?" His voice reverberates in my ear.

I moan softly. He's *really* good at this.

He removes his hand, then twists it back and forth, commanding the vines to snake their way further up my legs, all the way to my hips. They squeeze me delightfully, digging into my soft skin.

Saif backs up and admires his work. I can see the effect it has on him through his jeans. He spends several minutes running his hands up and down my body, planting kisses at random. I shiver and moan with each one.

Then he waves a hand again, and my wrists are temporarily freed. My arms fall to my side, but then the vines wrap around them from a new angle. In another second, they've bound my wrists behind my back, twisting up to my elbows, pushing my breasts out.

The vines around my legs pull me to the floor, and force me to kneel at Saif's feet, though my knees hover above the floor for just a second before they land, so as not to hurt me.

Another vine winds under my chin and pushes up gently, tilting my head back so that I'm looking up at him. My pussy is so wet that I'll be surprised if I don't start dripping onto the stone floor soon.

"You look fucking amazing like this," he says shakily.

I rake my eyes up and down his body. "You look pretty fucking good from this angle, too," I say, my voice thick with lust.

He unzips his jeans and pulls his cock out of his boxer briefs in one smooth motion. With a twist of his fingers, the vines raise me to just the right height, and he shoves himself into my mouth, then he braces himself against the wall, moaning as he pumps back and forth.

I moan too around his girth, and he shudders. I close my eyes and focus on the sensations shooting through me, when a thick vine begins rubbing up and down across my clit, curving with my body, and I moan louder against him.

He doesn't shush me like he has before, he just continues thrusting steadily, his vine bringing my desire to a fever pitch. I come undone not long after.

He pulls himself out of my mouth and backs up, panting heavily, his hands on his hips, and I shake with the last ripples of my orgasm.

He waves a hand at a nearby square table, and the various potted plants spring to life and walk themselves off the table, coming to rest safely on the ground. Even in my distracted state, I marvel at his power.

Then he turns his dark eyes on me once again, and I'm instantly engrossed in him. He tilts his head to one side and strokes his beard. "I'm not sure if I should make you come on your stomach, or your back. You're so pretty in both positions."

I bite my lip as he looks at me. Finally, when the anticipation is about to break me, he waves his hand, and the vines lift me toward the table, bending me over it with my ass facing him, my hands still bound.

The vines around my legs release me for just a moment, then wrap around my ankles and the legs of the table, spreading me wide. I pull against them, but they hold me fast.

Saif approaches me from behind, and squeezes my ass with one hand while running the other up my back to tangle into my hair. I shiver in delight and lean into his touch.

He trails his nails back down my spine, then kneels behind me, kissing up and down my thighs, putting his mouth as close to my pussy as he can without actually kissing it.

"You're such a tease," I breathe out.

"And *you're* so anxious for me," he says, laughing seductively. He runs a finger across my soaking entrance to illustrate his point, and I moan.

Finally, he puts his mouth right where he knows I want it, and I bite back a loud whimper. His vines hold me in place as he eats me out from behind, running his tongue all around me, his close-cut, velvety beard tickling my clit and making me jump a million little times at the sensation.

"I'm close," I whisper into the table a few minutes later. He chuckles against my clit, and it rumbles up through my center. Fireworks explode in my head.

"Perfect," he says.

Then the vines are moving again, and they flip me over onto my back with a soft *thump*, and I'm tied down once more, all four of my limbs stretched out and held fast to the legs of the table.

Saif looks down at me for a moment like he can't quite comprehend what he's seeing. He tugs on his cock a few times, groaning softly.

"You are *so* fucking beautiful," he says, sounding almost lightheaded.

I can't think of any witty reply, so I run my gaze up and down his statuesque form. He's certainly *way* out of my league under traditional standards, but not once has he made me feel like it. He has only ever treated me like he's lucky to share my space at all.

It's mind-boggling.

Finally, my brain thinks up a response to his compliment. "Then show me what I do to you."

He looks dazed for a moment, like my words do something to him that he wasn't aware they could, then he just smiles at me and leans over to give me a deep kiss.

I kiss him back, drunk with pleasure. I pull at the vines, wishing that I could dig my fingers into him, but the fact that I can't only heightens my desire. I moan his name against his mouth, and he rumbles his pleasure back at me.

He straightens and shoves his erection as deep into me as he can, and covers my mouth with his hand just as I release a loud cry.

He thrusts in and out of me, hitting my G-spot, and I come undone in a matter of moments. I bite back a loud whimper as pleasure crashes over me in waves. His thrusting increases to a frenzied pace, then he pulls out and his cum shoots up over my stomach.

When he's done, the vines go slack and fall to the floor, and so does he. He sits down hard, panting. "Holy fuck," he breathes between gasps. "That was . . . intense."

I smile up at the glass ceiling as my orgasm subsides. "Got anything I can clean up with?" I ask.

"Yeah, let me grab a towel." He stands and looks around, then swears under his breath. "Shit. There isn't one in here. I'll be right back." He pulls his boxer briefs and jeans back on quickly and exits the solarium.

I lie on the table and look up at the gibbous moon above me, drifting hazily toward her apex. Maybe it's a good thing that I can't hear her right now. She might be scandalized. I smirk at her while I wait.

He returns a few moments later and hands me the towel, then once I move, he picks the plants up from the ground and places them back on the table. He must be zapped of energy if he's doing it by hand.

"So, did you like that?" I ask as I pull my clothes back on.

He thinks for a moment, then smiles at me sheepishly as he twists a pot back and forth until it's perfectly in place. "Honestly, yeah. I didn't think I would, at least not as much as I did. But it was fun."

I smile back at him. "Good. And for the record, you're pretty good at it. Are you sure you haven't done that before?" I laugh lightly, though I'm genuinely curious.

He blushes and clears his throat. "Well . . . I have, but I was, shall we say, on the other side of the equation."

I waggle my eyebrows at him. "I always knew those nursing major girls would be kinky."

He blushes again, rubbing the back of his neck. "I um, wouldn't know. *He* was an engineering major."

My eyes widen slightly. "Oh." I cup a hand to his cheek and he looks at me nervously. "If he broke your heart, just give me a name, and I'll go kick his ass when I'm done with Bleddyn," I say jokingly. Or, maybe only a little bit jokingly.

Saif's booming laugh has some kind of direct connection to my nervous system; I can literally feel warmth travel through my body at the sound of his joy.

"No need. Actually, I may have broken his." He sighs. "I was young and, truth be told, flighty. Not ready to be tied down. And he was talking about having kids." He looks somewhat horrified at the idea.

I chuckle with understanding as I stretch up to kiss him quickly.

"Well if you ever wanna look him up again, I'm always willing to share," I tease.

He rolls his eyes, smiling wide.

"Now go to your room," I command jokingly. "It's way past your bedtime, soldier."

We exit the solarium and he gives me one last long kiss at his door before he enters his room and shuts the door softly behind him.

I walk around the balcony to my room, feeling light as a feather. I gather a pair of pajamas and head to the bathroom for a quick shower, then come back and snuggle into bed with a romance novel.

The main character in this story is sucked through time to the Britain of more than fifteen hundred years ago, and ends up becoming a handmaiden to Guinevere herself.

I fall asleep just after her heart flutters when she catches Arthur's eye for the first time as he's taking a drink of wine from his simple golden chalice.

~ Fifth Full Moon ~

Ravine

This man is literally trying to kill me. I sit back on my haunches and glare at him as I scream my thoughts, annoyed for the millionth time that my lupine telepathy hasn't kicked in yet. I know it normally takes a long time, but I need him to know *now* how outrageous he's being.

Ludicrous, the moon concurs as she wraps me protectively in her beams; he's been outvoted. I flatten my ears back and utter a low growl to convey the message.

We're on the edge of a wide ravine deep in the forest, and though the stream below is innocent-looking enough, it's at least a thirty-foot drop. Probably more.

"You'll be fine." Diego holds the handle of his homemade rope swing out toward me.

I look back at him evenly. *Because I'm not doing it. I've seen this movie. Literally. No way in any of the nine hells am I swinging on that.*

My thoughts fall on deaf ears. Or deaf . . . temporal lobe? Actually, I don't know how exactly the telepathy works. I'm also not positive that's the correct lobe. I make a mental note to look it up in the library tomorrow, since I will not be perishing in this fucking ravine tonight.

I shake out my coat, then turn and begin to pad back to the path that brought us here, and Diego sighs behind me. That's fine; he can be disappointed in me all he wants.

At least I'll be alive.

"I guess you like it the hard way."

My vision flashes red. I turn to growl at him, but instead, it turns into a yelp as all four of my paws leave the ground. For one wild moment, I wonder if I've taken flight, but then I realize Diego has hoisted me up over one of his massive shoulders.

He grips his claws tightly into me. "Don't let go."

I howl in terror as he runs toward the ravine and jumps.

My howl cuts off when we're in midair. There is absolutely nothing between us and the rocks far below. We start to descend.

He's going to kill us both.

Then his free hand catches the handle of the rope, and we're swinging across to the other side. A moment later, we land on the opposite side of the ravine, tumbling together in a mad tangle of limbs.

When we finally come to a stop, he rolls onto his back, gasping for air. I'm shivering like a furry leaf, but I crawl to him to make sure he hasn't punctured a lung on a rock or something, even though that would serve him right.

Fucking bastard.

But as I reach him and gain enough control of my muscles to stand shakily, I realize that he's only gasping for air because he's silently laughing his fucking head off. Tears roll down his cheeks, and he wipes them away. I bark at him, but that just makes him wheeze harder.

I look for a spot on his suit to grab with my teeth. I'm going to drag him back to the edge of the ravine - by his neck if I have to - and toss him off the edge.

Finally, his wheezing subsides enough that he can form words. "Oh. My. God. Your *howl* when we jumped." He laughs again. If my fur weren't already red, I swear it would be turning crimson now with embarrassment. *He's laughing* at *me. Of course he is.*

I huff through my nose and swat him with a heavy paw. *Fuck you, I thought we were going to die!*

He pushes himself up to his elbows and snorts. "That fall wouldn't kill us. We're both super durable, remember?"

I freeze. *Wait, what?*

"Well, I mean it wouldn't tickle, but we'd be fine after —" He cuts off and turns to me, eyes wide. "Wait, what?"

Holy shit.

"Holy *shit!*"

You can hear me?

"I can hear you!" He stands up, runs his hands through his shaggy hair, and then puts them on his waist. "How are you doing that? This is only your fifth change." He smiles widely at me. It's so strange to see that expression on his face.

I shake my shaggy head. *Fuck if I know.*

"Maybe you just needed to yell at me *that* badly." He's still smiling at me, and it's positively blinding.

I haven't ever seen him smile this much. It lights up his entire face, and his chiseled features transform from sharp and frightening to hauntingly beautiful. *He looks like a fallen angel.*

I think for one frightening moment that he might be able to hear the thoughts that I don't specifically direct at him, but he doesn't react, and I take that as a good sign.

He suddenly frowns, and my heart sinks. "That was pretty much the last skill you needed to get control of, other than shifting at will, but we can't wait for that. Tomorrow I'll go to Auberon and let him know that your training is complete."

What about my human *training? What about my dagger?*

He shakes his head absently. "You're great with your dagger," he says simply.

I certainly don't feel like I am.

My stomach clenches. *But what if I'm not ready?*

He steps closer to me, puts his hand under my muzzle, and tilts my head up so that I'm looking directly into his eyes. "You are."

Alive

If I tell her I love her
*   Would she run away with me?*
*   Would she be happy?*
Could I keep her safe?

I stare down at the page, my pen poised over it. The questions sneer back at me. I already know the answer to all of them.

No. She wouldn't, and I couldn't ask that of her.

No. How could she be? She's happy *now* — with *him.*

No. Not without making her hate me, anyway.

I fling the pen down on the desk with a growl. *Fuck.*

Writing has always helped me work out my thoughts. Poems, articles, anything really, and since she got here, it's been the only outlet I've had. The only thing I can bare my soul to without causing the world to implode.

But she's scattered my thoughts to the wind; I can't even focus on the simple act of putting pen to paper right now.

I push myself away from my desk and pace back and forth around my room. I've worn a path in the rug by the time a summons flies under my door like a paper bird.

I grimace at the thought. *Fucking birds.*

I sigh, exit my room, and head for the East Tower to meet with the

King.

My decision is made. She can hate me if she wants.
At least she'll be alive.

~ Waning Gibbous ~

Choices

By the time I wake on the day before our departure, everyone is in a flurry of motion preparing for our mission. Throughout the day, a pile of supplies gradually forms by the door. There are bed rolls, a pot and pan that each fold up for easy storage, numerous cans of food, and several first-aid kits.

It reminds me of the time when I was seven and my mom had gotten the bright idea that she was going to take me camping for a long weekend. She had neglected, of course, to remember to pack anything that we would actually need, and so we drove back home late that night, tired, hungry, and angry. I shake off the memory and head to my room to double-check my backpack.

At one point in the afternoon, Valentina knocks on my door. She enters holding a suit not unlike the one Diego wears during full moons, except mine is a deep, regal emerald rather than royal blue.

"That's beautiful," I breathe. "Where did you get it?"

"I made it," she says simply.

I gape at her. "You *make* these?"

She makes a dismissive gesture, but there's a gleam of pride in her eye. "I like designing and making clothes. I made a few pieces of yours too, while you were still out."

I shake my head at her in awe. "You're amazing."

She hugs me and practically floats out of my room.

I smile after her, then fold the suit into my pack tenderly.

It's early evening when Diego, who has been meeting with Auberon all day, opens my door without so much as a knock, ignoring my indignant yelp.

"Emergency meeting," he barks before he turns and walks back out of my room, leaving the door wide open.

I follow him across the balcony and down the spiral staircase without protest; something in his expression had rattled me. *Something's wrong.*

We enter the East Tower, and I stop dead in my tracks at the sight of Saif, who is standing over Auberon, roaring at him. I can't believe my eyes. Have I stepped into another dimension? Or . . . *another* another dimension?

"Over my dead body are you sending her off with him alone!" He snarls. "That was *never* the plan! You can't do that. Not again."

I've never heard him like this, so loud and vicious. He sounds, for the first time, like the deadly weapon that he is. A shiver runs down my spine before I can suppress it.

His eyes glint dangerously, just like the scimitar at his hip, but Auberon doesn't blink; he merely takes a sip of wine from his chalice, ignoring Saif entirely. As he sets the chalice down, Diego slams the door, and everyone falls silent.

Saif turns and glares at Diego like he's going to vault over the table and strangle him. His mouth is twisted in rage, and his chest rises and falls rapidly.

Auberon gestures to Diego and me. "Sit."

I do so quickly, and Diego marches to his chair between my father and Hyun-Joo. Saif's eyes follow him the entire way as he lowers himself stiffly into his seat.

Diego pointedly ignores him.

I glance between the two men, wondering what in the hell is going on, when my father speaks.

He steeples his fingers. "Bastet is on the offensive."

I frown, trying to remember why that name sounds familiar, and then it dawns on me. "A nuisance for another time," I say quietly, recalling his words when he had spoken of this guerrilla leader, months ago.

He grimaces. "Indeed. Unfortunately, that time is extremely near."

"So what do we do?" I ask.

He sighs heavily. "We must decide whether the Order should be divided, and handle both problems at once, or remain intact, and deal with them back-to-back. Bastet cannot be ignored long. It seems she has cobbled together quite the little operation of Mongrels, and is moving to strike Lisanor. We cannot afford for her to take it."

I think quickly back on the maps of Tenazeryth. Lisanor is a relatively small town about a hundred miles Southwest of Arkenvale.

Something else about his sentence needles me, but I can't quite put my finger on what. Something that sounded contradictory, but before I can pinpoint it, my thoughts are scattered to the wind.

He continues. "But, if we don't strike at Bleddyn now, there's no telling how much longer it will be until we can find him again. I fear he may not stay in the Cuhloch Forest any longer with Bastet marching through the South. He'll take the opportunity to sew more chaos. You may not get another chance to get your justice for some time if you don't act now."

My thoughts whirl, and anger bubbles up inside me. I realize for the first time how much I *need* to bring Bleddyn down. I've known this entire time that killing him was my mission, but fear has dominated anger throughout my training.

That anger flares up inside me now, bright and hot. Bleddyn took my life from me, and now that he's in my sights, I'll be damned if he gets away with it. "We have to go after Bleddyn," I say with a furious conviction.

But Diego speaks at the same time as me, and our words coalesce together in perfect harmony – until they don't.

"We have to go after Bastet," he says, with his "And that's *final*" tone that makes me want to slap him.

Saif visibly relaxes, if only a fraction. It seems he wasn't expecting Diego to be on his side.

And neither was I.

I widen my eyes at the vampire incredulously. "What, and just let that monster go? This is exactly what you've been training me for."

He narrows his eyes at me. "Bastet needs to be dealt with."

"Bleddyn it is," my father says mildly.

I can hear Diego's teeth grind as he glances at Hyun-Joo as though looking for confirmation that he isn't hearing things.

She, too, looks taken aback by the King's disregard of his best paladin's wishes.

He glances back at my father from the corner of his eye for just a split second, and his lip curls in contempt, but he doesn't argue any further.

"Fine," he bites. "But Bastet still needs to be stopped." He points one of his long fingers at me sharply. "You and I will take care of Bleddyn, and the others will head to Lisanor."

Saif, whose spine is ramrod straight once more, and is gripping *Dhabiha's* hilt under the table, judging by his tense bicep, cackles derisively. "I don't think so."

Diego finally turns to him, his blazing eyes narrowed to slits, and his jaw tense.

They may have been on the same side a moment ago, but this is a different argument entirely. One they've been having for a decade.

"She's ready," he growls.

"She's not," Saif spits back. "She hasn't had enough time; she needs all of us to have a chance."

I flinch at that, but he doesn't notice.

Valentina looks at me from the corner of her eye, frowning.

He continues. "Where she goes, I go. I'm not letting you get her killed just because you want to make up for your past mistakes." Saif's words are like acid.

Diego rises from his chair all at once, and his claws immediately elongate and dig into the lacquered wood of the table. "You have *no idea* what you're —"

But Auberon's patience has finally worn thin. He smacks the table with an open palm, and his chalice rattles against the wood.

I flinch at the noise.

"*Enough.*" The room goes still other than Saif's and Diego's shoulders rising and falling with their heavy breathing. "Eilidh," my father barks, and I jump.

The irate look in his eye chills me to the bone for a moment, and I flinch back involuntarily, but then he blinks, and it's back to its normal, kind glow.

His tone softens as well. "I have come to value your input."

The familial bond lies in the air between us like an invisible string, tying us together.

"If you feel that you need everyone to go after Bleddyn, then that is what you'll do. We will just have to deal with Bastet quickly after that." He falls silent, waiting for me to make a decision.

Diego can bite his tongue no longer. "Your Majesty, with all due respect, she has no place making a decision like this. She and I can do this alone."

He motions to Saif. "Besides, if he accompanies her on this mission now, they will both be emotionally compromised. It would put us all in more danger."

I glare at him, wishing I had gotten a good swipe at him two nights ago while I still had my wolf claws. He doesn't look back at me.

Hyun-Joo speaks quietly, frowning at the table. "And we wouldn't want anyone on this mission to be emotionally compromised."

Diego closes his eyes in frustration.

My stomach twists, and I don't take any longer to think about it. I stand and face Diego, and when I speak, my voice is steady.

"Like it or not, this is my choice," I say. "It was *my* life."

He doesn't move a muscle as he waits for my next words.

"I choose Saif."

Something flicks across Diego's eyes that I can't quite discern. Anger, certainly, but something more than that. He almost looks . . . hurt?

I blink rapidly and turn to my father. "I choose everyone. We go after Bleddyn."

The King nods. "So be it. You will all go, and Bastet is our next top priority. You'll just have to hurry."

I raise my chin defiantly at Diego.

He looks at me for just one more second before he turns on his heel, walks out of the room, and slams the door behind him. His eyes in that second had been full of disappointment.

No one moves as we wait to see what Auberon will do.

"Dismissed," he says finally, glaring at the door.

We leave.

Soulmates

Saif brushes me off outside of the East Tower with a quick squeeze on my shoulder. "I've got an errand to run. I'll see you later." His eyes are still blazing dangerously as he exits the front door, and I let him go with a silent nod. He needs time to cool down, and frankly, so do I.

After I splash some water on my face in the bathroom, I trudge to my room and slump down on the bed, thinking about the meeting. I press my face into my hands and groan loudly.

"We need to talk," a voice says from the empty chair by my desk. I don't think I could have jumped higher if I was in my wolf form. Hyun-Joo materializes out of thin air as I hold my chest, willing my heart to slow down.

"I know they say 'fight or flight,' but I don't think the flight is supposed to be a vertical one," she comments dryly.

"What." I gasp. "The fuck."

She blinks at me. "We. Need. To talk," she repeats.

"Yeah well, I tried that already, remember?" I stand and reach for my door, ready to pull it open and fling her out if I have to. Not that I'm sure I could; she's infinitely stronger than she looks.

"You're in love with Diego."

My blood runs cold and I stop dead in my tracks, mid-stride. My mouth hardly moves when I answer her.

"That's ridiculous." It comes out strangled.

She stands and strides to me in one second. Her abrupt motion snaps the spell I'm under, and I back away from her until she has me backed against a wall.

I am getting *very* tired of being backed against walls.

Though the top of her head barely reaches my chin, she somehow makes me feel like the smaller one as she glares up at me.

"It's painfully obvious."

My mouth works silently for a moment, but her scathing look puts an end to it. I expect her to slap me. To threaten me. To ask me what burial arrangements I'd like for after she dispatches me.

A beat passes.

"Why are you toying with him?" She snaps. "Either fuck him or don't, but stop leading him on."

I literally tilt my head and shake it, thinking perhaps I have water from my earlier shower trapped in my ear canal. When no water reveals itself, I have no choice but to look at her incredulously.

"*What?*" It comes out as a ridiculous squeak.

She crosses her arms over her chest. "You're stringing him along one day, practically making out in his bedroom, and in the training yard, all while you're fucking Saif? Are you just using Saif to hurt Diego? *Why?*"

My head spins. "Making ou — *what?*" I am hopelessly lost. "My feelings for Saif have nothing to do with Diego! And what the fuck is this conversation?" I throw my arms in the air. "Diego is *yours!*"

At that, she puts her hands on her hips, throws her head back, and cackles. "Oh my *god*, how are you so clueless?"

I've reached my limit with this woman. "Look, I don't understand anything you're saying, so you either need to explain what you mean *really* fucking fast, or get. The fuck. Out." I clench my teeth as I spit the last few words.

She takes a step back, steeples her fingers in front of her face, and takes a deep breath. "You know what? You and I got off on a *really* bad foot, and I promised not to interfere, but we don't have any more time for you to figure this out on your own. I'm not confident we'll live long enough for that," she mumbles.

I'm not sure if that's supposed to mean that danger is frighteningly close, or that I'm hopelessly stupid. Or both. Either way, I cross my arms, stand as straight as I can, and do my best to be intimidating as I look down at her.

She is very much *not* intimidated. She looks back at me evenly for a moment, then rolls her eyes and walks back to sit in the desk chair. She points at my bed wordlessly. I wait a beat, grinding my teeth, then sit down heavily on it.

She hangs her head and rubs a hand across her forehead, her dark hair hanging in glossy curtains for a moment. If she weren't so goddamn frustrating, I'd be far too distracted by the smell of her citrus shampoo wafting at me to be mad at her. But she is, in fact, *so* goddamn frustrating.

"Okay," she says finally. "Here's the rundown. Diego and I came to the Order around the same time, about twelve years ago. I was only here a few months before the King showed up with him one day out of the blue. Diego was completely out of it, bleeding out all over the entrance hall. Saif was barely able to keep him alive."

I didn't know any of this, but I nod, pushing down my curiosity for the rest of that story. Now is not the time, but hopefully someday I'll get to hear the details.

She continues. "He had a rough time getting acclimated to his new life." Her voice is tight. "The details are his to tell, but just trust me on that. But he's, well, him, so within six months, Auberon made him the leader of the Order. Then, six months later, he fell in love. Head over heels, instantly. As soon as he first laid eyes on her. And he hasn't let himself get close to anyone else since."

She sounds sad, but not jealous like I would have expected. She pauses, and I decide to fill in what little knowledge I have regarding Diego's past.

"Saif told me there was a woman who had been attacked by a werecat, and that Diego . . . was too distracted to train her properly." I lower my eyes, not wanting to meet her gaze.

"Her name was Imane, and yes, that about sums it up. After he got back from that mission, he was practically catatonic for months. He blamed himself, he was inconsolable, and he only ate when I forced him to. I thought I was going to lose him, and it scared the hell out of me. He was my best friend. But that's all he's ever been. A *friend*."

I know I do not succeed in trying to keep the surprised look off my face. "Are you . . . not into men?" I ask hesitantly. I find it hard to believe that anyone who *is* interested in men would not find Diego attractive. Infuriating, certainly, not to mention arrogant, imperious, and intractable.

But attractive nonetheless.

She sighs and rubs her temples, then takes a deep breath, as if bracing herself. "I'm not *into* anyone. I'm not interested in sex or relationships." Her eyes are shut tight. "I love Diego dearly; he's my soulmate, but not a *romantic* soulmate. I realized a long time ago that I am not interested in having more than a platonic relationship with anyone."

She finally opens her eyes and glares at me, but this time, the glare is based on fear rather than anger. *She's been hurt before when she's told people this.* I feel a small twinge in my chest at her guarded expression.

"Oh," I say simply. "You're AroAce."

It's her turn to look surprised. I realize that I've never seen her look surprised. This woman is far too smart for that; she has everything calculated out far before it can hurt her. "I — what?" She asks incredulously.

"You're aromantic. And asexual." Then I remember she has been living in an entirely different world than me for the last decade, spending very little time on Earth.

"That's what people are calling it," I say, then clarify. "Well I mean, that term's been used for a while at this point, but it's becoming more widely used."

She blinks, contemplative. "Oh," she says softly.

"So, when I saw you on Diego's bed that time . . ." I don't finish the question. She gives me a small, sympathetic smile. She's never smiled at me before, either. Even this tiny one is incandescent.

"I let him drink my blood when he needs energy."

She says this as if saying she lets him borrow a cup of sugar to bake cookies. At my horrified expression, she raises her eyebrows at the center. "Because of the whole vampire thing?" She holds her hand out toward me, palm up. *You know.*

I do not.

"He drinks your blood?" I whisper.

She rubs her temples again, like a teacher who has had enough of their students for the day. It's a look I had perfected myself, in another life.

"He constantly talks about how smart you are," she mumbles, though I don't think she realizes I can hear her. "I think he's got his heads mixed up." She sighs and speaks at full volume once more. "What *do* you know about vampires?"

Various images sparkle across my mind's eye, but I settle on the basics. "Super speed, transforming into a bat, allergic to sunlight."

She looks briefly like she might smack me. "And does any of that sound like Diego?" She asks acerbically.

"No," I say in a small voice, rubbing one arm. Though I had ripped through books on every other supernatural topic I could find, I had deliberately slacked off on brushing up on my vampires. Every time I had touched a book about them in Arkenvale's library, Diego's condescending smirk had flashed before my eyes, and I had found something else to read.

Hyun-Joo sighs. "Crash course: none of that shit is true." She doesn't give me the chance to ask any more dumb questions. "Mostly, vampirism is more of a disease than anything, other than the Shifting aspect. His vampire cells attack his human cells constantly. Ironic, since they're also the thing that will keep him alive basically forever, but they need to feed to fuel themselves. He needs fresh blood about once every week if he gets a large amount, and every few days if it's a small one. So, I let him use my blood."

"Does it hurt?" I already know the answer, but I want to hear her say it.

She suffers so much because of me, he had said.

"Yes," she says matter-of-factly. "It does."

"How aren't you . . ." I mimic a clawing motion at her, and she looks back scathingly. "A vampire?" I finish, dropping my hand to my lap.

"Well, he doesn't inject me with his venom, clearly. He just drinks." She says this as if it's exceedingly obvious. I hadn't realized that vampires could control whether they release venom when they bite.

"Oh," I say lamely.

We're silent for a beat. Finally, a question I've been wanting to ask her for months bubbles out of my throat. "Why did you hate me?" I hope the past tense is the right one to use here, and she doesn't correct me. That's a good sign, at least.

She sighs through her nose. "He blames himself for you getting bitten. We had gotten bad intel on where Bleddyn was performing his next ritual, and we didn't make it in time to intercept you before you were taken."

She looks at me, anger flashing briefly across her features. "But you would have been fine if you had just run when I told you to."

A pang of guilt twists my stomach into knots. "I'm sorry," I croak.

She sighs again and crosses her arms. "No, I'm sorry. That's not fair; you were just a human with no training. I just wish I didn't have to see him hate himself for it."

I chew on my lip for a moment. "Why does *he* hate me?" It comes out as a whisper.

Hyun-Joo gazes back at me sadly for a moment, then shakes her head faintly. "He doesn't hate you, Eilidh," she says quietly.

I hang my head in my hands and sigh heavily. "This is all . . . so much to process," I say.

She makes a sound of agreement. "I know. But like I said, we're out of time, and you needed to know. He's going to try to do everything he can on this mission to make up for his past mistakes. He would die if he had to, but I can't lose him." Her voice breaks. "He's all I have. So you need to promise me that you won't let him get himself killed."

"I promise, Hyun-Joo," I croak.

She stands to leave, but hesitates.

"Is there anything else I need to know?" I ask quietly, terrified of what the answer is.

She says nothing for a moment, but then she puts her hand under my chin and makes me look up at her. We've both got tears in our eyes.

"He's in love with you, too." She drops my head and walks away.

She closes my door, and I collapse into my pillow just as a sob escapes my throat.

Betrayal

I slam the car door behind me and stalk through the city streets, flooded with a warm glow from the streetlights. Finally, I come to the dark alley that has come to haunt my waking hours, in addition to my nightmares.

The crescent moon on the sign above grins at me like a sadistic Cheshire cat. I grimace at it and ignore my urge to rearrange the wild ivy on the building's facade into a neat pattern. Nothing about this place deserves my help, or my energy.

Being here is an absolute betrayal against everything I've fought for. Against my home, and the man who took me in. Against myself. But I have no other choice.

And it's all because of Eilidh.

Her arrival at Arkenvale had been akin to tossing a lit torch into a building full of powder kegs. *It was only a matter of time before it all burned down around us.*

I steel myself, then shove the door open. The crowded room goes still as I draw myself up to my full height, trying to put on my best impression of Diego's condescending scowl. At the thought of him, the scowl deepens.

The bartender leers at me appraisingly, and then he grins, his razor-sharp teeth glinting in the light from the fire on the other side of the tavern.

I stare into his black eyes evenly, suppressing the urge to adjust my glasses.

"So, you've finally decided to join us?"

Distractions

Some time later, long after the sun has gone down, Saif comes into my room carrying a mug of tea, wearing a baggy shirt and sweatpants, and looking rather frazzled.

It's been a long day for all of us.

"Woah, can you see in the dark or something now?" He chuckles as he flips on the light, filling the room with its warm glow. Luckily, my eyes dried long ago; I had just been lying, unmoving, as my mind swirled.

I force a chuckle. "No, just had a little headache." I sit up and take the mug gratefully; my taste buds sing when the chamomile hits them. He sits next to me and puts an arm around my waist as I lean into him and sip the tea.

He stares off into space while I drink.

"You're quiet," he says, finally focusing on me as he puts my empty mug on the nightstand.

So are you. I smile wanly. "Just thinking about the mission."

He nods solemnly. "I'm sorry you had to see me lose it like that earlier."

I think back to him standing over my father, raging, and suppress a shiver.

"I was just worried about you. I couldn't send you off alone with *him*. I can't do that." *Not again.* The unspoken words hang in the air for a moment.

I lie down to put my head in his lap, and he strokes my hair absently. "I understand," I say quietly. I reach up, trail my fingers lightly across his cheek, and savor the sensation of his beard hairs pricking my skin.

He turns to kiss my hand as I do so, and heat blooms from where his lips touch my palm.

Hyun-Joo's words cut through my mind, but I try viciously to push them away. Every moment I spend with Diego, he's sneering at me, or laying me out flat while we spar. Nothing I *ever* do is good enough for him. I'm never fast enough, or strong enough. He can't stand me unless I'm in my wolf form, and even then it's just admiration for my physical strength.

That's not love.

But I think *this* might be.

I look into Saif's eyes, and he smiles at me warmly. I put my hand behind his neck and motion gently for him to lean down to kiss me. He complies immediately, and butterflies explode in my stomach when our lips meet.

He shifts and lies next to me, one hand in my hair, the other tracing the curves of my breasts, my stomach, and my hips. His touch is intoxicating; I wish I could drown myself in this feeling.

I trail my nails gently across his collarbone, then down his back, before I slip under the waistband of his sweatpants. I cup his firm ass for a moment, then move my hand around to his cock. He's already rock hard, and I stroke him up and down as he kisses along my jaw, my throat, and down to my breasts.

We remove our clothes in a flurry of motion, and he kisses me once again. His kisses are more hurried than usual, more desperate, and my body responds to his urgency in kind to show him that I'm not going anywhere — not without him.

I breathe heavily as he sucks on my nipples, and moves a hand to my clit. After a few moments, his fingers are slick, and I'm gasping quietly with each stroke.

"You love the feel of my cock in your hand, don't you?" He says quietly, moving up to kiss my neck again.

"God, yes," I breathe shakily in his ear. Him talking like this is *hot*.

He licks up my neck and breathes in my ear. "It'll be even better in your mouth." He shifts and pulls free of my grasp. In another moment, he kneels over my face, and I take his girth into my mouth.

While he thrusts as deeply as he can, he grips the headboard so hard that I worry that he might crack it, but he's too controlled for that.

I've got one hand on his ass, and the other one between my legs. I moan quietly against him as I curl my fingers to hit my G-spot, and use my thumb to frantically circle my clit.

Soon, I'm close, and then he grunts heavily. "Fuck, Eilidh, you're amazing."

All at once, I'm gasping around his length as my orgasm crashes over me.

Saif slows and pulls out of my mouth. Drool drips off of his length and onto my chest. "I knew you'd like that." He grins. He moves off of me, then twirls his finger in the circle through the air. "Turn around."

I do, and grip the headboard where he had just been digging his nails into it.

He presses the tip of his cock into my pussy just an inch or two, and I gasp as he pulls it back out. *Tease.* But then he rubs the tip farther up and pushes gently on that opening, and my stomach flutters.

He leans forward and kisses me on my shoulder. "Is this okay?" He asks quietly. It's been a while since I've engaged in this particular act, but it *was* one I enjoyed quite a bit when I did. His girth intimidates me for a moment, but I nod anyway. "Are you sure? Because we don't have to," he says sincerely.

If he stalls any longer, I'm going to explode. "Fucking do it," I hiss.

He doesn't ask again. He pushes himself into me slowly, inch by inch, and it hurts in the most delicious way possible. He kisses firmly all around my shoulders and neck as he does, then puts a hand around my mouth and I moan against his palm once he's deeper inside.

After a few shallow thrusts and several deep breaths to acclimate myself, I begin pushing back onto his girth, driving him deeper into me. He lets out a shuddering breath and tangles a hand into my hair, tugging with just the right amount of force. "Oh my *fucking* god," he breathes into my ear, then curses in rapid Arabic.

His words set me on fire. I moan his name, and he reaches a hand around to rub my clit. Soon, another orgasm starts. I remove my hands from the headboard and shove my face into my pillow just as I scream with pleasure.

His thrusts become frantic briefly, then slow as he comes inside me. When we're both finished, we collapse together, and he pulls me onto his shoulder, kissing me on top of the head firmly.

Love

Lying here in my bed with our dewy skin pressed together, I am suddenly overwhelmed by my feelings for Saif. For *him.* Not Diego. All Diego and I feel for each other is disdain, and maybe a small mutual admiration of our supernatural strength.

Hyun-Joo is ridiculous. And so is that fucking voice in my head.

"I need to tell you something," I say quickly, before I can change my mind.

He looks like he's going to fall asleep at any moment, but he rolls to his side and looks at me with a smile. "Shoot."

I look at his face and his dark, trimmed facial hair that feels like soft velvet when I run my hand over it, and realize that he's got a few gray hairs mixed in his beard that I hadn't ever noticed before.

Fuck. I didn't think he could get any sexier.

I clear my throat. "Um, so, you know how I was raised by my grandparents?" My voice shakes.

He frowns at my tone, then frowns further when he processes my words. "No, I . . . don't think I knew that."

My eyes widen. Hadn't I told him that? *Maybe not.* How could I have neglected to let him know about such an integral aspect of my life? *Way to go, Shaw.*

"Oh. Well, I — I was," I say lamely.

His eyes dance with concern. "Okay."

I take another deep breath. "Well, while you were gone a few months ago, I was reading in the library, and the King walked in and said he wanted to talk to me."

His expression clouds at that, but he stays silent.

I recount the story to Saif slowly, telling him about the photograph Auberon had shown me, about the details he knew about my mother. It's the first time I've said the words out loud. My tongue twists around them strangely; they're too foreign and outlandish to sound real. "Auberon is my father."

By the time I finish my story, Saif has rolled to his back, and he's staring at the ceiling, hardly blinking. I can see the gears in his mind whirring at dizzying speeds. He's silent for a few moments, then mutters so softly under his breath that I wouldn't hear him without my lupine abilities. "That's perfect."

I wince. If he's being sarcastic, I must have really pissed him off. "I know it's a lot. I'm sorry. I shouldn't have waited so long to tell you."

He just shakes himself slightly and breathes out, considering his next words carefully. I'm not positive he even heard me apologize. "Are you telling me that I just made love to a princess?"

I burst into laughter, but he's serious. My laughter dies away instantly.

"I'm not a *princess*. I'm thirty-one years old."

"Age isn't an indication of rank," he says, rolling back to his side to face me. "And last I checked, the daughter of a king is called a princess. Granted, it's been some time since I've seen a kid's movie but —"

I hold my hand up to silence him. "No, I." But I have no other words. *Holy* shit. *Am* I a princess? I try to picture myself in a giant ball gown, or riding in a carriage as it begins to turn into a pumpkin. I don't succeed.

I bring my fingertips to my temples. "I don't know," I say. He lets me process.

Then the other part of his sentence hits me. "Did you say made *love?*"

His eyes widen slightly and he searches my gaze like he's trying to gauge my feelings. Good luck to him with that, because I can't puzzle them out right now myself.

"Yes?" He looks terrified of what my response may be.

But I look at Saif now, at how his skin in the soft yellow light shimmers like polished bronze. His sharp jawline is enough to bring me to my knees. He's been caring for me for months, and sure, we had had a bit of a tiff, but he had just been concerned for my safety around Diego.

Diego.

No. I push his name and face from my mind.

Saif and I gaze into each other's eyes. Brown and green, each blazing in the dim light with this feeling. The strongest feeling there can be between people, no matter what form it takes. The reason people have lost their minds and fought wars.

He speaks first. "I love you, Eilidh." He's quiet, but his tone is steady, like he has rehearsed these words to himself many times.

"I've loved you since the day you woke up here in Arkenvale. Every morning when I open your door, I fall in love with you all over again. You're the fire that warms my soul, and keeps my heart beating."

He puts one hand into my hair. "You are my flame."

Tears prick the corners of my eyes. How do I even begin to adequately respond to that? I don't think I could, even if I spent every day of the rest if my infinite lifespan composing my reply.

"I . . . I love you too, Saif. I love you so much."

It isn't enough. But for him, it seems, it is absolutely everything.

He brushes my hair behind my ear, leans in, and kisses me tenderly on the mouth. I kiss him back, running a hand through his thick curls.

When we finally pull apart, he nuzzles me onto his shoulder and pulls a blanket up over us. "Sleep well, Eilidh," he murmurs into my hair.

I do.

I fall into a deep and peaceful sleep in the warmth of his arms. As I drift off, my final thought is how desperately I want to fall asleep in his arms for the rest of my life.

I don't feel him get up and leave in the middle of the night.

Departure

The next morning, I wake up alone in my bed. The sun is just beginning to rise as I gather my clothes for the mission and head to the bathroom to freshen up before we leave.

When I'm done getting ready, I go to the kitchen to make some toast, and I'm just spreading peanut butter on a slice when Saif walks in carrying two large baskets overflowing with fruits, vegetables, and herbs from the solarium.

I smile at him. "Good morning."

He returns my smile. "*Sabah al-khair*, my love."

My heart flutters at the word.

He gives me a tender kiss as he sets the baskets down.

When he pulls away, I frown slightly. He has dark circles under his eyes, like he didn't sleep well. I open my mouth, but he speaks before I get the chance to ask him how he's feeling.

"I'm just going to cut and prep these quickly before we head out. Mind helping? I know how good you are with your hands." He winks, and I blush.

He must just be nervous about the mission, and that's why he couldn't sleep.

We cut up the produce together as I munch on my toast, and he brews some mint tea for the road. It all feels so strange, this domesticity, but it's nice. *I could get used to this.*

When we're done, we carry the containers of food through the dining hall on our way to the front door. My gaze passes over the stained-glass figures in the windows once again. The sword, the chalice, and the stone. Simple, but beautiful. Delicate, but strong.

Everyone else is already in the entrance hall, checking and rechecking their packs, and even the King is there, ensuring that everything we'll need is with us. Once we've each triple-checked that we have everything, we're ready to go.

I turn to face my father and a lump forms in my throat. I hadn't even thought about how hard it would be to say goodbye.

He interprets my stricken face. "Everyone, kindly give Eilidh and me some privacy."

Looks are exchanged behind me, and I can feel the heat of Diego's glare on my back. *You haven't seen what he's capable of.* But just because he's my father's top soldier doesn't mean he *knows* him.

I grab Saif's hand as he moves to walk out the front door with the others. "He can stay," I say to my father, inclining my head to convey the message. *He knows.*

The King just nods.

When the front door has closed behind the others, my father opens his arms, and I close the gap between us quickly. In one second, I'm a little girl clinging onto her daddy, tears scratching at my throat.

I don't even know why I'm crying. We'll be back in a week or so, and I'll have gotten my justice.

And then we'll be on to the next mission, off to protect the innocent, and do good for our people.

But the little girl inside me doesn't understand that. She just wants to stay in the safety of her father's arms.

That's all she's ever wanted.

"I'm going to miss you," I say into my father's chest. He's only about four inches taller than me, but I still feel minuscule in this moment.

He runs a hand over my frizzy waves. "And I, you, dear girl." He turns to Saif. "Bring my daughter back to me safely, Saif Rahim. That is an order."

Saif bows so deeply that he faces the stone floor rather than my father. "Of course, Your Majesty. I'll do whatever is necessary to keep her safe. I swear it on my life."

Eventually, I step back and look up into my father's golden eye. He puts a bracing hand on my shoulder and looks to my thigh, where my silver dagger is strapped to me. "Make me proud, Eilidh."

I nod. "Of course, Father." The word is still strange in my mouth, but I have the rest of, well, forever, to get used to it.

Through the Willow

We exit the front door of Arkenvale and join the others, but instead of turning toward the garage, Diego walks East, toward the woods.

"Where is he going?" I ask.

Saif grimaces.

"Auberon told us this morning that with Bastet on the move as well, he doesn't think it's safe for us to go traipsing through the countryside. He wants us to go through our gateway here, then re-enter Tenazeryth at the edge of the Cuhloch Forest, near Bedivere."

My throat tightens. "We're going back to Earth?"

He squeezes my hand. "I've got you, *Lahabi*."

We walk for about an hour into the woods to the East of the castle. We don't pass the training area where Diego and I had been spending the full moons. Instead, we follow a small stream. Birds and insects sing their songs all around us as we walk.

Then, the stream widens significantly, and we enter a clearing. The water runs through the center, and just a few feet away from its bank stands a massive, ancient willow tree that takes my breath away. Its thick trunk twists up from the ground, forking out into several smaller sections. Its lush branches form perfect curtains, reaching down to the ground to caress the blades of grass and clovers.

The six of us walk through its trailing branches, and it feels as if we're passing through gossamer. The magical barrier lets us through without issue. Once we're all under the branches, Diego places a palm on the trunk, and the others do as well. I follow suit. He glances at each of us in turn.

"Ready?" Everyone else nods. His eyes land on me last, and I bite my lip, but nod as I squeeze Saif's hand tightly. Diego closes his eyes, takes a breath, and utters a single word.

"*Trafnidiaeth.*" I have the distinct feeling of falling through the earth and being whisked away by the roots of the willow tree. My stomach feels like I have just been tipped over a drop on the world's highest roller coaster.

I open my mouth to scream, but just as I do, there is solid ground under my feet once more. Though my legs are suddenly made of jelly, Saif holds me up easily as I pant against his chest.

"You did wonderfully, my love," he says into my hair as he strokes my back.

Diego, who is still standing just a few feet away, stiffens.

Everyone gives me a moment to breathe. But only a moment.

"Let's go," Diego bites out. I take one more breath and look around, and we're in a public park. I release Saif's hand and Valentina falls into step with us.

"Where are we?" I ask.

"Unity Island Park," she says. Seeing my blank stare, she clarifies. "In Buffalo." I nod slowly.

As we walk out from under the tree and pass through another invisible barrier, sounds explode all around us as though a switch has been hit. I hear birds chirping, people talking, and vehicles whizzing nearby.

I look back at the tree we had been transported to. It's a towering maple tree that looks like it's been here for hundreds of years. The leaves are the color of Martín's flames, and tears prick the corner of my eyes, wishing for the hundredth time that the trees in Tenazeryth could blaze with colors like this.

So the corresponding portal trees don't have to be the same both here and in Tenazeryth to work.

Fascinating.

We head East off of Unity Island as Diego consults a map.

"There's a car rental place about fifteen minutes from here. Once we're there, Martín, you go in and get us the vehicle." Everyone nods along. "Then we hit the road, and we'll be in Charleston by midnight at the latest."

"Charleston?" I ask.

Saif clarifies. "West Virginia."

I exhale slowly. There's a long car ride ahead of us.

We walk in pairs of two down the sidewalk, and I marvel at how normal it feels. This dimension has kept going in my absence; my sudden disappearance made no difference at all.

I wonder who even noticed I'm gone, I think with a pang.

It's late November, even though it feels like it's sixty degrees right now. Every year, Summer encroaches farther and farther into Autumn's territory. I clench my jaw as a large pickup truck rumbles past us, billowing thick black clouds from metal pipes. *No wonder.*

My job has definitely fired me by now, and my apartment has probably been rented off to someone else. *Is there even anyone who would have reported me as a missing person?* Not likely, unless the leasing company for my apartment building is somehow obligated to. Certainly not my only living relative this side of an interdimensional portal. She's too busy living her best life in Reno, far too preoccupied to care about her only child.

I had missed months of getting macchiatos at Tia and Kenji's bookstore. We had always been friendly when I was there, but we had never talked about our personal lives. They probably think I just moved, or found a different bookstore to haunt. *Maybe they think I've become a regular at the giant chain across town,* I think in horror.

It strikes me then that the only people in the world who *really* know me, who actually care about me - other than my father, of course - are right here.

I'm not sure if that makes me feel better or worse.

I don't realize I've slowed until Diego turns and snaps, "Stay together," before and he and Hyun-Joo continue striding down the sidewalk. Valentina and Saif had been hanging back a bit from the others, keeping an eye on me, letting me process my thoughts, and our orderly procession is beginning to fall apart.

I look at Valentina with tears in my eyes. She holds out her hand, and we walk together. Saif follows closely behind us.

"It's hard the first time back," she says quietly. "Brings back a lot of memories." Martín turns too, and he gives me an encouraging smile, though the corners of his eyes are tight. I can only imagine how hard being here is for them in particular, having been hurt over and over and shunned by everyone they ever loved.

Fifteen minutes later, as promised, we make it to the rental place. Martín shakes his arms out, does a few lunges, and slicks his braids back.

Valentina throws her head back and groans at the sky. "*Mátame.*"

I giggle. "What are you doing?"

He flashes me a bright smile as he pulls his braids into a half-updo. "Preparing to get us the most luxurious vehicle possible for almost no money, and every perk thrown in that I can." He points to the person at the counter inside, who is oblivious to the routine occurring just outside the window.

I squint at them. "I think that's a guy."

Martín stops his theatrics as though I'd doused him in ice water. "*Mi querida,* do you think so little of me? That my talents are limited to women?"

I blink and start to sputter. "No, sorry, I just didn't know you, uh, liked men?" I finish as a question and he smiles again.

"I like everyone and anyone, darling, and they like me. Just watch. Either that man realizes he's attracted to me right off the bat, or I get to watch the panic in his eyes as he figures it out."

At that, he strolls into the building and saunters up to the desk. By the look of things, the man at the desk did not, in fact, realize it off the bat. But Martín has barely been in there fifteen seconds, and I can see the man blushing from here.

I cock my head to the side in awe. "I think your brother has more magic than just controlling fire," I say to Valentina.

She puts her head in her hands, her locs falling dramatically around her face. "*Dios mío.*"

Not even five minutes later, Martín ambles back out, and I can see the man behind the desk watching him the whole time, as though dazed. He tosses a key fob to Diego with a wink.

"Here ya go, boss. Got a nice upgrade at no extra cost. And a phone number, but I didn't have the heart to tell him that *I* don't have a phone to call him with."

We head to a large, black SUV in the parking lot and pile inside. I take the third row with Saif, and Martín and Valentina take the middle, separating us from Diego and Hyun-Joo. They all talk for a few minutes while I focus on breathing and keeping myself calm, looking for colors.

It's okay. You're safe. Even if something did *happen, you have a healing factor now.* Saif holds my hand, but he dozes off within minutes. I pull him onto my shoulder and wrap my arm around him. Not long after, I'm dozing off as well, rocked by the motion of the vehicle. I kiss his mop of dark curls and yawn. *And you have him.*

The last thing I see before I fall asleep is Diego's crimson gaze flickering at me in the rearview mirror. That gaze follows me into my dreams.

Cemetery

"Eilidh." Saif nudges me gently, rousing me from my slumber. I stretch and look around. When I realize where we are, I freeze, positive that I'm still dreaming.

We're parked just outside the gates to a cemetery that I haven't seen in more than six years. I scramble out after him. "What is going on?" I ask.

Diego doesn't look at me as he answers. "It was Valentina's idea."

I turn to her, and her mouth is hanging open at him. "Oh, you motherf—"

I cut her off. "Why are we here?" I ask her sharply.

She gives him another scathing look before she answers me. "We *all* think that it would do you some good to visit them."

She takes my hand and leads me through the gates. She clutches me like she's afraid I'm going to crumble to the ground before we even make it.

I'm not so sure she's wrong.

We wind our way through the stones in silence as dark clouds roll across the sky. Eventually, we make it to the familiar spot, and I look upon the two names, tears stinging my eyes.

"Chester Shaw," reads the stone to my left. "Joann Shaw," reads the one to my right.

I gently take my hand from Valentina's and move to rest one hand on each stone. I run a finger along ribbons carved from granite, and a sunbeam that stings like ice instead of providing warmth. I had picked these designs numbly, still in shock.

Kianga's parents had helped me immensely with a lot of the legal and estate issues, but the ultimate decisions had fallen to me; there was no one else left who could do it. No one left who *would*, anyway. My mother didn't even bother showing up for the funeral.

She never even called.

Every scrap of them had been taken from me, and she couldn't be troubled to show her face for one day. To even *pretend* to care about me, or to ask if I was okay.

"I'm sorry," I whisper to them. "I'm sorry it's been so long."

They don't respond, but a cool breeze blows, carrying with it the smell of petrichor, and I know they forgive me.

I wipe a tear from my cheek, then realize that it isn't a tear at all. I tilt my head to the sky just as several more drops fall on my skin. I exhale slowly as drops begin to patter around me.

Rain.

It has been far too long since I felt rain. I smile wide and exhale shakily at the clouds, my eyes still shut tight. Then suddenly, the drops stop falling. I open my eyes, gasping at the loss of the sensation, and realize that Hyun-Joo has put a barrier above us.

I turn to her in supplication. "Please," I whisper, as the drops begin to fall in earnest atop the barrier. She gives me a long, melancholy look, but then she waves her hand, and the barrier above me recedes, though everyone else is still covered. But then Diego puts a hand on her shoulder wordlessly, and the barrier evaporates completely.

The six of us are drenched in moments. I look around at the others, a grateful smile on my lips. Then a loud clap of thunder crashes above, and I laugh, tilting my face to the heavens once more.

Hi, Pop-Pop. "When I was a kid," I say after the thunder has ceased.

"We would sit out on the porch during thunderstorms. He loved them, and so I did too." I rub my thumb over my grandfather's headstone, wishing desperately that I could sit on his lap for this storm, too. And for every storm for the rest of eternity.

I glance at my grandmother's stone. "She never really did, but she loved whenever her flowers would get watered without her having to do it." I emit a small chuckle, thinking of my grandmother puttering over her flower beds. I close my eyes, and I can see her clear as day, smelling a blooming yellow tulip — they had been her favorite.

"That sounds wonderful," Valentina says quietly.

I take her hand again and squeeze. "They were." I sniffle, and she squeezes my hand back tightly.

We listen to the thunder for several long moments before Diego finally breaks the silence. "We should get going." His tone - for once - isn't caustic.

It's almost . . . gentle.

I glance at him from the corner of my eye. Several sections of his rain-soaked, shaggy hair have fallen across his face, but he doesn't brush them back.

I swallow hard as Valentina squeezes my leg and stands. "I'll dry us off when we get back to the car."

"Actually," I say as she pulls me to my feet, "I have one more person I need to visit while we're here."

Her eyes flood with confusion. I look away, ashamed that I hadn't told her before now.

Saif's tone is stricken. "Kianga?"

I nod, then turn silently and walk back diagonally, a few more rows. The others follow me, but I don't look back at any of them. Saif whispers to Valentina behind me, explaining.

The stone I'm looking for is under an old oak tree. Rain drips through the orange leaves as I sit heavily against its trunk, just staring at her name.

Kianga Nabil.

The others crowd under the lush canopy as Valentina sits down next to me again and grabs my hand. Her presence gives me strength that I've never felt before while staring at this stone. I take a deep breath, and the smell of decaying leaves fills my nostrils.

"Kianga was the love of my life," I say, answering the unasked question, and I hear several sharp inhales around me. I can't look at Saif, but I clutch Valentina's hand like a lifeline as my mouth twists in a rueful smile. "She just never knew it."

I think back to the first time I saw her as another roll of thunder fills the skies. "We met on my fifth birthday. My mother had decided she wanted to do something nice for me, so she brought me to the library to sign me up for my first card. I'd been begging for one for forever."

I exhale quickly through my nose. "We walked in, and there she was. She was holding her father's hand while her parents spoke with the librarian. They had just immigrated from Egypt, and the librarians had been helping them with paperwork, and finding books to teach themselves English. I'll never forget the look on her face."

I can't help but smile at the memory of that fierce little girl who would change my life forever. "She saw me staring at her, and she jutted her chin out at me as if daring me to pick on her. I found out later that that had been happening a lot to her in just the few months they'd been here. But no matter how hard she glared, I didn't stop staring."

I take a shuddering breath. "She was - she never stopped being - the most beautiful thing I had ever seen."

Valentina reaches toward my cheek and brushes away tears that I didn't know I had shed. I continue; now that I'm talking about her, I can't stop.

I might not ever stop.

"I went over to her and asked her to help me pick out a book for my birthday. I don't think she really understood my words at that point, but she understood my intentions. She grabbed a book, and we sat and read it together. Then another. I would have sat in that library and read every book in the world with her if I could have."

I scooch closer across the wet grass to lay a hand on her damp headstone. "When my —" My voice catches. "When I was in the accident." I nod toward my grandparents' graves. "Her parents took me in. We graduated together, then took a gap year to just *live*. She had our whole futures planned out for us. She had such big dreams." I smile wistfully, but it quickly turns pained.

"Then, the day I turned twenty, she ran out to grab me some ice cream, just because I was in a bad mood. The store was just a few miles away, and she *promised* she would be right back. But then a massive thunderstorm blew in out of nowhere while she was out. It was dark, and her car needed new tires, but she had spent the money on my present instead of buying some." I pause, and I don't think Valentina is even breathing beside me.

"When the police showed up at the door instead of her, her mom fainted. A few months later . . . " I trail off and rub at the tattoo on my right ankle. Valentina looks down, and then back to me, understanding.

I clear my throat. "Two years after that, her parents divorced. There was just no more room left in their marriage for love; it was all taken up by grief. I haven't talked to them since then. They never blamed me," I say. "But I blame myself."

Lightning streaks across the sky.

Diego speaks behind me. "You mean you *blamed* yourself." He emphasizes the past tense of the word.

"No," I whisper harshly. Guilt presses heavily against my chest, cold, but familiar. Thunder roars overhead, and when it ceases, he makes a sound like he's going to argue with me, but I cut him off.

"The only thing they recovered from the car wreck was her pendant." I move a hand toward my rain-soaked chest, but stop in midair, just above my bare skin. "I was wearing it when Bleddyn attacked me. It was all I had left of her. And now it's *gone*."

Another flash of lightning.

The last word comes out as an angry sob, and then Valentina wraps her arms around me, squeezing as tightly as she can, holding me together.

In the next moment, Saif sits on the ground on my opposite side and rests a hand on my knee. "I've got you, *Lahabi*."

The three of us sit there together like that until the only drops on my cheeks are from the sky above. I finally stand, leaning heavily on Saif and Valentina.

"I love you." I plant a long kiss on Kianga's headstone, then turn and walk away as thunder rattles the earth.

Bravery

We do indeed make it to Charleston by midnight, or, more specifically, a huge state forest outside the city. The rain had stopped somewhere in Pennsylvania, and here, it's as dry as a bone. The leaves here, too, are hanging on later than they would have even a decade ago. The explosion of autumn foliage around us makes my heart sing.

As Diego drives down smaller and smaller roads into the mountain, I convince myself that there is no way that we'll be able to find a single tree out of what has to be millions, and we'll have to turn around and head back to the portal in Buffalo.

But eventually, the SUV has taken us as far as it can, and he still doesn't turn us around. "Tonight, we sleep by the car," he says as he puts the vehicle in park. "Everyone rest up. We have a long day ahead of us tomorrow."

We pair off in various spots around the SUV, and Diego takes the first watch, prowling around the perimeter like a lioness guarding her cubs. My watch is last.

Saif and I lie down with our sleeping bags nuzzled together on a thick blanket of fallen leaves, and he tangles his fingers in mine once we're both comfortable. "Good night," he says softly, rubbing his thumb across my skin. "I love you."

"I love you too," I whisper back, a small smile on my lips. I can't believe how easily those words come when I'm looking into his eyes.

I expect to be up long into the night, but it's amazing how tired simply riding in a car has made me. I quickly fall into a surprisingly restful sleep. I don't even hear Saif move or feel him untangle our fingers when Diego wakes him for the second watch.

I wake hours later to Martín shaking my shoulder gently, stifling a yawn. "Rise and shine *cariño*." I stand up and stretch, worried that if I close my eyes again for a moment I'll fall back asleep.

I glance at Saif, who is lying on his stomach, his arms folded under his head. How anyone can sleep on their stomach has always been a mystery to me, but the bigger mystery is how he makes it look so damn sexy. I lean back down and plant a soft kiss on his mop of dark curls.

I walk away, doing a loop around the perimeter of the campsite. I check on everyone in their sleeping bags, then realize with a start that the bag next to Hyun-Joo is empty.

Where the fuck are you? I check in the SUV, but Diego isn't in there either. I walk around the area again, chewing on my lip. *Should I wake someone else? What if something is wrong?* Just as I decide I need to wake Saif, a quiet voice hisses at me from the trees.

"Your stomping is loud enough to wake the dead."

I jump several inches in the air, turning as I do so. Dry leaves swirl and then crinkle under my feet when I land. Diego emerges from the trees.

"Can you for *once* approach me like a normal human being?" I hiss under my breath, my heart hammering.

He scowls at me and points to himself. "Vampire," he whispers back at the same volume.

I roll my eyes. "You know what I fucking mean."

He smirks coolly at that. "Sorry *Lobita*, I didn't realize your werewolf powers included flight. I'll try to stomp harder next time so you don't launch yourself into orbit."

I clench my jaw. "Go to bed," I bite.

He snorts. "I got all the sleep I need. I was going to tell Martín not to wake you, and that I'd take your watch, but I lost track of time."

I put my hands on my hips, and the corners of his mouth tighten. "What are you doing out there alone anyway? What if there's something dangerous?"

He doesn't answer for a moment, he just blinks at me like I'm an idiot, but then he cocks a thick eyebrow at me. "Pretty sure *I'm* the scariest thing in these woods. And I was just walking."

I stare at him incredulously. "You don't think you'll get enough of that later today?"

He doesn't answer, he just twists his mouth in annoyance, then turns and prowls to the SUV.

I crush a brown leaf under my foot and grind it into the dirt. *Just let him go. If he wants to brood, he can do it alone. Do not —*

I follow him.

He sits in the driver's seat and quietly closes the door. Anger flares up in my stomach. I open the passenger door and hop inside.

"Excuse you?" I say at normal volume once more. Hopefully, the glass of the vehicle is thick enough that no one else will be able to hear us. "I thought we were having a conversation."

He doesn't look at me, he just leans his seat back and puts his hands behind his head. "And now we're done."

I gape at him. "What the *hell* is your problem? What did I do to piss you off now? I know you hate me, but fuck, I didn't think I could get on your nerves in my *sleep*."

He turns to me abruptly and scowls; his eyes practically glow in the dark. "I don't hate you," he murmurs.

I cross my arms. "Well, it sure seems like it. It has *always* seemed like it." The last part comes out sounding more wounded than I mean it to.

He puts his hands over his face and groans.

I throw my hands up, hitting the roof of the SUV sharply in the process. "You know what, never mind. Fuck it."

I move for the door handle, but his hand shoots out to grab it before I can reach it. "What —" I turn, and his face is inches from mine. I recoil, but he doesn't move.

His next sentences are rapid-fire, like he's been trying to hold them back forever, and they've finally burst forth, like water from a crumbling dam.

"I can't sleep because I'm fucking *worried*, okay? I'm worried that I'm sending you to your death. That I didn't train you well enough for this fight. I'm worried that you'll get hurt, or fucking killed. I'm fucking *worried* about you because I l—" His mouth clamps shut and he clenches a fist as he turns away from me.

I realize I've stopped breathing, and inhale shakily.

He says nothing more; he just glares out the windshield, his shoulders rising and falling heavily. The silence between us is unbearably tense.

Finally, I can't take it anymore. "You did a great job training me." I pick at the fabric of my pants.

"Tch."

"Would I lie about something just to make you feel better?" I ask, annoyed.

He's silent for a moment, but when he speaks, there's a smile in his tone. I can just picture the smirk on the other side of his face right now. "I don't think Martín's hottest flames on your feet could make you do that."

I smirk too. "Exactly. So, you know it must be true. I've done things I never would have believed I could do because of you. Because . . ." I frown. "Because you pushed me so incredibly hard."

I pause for a moment in contemplation. "I've done nothing but doubt myself this entire time, but *you*." I gesture at him with my left hand, palm up. "You believed in me since the beginning."

I trail off and absently lower my hand to the center console as the realization hits me. It hadn't occurred to me before this moment, but he really *had* believed in me. He must have.

For months now, he's been making me swallow my self-doubt. Even though I hated him in those moments, had gotten countless cuts and bruises, and gotten my ass kicked consistently.

He has taught me that most of my limits are mental ones. And even when they're not, and I fail, he's made me get back up and try again. He's taught me that I *can* get back up, no matter what.

I blink rapidly, my mind whirring. Saif is always there too, but he's always telling me to slow down, to be cautious, that I'm not ready. But Diego has pushed me to my limits from the start, taught me how to give the middle finger to uncertainty, and come out on top in the end, despite some failures along the way.

I'm so lost in thought that I don't realize he's lain his hand over mine on the center console between us. When he inhales sharply, and I blink and see it there, my heart begins hammering. His hands aren't calloused from holding weapons like Saif's; they're as soft as satin.

I look up into his glowing eyes, and I can tell by the movement of his shoulders that his breath is coming more rapidly now.

His voice is low and quiet when he finally speaks. "I've believed in you since I saw you for the first time in that clearing. You were pulling on your restraints like you were ready to rip Bleddyn to shreds with your bare hands. And then you ran like the wind from *me*. You were so brave."

I shake my head faintly. "I was *terrified* in that clearing. That's *why* I ran. I was scared the entire time. I just. . . . I don't know. My instincts kicked in and I couldn't just lie there anymore. And when you —"

I close my eyes against the memory of his face dripping with Azaeroria's blood, and shudder. "I wasn't thinking. I wasn't even smart enough to run in the direction Hyun-Joo was trying to pull me in."

He raises an eyebrow at me, but for once, it isn't mocking or condescending; he's genuinely curious. "Do you think bravery means being cool-headed and fearless no matter what?"

I stare back at him blankly.

"Bravery is doing something in *spite* of the fear. You fought back. You ran. You did more than I did when I was attacked."

He casts his eyes down, and laces his fingers between mine. My fingers move of their own volition, curling up to clutch his hand right back.

I breathe deep, trying to calm my racing heart while I consider his words. *Had* I been brave? I certainly hadn't felt like it at the time, but maybe doing the only thing I could do with what I had at my disposal *was* the brave thing to do.

Maybe - sometimes - to run is the brave thing.

I wet my lips. "You think I'm brave?"

He tears his crimson gaze from our clasped hands and searches my eyes. "Of course I do," he whispers.

It's dark, but he's not even a foot away from me, and I can see well enough to make out his expression, though it's not one I've seen him wear before. It's as alien to him as fury had been on Saif's face when he was screaming at my father.

Diego looks . . . *vulnerable.*

He shifts, leaning in closer to me. "Look, I . . ." He shuts his eyes tightly, and growls through his teeth.

I hold him tightly and use his hand as leverage while I shift so that I'm sideways on the seat, facing him full-on. "You what?" I ask quietly.

He sighs. "I just —" He cuts himself off again, but he's leaning in farther still.

I can smell a floral tea on his breath, just like when we had last sparred together in the circle. When he had me pressed tightly against the ground, and slid a fang against the delicate skin of my neck.

I blink and realize that his face is nearer now, and also that I have lain my head against the seat to tilt my face up at him, though I don't remember doing that at all. Just had to get a better view of him, I suppose. *Or are you exposing your neck?*

I take a shaky breath. *What the* fuck *are you doing, Shaw?*

I have no response for the voice of reason screaming in my head, so I shove it away. *Nothing. We're just talking.*

Just holding hands and talking, as each streak of color in his irises becomes more and more visible. If he gets any closer, his long eyelashes are going to brush against my forehead. My breath catches at that thought.

I suddenly feel like I'm being sucked into a black hole. It's drawing me closer to Diego, and sparks are shooting through my veins with every millimeter that closes between us.

Hyun-Joo's words toll through my head like a bell. *He's in love with you, too.* My whole body trembles. But she was mistaken. No matter how close she and Diego are, she couldn't have been right about that.

Could she?

My heart is trying to beat its way out of my chest, and sweat is beading up on the back of my neck. I need fresh air, but the only oxygen in the SUV right now is swirling heavily between us, along with static electricity that might cause the vehicle to explode if it doesn't dissipate soon.

I grip his hand tightly, desperate for something to ground myself, and he pushes my hand into the center console firmly, like he knows just what my body needs from him.

As he puts his weight into our clasped hands, he inhales deeply through his nose, and I feel a few pieces of my hair shift when he exhales.

He tilts his head to the left, and his eyes find mine once again.

I'm frozen against the head rest. I should break the spell, should say something to reassure him once and for all and then get the fuck out of here. I should say something to get him to lean in closer — *no,* I mean, to back off.

Because he's *so* close now. *Maybe my speech can wait.* He searches my eyes a final time, and something shifts in his. The hesitation that has been weighing them down vanishes in an instant.

I take a shuddering breath just as he closes his eyes and leans into me. Crackling electricity explodes throughout my head, my body, and through the very air between us. I close my eyes, too.

Then I see Saif's face on the back of my eyelids, and I gasp sharply.

"I'mnotImane," I blurt out all at once. He freezes and snaps his eyes open, his lips no more than an inch away from mine. Heat radiates off of him, or maybe it's coming from my burning cheeks.

"What?" He croaks, a million emotions flashing through his blazing eyes. I can see myself reflected in his dilated pupils for just a split second, pale and trembling, before he leans back.

I take a ragged breath and lick my lips, swallowing hard. "I — I know what happened with Imane. I know that she . . . that she didn't make it. But I am not her." I'm scared to meet his eyes.

He pulls his hand out of mine then, and there's an intense pang in my chest. His eyes have turned as hard as diamonds.

"No, you certainly are not," he says icily.

He might as well have slapped me. I would have preferred that, in fact, to the way I can see the light recede from his eyes, and the blank mask slip back over his face once more.

I had just — what the fuck *had* I been doing? Trying to reassure him that he wasn't repeating his past mistake, I suppose, but instead,

I had crossed a line that I should not have. Again.

"Diego, I'm sorr—" But it's no use. He's already closing the car door behind him. I lean my head back against the window of the passenger door and bare my teeth.

"*Fuck.*" I don't try to stop the tears as they flow down my face.

World Upended

I wake everyone up with the sun. Everyone except Diego, who is sitting on his sleeping bag with his back to me, and Hyun-Joo, whom he gently nudges awake with the first rays of dawn.

Saif looks at me, his warm eyes full of concern. "Are you okay, love?" He cups my cheek and I lean into his touch.

I sniffle. "Just tired," I murmur. "This hour existing should be against some kind of international treaty."

He chuckles and kisses the top of my head. "You know, I always loved sunrises, even more than sunsets. They're the promise of a fresh start. Every day, the world wakes with renewed hope."

I wrap my arms around his waist and feel his heart beat steadily in his chest. "That's beautiful. I'll appreciate it in about six hours."

His booming laugh bounces around the campsite, and then he leans down and kisses me easily, with no hesitation whatsoever.

And without the world imploding as a result.

Guilt twists icily in my stomach. Nothing had happened in the SUV, but then again, *so much* had.

And none of it can ever happen again. I kiss Saif back fiercely. *And it won't.*

After we've gathered our things and eaten a hearty breakfast, we move out for the portal. I am reminded numerous times during the hike that being a treadmill runner is *not* the same thing as hiking through a wild mountain range.

"You know, I never trip over roots when I'm on an elliptical," I grumble as Saif catches me for the dozenth time before I topple to the ground.

But at least it's pretty. I pluck an especially large orange leaf from the ground at one point and show it to Martín. "Your favorite color!" He takes it and puts it on his head like a crown, then struts like a peacock until it flits back to the ground.

I giggle at him and turn to Saif, who smiles tightly back at me.

After about two hours in the woods, we finally come upon it. How Diego managed to find a single tree in this forest is beyond me, but I'm too tired to care. The portal tree is an enormous live oak that looks like it was plucked out of a fairy tale about a witch who eats little children. Its huge trunk and gnarled branches must hold countless memories. I gape at it as we approach.

Just as when we had walked through to the willow tree back in Tenazeryth, the feeling of walking through an invisible gossamer web sends shivers down my spine as we pass under the branches and approach the trunk. Once all our hands are against the bark, Diego wastes no time.

"*Trafnidiaeth.*"

Again, the sensation that I'm dropping through the ground, being whisked away by the roots of the tree, before being deposited back on solid ground at the edge of the Cuhloch Forest. Only now, we're under a towering pine tree.

"What does that word mean?" I ask the group as we plunge into the forest. I already miss the smell of the decaying fall leaves back on Earth. "What language is it?"

"It's Welsh for 'transport,'" Saif says absently.

"Hmm." I think for a moment. "'Transport' makes sense, but why Welsh? Wouldn't it make more sense if the gateways here could only be activated by an Indigenous language? Algonquian? Or an Iroquoian language? Or I mean, *any* of the other ones? Why *Welsh?*"

No one says anything for a moment, but I see several brows furrow. Valentina is the one to break the silence. "That's a good question," she shrugs. "Why have all the kings been white men at all when all the portals are in North America?" She shrugs again.

I gape at her. I hadn't even considered that, but of course it doesn't make any fucking sense. *Check your biases, Shaw,* I chide myself silently. *And ask your father when you get back.*

Diego makes an exasperated sound ahead of us. "Because they took Tenazeryth for themselves too, just like everything else. Now be quiet, and save your energy. We've got a long day ahead of us."

My mind swirls as we walk into the warm and silent forest. I stay at the back of the group, as far away from Diego as possible.

I notice after a while that the land here looks like it's dying. Dead trees litter the forest floor, and there is little vegetative ground cover. After several minutes of feeling unnerved and trying to pinpoint why, it hits me that I don't hear any birds. In fact, there isn't any wildlife anywhere.

"This forest is as still as death," I say uneasily.

Saif shivers beside me. "It's probably because of Bleddyn. He's poisoned it."

I make a thoughtful noise, and then we walk in near silence for the rest of the day. At one point, Saif walks over to Martín and mumbles at him. I can't hear everything over my labored breathing and the cracking sticks beneath our feet, but I catch pieces.

"Tonight . . . Give us . . . Alone?"

Martín glances over his shoulder at me and grins mischievously. I squint back at him suspiciously and blow a rogue hair away from my face. He looks back at Saif and nods, clasping the taller man's shoulder jovially. "No problem, *hermano.*"

We continue walking until the sun goes down.

By the time we find a clearing and Martín lights us a campfire to cook dinner - Hyun-Joo sets up a force field high above us to keep all the smoke from billowing up in one spot and possibly revealing our position — I'm dripping with sweat and utterly spent.

Once we've all eaten, rubbed our sore feet a bit, and Val has helped us each splash water on our faces, Diego assigns watches.

He looks as exhausted as I feel. I wonder, for a moment, if he actually *had* gotten any sleep last night, but then I remember the ice in his voice this morning, and how he had closed yet another door in my face, and I push my concern for him away.

I had extended an olive branch, and he had thrown it back in my face. *Clearly, he's madly in love with me,* I think caustically, glancing in Hyun-Joo's direction. *The man can't stand me.*

The critic sneers in my head wordlessly. I ignore it.

Hyun-Joo notices Diego's exhaustion too, and pulls him away into the woods, I assume to give him blood. Before I can stop myself, I try to picture how it works. Does he bite her neck? Do his fangs sink as easily into her skin as they had into mine? What would it be like for those fangs to slide into me as a human instead of a wolf?

I shudder and quickly halt my thoughts from going any farther. *Focus, Shaw. You're exhausted.*

Martín, seeing that Diego and Hyun-Joo have gone off, looks at Saif and me.

We're snuggled together on a log a bit back from the fire. He's staring into the flames, running his hand over my hair absently, and I'm lying across the log with my head in his lap. He's been distracted all day; he's barely said a word to me since this morning.

Martín nudges Valentina, then stands and stretches exaggeratedly. "Well, I think I'd like to get *some* exercise today at least, after all this sitting around. Dear sister." He holds out a hand to her. "Care to join me on a stroll and let these two get some . . . rest?" He winks dramatically at her.

Valentina looks up at him and rolls her eyes. "You're an idiot." But she takes his hand and they walk off into the trees. As soon as they're gone, Saif nudges me, and I stir. I had almost fallen asleep in his lap. I look up at him with a small smile.

"Want some tea?" He asks lightly. "I have something that will make you feel great after today."

I nod and watch as he goes to his pack, grabs some herbs, and puts them into his metal tea ball. He heats a kettle over the fire for a few minutes, then pours some water into a mug.

This man brought an actual ceramic mug on a mission through the woods to kill a werewolf. I smile at the thought. He's a creature of habit if ever there was one.

I can't wait to memorize all his idiosyncrasies. All the small, day-to-day behaviors like this one that make him *him*. Once we complete this mission, I'll officially be in the Order, and then . . . then I'll be home. With him. For the rest of his life, if he wants me. If he doesn't come to his senses and realize how much better than me he could do. Someone thin, or maybe someone incredibly fit like him. Someone who isn't an absolute wreck of a human.

I grimace. *Not even human.*

Werewolf.

I shake myself slightly. *Saif loves me,* I think firmly, silencing the critic's voice.

I lean against his shoulder while the tea steeps. It reminds me of something I had been meaning to mention to him. "I hope it's more of that hibiscus tea."

He looks at me questioningly. "What hibiscus tea?"

"The hibiscus tea you make for me during full moons," I reply, squinting at him.

He shakes his head distractedly as he dips the metal ball into the cup several times. "I've never given you any hibiscus tea. After your first transformation, I didn't bring you anything for full moons because I thought your stomach couldn't take it."

I frown into the mug and stare at the darkening water, which is quickly turning violet. "Well, there's been a mug of hibiscus tea on my desk every full moon for months. It helps my headaches."

He shrugs. "It must be Valentina. Have you asked her?"

My frown deepens as I recall Valentina trying to make tea for Martín as he wailed dramatically from the kitchen floor.

"No, I haven't. I guess it could be her." I shake away my confusion. It must be her; no one else would do that for me. Then something else nags at me. "What about the extra blankets those mornings?"

He shakes his head again as he removes the metal ball from the mug and sets it beside him on the log to dry. "She must have done that too. Once I'm asleep, I'm out like the dead. You know I'm not a night person."

I scratch my head, still frowning. He hands me the mug, and my thoughts whirl as I take the first sip.

It's fine. I'm a night person. Diego's voice from our first morning in the greenhouse reverberates around my mind like a gong has been struck. I nearly drop my mug, and Saif clasps my hands around it tightly.

"Careful, love. Drink up. It will make you feel better."

I hardly hear him; my mind is occupied with the memory of bumping into Diego in the hallway the night I first slept with Saif. A jolt runs through me.

I always make a few rounds at night.

Diego hardly ever seems to sleep at all. He's probably always wandering around the castle at night.

My heart begins to race as I sip the hot tea. I don't recognize the taste; it's bitter, but not undrinkable. It must be some special concoction for achy muscles, because my arms and legs start to tingle. I take another sip and lean against Saif.

He wraps his arm around my shoulders tightly, kisses me firmly on the top of the head, and sighs heavily into my hair.

I fit perfectly into him, and he's just as gentle and loving as always, but he's not the one I'm thinking about right now. Sweat beads up on the back of my neck.

Diego's the one doing those things for me. The realization hits me like a truck. He's been caring for me for months and never said a word. Never expected any thanks in return. Told no one, including me.

But *why?* My heart pounds in my chest as my breathing grows heavier.

He's in love with you, too.

My stomach twists, and at first, I think it's just anxiety. But then it twists again, and when I let out a small groan, Saif shifts.

"How are you feeling?" He's gazing down at me, his eyes tight in the corners, and glistening like he's in an immense amount of pain. I lean back in concern, swaying slightly. My muscles are like jelly, and my vision dims at the edges. I must have exerted myself today harder than I thought.

I blink to bring him back into focus. "Fine, I . . . Whatsamatter?" My words slur together. I breathe deep, trying to get a grip on myself as a tingling sensation runs from my neck into my limbs.

He cups a hand to my cheek, his jaw set. "I'm sorry it had to happen this way."

Disorder

I try to shake my head at Saif in confusion, but my equilibrium is completely gone, and I just end up pitching myself backward off the log, landing with a heavy thud in the cool dirt.

The mug crashes to the ground with me, shattering into pieces in front of my face. The hot liquid pools around me, rippling with each ragged breath I take.

"Wha . . . put . . . tea?" I slur, not even able to form the full sentence. He kneels beside me and brushes my hair out of my face.

"Just a bit of wolfsbane. Don't worry, it's only enough to incapacitate you until morning."

Hot tears run down my cheeks into the dirt. "Wh . . . why?" I croak.

His mouth twists grimly and shakes his head. "You wouldn't understand. Not yet."

He runs a hand through his dark curls as he stands. My vision swims as I try to focus on him. "Don't worry, *Lahabi*. No one will hurt you ever again." He clenches his fist.

Diego? I think hazily. *Is this about Diego?*

He continues. "Your father will be dethroned, and we'll all be better off." He sounds panicked. Almost deranged.

This is all to get back at my father and Diego for Imane's death. *Is her ghost really worth more than me?* I try to ask him, but my lips won't form the words. *Did you ever really love me?* The thought twists a knife in my gut, on top of the pain from the wolfsbane.

"Tricked. Me," I hiss slowly.

"No." He shakes his head fiercely. "No, I'm saving you."

I try to scream at him, but it just comes out as a pathetic groan.

Suddenly, a lanky form lifts me from the ground and carries me away from Saif. "Quickly now, and be careful with her," he says.

Whoever is carrying me growls at him; they don't seem to care for his direction.

I'm being carried hastily away from the campfire, and though I try to scream, all I can manage is a gurgle.

"What the fuck is going on here?" Valentina's voice pierces my hazy thoughts. All at once, a rushing wave crashes into the person holding me, and I fall to the earth. I can't catch myself, and I'm certain a few of my ribs would have cracked against the ground if the water didn't whisk me softly away.

Chaos explodes around the campsite. From where I'm lying, I can see everything, though the shapes swim in and out of focus.

Valentina is throwing daggers of water at a werewolf. *No,* I realize. *Not a werewolf.* This wolf is upright on two legs, and it's wearing a shirt and pants. My recall is slow and hazy, but I recognize this creature. Not from a book in my father's library, but from my childhood. I can see the book as clear as day. My grandfather read it to me all the time when I was little, and would put on voices for all the characters.

A wulver. Wolf-headed creatures that were never human, though they walk on two legs. They're Scottish fairy tales. They aren't real.

But no one has told the wulver that.

It's got a very real Celtic sword in one hand, and a silver chain hanging off the belt at its waist like a whip.

Saif is yelling, trying to close vines around Valentina's wrists, but she's too fast for the two of them; she slices through everything he sends at her easily, and keeps the wulver at bay with large waves.

"Val, stop! Just listen!" Saif screams, but Valentina is not in a listening mood.

I hear Martín in the distance, yelling his sister's name. I take a ragged breath, and when I open my eyes again, a second wulver emerges from the darkness between the trees. It advances on Valentina, who has her back turned toward it, fighting off the first wulver and Saif.

I try to scream a warning, but can only wheeze.

Martín crashes into the clearing a split second later and takes in the scene for only a moment before seeing the second wulver's ax move for his sister's back.

And Martín, the protective older brother, who used to distract their father so that he was the one to end up bruised and bloody instead of Valentina, who would literally burn the world to the ground for her. He does what he has always done.

He steps in to take the blow for his little sister.

Martín jumps between the wulver's ax and Valentina as the blade falls, and instead of landing in her back, it hits Martín's chest with a sickening squelch. The wulver freezes in confusion for a moment, and it's all Martín needs.

He reaches out, using the last of his strength to grip the wulver's arm, and the Mongrel goes up in a raging inferno. The light is blinding, and the heat is dangerously intense. In seconds, it's a pile of ashes on the ground, and Martín falls to his knees, blood spraying everywhere around him.

I choke on the acrid smell of burning fur and flesh.

"*No!*" Saif screams. Valentina turns to see what happened and freezes in horror.

Just then, Saif and the wulver are flung into the air with such force, it's as if an invisible wrecking ball had hit them. Hyun-Joo walks out of the woods from behind me, not sparing me a glance as she steps over my limp form.

Saif and the wulver recover quickly for having been thrown twenty feet through the air. He clambers to his feet, and then he and Hyun-Joo stare at one another for several long moments. He shakes his head at her, a pleading look in his eyes. "Please. Just listen."

Hyun-Joo draws herself up to her full height, then turns halfway back around to me, her eyes brimming with tears as she screams back into the trees. *"Diego!"*

Saif snarls in rage. The wulver grabs him and pulls him behind as it runs off. They disappear into the trees, and then everything is utterly, eerily silent.

It's all over in less than sixty seconds.

Diego crashes out of the trees behind me then, and in an instant, he's on his knees at my side. He rolls me onto my back and puts a finger to my throat to check my pulse.

I groan at him as he cups my cheeks with his hands. His glittering red eyes are bright with horror. I reach a hand to him shakily, and it lands heavily on his thigh.

"Who did this to you?" He hisses as he frantically runs his hands along my body, checking for wounds. His eyes dart around the clearing, looking for threats, then back to me.

"Sa . . . if," I gasp, writhing on the ground.

He shakes his head in disbelief. "No . . . no he was supposed to keep you safe. He was the better choice."

What the fuck does that mean? I try desperately to ask him, but my strength flits away from me like a will-o-the-wisp.

When he finds no wounds on me, he looks up at Hyun-Joo for help, but her gaze is not directed at me. He looks across the campsite, and his mouth twists in horror.

"No!" He rolls me gently back onto my side in case I vomit or try to swallow my own tongue, then jumps over me, running for the other side of camp.

I can see Valentina and Martín once again; Hyun-Joo and Diego are quickly by their side.

Valentina is wracked with sobs. "No no no no no *please!*" She clutches her brother to her chest, soaking herself in his slick blood. She slaps his face and shakes him. *"Martín!"*

He coughs once, and blood gushes from his mouth as he raises a shaky hand to her cheek. *"Lo siento,"* he whispers, and then his arm slides back down and lands softly in the dirt.

Valentina screams her throat raw as every drop of dew on the foliage around us explodes in a million different directions.

For what feels like a lifetime, there is no sound in the clearing but Valentina's wails. I reach a hand out to her hazily.

This can't be happening. I try to sob, but it just comes out as a faint moan. Hyun-Joo looks at me, finally, and sees me reaching for Valentina.

I have to do something. This can't be how her story goes. This can't be how Martín's ends.

Like hell.

Hyun-Joo nudges Diego and points to me. He turns, and, seeing my feeble attempt at clawing my way across the ground, comes to gather me into his arms and carry me over to the bloody scene. He doesn't lay me back on the ground, but instead cradles me in his lap as he sits next to Valentina and Martín's body.

I reach my left hand out, not to Valentina, but to Martín. His chest is cracked open, and broken ribs poke out at sickening angles. His eyes are still open, but they're devoid of everything that made him *him*. There is no mirth in them now, no fierce loyalty.

Hot tears run down my cheeks as I groan. *I'm so sorry*, I want to tell him. *You should have stayed away. I shouldn't have trusted Saif. I should have known what he was planning. I should have come alone with Diego like he wanted.*

Martín had always protected everyone else. He never had someone to step in and protect *him*. I clutch as hard as I can into his shoulder, my body spasming as my silent sobs battle against the wolfsbane for control of my muscles.

I shut my eyes against the fury building in my core, and wish desperately that I could magically stitch his wounds, clear the film from his eyes, and bring the smile back to his face. My nails dig deeper into his shoulder.

I wish I could fix this.

A tiny vibration buzzes to life in my navel. Another symptom of the wolfsbane poisoning, I think at first. But then the vibration increases, travels up through my chest, into my arm, and into the fingertips that are still digging into Martín's body.

Reddish-brown light pools slowly around my fingertips, and then shoots into him. *It's the same color as Mars*, I think wildly.

Valentina hisses. "What are you doing to him?" She reaches for my hand, but Hyun-Joo grabs her arm.

"Wait. Look."

The light spreads out from my fingertips, each small circle blending with the others until my entire hand is glowing, and I can *feel* it vibrating like mad, but my hand is steady.

Martín's skin moves of its own accord then, and the sight is so unnatural that I would vomit if I could, but my muscles no longer obey me. They only obey the vibration and the rusty glow. The skin slowly reaches for itself, coming together like I'm using invisible stitching to sew him back together.

His rib bones crackle and pop as they return to their normal positions. When his skin is seamless once more, the light flares up, blinding us all as it flashes out of existence.

Martín gasps.
Valentina screams.
I black out.

336

Strange Firsts

I come to not much later, lying on the ground a few feet from Diego, who is bent over a loudly groaning Martín. Diego is trying to wipe the blood off Martín with a shirt from someone's pack, but must be scared that he's going to harm him; his gentle wiping motion just spreads the blood around on both of them.

I realize, then, that Hyun-Joo and Valentina are screaming at each other. "I am *not* just going to turn tail and run! He almost killed my brother! I'm going to get that bastard and make him *pay!*" Valentina is more furious than I've ever heard her. I didn't even know she had a vengeful bone in her body.

Hyun-Joo makes an exasperated sound, as though this is the millionth time they've said these exact words. "It isn't *running* to take your resurrected brother back through the portal so he can get to a good fucking hospital!"

"Fuck you!" Valentina spits. "There's no reason you can't be the one to take him so I can get him justice!"

Hyun-Joo screams in ire. "Diego, talk to her! Give her an order! Do *something!*"

Diego is taking Martín's pulse. "Valentina, you have to be the one to take Martín to a hospital. If you go after him now, you'll be sloppy. It won't be safe for you or anyone else. You're emotionally compromised."

Hyun-Joo looks at me, sees me staring at her, and speaks anyway. I already know what she's going to say. She's said it before. "We wouldn't want anyone emotionally compromised."

Diego growls wordlessly.

"Fuck your orders. I'm going." Valentina sits down on the ground and cradles her brother's head in her lap. He's still not conscious, just groaning occasionally.

Diego and Hyun-Joo look at each other, communicating silently, and the fight goes out of her.

Tonight is a night of many strange firsts.

"Fine," she bites out, and stalks off toward her sleeping bag.

At that, Diego leaves Valentina with her brother and comes over to me. He scoops me up into his arms easily, then carries me over to my sleeping bag, which is still unrolled next to Saif's. He takes one look at Saif's sleeping bag and flings it viciously into the fire, smothering the flames.

Diego holds me in his lap for a few minutes, stroking my hair. I try to tell him that I'm sorry. That I should have listened to him, and come on this mission with just the two of us, but all I manage is a weak whisper against his chest.

"My. Fault."

He shakes his head fiercely, and if I didn't know better, I'd think there were unshed tears crackling in his voice when he speaks. "It's not your fault." He takes a ragged breath through gritted teeth. "What was that? That you did to Martín?"

I shake my head slowly against him and breath in his familiar scent. "Wish. I knew."

I slip into the inky void once again.

Written in Stone

When I open my eyes again, the first thing I realize is that it's dawn. The second is that I can move my limbs again. The third is that there is a huge, scorching presence behind me.

I roll over stiffly in my sleeping bag, and make contact with Diego's elbow. He's curled up on the ground just as he had been that one morning in the greenhouse. Except now, he's curled up next to me, so close that the heat from his body permeated the sleeping bag and kept me warm all night.

I yelp and recoil, and his eyes snap open. As soon as he sees the look on my face, he sits up and scans around the clearing. "What's wrong? Is he back?" He growls, his fangs sliding out of his gums, and I just gape up at him.

"What are you doing?" I squeak.

He snaps his attention back to me. "You looked petrified. I thought Saif was back."

My mouth works several times as I try to utter a reply, but then movement behind him catches my eye, and I realize that Hyun-Joo was curled up on the other side of him, though she's sitting up now, too.

"Eilidh?" I whip to my right, and Valentina is sitting up a few feet away. Martín doesn't stir from his spot next to her, but his chest rises and falls steadily.

Oh. We were just all huddled close together for warmth. That's all.

I blink as the hazy memory of Diego smothering the fire flashes across my mind. Indeed, Saif's sleeping bag is still mostly intact, though badly charred, on top of what had been a pleasant campfire last night.

I flush. "Sorry." I clear my throat. "Nightmare."

Diego casts his gaze at the ground, and I look away from the way his dark eyelashes brush the tops of his cheeks. "That's understandable," he growls.

He stands and holds out a hand to me, and I just stare at it for a beat. But then I grab it tentatively, and he pulls me to my feet, guides me over to a log, and helps me sit down against it.

"Eilidh," Valentina says, her voice strained. "What the fuck happened?"

I take a breath and steady myself. "Wolfsbane."

She hisses air in between her teeth. Hyun-Joo looks to the side, her mind whirring with the new information. Diego looks murderous.

"Why?" His voice cuts the air like a knife.

I curl in on myself involuntarily. There's only one answer that makes sense.

"Because of you," I say quietly, and Diego blinks hard like I've slapped him. "He hates you. He must have wanted to make you pay." I wince, knowing my next words are going to set him off. "For Imane's death."

I'm right. Diego moves, lightning fast. He picks up a small boulder nearby and hurls it at a tree that explodes into a million splinters. "*Fuck!*"

None of us stop him; we let him rage. Several more trees in the immediate vicinity meet their untimely demise.

Finally, he comes back over, running a hand through his hair. His brow glistens with sweat. I avert my gaze.

Hyun-Joo glances at Diego, and then breaks the silence. "That doesn't make any sense."

I scoff at her in disbelief. "Well that's what the asshole who drugged me last night said, so I'm just telling you — "

She cuts me off. "No, I mean, I believe that's part of it. But he could have hurt you at any time before last night to get to Diego. Why did he wait so long?"

Valentina and Diego look at me, waiting for the answer.

I consider, just for a moment, feigning ignorance. But they deserve my honesty. They deserve to see the whole picture.

"He wants to hurt Auberon too. Wants him to agree to step down from the throne, I think." *At least, I hope that's the plan.*

"But why would kidnapping you be enough to get Auberon to abdicate the throne?" Hyun-Joo asks. "Sorry, but you're not even officially in the Order, and he definitely wouldn't step down if any of us were in danger."

I sigh wearily and hang my head. "He's my father."

None of them move for several moments. When I look up at them, they've all got incredulous looks on their faces. I sigh again. I wish that I had the photograph with me. That would make it all so much faster, not to mention more believable. I recount Auberon's tale as quickly as I can, and by the end, they're all staring at me in shock.

Diego walks away from us and bends over, his hands on his knees, looking vaguely like he's going to vomit.

Valentina shakes her head at me. "We just saw your father's grave yesterday. His name was literally written in stone."

I squint at her in confusion, but Hyun-Joo is nodding in agreement. I recall that I hadn't told Saif that I was raised by my grandparents before revealing this news to him, either.

Way to go, Shaw. I am truly, utterly terrible at opening up to the people I love. I hang my head in regret.

"Those weren't my parents. They were my *grand*parents. My grandparents raised me."

Realization dawns on the two women in sync. Hyun-Joo shakes her head. "*Ileon jenjang.*" I can guess the meaning of that. *Holy shit.*

Valentina looks at me then, her eyes glistening. "Why didn't you tell me?" She asks softly.

I wince and huddle into myself. "I don't know. It just — it hurts. It's easier to not talk about it."

She just looks away, shaking her head in small, agitated motions. "You didn't tell me about Kianga, either."

"I'm sorry," I whisper helplessly. "I just couldn't. She was my whole world. She was my sun, Val, and I was just her moon. Every time I think of her, it's like losing her all over again. Everything just goes dark and cold, because I know she isn't around anymore to shine. Please understand," I plead as I reach for Valentina's hand, but she pulls away from me, and I dig my nails into my palm instead.

The oppressive silence stretches on as Diego shakes his head at the ground and mutters to himself, imperceptible to the others. "She thinks she's the *moon.*" He chuckles to himself, then finally stands back up and comes back over to us, running a hand over his face roughly.

I shift uncomfortably. I know he's laughing because I think so highly of myself, but I have no better metaphor at the ready.

Hyun-Joo has yet more questions. "What about that rust-colored light? You *resurrected* Martín. How long have you been keeping *that* skill a secret?"

I shake my head at her. "I have no idea what that was. I was just wishing that I could bring him back and fix my mistake. It was the thing I wanted most in the world. What happened to him — it was all my fault."

Tears sting my eyes. "If I had just listened to Diego and made this a two-person mission. If I hadn't told Saif about my father the other day. None of this would have happened."

So many mistakes in so little time.

Hyun-Joo doesn't look entirely convinced, but for once, she doesn't fight me. "Well, we'll have plenty of time later to attend group therapy and figure out all of that, but right now, we have to focus on the next steps. I'm taking Martín to the hospital. You three need to find Bleddyn and put an end to him." She grimaces. "At least that will solve one of our problems."

I grit my teeth. "And then when I find Saif," I growl. The three of them look at me, but I don't meet any of their eyes. I think of Azaeroria clamping the rag over my face as I thrash helplessly, tied to a cold stone slab. Of Saif standing over me as hot tea pools around me on the ground.

I am sick and tired of being betrayed.

My jaw tenses with resolve. "I'm going to fucking castrate him."

No one says anything for a moment, but then a strange noise erupts from Hyun-Joo's mouth. It takes me a moment to process that she's *laughing*, and it's not the derisive cackle I've heard from her before. It's a genuine, mirthful laugh.

I stare at her, my jaw hanging open. When her laughter dies down, she wipes a tear from one eye and smiles at me.

"God, I wish I could be there to see that."

~~~~~~~~~

About thirty minutes later, we're all packed up and ready to head out. Valentina, Diego, and I have put on our battle suits that Val made for the fight with Bleddyn, but since we can't be sure that we won't be attacked before we make it to him, Diego had insisted that we needed
~~~~~~~~~

to be prepared.

His suit looks the same as the one he wears for full moons, except this one is navy. Valentina's is the color of Merlot, which complements her Black skin perfectly. Her eyes are fierce, and she's moving in a way I've never seen her before, clipped and disciplined. She looks like a woman who was raised on a battlefield.

I suppose, in a way, she was.

I pull my emerald suit on and realize that it is not, in fact, spandex as I had thought at first, but a much thicker fabric, though surprisingly stretchy and comfortable. And - thank goodness - breathable.

I pull my hair into a quick side braid. It frizzes everywhere, but it's as good as it's going to get. I strap my holster to my right thigh and secure my silver dagger. Its weight is reassuring, and I grip the hilt tightly.

Hyun-Joo has created a type of force-field gurney for Martín, who has stopped groaning, but I'm not sure if that's a good sign or not.

Valentina clutches her brother's hand and kisses him on the forehead. *"Te amo."* She lets go reluctantly, and then we all stand in silence for a moment, steeling ourselves for what we need to do next.

Hyun-Joo moves to Diego and gives him a fierce hug. He wraps his large arms around her and holds her close. A pang reverberates in my gut.

They really do have a special bond, but looking at them now, at the way they hold each other, it's obvious that it was never a romantic one. Their hearts are bound, their souls are intertwined, and that is as true a love as any.

When they release one another, Hyun-Joo walks to me, and I freeze. *Is she going to hug me next?*

But instead, she grasps my hands in hers and looks up at me fiercely. Her eyes are dewy, but her voice is steady. "Bring him back to me." I can only nod in reply. She turns on her heel and walks off without another word, Martín floating next to her. The three of us stare at her back until she and Martín disappear through the trees.

"*Vamos*," Diego says softly as he turns and takes off into the trees. Valentina doesn't take my hand to walk like she usually does; she strides purposefully behind Diego, her head held high.

We walk in single file farther into the silent forest.

Collapse

I can feel the wulver's disapproving glare on my back. *Like I give a fuck what she thinks.* I know she already thinks I'm a failure. *Because I am.*

Ruined. Everything is ruined, and it was all for nothing. Eilidh is still out there, oblivious as to what's coming for her. I grip *Dhabiha's* hilt so tightly that she vibrates.

And Martin. A sob rips free from my throat as the thick wall of thorny vines knits together. I don't try to wipe away my tears. Let them stain my skin. Just like his blood, which will forever be on my hands.

When the wall is complete, I collapse to the ground, shaking. I'm running on no sleep, and it's catching up to me. "You're sure Bastet got word that we're here?" I ask the wulver over my shoulder, and she just nods.

Quite the chatterbox, this one.

I don't bother trying to rise to my feet, I just collapse onto my stomach and put my head on my arms. "Fine. Wake me when she gets here."

The wulver says nothing.

~~~~~~~~~
~~~~~~~~~

I'm awoken by a mighty crash, and I jump up and unsheathe *Dhabiha* before I've even consciously registered what happened.

"Holy shit," I breathe as I slide her back into the scabbard.

A midnight blue wyvern the size of a school bus has dropped from the sky. The woman riding it jumps off gracefully and lands lightly on the balls of her feet, then turns and bows to the wyvern.

My eyes widen as I take in her striking outfit. *She sure knows how to make an impression.*

Bastet turns to the wulver. "What the fuck happened? *Where* is Auberon's daughter?"

Her voice sets off an alarm bell in the back of my mind, but I shake myself. *I'm losing it.* I need more sleep, and a chance to actually process what I've done.

The wulver jerks her head at me. Though the upper half of Bastet's face is covered in a cat mask, I can feel her withering glare.

"The Order happened," I growl furiously.

"Was it Diego?" Bastet's voice is razor-sharp, but still, something about it burns through me like whiskey.

It takes me a moment to formulate my response. "No, actually it wasn't. I wouldn't have made it out of there alive if it had been him," I mutter grimly.

Neither one of us would have.

Bastet steps toward me, and I have to actively avoid looking at the hypnotic swaying motion of her hips. I shake myself again.

She stops a few feet away, and I gaze back at the thick material covering the eye holes of the cat mask.

"I should have known it wouldn't be so easy," she says, and before I have time to reply, she pulls the mask off. "Guess I'll have to get the little *princess* myself." She looks down her nose at me, and it's only then that I realize I've collapsed to my knees.

I think my lungs have collapsed too, given the fact that I am suddenly unable to breathe.

Perhaps the world itself is collapsing.

No. That's impossible.

"What's wrong, Saif?" She purrs. "You look like you've seen a ghost."

Collision

Just before sunset, we come upon a clearing occupied by a small ring of four small, seemingly abandoned, log cabins. Vines have taken over most of their outsides, and two of them have broken windows. One doesn't even have a front door. It's the first sign of habitation we've seen since coming through the portal back into Tenazeryth.

Well, former habitation. Maybe Bleddyn had run off the occupants just like he had all the wildlife.

Diego consults his map, his brow furrowed. "This place isn't marked on the map." Then he growls and crumples it, shoving it roughly into one of his pockets. "Let's search the cabins. If they're empty, we can crash here for the night. We shouldn't be more than a few more hours from where Bleddyn is."

He pauses, running his hands through his hair, his mouth twisted in annoyance. "Assuming Saif's intel wasn't wrong. Or a trap."

He stalks off, mumbling under his breath in Spanish, and Valentina and I follow behind him.

She hasn't spoken to me all day. I don't know how to begin to apologize to her for keeping so many things from her. Though it hadn't been intentional, my intentions don't matter; I had hurt her.

My heart twists. *She must think I don't trust her.*

We sweep each of the four cabins, but there's nothing in any of them. Quite literally nothing — not even any furnishings. I expect to walk in and see dinner plates still on the dining tables, or at the very least, mattresses stripped bare, but all four of the cabins are absolutely devoid of any evidence that they had once been inhabited. The flight of the residents here had been planned, and thoroughly executed.

In the only cabin with fully intact windows and doors, Diego finally sets down his pack. Valentina follows suit, and I lean against a wall and slump to the ground. None of us speak.

The silence stretches on painfully. No one breaks it.

We all sit against a different wall and eat provisions from our packs. I finish first and try to sit in silence, but the sound of the other two chewing sets my teeth on edge. I stand, tap the silver dagger strapped to my thigh in its holster, and head outside.

I walk to the diagonal cabin and head around the rear. I take my dagger and draw a large "X" in the wood. This dagger, it seems, does not dull. I've had it for months now, and have never once had to sharpen it, despite slashing and stabbing it into straw bales and wooden dummies every day.

I back up ten paces, nearly reaching the edge of the ring of trees, then fling the dagger at the "X." I miss fantastically, but I at least get it to stick into the wood, albeit about five feet to the right of my target. I walk to the dagger, pull it out, and try again.

As the sun fades completely, I realize that I can still see perfectly fine in the dim twilight. I look up into the sky and my eyes land on the moon instantly, easily visible through the barren branches. She hangs above me, watching my progress silently, but she's partially turned away, only in her waning gibbous form tonight. *Odd.*

I'm able to see in the dark as a wolf, but this is the first time my night vision has presented itself as a human. I decide that I'm not going to question it right now; I table it for later. I pull my dagger out of the wall and continue.

At least another hour goes by, and by then, I've hit the center of the "X" numerous times. I have practiced running away from the cabin and flinging it behind me while in motion, tumbling and throwing it from my knees, and even a few times from flat on the ground.

I don't hit it every time, but it's always reasonably close. If my target was a person - or a werewolf - my dagger would have buried deep into their flesh. Grim satisfaction fills me.

I decide to do one more throw, and then try to go back and get some rest. Hopefully, Diego and Valentina have long ago fallen asleep, and I can slip in without any awkward tension. I lean against the wall of the cabin for one moment to breathe, then I sprint away.

After a few steps, I turn and slide on my knees (thank goodness for this thick suit), and fling the dagger as hard as I can back toward the wall.

At the exact moment the hilt leaves my gloved fingertips, I realize that Diego is standing directly in front of the "X" on the wall.

I open my mouth to yell at him to get out of the way, but at the last second, he steps to the side and grabs the hilt of the dagger out of midair.

The tip of the blade hovers inches away from the very center of the "X."

I stand, thunderous. "What the fuck are you doing? I could have killed you!"

He scoffs and rolls his eyes. "Please."

I clench my fist and growl.

He narrows his eyes. "What are *you* doing? You should be sleeping! You have to kill a monster tomorrow, in case you forgot."

I stalk to him and grab for my dagger, but he reaches up and sticks it into the wood of the cabin, far above his head, and even farther out of my reach.

"I'm *fine*," I bite out, looking up. I consider jumping for my dagger, but I refuse to give him the satisfaction. I cross my arms and glare up at him instead. "Where's Valentina?"

"Asleep," he says. "Where you should be. Now come to bed," he snaps, jerking his head toward the other cabin.

I bristle. "Stop barking orders at me."

He puts his hands on his waist. "I'm your commander."

"You still don't get to make all my decisions for me!" Something he had said last night nags at me, and I'm too angry and exhausted to follow my better instincts and stay silent.

I glare at him. "What did you mean, Saif was the better *choice?* Choice for what?" I grit my teeth. "Choice for *who?* Who gets to make it?" I whisper the last sentence furiously.

He gazes at me for a long moment, a million emotions flashing through his eyes, though his face is completely blank. Then he looks away and sighs deeply. "Don't worry about it."

I let out a loud cry of frustration and begin pacing back and forth like a caged animal. "Why is everything so goddamn difficult with you? Why can't you ever just *talk* to me?"

He only ever *really* talks to me when we're alone during a full moon. Every other time he's around me, he's sneering condescendingly, or snapping orders.

He crosses his arms, still not looking at me. "There's nothing to talk about."

I stalk to him and bend my neck back to glare up into his infuriating face. "I can't fucking *stand* you!" I shove against his chest with one hand, but he doesn't budge. Because of course he doesn't.

He smirks and puts his hands on his hips. "Yeah, keep telling yourself that *Princess*. Maybe eventually you'll believe it." He cocks his head to the side and grins mockingly.

My nostrils flare. I want to knock that grin off his face.

"Don't call me that." My teeth are clenched so hard I fear they may break.

He leans down toward me close enough for his blazing eyes to fill my vision. "Or what?"

My vision flashes red, and my hand moves, lightning fast.

I get exactly one hit in, snapping his neck to one side. He stands, unmoving, in that position for a beat.

As he turns back to me, chuckling and licking blood from the corner of his lip where I had made contact, there's a dangerous glint in his eye.

"You can do better than that, *Lobita*."

I take a second swing.

Before I can make contact though, he grabs my wrist, twirls me around, and pins it above my head, slamming my back into the rough wood of the cabin wall. I groan through gritted teeth.

I hang onto his arm for leverage, then rear up and kick out viciously, both feet aimed at his solar plexus.

He blocks my kick with his free hand, grips tightly into my soft waist, and shoves his hips between my legs, pinning me between himself and the wall. Then he grabs my other arm and pins it above my head as well, immobilizing me.

I thrash wildly, arching against him, but he pushes his full weight into me, crushing me against the cabin wall. I bare my teeth at him and growl in frustration.

"*Salvaje*," he rumbles at me with a smirk.

"Fuck you," I spit.

He looms over me, his face inches from mine. We're both breathing hard, and his pupils are so large that his eyes are practically pools of inky darkness. If I look much longer, I could drown in them.

I wonder for a split second what that would be like. *Maybe it wouldn't be so terrible.*

My eyes move to his thick lips. His fangs have popped out, and he must have bitten himself when I punched him, because they're slick with blood, glittering like razor-sharp rubies. A drop runs down his chin.

My whole body vibrates.

I look up to see him staring hungrily at the crook of my neck where he had bitten me the night of my first transformation. I can remember with perfect clarity how it felt to have him sink his fangs into me, and the euphoria that had followed.

I shiver.

He drags his heavy gaze back up to meet mine, and a fiery bomb explodes in my core.

"Fuck," he rumbles, almost to himself. There's a note of resignation in his tone, like something he's been keeping at bay for far too long has finally broken through his defenses.

I lean up into him as hard as I can as he brings his mouth down onto mine with a growl.

We collide with stunning force.

Explosion

I try to yank my wrists away from Diego's clutches, but he pins them both against the rough wood of the cabin with one forearm. With his other hand, he pulls me deeply into him, and our bodies curve together perfectly as I wrap my legs tightly around his waist.

He forces my mouth open roughly with his tongue, and we move together like a choreographed dance, taking quick gulps of air between kisses like we're drowning in a raging storm that keeps pushing us beneath the waves.

He tastes mostly of copper from the blood, but there's something floral underneath. Something familiar that I finally recognize.

Hibiscus.

I adjust my hands enough to scratch my nails along his forearm, and he lets go, growling deep into my mouth. He lifts me up higher against the wall so that I'm propped slightly above him, then he twists his hand up into my hair and pulls my head to the side so he can kiss my jawline.

As soon as my hands are free, I rake my nails up his back as hard as I can. He moans against my neck, and it's almost a whimper. It stokes the fire in my belly.

My hands move to his shaggy chestnut hair, and I grab fistfuls and tug. Our kisses slow a fraction, and it's all I need. I pull his head to one side and bite his muscular neck.

He moans, then pulls his head back, out of my reach, panting desperately.

"*¡Espérate!*"

I glare at him blankly, and he translates.

"Wait." His crimson irises are becoming more visible again. "I can't," he says between gasps. He interprets my expression before I even have to open my mouth to utter a word. "What if I hurt you?"

I don't know if he means physically, or something else — something far more permanent. But either way, I don't care.

His eyes are remorseful, but resigned. What a selfless leader. What a martyr.

What a fucking idiot.

I lean my forehead gently against his as I run my hands through his hair. Then I chuckle wickedly, yank his head sideways, and bite hard on his earlobe while my other hand rakes down his back. He lets out a higher-pitched moan than before.

"You know I don't break that easily." My voice is low and thick with desire, and he shudders.

This is, apparently, the only persuasion he needs. He trusts my judgment. After all the training he has given me, he knows that *I* know my limits, and my strengths.

He cups my ass with one hand, moves the other around the back of my neck, and slams my mouth back down onto his just as he adjusts me so that my pussy is right against the outline of his hard cock. He feels *huge*.

I moan against his mouth, and he pulses between my legs. Though our suits are thick, I'm quickly soaking through mine. The anticipation is going to drive me to madness long before I even get his pants off.

He grinds against me several times, and we drink each other in. Then, in one quick motion, he moves his hand out from under my ass, props me up against one knee, and rips ferociously at the zipper of my suit. In the next instant, he pulls it down to my waist, and unhooks my bra.

He kisses between my breasts, directly on my scars, then pulls one of my nipples into his mouth as he tosses the bra to the side. I arch against him as hard as I can, leaning my head back into the wall, and moan. He tugs on the bottom of my braid, pulling my neck back even farther.

"Holy *fuck*," I breathe. My mind is short-circuiting. I moan uncontrollably as pleasure erupts all over my body. I've never made a sound like that before, but then again, I've never been kissed like this.

I quickly clamp a hand over my mouth, but due to whatever biological codes that were written into us through eons of evolution, the noise works on him.

He pulls my hand roughly away from my face. "Don't you fucking dare," he growls. "I want to hear every sound those pretty lips of yours can make."

I whimper pathetically, and he releases a satisfied groan.

He begins grinding his hips in a way that rubs his cock directly against my clit, then moves his mouth from one nipple to the other, with a murmured "*Mierda.*"

Even I know that one.

I realize that I have stopped moving, too caught up in the pleasure that he's causing all over my body.

"Can I kiss you again?" I whisper into his ear, and he moves immediately, like he's been waiting for this request. He puts one hand behind my neck and slams my mouth down onto his.

As our kisses deepen, I dig the nails of one hand into his back and rub between his legs with the other. His tongue stops moving against mine for a full second before he's growling at me again.

I could get very used to feeling that growl reverberating against my teeth.

Abruptly, he sinks to his knees, and kneels between my legs.

I've never brought someone to their knees before. Something deep within me takes control.

I reach around his neck and yank hard at his suit's zipper. It comes down instantly, and I pull his suit down over his impossibly wide shoulders before I shove him over. He lands hard on his back, and I land on top of him, my palms splayed across his solid chest.

I grind into his rock-hard bulge. I was right; he *is* huge, and there's no way I'm not soaking him through both our suits. He moves his hips too, in perfect synchrony with mine.

I run my hands through the sides of his hair, my nails scraping his scalp. He closes his eyes and bites his thick bottom lip with one razor-sharp fang. Another drop of blood beads up around it.

I clamp my mouth over his again, licking his lips, tasting every bit of him I can. When I'm finally able to pull my mouth off of his, I brush my lips over his ear. "Let me ride you," I breathe.

His eyes widen with lust, but then he smirks again. "I don't think so," he shoots back playfully.

I tilt my head at him and frown. "You don't *want* me to ride you?" A thought creeps up in the back of my mind. "Or, do you want to stop?" *Oh god.* He's changed his mind. He thinks that this is a huge mistake. That *I'm* a mistake.

I start to rise off him, but his hands fly to my hips, and he pulls me back down onto his cock as it throbs against his suit. I make a sound halfway between a yelp and a moan.

"Of fucking course I don't want to stop," he breathes. "But you aren't getting off that easily."

Before I have time to wonder if that pun was intended, he flips me onto the ground, flat on my back, with a solid *thump*, and I emit a keening noise that is definitely more pleasure than pain. It should hurt, but instead, it makes the adrenaline surge through me harder than before. He must have pulled out my hair tie when he was yanking on my braid earlier, because my hair splays out under me as I fall to the ground.

He tugs my suit down over my hips, then flings it aside the second my legs are free. He doesn't break our eye contact as he does it. My pussy throbs in anticipation of whatever is next.

He leans down over me and kisses from my collarbone up my neck until his deep timbre is rumbling in my ear. "You have to come for me before you get my cock," he says wickedly.

I shiver and let out a desperate sound.

He kisses back down my neck, over my collarbone, detours briefly to suck my nipple again, then moves down my stomach. Then he's kissing down over my hips, down the outside of my leg, and down to my foot.

With each kiss he plants on my burning skin, he runs his hands up and down my legs, caressing me, and there's so much sensory input, it's like he's tapped into every nerve in my body.

He kisses around my ankle and then moves upward, this time planting his kisses on the inside of my leg. As he passes my knee, his kisses intensify. He bites my inner thigh; his fangs prickle me, shooting sparks through me, and shattering any rational thoughts left in my head.

He moves so that his mouth is hovering over my clit, and I nearly combust with desire. But he brushes his lips ever so slightly over it, then moves up again to bite the other side of my neck.

I take the opportunity to rake my fingers through his hair once more, and he moans into my ear.

He begins the entire process again, down the other side of my body this time. He plants an extra long kiss on my semicolon tattoo, then bites his way up to my inner thigh, leaving his marks on me.

I'm going to fucking explode.

Just as I expect to feel his tongue on my clit, he moves upward *again*. Part of me is annoyed and vibrating with anticipation, but then the other part of me is kissing him desperately, and silently begging him to never remove his mouth from mine.

As our kisses halt once more, his eyes are playful. "Don't worry darling, we'll get there, but I want to enjoy this more first." He trails a claw under my chin, and the fire in my belly becomes a raging inferno. "I've thought about having you under me far too often not to take my time with you now."

He pushes his fingers against my pussy, and I moan pleadingly. He begins rubbing my clit in a circular motion with his thumb, keeping his pace and pressure consistent.

Then his other hand grips my chin, and he forces me to look him in the eye. "Scream for me," he commands, and I do, loudly, as his middle two fingers slide inside me. They're thick, and *long*.

"Good girl," he growls slowly, and his words shoot through every nerve in my body like lightning.

I close my eyes to focus on the sensation, but he halts, and I whimper as I look up at him beseechingly. "Eyes on me."

He starts those intoxicating movements again, and I shatter like glass around him. His deep, rhythmic motion sets me ablaze, and he presses his free hand against my stomach to hold me steady through my orgasm, holding me together as I come undone.

"There you go darling," he breathes. "Come nice and hard for me."

I do.

Passion

When I finally stop gasping and trembling, Diego removes his fingers from my pussy, and I take a few dazed breaths. He's gazing at me intensely, like he's filing this image in his mind for future reference. Like it's something he never wants to forget.

I decide to give him a show to remember. I close my eyes, arch up, and pinch my nipples as I moan loudly.

He shifts, and a second later he's rumbling in my ear again. "Tell me what you want."

I hesitate, but then I find my strength in the depth of his eyes, and swallow my apprehension. "You," I whisper, running a thumb along his sharp cheekbone. "I just want you."

The blinding smile he flashes at me will be emblazoned in my memories for the rest of eternity. "You have me, *Lobita*. I'm not going anywhere."

Our lips meet again, and I clutch him tightly until he finally pulls back. "Do you want me to taste you?" He whispers in my ear, and I shudder.

"Fuck yes." I don't *mean* for it to come out as a beg, but he seems to enjoy that it does.

His smile turns wicked. "As you wish," he rumbles.

My pussy throbs. In half a second, his tongue is directly on my lips, and then he's pushing them apart. He's working for this. He *wants* this. He wants *me*. The thought is too absurd for my brain to comprehend.

His tongue hits my clit, wide and flat, and I release a high moan as he circles all around it. He sucks on it, kisses it, and nibbles it gently with his teeth, and I'm drunk with pleasure. Then his fingers are at my entrance again, and he slides them in easily.

I scream with ecstasy.

He moves his long fingers inside me as he buries his face in my soaking lips, then curls them to find my G-spot. His rhythm is perfect. He shoves his other hand under my ass and squeezes hard.

Fuck. He knows everything I like.

I've lost all control. All my nerves are going haywire. I have to focus on something else quickly before I spontaneously combust. I move my foot under him and begin rubbing it against the hard outline of his cock.

He shudders and gasps, then utters a harsh "Fuck" against my clit. I match my rhythm to his. I thought this would be a distraction, but my brain is a traitor — it just enhances my pleasure. It's over not long after that.

I tug his hair harshly as waves of ecstasy explode from my center and crash throughout my body. He moans against my clit, and I arch back again and scream with pleasure. He doesn't change a thing — he keeps the rhythm he used to tip me over the edge, and that keeps the orgasm going for what feels like an hour.

Finally, it subsides enough that I can catch my breath. I'm lightheaded, and the only thing I can hear is the blood pounding in my ears as he finally begins to slow. Mercifully. Infuriatingly.

His eyes move slowly up my body before they meet mine. They're completely dilated again, dark as pitch. He moves to a kneeling position, and his cock pulses against his suit. He wipes a hand across his chin, where he is soaked from my juices.

Then he takes the two fingers that were just making themselves acquainted with my G-spot, puts them in his mouth, and sucks on them. As he removes them, he gently drags them over his tongue as he looks me in the eye.

"Fuck," I breathe shakily.

He's unbelievably sexy. He's ethereal. He's infuriating.

He smirks as if he can read my thoughts. "Looks like you *can* stand me after all." His musical voice is deeper than usual.

"Only when your mouth is too busy to say something stupid," I throw back at him.

The other side of his mouth twitches up and now he's fully smiling, his fangs glinting like daggers. I have the sudden mad wish that he would sink those fangs into my throat again.

I sit up slowly, my muscles still not completely done shaking with pleasure. "It's my turn to make *you* scream," I say.

His eyebrows perk up in the center just a bit. "Let's see what you've got."

We collide once more.

He tastes of frenzied lust — he tastes of *me*. And he had loved that taste. That drives me wild in a way I didn't know it could.

My hands knot in his shaggy brown waves again. They're thick and silky, and it's so damn satisfying to run my fingers through them. I pull his head to the side and bite his neck, just in the crook where his blood pulses under my teeth. He moans in my ear.

I move my hands to his hips, where the bottom of his suit is just begging to be pulled off him. I oblige, and realize that there is in fact another layer of fabric. He's wearing compression shorts under his suit, but they don't do very much — it's impossible to completely compress everything he has underneath them. I rip them off him and toss them aside.

His massive cock springs free, and it bobs up and down with each pump of his heart, like it's beckoning me. I shove him down to the ground once more.

He pulls me with him, and then we're entwined together, our breath rapid, our skin hot and dewy with desire. He gives me another deep, desperate kiss as his claws dig into my waist.

I back my ass up as I move down his wide chest, then down his washboard stomach. I kiss each of his hips while my hands grip his ass. He arches up involuntarily, but I kiss down harder on his hips, pushing him back down into the ground.

I wrap my hands around his cock, one over the other, and there's still some of him to spare; the tip points skyward as his length pulses in my hands.

I move my hands up and down a few times, feeling all of him. The tips of my thumb and middle finger just barely touch when I squeeze gently. He throws his head back, eyes closed, and moans. I can make him do more than that.

I lick around his tip with a wide, flat tongue. Then, all at once, I shove as much of him into my mouth as I can take — which is only about half of his length, thanks to my godforsaken gag reflex.

Shouldn't supernatural powers give you supernatural deep-throating abilities for supernatural dicks? *A tragedy.*

"That feels fucking amazing," he growls. I moan against his cock, and it pulses in my mouth. To hear this man actually praise me is driving me absolutely *wild.*

My hands work his base as my mouth moves up and down the top half of him. Our eyes lock, and he moans loudly. He digs his claws into the earth beside him like the gravity has been switched off, and he's afraid he's about to spiral into orbit.

I take a second to take in the sight of him. I don't know when - or even *if* - I'm going to get this chance again, so I'm going to enjoy the sight while I can. Commit it to memory, etch it into my mind's eye permanently.

Fucking hell. He's gorgeous.

I can't take it anymore. I bob down, pushing him as far into my mouth as I can once, twice, thrice, then quickly dislodge myself and crawl back up until my hips are over his.

I'm soaked again, and I press the tip of his cock to my opening, but his size is intimidating. His dark gaze bores into me like he knows exactly why I'm hesitating.

"You can take it, darling."

"Yes, sir," I breathe. I push my hips down hard, taking as much of him as I can at once. He groans loudly, and I suck air in through my teeth as he stretches me.

There's too much of him at first, and not enough room inside me, but after several long thrusts in and out, he fits perfectly. As soon as we're sealed together, he lays back his head and *whimpers*.

The sound of his pleasure snaps my brain into pieces, and no rational thoughts are left. It unleashes something primal in me. Something carnal. I need to hear it again. I need to hear it *forever*.

I move on top of him in steady, circular motions, moaning from the perfection of the angle; as I move my hips, his girth rubs my clit with each slide in and out of me. I'm upright at first, my hands splayed out across his lower abdomen. But soon, I'm crumbling down, too wracked with pleasure for my muscles to hold me up.

I lie on his chest, and my hair spreads out in a fiery pool around him. He wraps one arm around my back and digs his claws into me, and it should hurt, but it doesn't. It feels fucking *amazing*.

His other hand moves to cup my ass, then he pushes me onto his rock-hard erection over and over, driving himself deeper into me than I thought physically possible. He's giving me leverage, and we're using it to our mutual advantage.

He groans loudly. "I've thought for *months* about how you would feel on my cock, but I never imagined it would be this fucking good."

I scratch my nails down his chest as I come down onto him, and there's that whimper again.

Goddamn.

He follows it with a "Shit," and begins to pant in earnest. Our breath synchronizes as both of us gasp for air between our moans of pleasure. Mine quickly rise higher in pitch.

He clamps his mouth over mine as he tangles his hands tightly into my hair. He tastes of salt and copper, and I've never tasted anything more delicious.

We move as one. With each thrust up into me, he lets out a low moan against my mouth. This man is making more noise than any partner I've had in the past did, and it's driving me absolutely wild. Hearing the effect my body has on him is more rewarding than he could ever know.

When I've finally regained some control of my muscles, I push myself up and lean back until my hands rest on his muscular thighs, just above his knees.

At this new angle, he hits my G-spot with incredible force. He moves his hands to cup both my breasts, his thumbs circling my nipples.

He's thrusting so hard up into me that my knees have lifted off the ground, and we're fused so closely together that I'm not even sure we're two separate people anymore.

I've never felt this incredible. My body has taken over, and seems to know exactly what to do and what it needs from him.

"I want —" I clamp my mouth shut. I'm not sure why I spoke in the first place. It's not as if I can form a rational thought at this point. I try to act like I didn't say anything.

He notices.

"What do you want me to do, darling?"

"No, I." I gasp for air as he switches the tempo and slows a bit. "Nothing. Just this," I breathe. "Please don't stop," I whimper.

He bares his teeth at me, then puts his hand up into my hair and pulls me down toward him, forcing me to look into his eyes.

He stops moving his hips, and we're momentarily motionless, still sealed together. It's incredibly distracting.

"Use your words, and tell me what you want," he bites. I break under his gaze, and then my mouth voices what my mind hadn't worked out it wanted yet.

"I want to feel you pulsing inside me, Diego," I hiss. "I want you to fill me up."

His smile nearly blinds me. He lets out a deep rumble between his teeth and pulls me into a deep kiss.

"Good girl," he growls again when he pulls away.

He sits up abruptly, not even needing to use his arms; those are occupied with shoving me off him and onto the ground. I hit the earth with a yelp that is more pleasure than pain, smiling widely.

Then he's on top of me, looming over me once more. He's so close and his shoulders are so wide that his rich skin fills my vision.

He dwarfs me, but unlike when we've sparred together, and the sheer size of him seems to activate my fight or flight response, I feel secure with him now. Protected. His eyes are narrowed just slightly, and it lends an intensity to his gaze that normally infuriates me, but now sends shivers of delight down my spine.

He uses one hand to squeeze my neck, pushing exactly right against my pressure points. I start to feel delightfully dizzy.

He kisses me again, and maybe it's the fog in my mind, but it seems . . . tender. Not rough, and not desperate, but deeply passionate. The kind of passion you only gain with time and familiarity, not the kind that intensifies your every move and burns out in a flash. I lick his bottom lip and moan into his mouth.

He slides his cock into me then, and my hips rise to meet his as he moans an elongated "Fuuuuuck" in my ear. I breathe out shakily, my whole body vibrating with pleasure.

Again, we move as if choreographed — like we were made for this. For each other. His pace is slow, but hard, and his considerable length slicks against my clit with each deep thrust. He grunts into my ear with each one, and I moan in answer.

I realize my nails are digging into his shoulders; I'm clutching him to myself like he's a life preserver that's been thrown to me just as I'm about to drown. Like he's the only thing in the world worth holding.

I don't release him. I dig my nails in harder, and he exhales shakily.

He brushes his lips against my ear and I shiver. "You're doing so well taking all of me."

I make a pathetic sound. *Please, Universe. Never let this end.*

His breathing becomes more haggard, and he begins muttering curses in Spanish. After he's strung together a full monologue, he leans into the crook of my neck and bites me in earnest. His fangs sink easily into my skin, and his venom burns through the last inhibitions left in my mind. I scream in his ear, high with pleasure.

He removes his fangs as he slides his arms against my shoulders, framing me underneath him, then he tangles both his hands in my hair and leans his forehead against mine.

"Fuck, Eilidh. You're making me come," he breathes against me.

It's the first time he's said my name, and the way it sounds in his mouth is more than I can take. It shoots through me like fireworks as his thrusting becomes frenzied. It sets me ablaze. I was right on the edge, and he just shoved me over once again.

"Oh god," I moan in his face. "Diego." And then I come too, my orgasm cascading around his cock as he slides in and out of me. He pulses over and over, filling me up as I had commanded him to. His eyes are little more than slits as a third and final whimper escapes his throat.

"I can feel you clenching around me," he grunts. "You feel *so* fucking good." He clamps his mouth over mine then, and we kiss one another like the only oxygen left in the world is in the other's mouth.

Finally, he slows. We both gasp for air as our heartbeats slow together. Seconds crawl by, drunkenly hazy, and then he slowly lifts himself off of me, his skin glistening with sweat.

He pulls out of me for a final time, shuddering, and my body immediately misses his perfect size and shape. It leaves me with an aching need. I want him back inside me. *Need* him back inside me. I don't want this to end.

But everything has to eventually.

Brighter Than the Sun

Diego hits the ground beside me with a solid *thump*, then puts one hand behind his head and the other on my thigh, absently rubbing his thumb back and forth across my dewy skin.

Lying next to him like this is too strange, too intimate. Which should be ridiculous, since we just spent so long fucking. But sex is different than intimacy. I know that all too well.

He breathes a long sigh of satisfaction. "You are fucking magnificent."

I stare at him, incredulous. We aren't fucking anymore, so who the hell is this man, and where is the cold and distant vampire I know?

"What?" He asks, looking sideways at me.

"I just . . . wasn't expecting the compliment I guess," I mutter at the ground.

He rolls to his side to look at me full-on. His pupils have returned to their normal size, and his irises are nearly maroon in the moonlight. "Why?"

It's a simple question, but it's loaded like a fucking gun. I narrow my eyes in sudden anger. "You know damn well why."

He furrows his brow. "I don't."

I snap.

"Because you never compliment me. You've never once told me

that something I did was great, or even good. You just comment on what could be better. Nothing I do is *ever* good enough for you."

My last sentence slices the air between us, but instead of getting up to storm off, he sits up straight, rising above me. Now he's looking down his nose at me again.

Great.

"I thought you had figured it out by now. I was hard on you because if I hadn't been, you would be walking to your death tomorrow." The arch to his eyebrow says that he thought this was obvious.

I practically feel my hackles rising. *Condescension. Again.*

"You still could have told me just *once* that what I was doing was right! Maybe if I had thought for one *second* that I was good enough for you I wouldn't have —" I bare my teeth and turn away. Saif's face flashes before my mind's eye and I growl in barely-concealed anguish.

"You know what? Never mind. It doesn't matter now." I stand up shakily to pull my clothes back on, taking deep breaths. I am *not* crying right now.

"Eilidh," he says firmly.

I don't look at him.

He sighs heavily and pulls his suit on silently.

I zip my suit and look up at my dagger. It's stuck in the wood of the cabin about ten feet off the ground, but I'll be damned if I'm going to ask him for help right now.

I take a few steps back, then run at the wall, propelling myself upward to snatch it out of the wood. As soon as I land back on the ground, I shove it in the holster on my thigh, and begin to walk back to the cabin where Valentina is sleeping.

I don't make it two steps before Diego's hand lands on my shoulder. "*Eilidh.*"

I turn and try to strike him, and he grabs my wrist again. But instead of shoving me up against the wall and fucking me senseless this time, he tilts my chin up to look at him. I glare.

"You aren't *good enough* for me." I flinch like he had slapped me, but he continues. "You're *too good* for me. I tried so hard to not let myself fall for you. I was terrified that if I did, you'd end up just like *her*. And even if you didn't, so what? My love for you doesn't change what I am, and it isn't fair of me to ask you to deal with that. Not when you already had a good man."

He growls at the ground through bared teeth. "Or so I thought," he bites out bitterly. His voice is gruff, like speaking these words causes him immense agony. "I thought he was a good man," he mumbles, more to himself than me.

I stare at him, blinded by the brilliance of his eyes. "Your what?" I whisper shakily.

He doesn't reply at first; he just looks at me, willing me to interpret from his gaze what he doesn't know how to put into words. His irises dance like a deep red fire, blazing with emotion.

Those eyes scream so many words at me, even when his mouth stays silent. He has been screaming it in a thousand ways, for months, and I hadn't heard him. My lip trembles.

He curses softly in Spanish, then takes a deep breath.

"I love you. I love you more every time I watch you push on, despite your pain; every time I watch you get up after you fall."

I blink up at him in stunned silence, and he tucks a hair behind my ear.

"I love you. When I'm with you, my soul comes back to life. You light up the entire world, like the sun has come out after *years* of darkness."

Tears well up in both our eyes, and he shrugs helplessly.

"I *love* you. You think you're just the moon?" He scoffs and shakes his head at me. "You burn brighter than the fucking sun, Eilidh, and I would happily set myself aflame if it meant that I could bask in your light."

He leans down and kisses me, tangling his hands up into my hair, and there is nothing else in the universe but his lips on mine, and the feel of his arms around me. I wind my arms around his neck and clutch him like he's the only thing left for me in this entire dimension.

Maybe he is.

When he finally breaks our kiss, he pulls me in tightly and wraps his tree trunk arms around me.

I crumble.

Tears come hot and fast and before I can stop them, they pour onto his chest. The only movement he makes as I sob against him is to stroke my hair.

"I'm a fucking idiot," I gasp against him.

"No, you aren't," he says quietly.

"Yes, I am!" I insist. I pull back and look up at him. His face is grave, and his ruby eyes are sympathetic. "Why did I *trust* him?"

Diego is silent for a few moments and his Adam's apple bobs. "Because he was kind to you," he finally says, his voice tight.

I scoff, disgusted with myself. *Pathetic.* "And look how that turned out."

He tilts my chin up once more. "You aren't the only one he deceived. We all —" His voice breaks, and my eyes widen in alarm. He takes a second to clear his throat. "We all trusted him, and we've all known him for years."

He holds me tightly and kisses the top of my head. "I even trusted him with you," he whispers into my hair, and I squeeze him as hard as I can. I breathe in his aloe and cedar scent, and instead of my pulse quickening, it slows. The smell of him has become familiar and calming. He smells like . . . home.

I'm suddenly exhausted. "I'm ready for bed," I say, my face still buried against him.

He doesn't hesitate. He picks me up, cradling my shoulders and the backs of my knees, and carries me to the cabin where Valentina, mercifully, is still asleep. If she had woken up and heard the noise we were making . . .

My cheeks flush as Diego lays me down on my sleeping bag. "You sleep. I'll keep watch," he whispers as he kneels beside me.

I start to protest, but he holds up a hand. "I'm fine. I promise." He leans down and kisses me once more, and it's all I can do not to lose myself in the taste of his lips again.

"Hey." I hold his forehead to mine for a moment before he can pull away, and I look into his supernova irises. "I love you, too," I whisper, and he smiles warmly.

As I drift off to sleep, the last thing I see is his ruby gaze.

Through the Tunnel

When he wakes me the next morning, Valentina is already up and rolling her sleeping bag. I want so badly to go to her, but she still doesn't speak to me, even when she fills my water bottle for me, and I don't want to piss her off more. I decide to just give her the space she needs for however long she needs it.

We eat our breakfasts in silence as we walk further into the forest. I swear it's getting darker the farther we walk, despite the sun rising in the sky above us.

That can't be a good sign.

Diego leads the way, Valentina walks a few steps behind him, and I trail behind the two of them. I'm not sure if it's just my imagination, but I swear there is actual electricity flying between Diego and I, and I wonder if Valentina can feel it.

We walk for several hours. Finally, we approach a solid wall of trees, brush, and brambles interlaced with thorny vines.

"Well, this doesn't look natural," I say as I tighten my ponytail.

"It's not." Diego growls, his voice is tight. "It's Saif."

My stomach twists. *Of course it is.*

Diego uses his vambraces to slice through the vines, which end up being at least five feet thick. Once he's through, we see a long, dark tunnel.

"Why the hell did he block the tunnel? Doesn't he want us to make it to Bleddyn?" I ask.

Diego purses his lips. "I have no idea how that man's mind works."

We step inside, and it's like someone has flipped off a light switch. I blink in the darkness, and then I can see once again. I look around in confusion. Diego is looking right at me, but Valentina is taking slow, deliberate steps, her hands outstretched, clearly struggling to get a sense of her surroundings.

I step to her and take her hand, but she pulls away from me at first. "Val. I've got you." She presses her lips into a thin line, but nods.

Diego gives me a moment as we walk to volunteer information. When I don't do so, he breaks the silence. "So, when did you start being able to see in the dark as a human?"

I sigh as Valentina scoffs beside me. "Probably five years ago or so," she mutters.

It hurts, but I understand her frustration. "Last night." I look at Diego pointedly.

He clears his throat. "Well, that will probably come in handy."

We walk along for fifteen more minutes before we turn a bend and see a dim light at the end of the tunnel. After another few minutes, we finally hit the end, blinking as our eyes adjust to the light, though it's still as dim as twilight, despite it being around midday. I glance up at the sky, but the moon isn't visible; roiling clouds have shrouded her from me. I swallow hard and look at what lies ahead of us.

I do not like what we see.

The tunnel opens up into a clearing that is ringed completely with yet another wall of an impassable mixture of ivy and thorny brambles, though this looks like natural growth that has formed over decades. *Or centuries.*

There are about fifty yards of clear space in front of us, but at the other end of the clearing, the facade of a massive Gothic temple looms.

Its spires reach toward the dim sky menacingly, and the black stone is covered in wild vines.

I grit my teeth. *Bleddyn really* does *have a flair for the dramatic.*

Valentina grips my hand tightly. "I feel like a rat in a maze."

I squeeze her hand back. "I don't think there's any cheese at the end, though."

She closes her eyes. "No. There's justice."

That fucking word again. I think about it as we walk across the clearing. It's what I've been working toward for more than five months, but the word sounds so heavy now, so impossible to attain.

Imane died fighting the creature that had ruined her life. Where is *her* justice? Maybe I too, would meet my end, under the austere gaze of this ancient, abandoned temple. Maybe *that* is the justice, that I will die just as she had. Maybe then the scales will be balanced, and the Universe will have righted itself.

I think of Martín and Valentina, and how much they have suffered together their whole lives. Certainly, they received no justice against the world for pushing them out, or their father, which may be why Valentina is so desperate for it now. Maybe she wants to punish Saif for the wounds that her brother suffered at the hands of an entirely different kind of monster.

And finally, I think of Bleddyn. The monster that changed me, nearly ripping me to shreds in the process. He's killed countless women over the years. My father had said that he's been after Bleddyn for a long time. How many women has he killed in his search for a new mate? Surely, his victims deserve their justice?

My stomach twists. But who am I to carry out the sentence? There is no judge in this scenario. No jury. How can I be the executioner? I'm a librarian.

Besides, killing him won't bring them back, and their families will never get the closure they deserve. But it will make me feel better, right? My resolve hardens slightly.

Killing him will prevent future harm, and Bleddyn took my life, so I will be taking his. An eye for an eye, just like Hammurabi intended.

But did *he take your life?* A small voice whispers in my head. *What did he take from you?*

Everything.

A tiny apartment? Utility bills? Certainly not family.

But how could he have taken that? I have no family.

And then Valentina squeezes my hand absently like she doesn't even have to think about it. She hasn't let go of me, despite no longer being in the tunnel. I think of Hyun-Joo, acerbic but honest, never failing to tell me exactly what I need to hear, even when it hurts. Of Martín making me collapse with laughter against the kitchen island. And Saif . . . well, the man I had thought he was, at least.

I think of my father. If I hadn't been changed, I would never have met him. I had dreamed of having a father since I was old enough to comprehend that he was missing, and now I have him. I had been given a second chance at having a real relationship with a parent.

And then I look at Diego, the man who has molded me into a warrior, and has never let me doubt myself for long.

We finally come to the front steps of the temple, and my ears ring piercingly as Diego climbs them and approaches the door.

Bleddyn hadn't taken a family from me.

But he had given me one.

Oh, god. What the fuck am I doing?

"Diego, wait —" But I'm too late. There is no turning back now.

As Diego puts his hand on the handle, the door smashes open. He's thrown back, and his head hits a stone pillar with a sickening *crack*.

"*No!*" I begin to dart up the steps, but then a deep, rumbling growl from the doorway freezes me in my tracks.

Bleddyn steps out of the darkness of the temple's interior.

He doesn't deign to look at Diego's limp form. He looks down from the top of the steps, teeth bared at Valentina and me.

You've finally returned to me, beloved. It's good to see you again.

I toss my pack to the ground and unsheathe my dagger as ice spreads throughout my stomach and into my limbs. "I can't say that the feeling's mutual."

His mouth splits open in a menacing snarl, and his glowing eyes narrow. *What a shame.*

He lunges.

Justice

Valentina and I tumble in opposite directions, but he's not focused on her at all. He swipes at me with one massive paw, and I feel the wind against the back of my neck.

I turn and prepare to slash at him with my dagger, but then a whirlpool suddenly appears around him. *Val.*

"Go wake Diego!" She screams. I don't hesitate; I run up the stone steps, drop beside him, and put an ear to his chest. His heart beats steadily, and when I shake him, he groans softly.

I look at the scene below us. Bleddyn has broken through the whirlpool, and now Valentina is throwing long needles of water at him, chasing him in the opposite direction of the temple.

I probably should have read up on first aid and concussion protocol, but unfortunately for him, I hadn't, and there's no time to develop a decent bedside manner. I slap him, and his eyes flutter open. He blinks several times to focus on me, then brings a hand to his cheek.

"Did you just slap me?" He asks incredulously.

His pupils look normal. That's as far as my diagnostic capabilities extend.

"Sorry, but we can't have you sleeping on the job right now. Val's holding him off, but she's fading fast."

"Who?" He rolls to his side to see for himself. Indeed, Valentina has been throwing everything she's got at Bleddyn to keep him off of me, and her needles have devolved into spheres. Bleddyn has run to the far end of the clearing, but he's advancing back on her now.

"*Carajo.*" Diego stands, wobbles for a moment as he shakes off his pack, then takes off running down the steps.

I'm right on his heels at first, but then I dart to the right, in the opposite direction of Valentina. I have to draw Bleddyn away from her so she can catch her breath, and I bet that he's going to go for me again, just as he had with his first attack.

I'm right.

Bleddyn changes course and begins running at me. He'll be on top of me in seconds. I brace myself, preparing to bury my dagger into him as many times as I can before he rips me to shreds.

But then Diego jumps between us, loosing arrows from his vambraces, and runs right at Bleddyn. As the two near each other, Diego launches himself into an arc and comes down on Bleddyn's back, where he slashes down viciously with the swords protruding from the vambraces. Bleddyn howls, and his pace slows, but he doesn't go down. I hold my dagger facing back toward my elbow as Bleddyn barrels toward me.

I might as well be bracing to slash at a freight train.

"Run!" Diego screams.

Fuck that.

Just as Bleddyn reaches me, I do the only thing I can think of, and it's incredibly stupid.

I throw myself back on the ground and hold the dagger blade up in both hands as Bleddyn runs over me. The blade digs into his underbelly, his own momentum ripping flesh and fur off in chunks.

Blood rains down on me, and then one of his massive back paws lands on my right knee, and I hear a sickening crunch as it's slammed into the ground. I scream out, blinded with blood and pain. I don't even realize the blade is gone from my hands until Diego screams at me to get up and finish Bleddyn off.

I roll to my left, favoring my right knee, and search the grass around me frantically for my dagger. I wipe blood from my eyes and look at Diego. Bleddyn is clearly wounded, but he isn't going down without a fight.

I watch as he rears up like a horse, and slams backward into the ground, not unlike I had done a moment ago. Diego jumps off at the last second to avoid being crushed as blood spurts from the werewolf's stomach, and I see the hilt of my dagger buried in his abdomen as he rolls.

Fuck.

Valentina kneels at my side, takes one look at me covered in blood, and raises her hands as if she plans to douse me.

"No, save your energy, I'm fine." She frowns but lowers her hands.

Bleddyn stands and advances slowly toward me. His movements are jerky, and he's clearly in an immense amount of pain, but he doesn't stop. Blood is dripping down his back from where Diego had stabbed him, and from his underbelly into the grass.

It's not too late to join me, beloved. Give me the word, and I will dispatch these two. We can be together forever.

"Eilidh," Diego barks. "He's trying to get in your head. End this before his healing factor kicks in."

I show him my empty hands, and he mouths several silent curses before setting his jaw grimly.

Bleddyn turns his glowing gaze to him. *This one's scent is all over you. I see you have not been lonely in my absence.*

Valentina inhales sharply, and I clench my teeth. Bleddyn does not seem concerned with making this conversation private. That's a discussion for later.

Diego is done waiting. He jumps at Bleddyn once again, who is finally forced to engage. Diego's blades clash with Bleddyn's claws as the two collide. I watch for a moment, helpless.

The dagger is the only thing that can kill him, the only weapon of pure silver we have. If I can't get it, we're fucked.

I push myself up to my knees, and though my right one screams at me in protest, I grit my teeth and stand, and it doesn't give out on me. That's a good sign, at least.

"Val, can you pin him to the ground or something so I can get the dagger?" She looks at Bleddyn, who is lunging to and fro, albeit slowly, due to his injuries, as he does battle with Diego.

She's covered in a layer of sweat, and I worry she might not have the energy left, but she nods grimly. "I can try, but you'll have to be quick."

I test putting more pressure on my knee. I don't know how quickly I'll be able to move, but it's our only shot. "Okay."

She doesn't waste any time. A geyser of water explodes from her hands and it crashes into Bleddyn, who is knocked back to the ground. Diego jumps away and pants to catch his breath. She lifts her hands to the sky and the water arcs like a rainbow, landing on Bleddyn and pressing him against the ground.

I run.

It's fortunate that he's not any farther away, because my knee finally gives out a few steps from him. Muscle memory from a lifetime ago kicks in, and I slide the rest of the way to him as if he's home plate, my left knee bent underneath me.

Just as I grip the hilt of the dagger, the water stops falling, Bleddyn twists around to stand, and the dagger yanks free of his flesh with a sickening squelch, covering my hands with yet more blood.

He turns, snarling, his long teeth glinting like blades, and my reaction is pure instinct. I slash at him with my dagger and connect with his nose. He rears back and howls in fury, then brings down a front paw on my chest, crushing me into the ground.

I slash up at his leg wildly, desperate to sever a tendon or ligament, or anything that will get him off me so I can breathe again. Then I hear the squelching *thunk* of a blade landing in flesh, and the weight on my chest is gone. I gasp for air as I see Diego grappling with Bleddyn, one of his blades deep in the werewolf's chest.

Bleddyn's howl is deafening as he flings Diego away. I roll, preparing to fight sitting down if I have to, but the wolf collapses, pawing frantically at the wound in his chest. His howl turns to a whine, and I look in bewilderment at Diego, whose mouth is set in a grim line.

Bleddyn's breathing becomes labored, and his tongue lolls out of his mouth, but his telepathic voice is as strong as ever.

Don't you want to know who wanted you gone in the first place, before you dispatch me? Why the succubus brought you to me?

Diego squints at the werewolf. I turn to Valentina, who is just pushing herself up off the ground. She must have collapsed after her last geyser. She, too, looks at Bleddyn with confusion, so he's once again speaking for all of us to hear.

"She worked for you," I say shakily from the blood-soaked ground, clutching my dagger in two hands.

Yes you little fool, but that's not how this started. There was another who had gone to her first, who wanted you disposed of. That's what the succubus was hired to do. But they didn't know she was working for me.

Diego strides toward me quickly and pulls me to my feet, supporting me so I can stand on my right leg. "He's stalling. Finish it."

Bleddyn's glowing gaze moves to Diego as he labors for air. *Beware this one, girl. His touch is poison.*

Poison. My vision flashes red.

"Where is Saif? Why is he working with you? Is he the one who hired Azaeroria?"

I have no dealings with that man.

"Liar!" I snarl. "You're working with him, and with that wulver that tried to carry me off. Here to you, I assume. So where is he?"

Bleddyn's mouth splits wide in a toothy grin, and blood drips from his fangs onto the grass. *There are many more pieces to this puzzle that you have yet to uncover. But you will, in time.*

I rip free from Diego's grasp and limp toward Bleddyn. My knee protests, but it's better than it was even a minute ago — my healing factor must have kicked in. Bleddyn's however, has not; blood flows from the wound in his chest like a river.

I kneel beside him and meet his glowing gaze evenly. "Who hired Azaeroria?" I growl. "What is their name?"

His breath comes in gasps now. He's going to die before I get an answer. I grip my fists into his matted neck fur and shake him. *"Tell me!"* I scream.

Two final words scrape through our heads.

Arthur Pendragon.

Rage washes over me. *He's still lying.* I stab him in fury, my dagger burying deep in his chest with a squelch before I rip it back out of his flesh, and more blood seeps out over my hand.

Like cutting into a fucking cake.

The light flees from his glowing eyes. I release him, and his head thuds to the ground.

Valentina's shaky voice breaks the silence of the clearing. "Arthur Pendragon is just a fairy tale."

But Diego and I look at each other, and I recall his words from long ago. *So is the Big Bad Wolf.*

"All the stories are true," I hiss.

Prepared

I crawl backward away from Bleddyn's corpse, choking on the smell of blood and gore. Exhaustion ripples through me as the adrenaline stops coursing through my veins.

I look down at myself and gag. I'm caked in sweat, dirt, and congealing blood, and covered in bits of fur. I crawl a few more feet away, then vomit into the grass.

After my retching turns to dry heaves, I stand shakily and stumble toward the temple as the cloud above us begin to dissipate. Soon, the sun beats down on us. Diego and Valentina follow behind me silently. Neither of them reach for me.

I slump down on the steps, curling in on myself, and press my forehead into the cool stone. The three of us sit in silence for quite some time.

"Val, I hate to ask you, but do you have anything left to at least get the blood off?" I gesture at myself and suppress another gag as I sit up.

She approaches me silently and waves a shaky hand over me. A gentle stream of water hits me, and I scrub at my skin viciously. By the time she's spent once more, I've at least gotten the caked blood off my face and arms, though my fingernails are filthy, and my hair — I gag at the thought.

"Thank you," I whisper.

I turn to Diego, who is lying down in the grass a few feet away. "How did you wound him that badly?" I ask quietly. "Only pure silver can do that to a werewolf."

He says nothing for a moment, then sighs. "The short blades *are* pure silver. I replaced the old steel ones." He lifts one arm, and the blades flash at me in the sunlight.

I blink at him in confusion. "When? Where did you find that much pure silver?"

He looks back at me evenly. "I started looking the moment you agreed to this suicide mission. I wasn't letting you try to kill a werewolf with a fucking letter opener. I was prepared this time."

Not like with Imane.

His words hit me hard, harder than is probably reasonable. But I don't care.

"You never thought I could do this," I say quietly.

"It was just a precaution." His jaw is set.

"A precaution you only took because you thought I couldn't do it."

"Because you shouldn't have been the one to *have* to do it!" He yells, sitting up to glare at me.

Valentina looks between us cautiously.

"Auberon is *insane*! Literally insane! You can't pluck a regular woman from her cushy life and expect her to become a warrior in a matter of months! He should have learned that lesson after he got Imane killed!"

I've never heard him quite this furious before.

But I'm furious too. *Cushy life?*

"I thought *you* got Imane killed," I snarl.

I may as well have flung my dagger at him. His eyes fill with hurt, and I regret my words immediately.

"Diego, no, I'm sorry, I — I didn't mean that." My voice quivers.

But his face is stony. When he finally speaks, it starts low and clipped, then steadily increases in volume. "Yes. Her blood is on my hands, but it's on his, too. And *I* learned from my mistakes. *I* knew better this time. That's why I couldn't let myself get close to you. Why every day having to train you was *torture*. Spending every full moon with you because no one else could. Seeing the way you overcame every obstacle I threw at you to try to get you to realize what madness this all was." He's yelling by the end of his rant.

"That's why you told me to be careful of my father that night in your room."

Valentina goggles at me.

"You think he's unhinged. That he's dangerous."

Diego sighs and runs a hand through his hair. "I *know* he's unhinged and dangerous. Trust me. He's going to get you killed." He gestures at Bleddyn's corpse. "*That* was not something a sane person sends his own daughter to do if he wants her to live."

I want to argue with him more, but I am utterly exhausted. I lean back on the stones and glare at the clear, blue sky. "Before you opened that door, I wasn't even sure I *wanted* to kill him."

He and Valentina gape at me.

"He." I gulp. "He gave me you two. All of you." My voice breaks, and Val's expression, at least, softens with understanding. Diego just glares at the ground.

None of us say anything else for several long moments.

He finally breaks the silence. "It was either him or us; there was no room for mercy. We did what we had to."

I sniff, but he continues. "And *you* didn't see the havoc he's been wreaking. The bodies he's left in his wake. I'm glad that fucking monster is dead."

A chill runs through me at his glacial tone.

The silence stretches between us until Valentina stands. "I'll go sweep the temple, and make sure no one else is waiting for us."

I start to stand, but she puts a hand up to stop me. "You rest."

Diego, however, strides up the stairs past us, not bothering to look at me again. "You aren't going in there alone."

She looks for a moment like she wants to protest, but then she just shakes her head and follows him.

As they climb the steps and enter the temple, I try to process Diego's words. He had been trying to get me to quit. He hadn't thought I would succeed.

And he was right, I think bitterly. Tears roll down my cheeks before I can stop them.

I'm still crying silently when Valentina exits the temple and calls to me that it's all clear. I stand and make my way up the steps slowly, trying to staunch my tears before she can see them. I don't succeed.

When I get to the top of the steps, she opens her arms wide, and I lean down to bury my face in her shoulder. She holds me until my tears are dry, then leads me to the front room of the temple. We lay side by side in the darkness and fall asleep.

Communication

When we wake and exit the temple, Diego is sitting on the top step, looking out at the clearing. He stands without a word, and the three of us walk back through the tunnel. I don't look back at Bleddyn's corpse.

Our journey back to the portal is a painful blur. We stop along the way to wash as much as we can in a small stream, and sleep in the same cabins we had on our way here. My heart hammers when I look at the one that I had been behind when Diego —

I can't continue the thought right now. I grit my teeth until I fall asleep on the floor beside Valentina. She has apparently forgiven me for keeping pretty much every meaningful thing about myself from her. I will still need to give her a proper apology, but for now, this is good enough. Her presence is enough.

After another day of silent hiking, we make it back to the gateway. When we finally make it back to the SUV about two hours later, Hyun-Joo is waiting for us.

Valentina runs to her, and Hyun-Joo nods reassuringly. Valentina collapses with relief and sobs. It's my turn to hold her together, so I do. I hold her until she stops shaking.

Diego approaches Hyun-Joo, and she reaches up high to put a hand on his cheek. He leans into it for a moment, then scoops her up into a hug.

I smile faintly, glad that, even though I'm not sure what's going to happen between us yet, he'll have her no matter what.

"How are you feeling?" She asks him softly. He just shakes his head. She takes his hand, and they walk into the trees for privacy.

"So, what's going on there?" Valentina asks quietly, and I start. I had almost thought she had fallen asleep against my shoulder. "I always assumed they were together, but if you and he . . . I mean unless they have an understanding, or . . ." She trails off.

I sigh. It's not my place to out Hyun-Joo, as much as I am sick of hiding things from Valentina.

"They're just friends."

"Okay," she says simply. "And you and he are . . . what?"

I close my eyes. "Apparently, not talking."

She makes a thoughtful noise. "But what Bleddyn said. Was he right?"

I swallow. "Yeah," I say tersely.

"When?"

"When we stayed in the cabin. I was training with my dagger, and he came to try to get me to go to bed. I hit him, and he kissed me. And, well." I blush. I can almost feel the wood of the cabin digging into my back again, and goosebumps erupt over my skin.

She whistles softly. "Hey, good for you."

I open my eyes wide and stare at her in shock. She barks a laugh. "Hey, I'm a lesbian, not blind."

I cackle at that. It feels so good to be having a normal conversation again after everything that's happened. I lean against her, and we both chuckle easily. When my face hurts from smiling, I turn to face her.

"I'm sorry that I'm the world's shittiest communicator, Val. I'm so used to being on my own, that I kind of just forgot how to. But I promise, I will work on it." I squeeze her hands.

She smiles. "Apology accepted. And, deal. But I swear, if I find out you're hiding anything else major from me, I'll put you in a dog cone for the next full moon."

We're still laughing as Diego and Hyun-Joo walk out of the woods. He looks a little better, his eyes glittering a bit more than they had, but still not as bright as they could be.

Hyun-Joo looks more spent than she usually does afterward. She's paler than normal, and shadows jump out starkly from under her eyes. He must have needed more blood than usual, and it still hadn't been enough for him.

"Let's go get Martín from the hospital, and get the hell home," Diego says. He folds himself into the driver's seat of the SUV, and the rest of us climb in as well.

I'm too exhausted to even be consumed with my phobia; I sleep in the middle row next to Valentina until we get to the hospital, but wake with a start when she slams the door shut after jumping out. Diego is still maneuvering into a parking space, but she was done waiting.

Hyun-Joo gets out once he's parked. I'm unbuckling to follow them when Diego reaches around and lays a hand on my thigh. I freeze.

"You and I are still a mess. We probably shouldn't be going into a hospital right now, unless we want to be forcibly admitted to the psych ward."

I look down at myself, but of course, he's right.

I'm disgusting. Nearly a week in the woods would not be kind to me under normal circumstances, but add in the layers of blood and werewolf fur, and I must be truly repulsive.

Maybe I should have slept in that stream.

"I would sell my soul for a hot shower right now," I say wistfully.

He makes a small sound of agreement.

We sit in silence for several minutes while I bounce my leg and pick at my nails. Finally, Diego speaks.

"Eilidh." I freeze. My name still sounds so foreign in his mouth. "Talk to me," he says as he turns around in his seat to face me.

I grab my elbows across my chest and look just past his head. "Hi," I say softly.

He closes his eyes and sighs. "Look, I didn't . . . I just didn't want you to get hurt. I couldn't do that again."

I blink rapidly, and bite the inside of my lip, warding off tears. "I just don't understand why you acted like you thought I was so strong and capable, while the whole time you were preparing for me to fail."

He makes a frustrated sound. "You *are* strong and capable. Just because I wanted to have a backup plan, doesn't mean I thought you couldn't do it. It would have been stupid to go into that fight with only your dagger. And it worked, didn't it?"

I narrow my eyes at him, but shame freezes my stomach. I turn and lean my forehead against the glass of the window.

He was right, wasn't he? You lost the dagger, and you would have lost the fight if not for him. You weren't strong enough. You were not enough.

I swipe a hand across my eyes angrily.

What else is new?

I hadn't been enough for my mother to care about me, or to stay. I wasn't brave enough to stay in that car and die with my grandparents. I could have made Kianga stay home that night, but I didn't fight her hard enough. I hadn't been enough to hold her parents together either, and had lost the last remaining scraps of my second family because of it.

I take a shuddering breath.

But my father thinks I'm enough. He trusts me. He believes in me. My thoughts wander down a painful road.

Who would I have become if he had raised me?

Would he still have decided to come back to Tenazeryth, or would he have stayed in New York? Would he and my mother have stayed together? Would she have wanted me, then? Would I have had both parents instead of neither? Hot tears roll down my cheeks.

Diego lays a hand on my knee, and I jerk away as if his touch burns me.

"Eilidh —" He rasps, sounding wounded.

But then his eyes flick to the entrance of the hospital, and he grimaces. "There's Hyun-Joo." He turns back around. "Look, we'll talk about this later, okay?"

I don't respond.

Order Restored

Diego pulls up to the pickup area just as Valentina exits the door, supporting Martín, who is walking stiffly — but at least he's walking.

I hop in the third row of seats as he climbs gingerly into the middle row. He grins at me as he lays down to put his head in his sister's lap.

"Eilidh, *mi héroe.*" I reach over the seat and grip his hand tightly, a teary smile on my face. He squeezes back, though his grip is shaky.

When they're all in, Diego gets us back on the road. We only go a few miles before he pulls into a travel center.

"We should all clean up here while we can. They have showers."

"I'll wait in the car with Martín," Valentina says. "I'll just run in quick when you guys are back." Diego nods, and he and Hyun-Joo get out of the car.

I climb over the seat, careful to step over Martín, who pats my hip playfully as I'm straddled over him, trying to extract my second leg from the back seat.

"Sorry, *roja,* I'm in no shape for that now, but maybe another time." I snort, and Valentina smacks him gently on his cheek. He smiles and closes his eyes again.

When we enter the travel center, Diego pays for our showers. I enter my assigned room and nearly cry with joy; the entire space is a shower. There are two shower heads on opposing walls, a bench to one side, and all the hot water I could ever need. I spend the next twenty minutes scrubbing every inch of my hair and body several times over.

After I towel myself dry, I put on the last set of clean clothes that had been in my pack: black athletic leggings and a moss-colored sleeveless turtleneck top.

After I'm back in the SUV, Valentina heads inside. I take her spot next to Martín and cradle his head in my lap. He smiles gratefully at me and closes his eyes. His breathing is even by the time Diego and Hyun-Joo return to the SUV.

Valentina comes back out no more than five minutes later, and then we set off for Buffalo.

Diego, Valentina, and I recount the story of the past few days to Hyun-Joo and Martín. By the time we're done talking, it's well past dark, and we're only a few hours from Buffalo. I fall asleep for the rest of the ride, sprawled alone across the back seat.

I dream of Saif, and wake with a throbbing ache in my chest.

Diego takes the SUV right to the portal in Unity Island Park. I yawn and stretch as I step out into the darkness of the night. "Aren't we dropping this back at the rental place?" I ask, gesturing at the vehicle.

"No. They'll find it eventually." Diego sounds utterly unconcerned.

I cross my arms, still prickly because of how sweet the dream of Saif had been. "That's shitty. We should take it back."

He frowns at me, one eyebrow raised. "Why?"

"The same reason you should put your cart back when you're done at the grocery store." I set my jaw stubbornly. "It's the right thing to do."

He pinches his nose and inhales deeply. "Fine," he says finally. He gestures at the rest of the group. "You all go, we'll catch up."

He gets back in the SUV, and I climb stiffly into the passenger seat beside him. I hadn't intended to go with him, but I'm too tired to argue, and I guess it's only fair, since I was the one who suggested it.

When we get back to the rental building, he parks it right by the front door and drops the keys through the mail slot in the wall of the building.

"There," I say, sticking my chin up at him. "Don't you feel like a better person already?"

He rolls his eyes. "You'll probably hit me if I say no, so sure."

I crack a small smile despite myself.

We walk slowly through the city back to the park. I memorize as much of it as I can; I'm not sure when I'll be back in my dimension again.

I shiver against the night air, and Diego stops to pull a dark blue cloak out of his pack.

"I don't need —" I begin to protest, but he throws it over my shoulders and walks away without a word. It nearly swallows me whole; the hood acts like horse blinders, blocking out the world around me.

I stare after him for a moment, then hurry to catch up, clutching the cloak around me. It reminds me of something I've been meaning to ask him. "Why did you bring me blankets and tea for full moons?" I ask when I reach his side.

"Because you needed them," he says simply.

"But how did you know that?" I press.

He hangs his head for a moment, like answering me is a massive inconvenience, then shakes his shaggy hair out of his face once more. "When I checked on you the night before your first transformation, you were tossing and turning, and trembling like a leaf."

"That's how I always sleep."

He rolls his eyes. "No, it isn't."

I grimace at him. "Please tell me you don't climb in my window and hover over me at night."

He scoffs. "*Asqueroso.* I'm not a fucking creep. I just peek in to make sure you're okay, just like I check on everyone."

I raise an eyebrow at him. "What are you, a nervous first-time father?"

He winces, then shakes himself slightly. "I'm the leader of the goddamn Order. It's my job to make sure you're all safe."

I'm silent for a moment. "And the tea?" I ask as we cross the bridge back to Unity Island.

He shrugs. "You said you had a headache, and hibiscus tea has always helped mine." He says it as if that's all there was to it. I was hurting, so he stopped it. I pull the cloak tightly around myself once more as we walk through the dewy grass toward the giant maple tree.

When we make it to the portal, Diego places a hand on the trunk of the tree, and then pauses. "Would you like to say the word?"

I bite my lip and gaze up at him from under the hood of the cloak. "I guess I can try, but can I practice it first? If I pronounce it wrong, am I going to end up in a scary back alley somewhere?"

His mouth twists into a diagonal line. "No, it just won't work."

I nod. "Right, right. Of course."

"*Trafnidiaeth,*" he says, and I try to mimic the sounds.

"Fav-knee-keth."

"You're a natural," he deadpans.

I throw my head back and make an exasperated sound at the quarter moon. She commiserates with me.

It takes me several more times to get my mouth to wrap around the word correctly, but eventually, he's satisfied. I secure the cloak around my shoulders, adjust the hood around my face, and place my hand on the trunk of the tree as I take a deep breath.

"*Trafnidiaeth.*" We're sucked through the roots to Tenazeryth.

As soon as our feet are stable on the ground under the willow tree, all hell breaks loose.

Bastet

A chain wraps around my waist like a whip and yanks me viciously to the ground. I let out a yelp in pain as I collide with the earth, and all the air is knocked from my lungs. Diego moves toward me, but then a wulver steps between us, swinging a sword at him. He isn't wearing his vambraces to stop the blow; they're folded up in his pack. He jumps out of the way, rolling out from under the cascading branches of the willow tree.

I roll over to my hands and knees and gasp for air, looking desperately around the edges of the cloak hood to figure out what the fuck is going on, then I turn enough to see the wulver approaching Diego with its sword raised. He tenses, bracing to fight with only his fangs and claws to protect himself against an enemy that is somehow even taller than he is. A furious growl erupts from my throat as my nostrils flare.

It's the same wulver that had been working with Saif. I can tell by its scent.

My vision flashes red. He isn't fighting this Mongrel alone.

Like hell.

The wulver slashes at him with a mighty swing of its sword, and something deep within me snaps as he dodges the blow. In an instant, my teeth and nails elongate, and my muscles are expanding under my skin, from which red fur sprouts.

I distantly realize that I've just shifted into my wolf form, even though it's only a quarter moon, but I don't have time to ponder it.

I leap at the wulver, dig my claws into its back, and bite down on the shoulder of its sword arm. It howls with fury, reaching around to tear at me, Diego completely forgotten.

I pull it to the ground and the two of us roll. It's taller than I am, but I have it beat in raw power. As long as I can keep it off its feet, I have the advantage.

Then Diego screams. *"Down!"*

I look up just in time to see the blade of an ax swinging toward my head. I throw myself to the ground and scramble away from the blade and the wulver.

What the fuck was that?

I turn back around, teeth bared, ready to fight, but the woman who had swung the ax at me is helping the wulver to its feet. The fan ax reaches to her shoulders as she digs the end of it into the ground to brace herself.

She's Black, about six feet tall - a foot shorter than the wulver - and built like . . . a goddess. She's wearing an Egyptian bead net dress over a cream undergarment that accentuates her thin waist and thick hips. Gold manacles circle her wrists and ankles, contrasting brilliantly against her rich mahogany skin. She's got a thick Wesekh collar around her neck with a black cat head in the center.

Long crochet braids fall to her waist, adorned with a plethora of golden beads and cuffs. The upper half of her face is covered by a black cat mask with intricate gold detailing; the eyes of the mask are covered in a material that hides her eyes.

There's only one person it can be.

Bastet.

And this - to paraphrase my father - rag-tag guerrilla leader is not a Mongrel, like I had assumed she would be. She's either a Mage or a

Shifter, though neither option makes any more sense than the other. How is she working with Mongrels? And *why?*

Why is Saif?

None of this makes sense, but I don't have time to dwell on it. Bite first, ask questions later.

Bastet and I stare at each other for one more moment, but then she apparently decides that I'm not worth her time, and turns to Diego, who is rooted to the ground at the sight of her.

He holds his hands out. "Wait!"

She does not.

She twirls her fan ax and lunges at him. I dive after her, but then the wulver steps between us and swings its sword at me. I snarl and dodge the attack, then lunge for its long legs. It delivers a quick kick to my chest, and I yelp in pain. I back up, trying to find a good angle to attack, and look briefly at Diego to make sure he's okay.

He is not.

Bastet is a blur. She whirls her fan ax like it's one of her limbs. Diego is at a disadvantage; her mask covers her eyes, and he can't see where she looks to make her next move. She also seems to know all his classic tricks, like the way he does a double feint before actually moving in for the attack.

He tries to pin her against a tree to limit her range of motion, or get her to drop her ax and fight him hand-to-hand, anything to give him the advantage. But no matter how he maneuvers, she fights him back, darts away, or jumps at a tree and flips back over him. She may not be a Mongrel, but she's definitely more feline than human.

Diego can't get close enough to bite her, and he's fading quickly. He still hasn't had enough fresh blood.

Why didn't I let him use mine?

If he can't finish this quickly, or if I can't get to him, then he's dead, and it will be my fault. I snarl in fury.

The wulver, meanwhile, is giving me far too much trouble to be of any help to him. It swings its sword with such force that when I duck and it hits a sapling instead, splinters fly through the air as if it had been struck by a cannonball.

One hit and I'm done, silver or not. The blow might not kill me, but I'd rather not be sliced in half either way, and I don't want to test how far my healing factor will actually go.

My wolf form is cumbersome, particularly when fighting against an opponent like this. I'm used to sparring against men - and monsters - who are huge, lumbering targets, but it's lean and quick. It moves with the discipline of a seasoned soldier, and wastes not an ounce of energy on any superfluous motions.

I should have sparred more with Hyun-Joo when I had the chance.

I risk a glance across the clearing and howl in fury as Bastet does an acrobatic flip over Diego, and slices at him with her ax. He's fast enough to move so that the blow slices through his side, spraying blood everywhere, rather than chopping him in half, but as he grabs at the wound, she kicks him in the back, sending him flying face-first into an oak tree at the edge of the clearing.

He crumples, and for one agonizing second, in which the entire world stops turning, he doesn't move. I freeze and stare in horror. *No.*

The wulver doesn't hesitate. It unfurls the long chain from around its belt, and wraps it around my neck in a flash, shoving its foot into my back to throttle me. The chain cuts through my fur, into my flesh, and as I snarl in pain, I realize it must be pure silver, because it's burning me and zapping me of the last remaining bit of my energy.

But I'm too focused on Diego to care much about what happens to me. Bastet is taking purposeful steps toward him, raising her ax, poised to sink the corner of the blade in between his shoulder blades.

I release a piercing howl, and then it turns into a bloodcurdling scream — I've shifted back into a human. Apparently, the wolf form only holds when I'm furious, not when I'm terrified.

"*NO!*" I shriek at Bastet wildly, choking on the chain around my throat. The wulver is now much larger than I am, and I'll be out in another few moments, if not dead. I thrash, and the hood of the cloak falls back enough so that my hair pops out and cascades in frizzy waves all around my shoulders. I feel strands rip from my scalp as they tangle with the silver chain around my neck.

"Get away from him! If you touch him, I'll fucking kill you! Get *away!*" I scream, and there must be at least a drop of humanity left in Bastet, because she lowers her ax just a fraction, turns to me, and then does a double take.

Diego makes a noise - finally - and rolls onto his side to gaze warily up at Bastet. He puts his hands out placatingly once again as she looks back and forth between the two of us, her mask preventing us from discerning her thoughts.

There's a beat of silence, and then she pulls the mask up over her face and drops it to the ground. Diego lets out a horrified, incredulous sound.

"*Imane?*"

But she pays him no attention; her brown eyes are locked on mine. She puts a palm out to signal the wulver to let me go, and I drop to my knees, every ounce of strength having fled my body, but not due to the silver chain. My mind does not comprehend what I'm seeing.

That's impossible.

I look into Bastet's eyes as she steps toward me, her face twisted with confusion and horror, mirroring mine.

She has a hardness in her eyes that was never there before, and her features are significantly more angular than I remember, hardened like the rest of her, but I'd know that face anywhere.

In a million different forms. In a million different dimensions. In this life and the next. I see it every night in my dreams, even though I haven't seen it in person since a stormy summer night more than eleven years ago.

My jaw quivers, and my vision dims at the edges. I don't have enough control of my arms to try removing the chain from around my neck as she finally reaches me, and I stare unblinkingly up into the face that I know better than my own.

"Kianga?" I choke out, and the chain prevents me from inhaling again.

Diego screams my name as the world goes black.

PREVIEW OF BOUND BY ANCIENT BLOOD

A Ghost From the Past

I wake up in a cell.

It's not the one in the greenhouse at Arkenvale, but rather a dark, damp, stone cell. The only light comes from a small window, maybe a foot wide, at least six feet above me.

I groan and roll over, my eyes still fluttering open slowly.

Saif is sitting on the floor, wearing a rumpled cream tunic over black slacks and black loafers, staring at me through the thick bars. He looks like he hasn't slept in days.

I push myself up and crawl toward him. "Saif, thank god, get me out of —" But then my memories hit me all at once, and my blood freezes.

This man is no longer mine.

I throw myself back and hiss through my teeth.

He grimaces, his eyes glistening as if he's in pain.

I stand in fury and stalk to the bars as he stands and dusts the dirt off his pants. I don't bother to swipe at the dirt all over myself.

"Where the hell am I?" I growl.

"Tal Basta," he says calmly, adjusting his glasses.

"And where the fuck is that?" I bite through my teeth.

"All in time, my love." He turns away from me, and I look around frantically. All I can see are sandy stone walls to my sides, and another row of cells across from me. They're all empty.

"Where is Diego?" I hiss, trying to keep the desperation out of my voice, but it creeps in, nonetheless.

He freezes and turns halfway around, clenching his jaw. "Don't worry about him."

If I could get to him through the bars, I would strangle him with my bare hands. "Don't walk away from me!" I yell.

He ignores me, and walks down a hallway to the right, out of my view.

I curse and throw myself against the bars, but they don't budge. I try pulling on them, pushing them, lifting them up out of the ground, and yanking them down from the ceiling.

Nothing works.

I scream and punch one of the stone walls, scraping my knuckles. I put my fist to my mouth and try to take deep breaths. Freaking out isn't going to save Diego, wherever he is. Unless he's already . . .

No, I won't let myself even consider that.

After a few minutes, my knuckles have healed themselves. I look around the cell walls for any spot that may be weak, or that I can dig into. Nails or claws, I don't care. I have got to get out of here.

There's nothing. The absence of my dagger on my thigh is like a missing limb.

I back up against the bars of the cell, then take a running jump at the tiny window high up in the wall. All I can see is midday sun shining on a rolling field of dead grass. I pull on these bars as well, even though I'd never fit through the window, but they don't budge anyway.

I circle the cell like a feral animal for what feels like an eternity. Finally, I hear footsteps approaching. Thinking it's Saif, I press myself against the stone wall, prepared to grab him through the bars as soon as I see him. A figure walks into my view, and I snatch at them as fast as I can.

They're faster.

They grab my wrist and pull me hard against the bars. My head slams into the metal, and then they shove me back onto the ground. I hold my head and look up, wincing.

My dead best friend stares back at me coldly.

Her frigid eyes are vibrant brown, shot through with streaks of honey and apricot. I've had the pattern of her eyes memorized since I was five.

She used to wear a small stud in her nose, but now it's a gold ring. Her left brow is pierced too now, and small gold spikes protrude through the skin above and below it. Her rich mahogany skin is flawless.

She's wearing a simple gold tunic over tight black pants and knee-high black leather boots. Her crochet braids are still adorned with various gold beads and coils.

She's, well, a goddess.

I choke out a sob. "Kianga."

Her expression tightens even further. "What the hell are you doing here, Lee?"

I wince; the old nickname that only she could get away with calling me stings like an old scar being ripped open. "I have no idea; I woke up here."

"No. What are you doing *here*?" She gestures wide. "In this nightmare fucking fairy-tale land?"

"I." My mouth works silently as I try to come up with a succinct answer. "I'm a werewolf," I say, shrugging helplessly.

Her mouth is a thin line. "Yeah, I gathered that."

My eyes sting, but I'm afraid if I blink, she'll disappear. "What are *you* doing here, posing as an Egyptian goddess?"

She doesn't smile. I had always been able to make her smile so easily.

"Trying to kill your father."

Eilidh, Saif, and Diego will return in Bound by Ancient Blood,
along with new friends — and old ones.

Translation Table

Chapter	Original Text	English Translation
Sacrifice	¿Qué carajo?	What the fuck?
Waking	Sabah al-khair	Good morning
Lobita	Qué deseas?	What do you want?
	Tonto	Moron/fool
	Roja	Red
	Lobita	Little Wolf
	Et tu	And you?
Celebration	Señorita	Miss
	Cabrón	Bastard
Blades	Dhabiha	Sacrifice/offering
	No puedo más	I can't anymore
Hopeless	Hermano	Brother
	Akh	More a sound than an actual word; conveys hopelessness
The Morning After	Qué maravilla	How marvelous
	Lahabi	My flame
Diego's Warning	¡Cállate!	Shut up!
Saif's Warning	Shloonich	How are you?
	Al bab tejeek menh reeh sedh westereeh	(Expression) Close the door on people who are bad for you and protect yourself
Sand	Carpe noctem	Seize the night
Moonlit Forest	No malo	Not bad

Chapter	Original Text	English Translation
Afraid of Falling	Mamacita	Little mommy/hot mama
Boiling	Traición	Betrayal
Apology	Disparatada	Ridiculous/Absurd
	¡Ay por Dios!	Oh my God!
Concession	Loca	Crazy
Eternity	Ana uhibbuki	I love you
Weakness	Obstinada	Stubborn
	No es obvia?	Isn't it obvious?
Through the Willow	Trafnidiaeth	Transport
	Mátame	Kill me
	Mi querida	My dear
	Dios mío	My God
Bravery	Cariño	Dear/sweetheart
Disorder	Lo siento	I'm sorry
Written in Stone	Ileon jenjang	Holy shit
	Te amo	I love you
Collision	Salvaje	Wild
Explosion	¡Espérate!	Wait!
	Mierda	Shit
Order Restored	Mi héroe	My hero
	Asqueroso	Disgusting

Acknowledgments

This book is for the little girl who was told to get her head out of the clouds. The girl who was made to feel like her stories were a burden. Who was told that no one would listen to her.

This is for the teenager who started and discarded countless stories about young women just like her who would fight to make a difference. Who were powerful, and courageous, and loved. The girl whose heroines would defeat the bad guy, even when she couldn't do it for herself.

This is for the teachers who saw the spark in that girl, and fostered it. Who believed in her.

This is for the broken woman who had no one to turn to but herself.

You did it. And I'm so proud of you.

Thank you to my friends, who - for whatever reason - put up with me.

Thank you to my family — the ones who were assigned to me by the Universe, and the ones I have found along the way.

And thank you, dear readers, for joining me on this wonderful, incredible, terrifying journey.

I hope you'll stick with me until the end.

About the Author

Maria J. Hart was born and grew up in Pennsylvania, but she was raised in hundreds of different fantastical worlds that she found through books, movies, and video games. She is the author of The Blood of Tenazeryth, a collection of paranormal romance duologies and related works. She still resides in Pennsylvania, but now works in fantastical worlds of her own creation. Her hobbies include collecting books and comics (she sometimes even reads them), bothering her political representatives to be better humans (they are not generally receptive), and attempting to befriend the squirrels in her backyard (who are marginally more receptive than the politicians).

You can connect with me on:

🌐 https://linktr.ee/MariaJHart

🐦 https://x.com/mariajhart

📘 https://www.facebook.com/profile.php?id=61561681965678

🔗 https://bsky.app/profile/mariajhart.bsky.social

Subscribe to my newsletter:

✉ https://substack.com/@mariajhart

Also by Maria J. Hart

BOUND BY ANCIENT BLOOD

Eilidh grew up reading fairy tales full of brave heroes, easily identifiable monsters, and true love conquering all. But now she's living in a fairy tale world herself, and it is nothing like the stories. Now, the heroes make disastrous mistakes, the monsters disguise themselves as friends, and true love isn't enough to keep the world from shattering into pieces.

Eilidh has mastered one of her supernatural abilities, but there's something else sparking to life within her that she will have to learn to control before it's too late. This power could be enough to save the world - or it just may be the thing that destroys it.